La Vida Doble

La Vida Doble
A Novel

ARTURO FONTAINE

TRANSLATED BY MEGAN MCDOWELL

YALE UNIVERSITY PRESS ■ NEW HAVEN & LONDON

The Margellos World Republic of Letters is dedicated to making literary works from around the globe available in English through translation. It brings to the English-speaking world the work of leading poets, novelists, essayists, philosophers, and playwrights from Europe, Latin America, Africa, Asia, and the Middle East to stimulate international discourse and creative exchange.

Yale University Press books may be purchased in quantity for educational, business, or promotional use. For information, please e-mail sales.press@yale.edu (US office) or sales@yaleup.co.uk (UK office).

Set in Electra type by Keystone Typesetting, Inc. Printed in the United States of America.

Library of Congress Cataloging-in-Publication Data
Fontaine Talavera, Arturo, author.
La vida doble : a novel / Arturo Fontaine ; translated by Megan McDowell.
    pages cm. — (The Margellos World Republic of Letters)
ISBN 978-0-300-17669-8 (clothbound : alk. paper)
1. Women revolutionaries—Chile—Fiction. 2. Mothers—Fiction. 3. Chile—History—1973–1988—Fiction. 4. Chilean fiction—Translations into English. I. McDowell, Megan, translator. II. Title.
PQ8098.16.O5V5313   2013
863'.64—dc23   2012047817

A catalogue record for this book is available from the British Library.

This paper meets the requirements of ANSI/NISO Z39.48–1992 (Permanence of Paper).

10 9 8 7 6 5 4 3 2 1

And I am dumb to tell the hanging man
How of my clay is made the hangman's lime.
—Dylan Thomas

Lo que hace un hombre es como si lo hicieran todos
los hombres.
(Whatever one man does, it is as if all men did it.)
—Jorge Luis Borges

L'examen de conscience est un jeu crépusculaire oú le
scrupuleux perd à tous les coups.
(The examining of conscience is a crepuscular game
where scruples lose every time.)
—Régis Debray

CONTENTS

La Vida Doble

ONE

Can I tell you the truth? That's a question for you. Are you going to believe me? That's a question only you can answer. All I can do is talk. It's up to you whether you believe me or not.

I left the currency exchange with all the money on me. Thirty thousand dollars in cash, and a little over four million pesos. Canelo was next to me, Kid Díaz or Kid of the Day, as we called him, was a bit behind us.

"Run, Irene!" Canelo shouted at me. "Run!" And doubling over just as we'd been trained to do, hunching down and moving sideways to minimize exposure to the enemy, he covered my retreat, scattering lead from his Smith and Wesson .44 Magnum revolver. But not me. I ran for a stretch and then walked a few yards. When I saw that none of the people fleeing in terror from the sound of the bullets took any notice of me, panic overcame me and I threw myself to the ground and hid under a parked truck. Inexplicable, in a trained combatant like me. I told myself: I'll wait for the bullets to stop and then I can get out and walk away naturally. But really, when the moment of truth came, I chickened out. And I had the money on me. Those are the facts. An instant before, anything had been possible; an instant later, destiny had me cornered, the bridge was cut off, I couldn't go back. Never again. I get dizzy thinking about it. But that instant existed, that free and open field was real, and a tenth of a second later it had disappeared forever: I was a prisoner.

The acid of fear dissolved my spirit. I wanted to survive. I wanted more time. I panicked at the thought of living through the duration of my death. Fear of the annihilating wounds, the agonizing and inexorable proximity of the void, and in the meantime the torturous bleeding out that slowly transforms living into dead. I think of Canelo: there was, of course, an instant when he could have escaped and survived the way I did. But he didn't do it. Did he think he could face battle and come out of it alive? Did he even ask himself that, or did he do his duty out of instinct?

As I look out the window at the Baltic Sea, hulking ships are coming into port. And I imagine my daughter, Ana, on a lonely fishing boat at dusk, tipping my ashes from their urn into the sea off the coast of El Quisco. From here in Stockholm, Chile seems like a slim cornice suspended between the Andes and the ocean. What I'm telling you now happened there, a long time ago. I have a good memory. Not as good as Gato's, of course. There's no one with a better memory than him. You know what? He could remember entire portions of a person's testimony during an interrogation and repeat them the next day to demonstrate a contradiction.

Hey, speak a little louder. Raise your voice, OK? I'm getting pretty deaf, let me tell you. I always thought deafness would be silence, darkness, an absence, the same way blindness is. But no. Deafness is a constant noise, a buzzing in your head that keeps voices and sounds from reaching you and forces you to hear only what's going on inside you. Deafness more than blindness, I think, leaves you alone, with no company except your own unceasing buzz.

And so, without dropping my leather purse that was bulging with bills, I crawled under that goddamn truck. Some people went running past, but there were no more shots fired. I peeked my head out from under the truck and saw a gun pointed at my head. It was a relief. The mission was over. The guy aiming the gun at me was a young kid, skinny, not very tall, blue jeans, green shirt. Was it fear that made him breathe so hard? No one would have guessed he was an agent. I never found out his name. Later, I would meet him again in the nightclub at that house in Malloco. But I don't want to tell that part yet, I want to go in order; it isn't easy, though, memory doesn't work that way.

4

I dropped the purse slowly so he wouldn't get frightened and shoot me. He kept repeating his order like a madman. I didn't feel guilty in the slightest. I was shaking, but inside, a delicious peace was overtaking me. I no longer had to choose. Everything had been consummated. Though of course, it hadn't. Another man came, very tall and agitated, with a thin moustache and salt-and-pepper hair. Someone else I couldn't see came up behind me and roughly twisted my right hand behind my back until it hurt; they ordered me to put my left hand on the nape of my neck. I felt a cuff closing around my left hand and a painful yank on the right, and my hands were immobilized behind my back. I saw the man's violent eyes and I heard a shout. They were waving the bills in front of my face and I was saying that yes, they were mine. I never found out who that tall man with salt-and-pepper hair was. They must have transferred him to a different unit soon after. And the kid with the green shirt held my own Beretta to my temple.

Just then, Macha appeared. They called his name and I turned to face him. As I recognized him, I thought: *Canelo is dead.* That's what I thought as my eyes suddenly met his and my body was petrified. He had killed, he had killed recently. I had no doubt. He was coming from killing Canelo. I didn't know it was possible for a person's gaze to be so intense and direct and simple. I didn't dare lower my eyes out of fear that the moment I did, he would kill me. But holding his gaze was insolent as well and he could kill me for it, so I slowly lowered my lashes.

Of course, we had been told about him; I had even seen a photo that someone managed to take of him from far away, but it was blurry and he was hard to make out. He had been shot in the leg once during a raid, and he limped a little. They never found out who fired the shot. It could have been friendly fire. Most likely. It was said that he handled us, he was the chief operative charged with wiping us out. That much we knew. And he knew that we knew. I don't think he ever found out who our source was, but he must have suspected it was someone close to him. Once, we managed to leave a warning message on the windshield of his white car, a .8 Corona, which was in the parking lot of the guarded building where he lived. He moved to a new apartment and traded his car for a Toyota 4×4, red. And in less than a month he found the same kind of warning on its windshield. I didn't participate in those missions. I never knew how they did it. But now I think I know who our contact inside Central was. Yes. Maybe.

And one day we threatened him by putting a false bomb in his son's preschool classroom. Four years old, the kid must have been then. It was my job to go to the "meet" and hand over the Vietnamese IED they used to a combatant from another cell. A cone made out of a simple cooking pot filled with screws and nails. But someone warned him. We never would have set it off. It didn't even have a detonator. Macha went to the kindergarten himself with three cars full of thugs from Central who went running in and disarmed the device. Macha came tearing out of the building clutching his little boy in his arms. He put him into a different preschool, enrolled under a false name. It was our third warning. So he would look the other way, to get rid of us.

Another time, we undertook an operation to assassinate him as he was leaving his lover's house. But the man who came out of the house that morning at daybreak, the man who died riddled with bullets from our AK-47, wasn't him but another agent. Failed operation.

When I raised my eyes again, Macha was speaking quickly and sharply to the tall man with the moustache. He checked the time on his Rolex metal-band wristwatch. He put on a pair of Ray-Bans with metal frames. His back was upright, broad and straight as if there were an iron bar going through him from one shoulder to the other. When he put away the lens case, his dark suit jacket fell open and I saw the shoulder holster for his gun. I heard movement, a slight whisper behind me, just before a blindfold covered my eyes. When everything went black I died, though I didn't know it yet. Not, of course, the way Canelo died, Canelo, who was now firmly fixed in the eternity of heroes. But I knew that sister Irene had also fallen that day on Calle Moneda, and I was the one who had killed her.

TWO

Days are no different from nights, and everything unfolds within a gaseous atmosphere shot through with terror. If only there was some way to describe what happens to you while you're in there. What are you? An animal driven mad by the horror? Where are you? What do you hope for? From the moment they put the blindfold on, you are no longer you, and you enter into a nightmare filled with indefinite shapes, in which the stupor of fear, the sudden blows and startling pain gradually bewilder you and break you down. *A cry to summon all this and a tongue to hang myself from it.* Then you tell yourself: this was the truth always, the one my professors taught me, and in the university quads no one no talked about anything else. We are this impalpable flux; I never used to believe in intangible substances, in sacrosanct identities or timeless essences. Then I remember and repeat the lessons I learned in university: I am a slave because I chose to keep my life in exchange for my freedom, et cetera, et cetera. There were brothers and sisters who didn't let themselves get captured, and they sacrificed their lives. Not me. They were unbound, they ascended and stayed free, suspended above life and death. They are our heroes. The others, the agents who martyred them, admire them. If we are respected, it's because of them. If we are feared, it's because of them. I was trained to be like them, but I couldn't do it. Canelo did.

And so the master will rule over sister Irene, and little by little I will be worn away, I will become a thing to him, I will be his slave. Not Canelo, who went free. He put his dignity and freedom above his life. Excessively grand words? *Theirs not to make reply, / Theirs not to reason why, / Theirs but to do and die.* Not me. The master would slowly bend me to his will as though I were an animal that belonged to him. The face you cannot see becomes all-powerful, my terrifying *deus absconditus*, my hidden god. That was what was happening to me. But I'm getting ahead of myself. For now that moment of surrender builds in me though I do not know it. *No one commits suicide alone.* I am growing ever more exhausted, I do know that. We were trained to endure this. But I never imagined how the simple physical exhaustion chips away at you from inside. A person can die in that place from sheer tiredness, sheer discouragement, sheer solitude. It's a moribund life I'm living. You don't need them to kill you in order to die. You move steadily away from yourself until you leave yourself behind, and that's what dying is. There is an imperceptible surrender; it's this exhaustion that weighs on you and bends you that finally forces you to succumb.

The pain is forging my being although I don't know it yet. It always does. The flame that softens and shapes the metal. It's a matter of reaching the right temperature for each person. And they wanted more from me, always more. You have no idea what that is like. You can't imagine. You become a cockroach that everyone has the right to trample and crush. They tell you this. You know it's the truth. You can disappear forever at any moment. You live on borrowed time; you live as long as they want you to.

One of the thugs spit on me, just because. "Rat," they called him, Rat Osorio: an insignificant being, short and vulgar, with red hair full of dandruff and plastered to his skull, and elongated ears. They called him in to work the crank. I started to cry. Rat became furious, called me hysterical, and slapped me with his open palm. He kicked me to the ground. That was all, but it wasn't all. "Hysterical bitch," Rat said to me, looking at me with a mocking smile. "Bitch," he repeated slowly. "Adiós, bitch," and when he was leaving he turned around, wearing the same mocking smile; he said it again, just because. Do you understand? That was horrible. Worse than many other things.

Death will start to seem benevolent and good. Death is now the only hope. *In those days men will seek death and will not find it; they will long to die, and death will flee from them.* Because—you know?— there is always hope. We are always waiting for Godot. It's just that at a given moment, Godot becomes death and death doesn't scare you anymore. As long as the agonies it brings are not too painful. What frightens you is the physical pain you must endure in order for death's door to open. Your minimal future as you wait for the void also leaves minimum room for your past. I never knew that before: the past is yours only if there is something ahead of you, memory only exists and makes sense if there is a future. Otherwise, your memory stops working, it seizes up and forsakes you. That is what kills you. Time has run out and you are almost nothing, almost a thing, and in any case, not you. They have emptied you. And still you survive, with the useless tenacity of a crushed insect still waving its legs.

The interrogator's pleasure diminishes as I am slowly reduced to be merely his object. He builds himself up as my conqueror as he stamps out my freedom little by little. I must be subjugated and enslaved, but I must not become a broken-down machine. And so he likes it when I scream, when I refuse, when I resist.

I repeat to myself the lessons I learned in my university days: he recognizes his dominion over me in my shudders, my uncontrollable howls, my humiliating pleas, my unconditional subjection, my fear; my fear that penetrates my body like a tattoo. But the truth is that none of this is any good to me, these reflections do not save me, and the only thing I want is for the fear to stop.

None of what I learned sounds real, now. Even thinking as I'm doing now, from a distance and after so many years, is a form of running away. I think because I couldn't break my chains. I think and think about why I let them imprison me. Because when Canelo shouted at me: "Run!" And I heard him and saw him get in position to fire defensively: "Run!" And I ran, I ran zigzagging among the people, just as we'd been taught, I ran some fifty yards to Calle

Moneda, I hurled myself into the street to cross it, as we had been taught, but when I saw that parked truck I threw myself to the ground. I want you to picture it clearly. The sky was gray that fall morning in Santiago, but everything was clear. The street was well lit; there were distinct shades and contours. And there was an instant that existed, there was a precise tenth, an exact hundredth of a second when, instead of going on, I threw myself to the ground and slid beneath the truck. And that infinitesimal moment froze my biography.

I chose to survive. Did I choose? Can we choose? Something perhaps chose for me, my fear, my survival instinct, who knows? I didn't lie to myself: I knew they would find me, I knew I was turning myself over to them. Although I didn't consciously think of it that way. No. I told myself the trick was smart in its naïveté, it was something that any pedestrian might have done out of pure fear. The sound of bullets, the bursts of rapid fire and the pauses between them, the running footsteps and the shouts, and those long, frightening silences. First came the Smith and Wesson .44, then the agents' CZs. Because, just as we'd been taught they would, they drew those 9mm CZ 75 Lugers made in socialist Czechoslovakia and sold to a dictatorship that would use them to kill socialists. And more and more shots were fired; and surely the other three brothers were also fighting. The strange thing was that our AK was silent. I knew that weapon well, I could assemble and disassemble it blindfolded. Though even dirty and caked with mud they would still shoot straight, we always had to keep them like new. I was sure I didn't hear our AK.

Nothing I think gets me out of here. This stubbornness is a form of subsistence, a way of continuing to be me thanks to the guilt that is my past, the only bit of it that's still alive. That day, all my hopes were emptied out and turned into regrets.

And the burn never stops stinging. Could things have happened some other way? Was it mere chance? But isn't chance just the name we give to the reason we do not know? Were there, then, objective reasons? Then I return to how the events took place; I return, then, to the pain that exists within a time that expands and defers, that doesn't pass and won't allow me to forget for one minute the density of its presence. Pain is jealous like no other.

Once it has stopped, it's hard to understand what happened. It's a vertigo you cannot re-create. There is an impassable abyss between who you are under that pain and who you are one second later. There is no bridge between the two points. You ask why they are doing this to you. Images go by, they turn on and off, and you try to put them in order: my fingertips covered in layers of hardened glue, my awareness of Canelo behind me, the woman with glasses and the black Bic pen who passes me the receipt through the teller window—she is "fixed," we'd been informed, she will collaborate—the sketch I drew spread out on the dining room table in the safe house—it's the night before, we're going over the plan in detail—my drawing of the bars that protect the safes, the lying silence that follows Canelo's shouted order, the sound of the dial on the door of the Bash safe, the used bills encircled with elastic, my spacious black leather purse open, the sound of the purse's clasp closing. All of this is clear and makes sense. You knew it would be like this.

This is a fight for information. You are in a process of *truth production*, your body will be the living truth. And so they ask you for "the meet," where was "the meet," fucking cunt, tell us and we'll leave you alone, shit. Half a minute later they come back and the information you gave them was worthless. All is once again incomprehensible. And the spasms start up again, your body leaps, it lashes out uncontrollably, you are an insane doll hurting itself. It's an unbearable explosion that comes from within and that your own organism retains, convulsing, a crash of opposing waves in which your body is no longer yours, it escapes from you, breaks away, and nonetheless you go on suffering with endless ferocity. You want to give it up, your body, to let it go and keep your soul. Because it's your soul that can't take any more pain and terror and wants to flee. It can't, of course. Like feeling the rhythm of music without a body. I try to travel back through my memories. It's what we've been taught to do. But I can't think about anything now, and I moan, I shout for them to stop, but the gag swallows my shouts and I hear a groan rising from my guts. The impotent writhing hammers your impotence into your brain. Its counterpart: the power of that treacherous voice that gives and takes away this pain that is splintering you. For this to stop, you have to raise a finger. If you do, it's to confess, to denounce. The word you deny them is the only thing left of you. If it doesn't come, they punish you. The pain moves. Your own pain drives you mad, dislocates you. My pain is my pain. No one else can get inside it.

THREE

All this is what I say now. At the time . . . That experience of mine, only mine in that here and now, was everything, and it erased everything. No one else existed. That was the idea, as I see it. Only me, tied up and splayed out and shaking; me, invaded and run through by that evil flow that shot into me and dispersed. Just me and them, the ones who have the power to put a stop to all this. The pain ceases and yet—how can I explain—what has just happened goes on terrifying you. That's what fucks you. We're in another pause. When? It could start up again, right now. These memories are all confused for me. I'm putting this material of vague, nightmarish horror in order for your benefit, and for mine. I've spent years and years with all of this pent up and eating away at me from inside. I didn't want to talk about this. I didn't want the obscenity of these detailed descriptions that only dilute it all. I didn't want it. But I'm the one who does what I don't want to do. That's who I am.

Since I was a little girl, I've been that way. Obedient and scrupulous. Ever since the convent school where I lived in reverential terror of the nuns, whose authority I blindly obeyed; ever since, later on, my mother made me shave and wax my body; ever since I yanked out the first hair that sprouted from my nipple—so Rodrigo wouldn't see it—because yes, sometimes I get long hairs growing from my nipples; men think it doesn't happen to women, but it does to me. And it's those same nipples that two little pinchers are now biting into, two little metal clamps tormenting me. I'm not at all sure about the things I seem sure about. In that place, time stretches out like gum and loses its shape. You float, trapped in confused scenes made of spongelike material. I string together shadowy blotches; that's what I do when I tell you all this. I know I should construct a metaphor. A metaphor of the absurd, for example. But as you know, in the absurd no one is guilty. Here, yes.

The sound of water from a hose. An old voice tells you, as if talking to a baby: Get up, child. Let me get some water on you. An old woman who does the cleaning here. I hear the footsteps of her rubber boots. The smell reaches me, and it's a smell that is terrifyingly mine. I obey, ashamed, and I stand up as best I can and I show myself. It's offensive, I know. And? The stream of cold water. Now I remember that when they made me get undressed and they tied me to the metal bed frame, a woman shaved me. I *am* a baby, then. I'm tired. The shame leaves me. My body belongs to them and I let it go. *Behold the handmaid of the Lord; be it done unto me according to thy word.* My flesh suffocates my conscience. But my freedom to refuse survives. They want to take possession of that when they go to work on my body. Let the fuckers throw water on me, then. Let them take their time. I have to endure five hours. They take it all calmly, though they are diligent as well. They know they are racing the clock. If I give them the "alternative meet" in time, they can catch the rest of my cell. If I don't, the others will vanish and the trail will go cold.

It hits, and the shock is even stronger. The first moment is always the worst. You flail out, and it's as if your arms, legs, and head were going to be severed from you. You feel that they are taking you apart; they're going to tear you to pieces. The unbearable pain and trepidation. The straps hold you down; otherwise you would go flying through the air. The pressure of opposing forces crushes you. I am a body that escapes from its body, a being that dislocates from its being. It's an impossible escape. It's suffocating. It's desperate. I lift a trembling finger. I can't take any more. I have to give them something.

"The meet," I say. "I'm going to give you the meet. We . . . we . . . agreed . . ." I'm panting and my tongue is awkward and swollen. "We agreeeed . . . to mee . . . meeeet in Caaaa . . . in Caa . . . fé Haití, the one on Caaaaaalle Ahuuu . . . mada."

Silence. It's the lie that Canelo, ever prepared, had made up for me. Canelo protected me. I'm overcome by a terrible sorrow for him, for myself. As I think of him my resolve hardens; I want to be faithful to him, like a widow who wants or needs to be faithful and is resolved to stay true unto death. Why didn't I ask him more about the war in the desert of Ogaden? He didn't like to talk about that. Once, he told me about how that arid African soil trembled under the Soviet T-55 caterpillar tanks as they advanced toward the enemy. And another time he told me about that night, the night of the decisive attack, just before his column set off on the secret march to place themselves behind enemy lines, when General Ochoa came in person to rally them. He remembered almost nothing of what the mulatto had said to them, except: "If anyone falls prisoner, die in silence. Real men don't talk." That, Canelo remembered. And also: "The truth was invented not to be told."

I ask for a little water. "No," the chief interrogator, or the one I assume is the chief, tells me calmly in his whistling voice. And the word "no" immediately does what it says. That soft voice of authority is expressed in my behavior. I want to endure. I think of our songs by the fire in the mountains, I think of those long nights of conversation while we waited for a mission in some safe house. I can't betray the loyalty that ties me to my brothers, I can't endanger them, I have to be the one to interrupt the chain of denunciations before one link hooks into another and that one into another and on and on. Not because of what they would say about me. It's my reputation with myself that matters. I feel united with my brothers, we have a common dream, and I feel that I won't be me if I abandon it. Something like that—though not that, because there's no time for words in my head—is what sustains me.

"What else?" he asks me. I say: "There's a maaaa . . . man, we would find a . . . a . . . a man in a graaaay suit there, they said, drinking coffee and reading a n . . . newspaaaaper . . . *Laaas . . . Laas . . .*

Últiiimaas Noooo . . . Nooooti . . ." The guy with the hoarse voice shouts at me. I don't understand and I keep quiet.

"They're asking what newspaper it is," the other one breaks in. My mouth fills with foam.

"I aaaalready told you: *Laaas Úuultimas Noooticias.*" They shout something, I don't know what. Someone left the room and closed the door.

"And what was your second meet, the 'recovery meet'?" I answer quickly, encouraged by my own lie:

"Caaanelo had to giiiiiive me thaaat."

A tremendous blow resounds on the metal table. "Good for nothing! Don't feed us garbage, bitch. You know you gotta give us information we can validate. Got it?" It's the one with the low, booming voice. "Give us something that's true. And don't waste any more time, you cocksucking whore. Don't think you're gonna be some kinda hero, that kind of shit don't get you anywhere here. Ain't no one stands up under this shit. Ain't no one. Sing, if you don't want us to fuck you up, you cocksucking bitch."

"I aaaan . . . swered your queh . . . your question, sir." I couldn't do anything but stand by my lie. And he, insidiously:

"You did? You answered my question?" And to the other man: "Go on, then! Let her have it!" And to me: "Let's see if you under-stand my questions now, you shitty whore." I beg them not to. I plead, I ask for mercy, I cry. The humiliation of that, of not being able to control myself. I let out a wail as they stuff the rag back into my mouth.

Enough, isn't it? Let's leave it at that. I don't want to go on. It's too much. I don't like your curious eyes, I don't like the corners of your mouth; there's something obscene about them. I feel like I humili-ate myself, I get myself dirty as I tell you this. And it's pointless. You don't understand anything. You could never understand. The words grope me. They are foreign like the hands that grope me and tie me up. You can't get at what I lived through by talking, you understand? It's better not to try to imagine what can't be imagined. Because you can only act by means of that body that they've usurped. You can't act, then. There are only blocked possibilities. Your body connected to the enemy's brain to turn it against you. The skin of your back pricks and burns from so much contact with the springs of that horrible bed frame. And the machine becomes violent, and you twist and contort splayed out on that nauseating frame.

They stop: "You gonna talk now, you fucking bitch?" I don't react; I want to say something but I am half dazed. "You want her? Go ahead, stick your sausage in her ass."

"You crazy? This whore is so ugly I wouldn't fuck her even if she was sucking me, not even if she begged me on her knees, the bitch." The touching, their fingers, their mocking, their boorish language— listen to the ridiculous word I use, "boorish"—I don't know why it humiliates me so much. I already told you that. The degradation of a simple insult, a taunt.

"You're not convinced? All right then. You asked for it, whore. Quit your whining! . . ." In one jolt I am yanked out of my being. The vibration hammers into me and radiates through every fiber of my being. My musculature has come undone in a frantic dance that disarticulates my bones. I cry out. What I hear is someone else's voice. It's just like in my nightmares: my voice won't come. I'm losing my senses and the mortification does not let up. It penetrates into every molecule of my body. If this lasts any longer I could go insane. I am afraid of that. I am about to cross the threshold. I shout, I keep shouting and contorting inside a funnel of horror. I can scarcely make out the murmur of that high voice. "Stop. She's had it . . ." I'm exhausted. They tell me to sit down. I try and I lose my balance. A woman helps me. It must be the same old woman who shaved and washed me. She sits me down in a chair. My entire body is shuddering. I ask for water and the hoarse voice says no.

More questions. Where was the "upper meet"? Have I reached the moment of truth? How much time has passed? Fewer than five hours, surely. I take a long time in speaking. My numbed, awkward tongue. My shoulders hurt, my hips, knees, wrists, ankles. I try to calm down. The "upper meet," they ask me. I am terrified. That last time was even worse. It seems it can always get worse. It was the water, I think. The water made it hurt more. I know what I should do: give them something so they leave me alone. "The meet . . . ," I say shivering and unable to stop, ". . . the meet was in the meeeeetro staaaation Los Héroes, on the platform of the traaaain going weeeeest. That's where Canelo would be waaaaaiting for me." Another blow to the table.

"And who gave the order to Canelo?" The question means I'm still in danger. I'm strangled by thoughts of the terror that was and is to come, of his freedom to do what he wishes with my body. If only I could shut off my imagination, lock it away. I explain, stuttering, I explain in disjointed syllables and broken words that I dooooo . . . don't know, that I had no reeeeeason to knoooow.

The door opens and closes. It opens again and the shout startles me. The man with the hoarse voice tells me they have located two waitresses from Café Haití who were there this morning. Both of them confirmed, he shouts at me—and his voice breaks in rage—both girls confirmed that not at the time we were leaving the currency exchange with the money nor afterward was there a man in a gray suit reading *Las Últimas Noticias* and drinking coffee. "You lied, you stupid cunt." The voice lowers, the chords worn out. "What're you thinking? Who do you think you are? You disrespected us, you know? That hurts my feelings. And when my feelings are hurt I get angry and I start to feel like melting you into the metal of that frame you're on. Some fucking nerve, know what I mean? We're intelligence agents, we're professionals, you know? Or who d'you think you're dealing with, down here? You, you think that just because you got good tits we ain't caught on that you've been trained to handle this shit? Huh? Sure, she plays possum, the bitch. You really think we'd let you pull one over on us like that? You held up a currency exchange, you stole thirty thousand dollars, four million Chilean pesos on top of that, and there were armed men with you. What is that, cunt? A little game? Stick her, go ahead, we gotta stick her! Now you're fucked!"

A pause. Movement. The smell of alcohol, a pressure in my right arm, an elastic band, the prick of the needle, the pain of thick liquid going in. I know what it is, what it must be, what they taught us it would be: Pentothal. I let myself go. A calm comes over me. I feel dizzy, I'm going away, maybe I'm dying, and that's for the best.

The shouts wake me up, the questions, blows from a rubber hose on my thighs, on my arms, my stomach; more shouting. "Go on, Rat, turn it up, shit! This fucking cocksucker still hasn't understood anything . . ." His booming voice moves into me and fills me up as if I were an empty balloon. He doesn't have a face or body, only that booming voice that's connected to the instruments connected to my body in pain. The next charge hits hard. I am a sack that takes on shape according to his orders. I am a glove that fits his hand, mere femininity waiting for the structuring vector, the solid rod. The metal springs that wound my raw back, the gag that steals my animal cries, my piglike squeals—because that's what they've turned me into, a sow that squeals with her snout muzzled as they set about killing her. The jolt makes me howl again behind the rag and my body thrashes; then it is onslaught, shit, convulsions.

I enter into a petrified state, far removed from myself. I see myself as a child at the seaside in El Quisco, I smell the salt on the breeze, I see the reflections of light on the water as it washes over the sand, I hear the soft whisper of the foam near my feet . . . All this happens fast, very fast, and it's as if it is hanging outside me. As if parts of me were breaking off, parts of my memory, and the person I had been could now observe me from outside. Because I'm going, that's what I tell myself; this is dying, I tell myself, and I wander unstuck from my body, and it's a relief to die . . . A bucket of freezing water wakes me, frightened, and I'm back in my body. They won't let me die.

The other one is talking, the serene one, the one with the falsetto voice. It pacifies me. I wonder if the "truth serum" has softened me or given me some kind of brain damage. My heart is pounding. It's hard to breathe. That scares me. He wants to know if I know Bone. I tell him no. I'm exhausted and it feels better to tell the truth. My thirst is desperate. He asks me if Canelo knew Bone. I tell him I'm not sure, that I think maybe he did, but he never talked to me about him. The other one, the one with the hoarse voice, starts to laugh. "Fuck this whore. I'm bored, Gato." And that's how I found out they called him Gato. "The contact above is Canelo, dead; the contact below, a man reading *Las Últimas Noticias* in the Café Haití who was never even at the fucking Café Haití. This one's trained, man, can't you tell? She's a trained terrorist . . . She's carrying a Beretta when we pick her up, after a robbery and shootout where three men died, she's got thirty thousand stolen dollars on her, but no, she doesn't know anything . . . This fucking bitch is squeezing our balls, man. And it's fine if she wants to touch them, but I don't want the bitch counting up the wrinkles . . ." Laughter, several masculine laughs. I want to placate them and I think: How? And him: "I'm bored. She's all yours, Gato. You know where I'll be. Bye."

A door slams.

Then the calm voice became nervous and told me that Ronco, and that's how I found out they called him "Ronco," was crazy, capable of anything, you know; that Ronco was one to watch out for, see? He was out of control; I had to be responsible; I was going to regret this later; that all this effort and suffering, see, was for nothing, nothing.

They make me sit down again. The same woman helps me. Then Gato, in his calm falsetto voice, asks me why in our newsletters there is never a photo of Bone and there are so many photos, but all almost the same one, of Commander Joel. Gato doesn't insult me. It's a question I wasn't expecting. I don't know how to answer. "Didn't Canelo ever tell you what commander Joel Ulloa looked like? And you want us to think you're not lying to us. And he never described Bone to you? Why don't you just talk, already?" he insists in his soft little voice. "Why not? What difference does it make? We're all in this together, don't you think?"

I let out a "No!" I say: "It's not true! Your side doesn't have ideals. We're fighting for a world . . . a new world. Your side is only fighting so that we don't win." Silence. That silence frightens me. From a distance, as if I were hearing it from underwater, it seems like a door opens. I'm sitting, naked, on a hard chair. I must have been some three steps away from the bed frame. He repeats:

"Did Canelo ever meet Commander Joel?"

"I don't know. I assume so."

It was the pure and simple truth.

"But you didn't?"

"No."

It was hard for him to believe. I was tricking him, he told me. "How do you keep the allure, the unity, of a movement that never meets with its highest leaders? The members of a cell are contacted by the head of the group, and sometimes, they only meet to go over a mission and, later, during the operation itself. OK. We know that. But the leaders of the movement, how can they lead if no one or almost no one ever sees them or meets them in person? You could all be a shadow movement that Central agents invented . . ." He laughs.

FOUR

A crash in my ears. I'm stunned. No. Two simultaneous, awful blows have fallen, one on each ear. I take a step. My eardrums are buzzing terribly and I lose my balance. I'm blind and deaf. The room comes unmoored and spins away from me. I can't find the chair. Something . . . something sudden and horrible.

I'm terrified. Why did I stand up? Someone came up behind me and I didn't hear it. I'm confused. I'm going to fall down. I feel nauseated. If I could only sit down. Where? I'm lost. No. Now I start to retch. I'm no good to them anymore. They must be looking at my exposed flesh, dirty, foul smelling, doomed. Why is that woman trying to put clothes on me? These men have seen my breasts that I used to find pleasing and that some men, like Rodrigo, found marvelous, and my deep belly button, and my long legs with their soft skin that I used to care for with lotion, and my behind, my good-looking ass that was still high and firm. But now I don't feel like covering myself with anything. Because I'm nothing else besides my body, and they have subdued my body and turned it against me. By dressing me, they only humiliate me again, because they've had me naked.

I think while they put shoes on me. I think, hooded, trying to think. Or maybe I don't think. But I believe I'm thinking about something or feeling something. That's why I tell myself: I'm still alive. Surely I think: What's going to happen now? They're taking me out of here. There is an abrupt change in the temperature. It's cold. Are we outside? My legs won't respond. They pick me up. They carry me.

I don't hear the sound of cars. It must be the middle of the night. I hear a turn signal. I think it comes from the front of the car. They've thrown me into the back of a van. I don't hold out any hope. That is to say, I do. A change. That's something in itself. I am terribly thirsty. I should count so I can figure out where they take me. That's what we've been taught to do. One, two, three . . . twenty-four, twenty-five . . . At some point I get distracted and lose count. I think I got to seventy-eight. I think. It's useless at this point. It's all useless. I am terribly thirsty. We're going up and the car barely slows down at what, I assume, must be corners. Silence. We stop. A red light, I say to myself. The handcuffs bother me. I try to rub my head against something so the blindfold will loosen, but it doesn't work. Suddenly, a dry bump and we're on a dirt road. We go up a steep incline. The van stops, but no one gets out. Now we're moving more slowly; the road is full of holes and the van jounces like a cocktail shaker. The nausea comes back. We've arrived, it seems. I hear voices outside. The van is stopped with the motor still running. They keep talking. I should be afraid. I'm very thirsty. Are they debating? Impossible. This was decided before they took me out. What can they be discussing? What they should do with my body? But that must also be decided beforehand.

My heart jumps when they open the back doors. "Come on," they say. "Come on now . . ." I know that this unfamiliar and vulgar voice is the voice of death. It's a relief. It's over. They pull me out because, though I try, I can't move. They pick me up themselves, they support me almost lifting me, and they carry me again. People die, that's all, they kill each other, so what. That's how it's always been, and that's how it will always be. *Violence is the midwife of history* . . . And what will happen to Anita? I tell myself: I should beg for mercy. But I'm speechless. The horror. The call of death embracing me. I want its peace. One of them, panting, smells of onions.

"OK, hold on to this." A trunk, a tree trunk. I think of the Cross, of the wood of the Cross. I'm a Christ, I say to myself. Did I think it then, or later? I'm stepping on a root. I hear them talking. "You wanna say something? 'Cause this is as far as you get, bitch. Get it?

We're gonna shoot you. So: this is as far as you get. You know, you brought this on yourself. Or no?" I hear a shouted order, then: "For the last time, you got something to say?"

My tongue is responding now and I say: "Yes."

I smell the stink of onion very close: "Go on . . ."

I say: "I want, please, a glass of water."

The guy bursts out laughing. "She wants a glass of water, the princess."

I sense him moving away. I hear the murmur of the others. I don't think about death. I think: Did they go to get me some water? They must have some water in a canteen around here, warm water that tastes like metal, but water nonetheless. "Here," he tells me: "Take a drink, shit." As if by reflex I move my hands and the cuffs squeeze them painfully. He puts the bottle in my mouth and I smell the pisco. No.

"I don't want pisco," I protest. "I want water." He tells me:

"You're fucked, 'cause there's no water here; there's just this leftover pisco. And if you don't drink it, bitch, I'll drink it myself. So hurry up." He carefully pulls back my head and puts the bottle between my lips. A sip that burns, another. I close my mouth. I feel the pisco sliding into the cracks in my lips. I'm thirstier. "A little more?" And he brings the bottle close again. I drink. I drink even though I don't like it. But I drink enthusiastically. "OK! Enough. You're not gonna drink it all, bitch . . ."

He moves away, taking the bottle with him. I hear his steps crushing dry leaves. I'm thirsty, I think. The pisco made me thirstier. I hear another shouted order. The squad, I think, that is my firing squad, the one that's fallen to me. How many people? Two, three? A pause. My heart is beating and I hear it beat. Its last spasms. We're in the foothills, it seems. All is calm. The silence of night in the country-side. The stars must be out. I'd like them to lift my blindfold just so I could see the stars one last time. I think of Canelo, who knew how to confront death. I think: I should shout *Long live commander Jo* . . . I shout and now, yes, the gunfire rips the mountain peace to shreds.

A burst of gunfire is so violent, so long and noisy, I think. It doesn't hurt yet, I manage to think.

I came back to myself and I was still alive. It was terrible. I was stretched out on the ground and one hip was hurting. I'm badly wounded, I thought. They're going to finish me off. This tree root is bothering my hip. I think: Why are they taking so long? My head is spinning and the nausea returns. What is this? I hear laughter coming closer. Now they'll finish me. Why are they laughing, the fuckers? I feel the cold of a gun barrel on my temple. Why are they still laughing?

FIVE

A faint light above, through the barred window. I came to and I was in the same narrow, damp cell with unpainted concrete walls. I wasn't wearing a blindfold. My wrists hurt. But I could move them; my hands were free. I looked at myself, touched my body as best I could. My hip hurt, the skin of my back was stinging. They didn't kill me, I thought. Nostalgia for death. Something was left unfinished. And suddenly I felt happy, inexplicably, absolutely happy. I was terribly thirsty, but I had survived. Fuck, I thought. Nothing has ended, then. And Anita? A shiver raced like a cat down my back. And last night dying felt like a relief, but now I'm happy to be alive. Thirst. And I did it. I held out, shit. To be without the blindfold, to see that beam of light on the wall, to move my hands on my bruised wrists, to feel them free: that is happiness. My cell is frozen by now. They're fucked. I fucked them over. And why didn't my captors kill me if they knew I was no good to them now? They didn't break me, the fuckers. If they would only give me a glass of water . . . I'm shivering.

"Tomasa," she tells me she's called. Tomasa embraces me, and I still don't quite know who she is, and she kisses me and hugs me and lends me her blanket. She repeats in my ear: "I'm Tomasa, I'm with Red Ax."

And like a dark and fast-moving cloud crossing overhead, the memory of the tiled room, the cold water, the insanity that blots out the world . . . I'm trembling. I'm thirsty, I'm thirsty. I imagine the transparency of water in a glass. I see the water streaming out in the bathroom. I see the ocean at El Quisco, its blue, its infinite pound of waves. I see my golden skin in the full-length mirror in my father's room. I'm in my bikini and I look fantastic. I swallow saliva and my throat scrapes. I curl up on the filthy mattress and I cover myself with my blanket and the one Tomasa lent me. The dark cloud of the metal bed frame, the cold sensation of the tiles, the Pentothal injection, Ronco's hoarse order. I think about that place. It's as if it were a hole, and the floor was tilting and all the things in the world were sliding toward it like a pile of worn-out furniture, like a wave of wind full of wreckage to be swallowed up by the magnet of a gigantic toilet. Only Ronco and Gato were left, talking in that empty basement that looked like a bathroom but wasn't one, but would become one again in a split second if some diligent judge dared come to inspect it. In that place Gato's word creates all, including the detritus that is me. What will become of my body, naked, shaved, and torn asunder for them? His word is a mirror I cannot see.

Someone picked me up and left me thrown down on that cold cell's rough cement floor. I curl up, pressed close to Tomasa: now I'm happy. If they gave me a glass of water I would be completely happy. I think about Anita and my heart gives a jump. Is she getting up now to go to school? The table with its flowered tablecloth, the mug of Milo with milk, the smell of the bread my mother just toasted, orange marmalade, a clear pitcher full of water. My mother, I think. If it weren't for her, what would become of Anita? I smell the Christmas bread my mother makes. But we're not close to Christmas. I can't describe that smell of Christmas bread, but I can smell it. After all, my mother is my mother, I think to myself.

The sound of a key and I am trembling. A fat woman, in jeans and a belt with holster and baton, orders me to get up. She's short and smells of old sweat. She cuffs my hands in front of me and blindfolds my eyes. She takes me by the cuffs, and I walk behind her, blind and awkward. Behind me, a guard's footsteps. The smell of an infirmary. They sit me down like when I first got here, at the edge of a cot. Someone, a man with fat fingers, takes my pulse and my blood pressure. They weigh me. They take my temperature. The coolness of the thermometer in my armpit is pleasant. I think of my father taking me by the hand, sitting on the edge of my bed when I was a child and had typhus and a high fever. He still lived in the house then. My mother, when I got sick, would put on her serious face—her medical technician face—take my temperature, prescribe lemonade, and wait for "new symptoms." Examination with the stethoscope, ear exam, throat, they turn my eyelids inside out. "Say: AAAHHH . . ." It hurts: the little hammer on my knees, reflexes. They palpate my joints. All this calms me, makes me feel taken care of. I move my arms, my legs, my ankles. They palpate my breasts, my stomach, ribs, and spine. The sound of rubber, a glove, I relax, internal examination. I'm happy. After this they'll let me go. I ask for a glass of water.

The doctor doesn't answer me. "You're in good condition," he says to me. "A piece of advice: if you don't want them to damage you, give them everything straight away. Believe me, anything else is pointless, it's self-destructive. It's up to you whether you make it out of here or not."

My spirits fall. He is, obviously, one of them.

Back in the cell, the same guard brings me a green plastic glass. The water fills it halfway. Tomasa advises me to only drink a sip so it will last. Some hours later the fat woman brings me a full glass. I sleep. I wake up. They bring us a tray with a watery, lukewarm chicken broth, the kind that comes in a Maggi bouillon cube. I didn't know I was so hungry. The thirst hid my hunger. I fall asleep. I wake up and pace until I can't pace anymore, and then I doze and I sleep, perhaps, and I pace. I'm thirsty. I'm hungry. I'm cold. Tomasa wraps me up, she tells me to try to walk. I look for the light of the barred window. When I hear the key, my heart jumps: now they'll let me go. No. It's only a glass of water. We're hungry. Then, I sleep.

Until it happens. They blindfold my eyes, handcuff me, they take me along the hallway, they make me go down some stairs, and—godddamn it!—I'm in a room with a tiled floor that I recognize. They ask me the same things and I repeat the same answers. Pure fear. I don't want them to punish me for having lied, for not having told them more before. A moment later I'm splayed out on top of the bed frame, tied up, moaning, with a rag in my mouth, subjected to the same technology of pain. At times I hear Ronco's shout, but it's a shout that seems far away from me, and then it gets closer and moves away again.

And Gato's faked voice returns. No one will ever know what happened here, he tells me; none of it matters, he tells me. I let him talk. I hear him from so far away, from my crumbling self. He asks me what I think I will do. I tell him I am too exhausted to think.

SIX

C'est tout, that's all. I'm telling you all of this because you're going to write a novel, not an interview, right? How did you find out about me? Oh, you told me already, I remember now. Rumors, of course, those crumbs that feed the hunger of the curious. Why would a writer like you be interested in my wretched story? Anyway, you got lucky. If you had come to see me a while back I would have answered you the same way I did all the others: Not one word about that. End of story.

Call me Lorena. Not Irene. I want to be Lorena to you. You'll never know my real name. I live here in Stockholm under an assumed name with false papers. I have cancer; I am, as they say, "at death's door."

To die is to be gradually overcome by minutiae, indignities, trifles. Death is not of God. My illness sped up my aging. Now the filth is out in the open, the physical fatigue, my obscenely organic nature, and the fragilities of my infancy are sprouting up again. It's the second childhood, pure oblivion. *Sans teeth, sans eyes, sans taste, sans everything.* I can't dress myself: I need someone to help me put on my bra, to help me put on my stockings. It takes time; you have no idea how much. I can't go to the bathroom by myself, I can't walk by myself. This, and nothing else, is what it means to die. It hurts here, on my back; my skin is peeling off after so much time in bed. From the position I'm in. They put lotion on me. New pains crop up—stupid, unexpected pains. Sometimes I spend hours with this tube in a vein in my wrist so they can infuse me with chemotherapy or whatever else they feel like. I live vulnerable and propped up by those inoculations. The oxygen dries my throat. The cylinder is always next to my bed, and there are days when my lungs depend on it the same way I do the wheelchair or the nurse's arm when she helps me to the bathroom. Modesty dies along with a person. The dead are shameless. Sometimes the nurse punishes me with a twisted hatred. I ring the bell and she doesn't come, or she leaves the wheelchair out of reach. I call her too often, she says. It's possible. It's very pedestrian, this business of dying. And it is slow, it takes an eternity. She pressures me, negotiates her moments of independence. It's a dull, cruel fight, this final battle. If my friend Agda were alive, she would come and see me, she would take care of me. That thought comforts me.

As my illness progresses, the nurse both serves me more and enslaves me more. I am gradually immobilized. If you only knew how long it takes me to put on my shoes, even with my keeper's help. But she doesn't bend down, she doesn't put them on with her hands. She pushes the shoes to me with her feet, she kicks them, and if they make it on, fine; if not, another shot. She hates trimming my stubborn toenails that now grow curved and yellow. My keeper puts that job off longer and longer. When she finally does it, she's careless, and it's not unusual for her to accidentally catch my skin in the clippers.

And I dribble. I'm always dribbling when I eat. I move the spoon and fork awkwardly. I hate that. My shaking betrays me. Or if I manage not to spill, I choke. Even drinking water, I choke. I'm not having a metaphysical experience here, as you can see. When I saw myself in the mirror for the first time after chemotherapy, without hair, I thought I was looking at my skull. A cliché. Death is the greatest of all clichés. I live in wait for rigor mortis. But I won't be watching when it comes. One doesn't live through one's own death. That of others, yes, from the other side of the threshold, of course. The dead do not live. What I'm living now is the gradual loss of the capacity for being alive. Dying. For me, that's what life consists of now. And when the time comes they'll throw me out, they'll send me to that trash pile they call by another name, before my stench starts to horrify them and my face and hands—too white, and soon stained with violet—begin to disgust them. Above all, before that stench comes that the bouquets of flowers can't mask. That's what it's about, then, to die: to be left shamelessly exposed, meat no one bought from the butcher's and that eventually rotted. Then they dress you up in wood and cover you up with earth so they never have to see you again; you disgust them, and they weep, those people you disgust, poor things.

No one will go with you, of course. Nothing you've done before will be worth anything to you. And from now on there's no purpose, no task, not even the smallest one stays with you. For this voyage you won't bring a suitcase. I can feel my fear. To see death a step away, waiting for you like an abyss just a yard and a half away, and to be the one who's going to fall—it's atrocious, I tell you, just horrifying. I didn't want to die when Canelo fell in combat. Now either, you know; I don't want to die now, either. Even though when I was healthy, I did. And they're taking my life from me one bite at a time.

Do not go gentle into that good night. / Old age should burn and rave at close of day; / rage, rage against the dying of the light. Dylan Thomas. What do you know, I still have some memory left.

That's why you've come all the way to Ersta, Stockholm, to listen to me. I'm not kidding myself. You've come before it's too late . . . You're a crow with an ear for a beak. No one can understand this story. And no one would want to. It's useless. Only the edifying fable with its moral will remain, only the husk of the facts, the pornography of horror. We know that. But what gave it meaning, what made it human—that dies with us. I don't know how you'll use what I tell you, though I'm curious. I don't know if it will help you at all. I don't think a novel should repeat reality. Perhaps you should just imagine me on your own. You want me to talk to you about fingerprints, lock picks, chases, car bombs, manhunts, shootouts, and torture. But in the end what you're looking for is a moral adventure tale. That's what will get you a publisher. People love a story that confirms their prejudices. To recognize what they've already seen on TV: that's what they like. The truth is too disturbing, thorny, too contradictory and horrible. Truth is immoral. It shouldn't be printed. You won't write what I tell you. You're not going to like what you hear at all. I can read it in your eyes. *Hypocrite lecteur, mon semblable, mon frère:* Hypocritical reader, my double, my brother!

Ha, ha! Why am I laughing? You were saying you wanted my version. Don't ask me to give you yours, then. You have to listen to my story. That's why you came to Ersta. No one made you come here. You know what? I can smell your contempt, your virtuous-souled contempt.

Remember, when Dante reaches the bottom of Hell he finds the Devil crying. But he's still the Devil, and he doesn't repent. If he did, he would be in Purgatory, and he would have hope. The Devil doesn't repent and yet he cries, he cries hopelessly. There's something undignified about repentance and the desire for forgiveness, something Christianoid that bothers me. The Devil, even in defeat, stays faithful to himself and to his own contradiction. He punishes those he inspired and who have followed in his footsteps, he punishes them day and night, as he himself is punished. He is the supreme traitor.

SEVEN

Hate is human. There is nothing I don't hate. Tomasa hates only the other side. Not our brothers, not the ones who placed the bomb and blew up the bridge, not the ones she hid and who later fled, she tells me, leaving her at the mercy of these rabid dogs. I don't know what cell she's in. We try to maintain our compartmentalization. But I do know that they've brought her face to face with Chico Escobar and with Vladimir Briceño. There must be microphones in here, because she whispers it in my ear. "They want to know about the cash," she says.

I passed Briceño in the hallway. I'm sure they did that intentionally. His nose was broken, his shirt soaked in blood. We did as we'd been taught: we looked at each other like strangers. It isn't easy. How do two strangers look at each other in a place like that? Your surprise can betray you—the unexpected pleasure of recognizing a friend, though he's in the same situation as you—and so can an overly studied indifference . . . They're very alert to any signs.

"If they would just let me work," Tomasa says to me. "If they would just let me use my body for something. If only I could be a whore, I could do something and I'd at least be that, a whore. I want to prostitute myself," she says. You won't be able to understand that feeling. Even I can't understand it now, but I did back then. Who could I have been in those days?

If only they would let me shower. That's all I ask. As the days pass you can't imagine how important that becomes to me. I can't stand my own smell. Let me change these stinking clothes. Who knows how many people used them before me. They keep us in this basement in these gray, foul-smelling sweat suits and underneath them, nothing. I just want to wear underpants; I want to put on a bra, that's what I want. Clothes never used to interest me. But now . . . If they would only let me go out in the yard for a little while to feel the warmth of the sun on my face.

They've said to Tomasa: "Show us your tits, fucking cunt!" And she has lifted her shirt and done as they said. "Your nipples are really long," they told her. "Your nipples are skinny and ugly," they told her. And that time they didn't rape her. Me, I have pretty nipples. Tomasa screamed and they made me listen. She started to screech the moment they tied her up. I try to get used to it. It's impossible. She shouts like a wild boar. According to her, it protected her; according to her, it satisfied them and they weren't as hard on her. I've told her how I feel about underwear, what I would give for a Triumph bra. She doesn't care at all about that. As long as they don't rape her again, she doesn't care about anything. I want a bra. I feel so skinny . . . Who could buy me a bra? It doesn't matter if they have sex with you, Tomasa tells me, what matters is that they don't damage your insides. Gato rewards Rat or Ronco, she tells me, he gives them the go-ahead when he feels like it. Tomasa lent me a little mirror the other day. Somehow she gets her hands on those kinds of things. I saw the circles under my eyes, my sunken face, my elongated ears poking out from my greasy hair. My ears never used to stick out like that. But they do now. My breasts are smaller and more flaccid. Or am I imagining that? Surely that's why I don't interest them; they don't even want me to show them. I can feel their nondesire. I've heard that some women are forced to dance and they end up naked as showgirls, dancing and crying, naked as effigies of showgirls. In spite of everything, Tomasa and I laugh. I don't remember about what. But there are things we whisper about that make us burst out laughing.

I concentrate on trying to figure out what time it is, on following the sun between the bars of our cell's little window and measuring the shadows on the damp walls. The task keeps me busy. Tomasa got her hands on a deck of cards. That keeps us busy. She knows some tricks that amaze me. Tomasa tells me she imagines things, tells herself stories, dreams that she's free, that she's at her mother and father's house, that she's at a barbecue with high school girlfriends, that she's climbed up to place a charge on a high-voltage tower, or the column of a bridge; she dreams she's shooting at the enemy. That's how she kills time. I try to do the same, I try to imagine I'm crawling along on knees and elbows, soaked to the skin, in the Nahuelbuta mountain range, or with my heavy pack over my shoulder hiding out in the mountains and covering my tracks, or conducting a Vietnamese maneuver, or stashing an FAL rifle—one of those that donkey-kicks your shoulder when you fire—well-oiled and loaded in a hidden compartment under the floor of a house, or I imagine myself excavating a dugout to sleep in under the snow. I never manage to hold these images in my mind. And then, when they take Tomasa for another interrogation, her outbursts are truly frightening. She's already told them everything, surely. Why do they keep working on her? And I have to listen to it. And when my turn comes, they repeat their instructions: Raise your hand if you want to talk.

Days that are nights go by, merging into nights that are nights. I'm an animal reduced to basic desires: that they won't hurl one more blow or insult at me or take away my bowl of soup, the pillow or mattress, or the can that serves as a toilet in our cell. It's all happened to me. These are light punishments. I was punished for lying: four days with the same can, if I figured the time right. I can hear a bell, and that gives us a way to measure time. I hate to admit it, but it's the truth. The only thing left of that eviscerated time is the bell of a church that gives opiate to the people. It's like being locked in a medieval dungeon. Although in my situation now the priests are a help, even so, I repeat, they deal in resignation as consolation. Still and all I wait for those bells without which my dragging time would brush the abyss. It's an anemic present that evaporates and abandons me. The bells are the only human thing we have left.

Then, suddenly, they led me to a changing room and handed me a zippered plastic bag. There were the clothes I was wearing the day they arrested me. My purse, too, my wallet with the eight thousand seven hundred pesos I had with me that day, and my false ID card—everything except the thirty thousand dollars and the four million plus in Chilean pesos we had taken from the Bash safe in the currency exchange. They gave me a document signed by a military judge I never saw: provisional freedom. They had, they laughed, paid my bail with the money they found in my purse. I got dressed and they set me free at stop number 21 on Gran Avenida. There were no explanations.

EIGHT

They let me go in the afternoon. I did what our manuals taught us to do, to lose any "shadows," as we called them. "Tails," as they said in Central. But it's hard for me to walk in a straight line. The light hurts. The wideness scares me, the open space of the street. My first job is to lose my potential watcher. Useless, I thought. But I had to do it and I did it. I got on and off of two buses in a row, I walked along streets and then retraced my steps, I walked around the Central Station a couple of times, went out, and got on a third bus. I decided they weren't shadowing me. Finally, about four hours later, I got to my mother's house. It was a shock. My mother cried, so did the cook—everyone but Anita, who looked at me without understanding. Five years old, she was then.

I took a long, slow, hot shower and got into bed. I said I was tired and I needed to sleep. But I just lay there facing the wall. I couldn't get up. I wanted to be alone and not think about anything. My mother gave me some pills to help me sleep, and I managed to doze for a few hours. Ever since that day, I've never again been able to fall asleep without pills. Nor have I been able to sleep with the light off. I need a little light, otherwise I start tossing in bed and I can't sleep anymore. I woke up suddenly, startled and sweating. I was still in my childhood room.

When I left home to live on my own I didn't want to bring anything with me, and my mother kept things exactly as they were. It's as if I'd left home yesterday. There's an old Silvio Rodriguez cassette in my stereo. Those must have been the last songs I heard in this room. Everything is the same. Even a few old dolls with faded hair that I never gave away, which watch me from the shelf with staring eyes, open and empty, as if dead. I look at the little-girl curtains my mother never changed: they're sky blue with red, green, and yellow balloons. Behind them the flowers of the apricot tree press against the window. I look at the clock. Time doesn't pass.

My mother comes in and it's as if she'd woken me up in the middle of the night. Seeing her there disconcerts me. She's gained weight; I'm annoyed that she's here and interrupting me when I need to be alone. She opens the window so the scent from the apricot tree can waft in, but I sneeze and sneeze, waves of sneezing: I'm allergic to the pollen. If we were at the beginning of spring, with a little luck I could reach out my arm and grab an apricot. That's if the pigeons didn't beat me to it, or the damned ants. I stay there lying in bed, not thinking of anything. I used to love the flowers on the apricot tree. I try to smell them the way I used to, but I can't. I close the curtain. "I'm not hungry," I tell my mother. I bark at her, more like it: "I'm not hungry! Don't bother me, please . . ." I curl up and shrink from her. I want to be alone in the dark.

"I didn't mean to bother you," says my mother. "Quite the opposite . . ." She looks at me. I should apologize, but I say nothing. Finally, just when I'm about to utter the words, she makes a half-turn and leaves, gently closing the door. I should call her back and give her a hug. I freeze up.

My mind jumps around: the rough stubble on my father's chin against my face, Rodrigo's back as he plays paddleball on the beach, Ronco's shout, my grandmother's deeply wrinkled cheeks. And the rancid smell of the nuns in school, Gato's sibylline voice, the pain in my wrists, the pain on my back from the electrified bed frame, the feeling of Canelo's short hair in my hand, the dry sound of my leather purse closing with the money inside . . . My memories bounce off of hard glass.

I'm empty, I need deliverance, but there is none. Sighs escape my lips. And my sighs are the howls of an animal that has lost its vocal cords. Even stretching out in the bed is an effort. I doze curled up. Nothing will move me from that position. Except the anguish squeezing my guts; then I arch my body as though trying to wrench away from myself. How long will it last? What can calm me? It's hard to breathe. I'm desperate. The floor sinks down. I'm the one who has to end this. I should do now what I should have done with my Beretta in Calle Moneda. I'm resolved. Yes, now. There's no hysteria. I'm reasoning coldly. No one can endure this anguish. It's the only way out. But not now. As soon as I have the strength. I'll go to my mother's bathroom and swallow the whole box of sleeping pills. That's the answer. This is impossible to bear, it's inhuman. The decision calms me down.

Until Anita comes in and climbs in bed with me. She makes me laugh. I hadn't remembered her laugh, and when I see it spill from her mouth, it makes me laugh, too. When she leaves my room, I fall back into the abyss that opens up for me and leads to another abyss, which also opens up and drops me into yet another abyss.

My mind wanders to Liv Ullmann's face in the black-and-white film *Persona*, by Bergman. The scene goes like this: Liv is in bed in her white nightgown, smoking, motionless while she listens with enormous attention to what Bibi Andersson is telling her from the armchair. Alma! Of course, Bibi Andersson is Alma, the nurse, and Liv is an actress—I forget her name—who is sick, withdrawn deep into herself, barely moving and refusing to talk. Bibi, who is Alma, talks to her and likes that Liv listens.

What Bibi, the nurse, is telling her about is a strange sex scene with some very young boys at the beach. She and a friend were sunbathing naked when these unknown boys came along and started to ogle them. Her friend said to her: "Let them look." And Bibi, inexplicably, stayed there, naked and lying face down. Her friend stayed on her back. One of the boys, the braver one, came closer, and her friend took his hand, helped him take his clothes off, and they began to make love. Her hands squeezed the muscles of his buttocks while he penetrated her. Then Bibi wanted to have sex with this same boy; she did, and she got very excited and came immediately.

Then the other boy came over and her friend started to play with him, and he came in her friend's mouth; she touched herself then and when she came she cried out . . .

As Bibi's story goes on, Liv's face, listening, becomes larger. The hand with her cigarette covers her thirsty mouth. It's a kind of modesty that gives us pause. Later that night, Bibi goes on saying, she made love with her fiancé and it was better than it had ever been before or would be again. She can't understand how the whole thing happened.

The silent profile of Liv's face continues filling the screen. The light seems to sculpt that face in stone. The forehead, the eye, the outline of the nose, the contour of the lips, all chiseled by light. It's an inhibited and emotional face. Moved by what she hears. Her full lips, made for kissing, are hesitating, about to open. Something is transforming her from inside, but she holds it back.

It's extraordinary! Liv just listens. And that's what Bergman filmed: a woman listening.

Time is beginning to stick to the curtains. Beyond them, hidden, are the flowers of the apricot tree. A black claw reaches into my stomach and squeezes me from inside. If this doesn't stop, I know what I have to do, I tell myself. It doesn't make me sad. It's not revenge. I think that I should prepare my mother, my father, Anita. But how?

So, how did it come to this? I tell myself: I have to go back to my mother. I must. My mother: smart, ugly, but well shaped, good breasts, good legs. I've told myself this story before. A woman who works in Radiology at the Salvador Hospital feels that her face doesn't belong to her, she's insecure about her looks—but not about her intelligence. She wins the love of a tall, muscular, beautiful man. He's a talented tennis player but not, of course, a professional. He's a businessman. He works with his father in a small workshop in the neighborhood of Carrascal. He buys tree trunks in the south, brings them by train to Santiago, and makes them into boards, planks, and panels. For doors and windows, for floors. That's what my father makes and sells: doors and windows.

Now it strikes me as a poetic trade, but not back then. The best wood is rauli beech or holm oak. Sometimes he's contracted for a walnut door. His father still gets to the yard at six in the morning and is annoyed if his son—who must be over forty by now—isn't there yet. My grandfather is Catalan. He's the one who taught my father all the tricks. My father told them to me. How to use the spray gun to lacquer pine particleboard; how to work the table saw and the circular saw; how to add a hundred years to a young rauli or roble beech by darkening it with cedar extract so it passes for a strong, ancient beech; how to kill the yellow spots on chestnut by rubbing them with a soft bitumen-soaked cloth, so you can sell it as oak, which has such a similar grain; how to disguise a knot, which mordant to use, which aniline (if one is disposed to use aniline), how to get rid of the pores using a rag soaked in alcohol, powdered pumice stone, and a few drops of varnish; how to apply—just the way foreman Vicente shows him—a very thin layer of shellac, and then sand it and apply another coat, so the wood gradually takes on, layer upon layer, as the fumes evaporate, that singular caramel tone of a real lacquer. Master Vicente knows how to keep varnish from getting that fatal roughness that looks like an orange peel. He taught my father to do battle with those gray spots that form, using benzoin mixed with oil and, afterward, polishing it with the palm of the hand covered with a mixture of Venetian tripoli, water, sulfuric acid, Vaseline, turpentine, and alcohol. You have to smell the wood, my grandfather tells him, you have to touch it, love and taste it. It's the only way the wood will give itself over to you. The finest varnish contained lacquer, sandarac, and white elemi. What his father absolutely never taught him, but Vicente did, was how to make a good "prison rotgut" by mixing tea and lemon with the alcohol for dissolving shellac. The first time my father got drunk it was in the workshop on that cocktail of Vicente's.

My mother is totally uninterested in this world of wood. She falls in love with a good-looking, healthy, vigorous man, who handles his

Jeep well, who patiently teaches her to play tennis, and who takes her on vacation with his parents to the beach at El Quisco. They get married, they have their first child—me—and they're happy, except that the second child takes its time in coming. Tests.

That's where they are when the drama unfolds. One night, when he's told her he has to stay late at the workshop to receive a shipment of larch boards arriving from the south, she follows him, sees him go into a restaurant, waits a while, and finally, gathering up her courage, she goes in and sees him at a corner table with "another woman." My mother goes over to them striding like a queen (according to her), and when she gets to the table she realizes she doesn't know what she's going to do. My father watches her, pallid. The woman is gorgeous and young. She waits, flabbergasted.

Then my mother can think of nothing better than to introduce herself to the stranger, to reach out her hand and say: "I'm this man's wife." And the woman stands up, shakes her hand, lowers her eyes, and says: "I understand, ma'am." Then my mother faces my father. She shouts: "As for you, I will not greet you, and I never will again, you little shit!" And in a single motion she grabs the glass of wine and throws it in his face. She leaves the restaurant walking like a queen, leaving a tomblike silence in her wake.

My father will defend himself, he'll say it was a casual fling. He will apologize. My mother will reject him. My soul will be torn in two. I tape a photo on the wall of my room of my father playing tennis, hitting a backhand. His body stretches out like a rubber band. The effort is concentrated in his face. My mother can't forgive him. My father pursues her for months. Nothing.

Until he finds someone else. She's attractive, with a pretty face, and fourteen years younger than my mother. She plays tennis well. My mother is devastated. I stay with her; it's what I have to do, but inside I'm contemptuous. I'm eleven years old. I loved and still love my father. I go to his new house in Ñuñoa with its terrace of grapevines, its apple tree, two plum trees, and, at the back, an old olive tree with gnarled branches; and there's Master, a purebred German shepherd that I adore. I still go with my father to El Quisco, to the same rustic wooden cabin he's always had. We take Master with us. When we arrive, I smell the salt and the stale air. We have to ease open the windows and air out the sheets. I like to see them hanging in the sun, so white, changing shape as the wind takes possession of them. They change colors, taking on a new brilliance. I like to be there by the sea, alone with him. Not with his new wife. I watch him in the mirror while he shaves. Why couldn't my mother keep him?

As soon as my father remarries, I don't like going to his house in Ñuñoa anymore. But I go. And he worries about me. He calls me more often than I'd like. One day he takes me with him to the South. I'm fifteen years old and I love the idea of traveling alone with him. His wife is almost always with him when I see him. We're going to look at a forest. We travel by plane to Temuco and stay in a hotel. I feel so grown up and happy. The next day a Jeep comes to pick us up. It's a long ride up a mountain track. To one side is a ravine, to the other, dense, wet forests, immense ferns, climbing vines. My father explains that the land isn't his, only the machinery, which, he tells me, required taking on "severe debt" to buy. We turn onto a wider road. After a few minutes the noise starts. A truck goes by carrying tree trunks, then another truck. We get out and continue on foot. My father talks to the guy who came to pick us up.

Suddenly, horror. A machine moves among the trees, takes hold of one with two steel arms, and cuts it down. The embrace lasts about a minute. When the trunk falls, the earth trembles. Other talons grab the trunk that fell and they strip it in no time, removing its branches. The earth thunders again: another tree has fallen. A crane picks up the freshly stripped tree and throws it on the truck. In less than five minutes a life that took over eighty years to reach that immensity has ended. Another tremor: the machine felled another tree. I ask my father if we can leave. He is surprised. He's brought me here to show me his new machinery. He tells me again that he's gone into debt so he can buy it. I start to cry and I don't stop until we get back to Temuco.

My father tries to console me but he can't. From that moment on he won't be able to. I can't see him the way I did before. I'm fifteen years old now. From that day on his presence in my life will gradually diminish, and later on, when I start university, he will be an enemy. But it hurts me, and he remains in my thoughts, speaking to me from there, always very close to me. If I go to him because I need something, he never fails me. Almost always what I need is money, and he gives it to me, no questions asked. He gives it to me happily.

Some two years pass, and I find out that things are going badly for him. He's had to turn all the tree-harvesting machinery over to the bank, and he's barely maintaining the workshop. He's sold his house, his stock in the tennis club, his car. Now he rents a duplex that doesn't have a garage. He uses a canvas to cover the used Taunus he bought. He mortgaged the house in El Quisco. He's sad, embarrassed. I know what I should feel, I try to convince myself to feel it, but the rage is stronger. I like how the anger overcomes my compassion. I'm losing sight of him. I have a boyfriend, Rodrigo, an animal, a tender animal.

I found a notebook at my mother's house. Eighteen, I must have been when I wrote it. I was in college. It's a diary but not a daily one, a notebook swollen full of banal notes, dried flowers, matchbooks and scraps and napkins and cards, everything glued in. It's one of the few things my mother sent me from Chile when I came to Sweden. A few weeks ago, when I found out you were coming, I reread it. Nothing worthwhile, I'd say. Except for a couple of folded pages that fell out of the notebook and that I don't remember writing. But the handwriting is mine from that time. Look, if you go over to the dresser, next to the TV, you'll see a couple of folded sheets of paper under a little statue of the Virgin of Guadalupe. Why a Virgin of Guadalupe? A Spanish priest brought it to me. You know, this home is part of Ersta Diakonianstalt. They're Protestant, but every week a Catholic priest comes. He assumed that I must be Catholic because I'm Latin American. I told him I'm not, not anymore. But he insisted. He wanted to pray with me, and finally, I gave in. He left me that little statue as a gift. To help me start praying again. Do you think it helps to pray if you're not a believer? There! Underneath. See them? Give them to me. You won't be able to read the writing. I'll read them to you.

"My father always sticks his nose in. I saw it all coming. He'd like to plan and control every second of my life. He thinks for me. It's not that he wants me to be like him, not that. He wants to invent me. And so he attempts the impossible. His love suffocates me. I should just leave, I know. And when I say good-bye, I don't know why the tears come to my eyes, tears I can barely hold back. Then his demanding, loving gaze will infiltrate me, and I forget the suffocation and my anger. What I remember then is his capacity for utter devotion to me, his conversation that comforts me, his care for me, and his blind faith in me moves me then, that hope of his that encourages and then punishes me; his unconditional nature, too, and my own confidence—less every day, of course—in his ability to take charge.

"How to regain those earlier times when I was a little girl, those moments when we understood each other without trying, and just being with him was fun. Back then there wasn't this pressure or these heartaches, the neglected duty, my anguish over not accomplishing what I've promised myself, though deep down I know it's just my own youthful ambition and he's to blame, he's the one who implanted this feeling of specialness in me. Back then I didn't have this critical and evasive gaze. I blame myself. Myself, and my mother. It's my endless adolescence. They explained to us in school over and over what it was all about. Is it possible to return to a previous state? Or if not, when will I be old enough to leave all this behind? And it's not a question of getting some physical distance—we already have that. He filters into my mind. The other day I was flipping through his books, which are few, and I came across a verse. It said that the father, even dead, has 'fear within me, within my very hope.' It was a quotation from Rilke, and he had underlined it himself. It was a self-help book for fathers. I think it must have been a gift from his wife, who isn't very intellectual, shall we say. But the only parts that were underlined had been underlined by him. In my solitude, that uncertainty of his sneaks in and I can be, in part, how I think he might want to be if he were me. Only by keeping my distance can I manage to be myself and also coincide with him. And be at peace. But only partially. Because there's an equally strong and insistent force that makes me want to be definitively separate from him, that urges me to live as though he had never existed. And when the good-bye comes, the very moment I've been looking forward to, sometimes my eyes fill with tears. And it's not that the separation is going to be long, no. Because it's not my departure from that duplex of his, with Master playing in the front yard, that separates us. My departure is just a pretext for that long embrace that we give each other always and never."

That's it. Well, you can tell I was in college and I was trying to write with a certain style, right? How pretentious . . .

NINE

I come out of my childhood room and I search among my mother's jars and bottles. I draw an almost boiling bath, a bubble bath. I use her verbena soap, her shampoo, her conditioner with pure olive oil, I dry off with her fluffy towel, I spread her almond-scented lotion over my legs, my arms, over my diminished breasts. I trim my toenails, I use her lotion for cracked heels. I take the top off her bottle of nail polish; its smell would make me dizzy now. I open her makeup box and that palette of colors calls out to me; I'd like to make an abstract painting with my hands. But its shades confuse me, I don't know how to begin, and I go back to bed with my hair wet.

I return to the apricot tree. I try to imagine the way those ripe apricots looked shining in the afternoon light. As I said already: beyond the curtains I don't open there are no apricots yet, there are flowers plastered against my window. I glance at the bedside table: a pile of pages stuck to old glue. No covers. Dry, yellow pages: "Would I find la Maga? Most of the time it was just a case of putting in an appearance, going along the rue de Seine to the arch leading into the Quai de Conti, and I would see her slender form against the olive ashen light . . ." I turn to page 48: "I touch your mouth, I touch the edge of your mouth with a finger, I am drawing it as if it sprang forth from my hand . . . ," and to page 428: "As soon as he began to amalate the noeme, the clemise began to smother her and they fell into hydromuries, into savage ambonies, into exasperating sustales." So many times I had dreamed with open eyes over this book . . . I start to fall asleep. It's wonderful to be able to doze like that.

Suddenly, I hear my father's voice.

My door opens and he's really there, sitting at the edge of my bed, his big hand caressing my hair. He looks younger than my mother. I smell his same old Yardley cologne. It smells of lavender; it is what remains of his old life. That, and his suit made of good cloth that's grown shiny and worn with use. He's a youthful and handsome old man, with his shock of white hair falling over his ears. It's strange to see him there in my mother's house.

When he heard me crying he put his arms around me. The only thing I wanted was to again be the little girl whose father could make everything right with the world. I'm sure that's what he wanted too. It felt wonderful to burst into tears in his arms; I felt myself growing calm little by little, though I didn't stop crying, pressed close to him and wanting to never let go. I wanted to go with him to El Quisco, I told him, that very day, to swim in the sea, play paddleball on the beach with him . . . I made him lie down next to me on the bed. I laid my head on his chest. I felt the thin cotton of his shirt and the cold silk of his tie on my cheek. I felt his beating heart against my ear. "Daddy," I said to him.

It was dusk when I woke up. How long had I slept? There was barely a trace of light floating behind the curtains. Then he started talking to me, he told me he loved me so, so much, and that for all these years he had thought of me every day, every day. He was talking in a soft murmur, and I took refuge in his tenderness. I felt that, like an incubator coaxing chicks out of shells, his warmth was bringing me back to myself, to what I had been, to a lost peace. Happiness had existed, and I could get it back.

Suddenly he was asking, in the same sweet and masculine tone, why I had gotten myself into this trouble; he said he had told me not to get mixed up in politics, it was a foolish thing to do under a dictatorship. I jerked away roughly and ordered him to leave the room. My teeth were chattering in rage. I couldn't speak. I couldn't control my jaw. He tried to soothe me, he told me he was sorry. I wouldn't relent, and I threw him out of my room. He told me that no matter what happened or what I did, he would always love me and I could always count on him. He closed the door gently. I tried to cry, but I couldn't.

TEN

My inability to coincide with myself, when did that begin? The distance from myself that I seem to have always felt, what caused it? And my resentment? I go back, then, inevitably, to the rupture that came from my parents' divorce, my harsh disdain for my mother after my father left—my mother, who didn't know how to keep him with her. Her efforts to be motherly only seemed like signs of her impotence. I go back to my father, the love I felt—the resentful love of an only child for the man who had left us both—my jealousy of his new wife, who was not my mother but who wanted to be something like it, and thus let me punish both him and her in revenge for my scorned mother. I go back to my intense devotion to Mary, virgin and mother who never knew a man's sex. She was my solace, she and my grandmother, my grandmother with her white hair that would turn yellow and her natural, easy laugh, whom I went to visit every afternoon.

And I'm haunted by my terror of the nuns, of their sparse moustaches and their rancid odor, their severity that intimidated and disciplined me; later, my disdain for them would grow, for their irredeemable infantilism, their sinful vigilance. I feel the desolation of the day of my first period, my disconsolate sobbing. I didn't want to stop being a little girl yet, I was still very short, and I couldn't, just couldn't accept that my childhood had ended so suddenly and with such strange discomfort, a pain down low in my belly, and this dark blood, viscous, foul-smelling, and mine—no, I didn't want to be a woman, not yet. But it was forced on me, just like my parents' divorce and the sudden death of my grandmother, who took the Virgin with her. She left me her embossed silver mirror. I still have it.

And then the fear of my body; fear of its desires, then, the desire at its core, in its hidden depths and cavities. And the humiliation of that market of little virgin whores in the parties and clubs, which our mothers prepared us for—with help from hairdressers, stylists, make-up artists, and aestheticians—marinating our bodies as if in a stew, transforming them so we could seduce brutish teenagers who dream of animal sex and flee from intimacy. I certainly couldn't make friends with either boys or girls at those animal markets.

I grew up alone and separate. I had the feeling that I was inert, and I needed to keep myself soft like clay, always soft, waiting and waiting for the man to arrive who would be able to give me shape. Because in spite of everything, I wanted my Pygmalion to appear, even if he was nothing but a beautiful animal.

But I didn't like the way I looked. I was pained by the women whose looks I did like, the pretty ones, the ones who felt men's eyes following them. I was saddened by other women's beauty. I wished I could just deflower myself. My mother would stay working at the hospital until very late. Her duty was to the sick. Her daughter would just have to understand. My mother never created a relaxed atmosphere where I could be myself. She didn't know how. This was never more obvious than when she took it upon herself to forcibly construct that "homelike atmosphere" and would start to make dinner, asking me to light a fire. My mother didn't like how I looked, and that made her feel desperate. She would have liked to have a very beautiful daughter. Who wouldn't? She used to inspect my hairstyle and would always suggest a change. The change that could make up for the beauty I was lacking. She says that to me with the cold calm behind which she hides her frustration. She says it while putting on her glasses and peering at me in the mirror with the same harsh seriousness she has when she looks at X-rays. She comments on my eye shadow, gives advice. She speaks like a doctor prescribing medicine. Then she smooths a lock of hair yet again, and her gaze becomes even harsher, as if she hates me for not being the beauty she wanted. That's how I feel. The pimples that sprout on my face drive her crazy. She wants to squeeze them. She can't resist. Same with my blackheads. She has to pinch them out of my skin. She can't resist. She'd use her teeth if she could. She's like a monkey picking lice.

And finally, my great love—because desire creates the object of desire—came to me, came to me while I was studying French language and literature at university and reading that *it's the Devil holds the strings that move us*, and adoring the *Black Sun of Melancholy*. I recited idiotically to my stupid and beautiful animal: *J'ai tant rêvé de toi que tu perds ta réalité*, I've dreamed of you so much that you're losing your reality. And it was true. I'd been dreaming of him for so long.

I met him on the beach at El Quisco. He hypnotized me as he played paddleball in his bathing suit. I found myself watching the deft movements of his lithe, hairless body—his legs that were firm and a little crooked, his slender back—and then lowering my gaze to his, how to put it, his unforgettable green bathing suit. Yes. The "gluteous" shapes beneath that green bathing suit were momentous for me. I don't think that word exists. It would have to be invented for him, for his "gluteous" form. I've never seen anything like it since. I shivered, and felt ashamed. He lost the game but he won me over.

And with him, I will dare to go out past the breaker zone, deep enough to swim. The feeling of floating in the ocean, as if I were free from gravity's force. Sometimes he lets himself float, other times he swims fast, driving his arms into the waves and showing me the strength of his grown man's shoulders before I lose him from sight. He dives underneath me, under the water, and reappears here or over there. If I got a bad cramp and doubled up and started to drown, Rodrigo would save me. It would be wonderful to be saved by him. Really, I wanted to dance with him. That's all I wanted, for the moment.

It makes me laugh to remember it. It makes me sad to remember. He came to pick me up to go to a bonfire at the beach. As we were leaving he said he'd left his sweater at home, and I went with him to get it. We went inside. The house was empty. His aunt and uncle had gone to Santiago and wouldn't be back until Friday, he told me, looking at me with his calm, direct gaze. A log cabin, all very rustic. We sat down on a wicker sofa on the second floor deck, overlooking the ocean. He put on music. We drank piscola. I took off my sandals and rested my feet on a little bamboo table. And then, I don't know how, we were dancing. Diana Ross's voice mixed with the sound of the nearby ocean. *Reach out and touch somebody's hand.*

Over his shoulder I could see the foam shining on the waves as they broke, lit up by the moon. The floorboards of the deck were spaced apart, and they felt rough when my toes went between them. That was annoying. But it was delicious when my toes would accidentally brush against his. When had he taken off his sandals? A big toe slid over my foot and pressed at the base of my toes. I lost the rhythm and missed a step. He held me firm and I felt the muscles in his chest pressing into mine. The image of his torso in his bathing suit flashed into my mind. My stomach tightened. Here. Like this.

That present, that now drains away without us noticing. What that now holds within it is the crash of waves nearby in the night, and a man's foot that brushes against mine and stays. Accidentally. We're dancing. That's all. And the separated boards of a second-floor deck torment our feet and obstruct their movement. We can't help but dance very slowly. *No matter where you are, no matter how far . . .* His face is pressed against mine. His tenderness makes me melt. *No wind, (no wind) no rain, (no rain) / Nor winter's cold . . .* I feel a thigh move between my legs. Its invasive touch unsettles. He's bringing me to a place I'd rather not go. I sense danger. *Do you know where you're going to?* But there's a hand with immense fingers that moves down my back and comes to rest along my spine with a smooth naturalness.

When that hand pulled me toward him I had no choice but to go. And then I felt the intrusive thigh wasn't alone, there was something else now, a firm mass. Was that what he was thinking about? My first reaction was repulsion and disgust, almost. But when I felt it so aggressive and firm and persistent, so foreign to the rest of a human being's body, I don't know . . . I had never imagined the curiosity that insolent, uninvited guest would provoke in me. Suddenly, I was laughing with my eyes closed and my head thrown back. Rodrigo's lips on my neck. A shiver went down my back. This was serious. I straightened up and my mouth landed precisely on his. We kissed with a calm that we barely maintained.

My first kiss . . . Anyone who forgets her first kiss didn't deserve it. Don't you think? Even if she has a degree in French literature and she's read all her Simone de Beauvoir, her Foucault, and her Derrida. Mine was in El Quisco, like I told you. The truth is, I could never forget. I don't want to, either. Even though Rodrigo turned out to be a bastard. But in that first encounter there was sensitivity, gentleness, tenderness. Nothing that hinted at the cruelty to come. Our heads moved apart, and the first thing I saw were his eyes narrowed in a smile. When I was able to disengage from those tender, kind eyes, my gaze went to his mouth that, also smiling, was waiting for me. *No wind, no rain, / can stop me, babe* . . . My stomach was being wrung like a wet towel. Something in him was escaping. My mouth sought his and I lost myself in it, I did battle with an ardent tongue, rough and formidable. We gasped for air and he held my hips and pulled me toward him calmly, surely. I don't know: his bare foot moved slowly over mine.

That night, back in my own room, I fell asleep with Diana Ross's voice in my ears. I thought about Rodrigo's sweet eyes, and I felt them next to me. It was a hot night, and every so often I woke to the buzz of mosquitoes flying over my sun-browned skin.

The next day I didn't see him on the beach. I was with his friends, but I didn't dare ask about him. I searched for him as though sleep-walking. Nothing. He'd disappeared. The next day, same thing. And so on. I was eaten up by longing. I slept badly. Then I would spend the day yawning, and the yawns turned to sighs on my lips. On the fourth day, let's see . . . Yes, I think it was the afternoon of the fourth day, I spotted him playing paddleball. I slowly brought my sun umbrella closer. While I walked over the sand I could look right at him through my dark sunglasses without disguising it. I untied my beach wrap from around my waist and carefully spread it out over the sand; I got my Nivea sunscreen from my bag and began rubbing it over my legs. I took my time. Was he watching me? I lay on my back with my straw hat over my face.

I didn't wait long. I heard a footstep, very close by; a dusting of sand and someone took off my hat. His chin, his nose, inches from mine, his disconcerting smile. Calmly, I got up, tied the wrap around my waist, and reached out my arm to take the paddle he was offering me, smiling, his face all full of sun. I noticed the white mark left by his sunglasses, his dripping hair, his eyelashes caked with sea salt. His hand . . . the paddle was still in his big hand with its big fingers. If it was God who made them, he shaped them with a lot of love, I felt. It was a hand, I felt, that would be able to hold a just-hatched chick and lift it without frightening it. I like men's hands. *Reach out and touch somebody's hand . . .* The ball went flying and there I was, awkward, terrible, of course. And him, agile and well timed, stretching and jumping along the shore of wet sand to hit the ball gently within my reach. We played for a long time. When, sweaty and exhausted, we dunked ourselves in El Quisco's freezing water, the sun was setting. Afterward we shivered with cold, together on my wrap watching the last reflections of light on the horizon, the beach almost empty, and we laughed and kissed with lips that were salty and trembling from the cold.

We went into his house hugging and laughing, and he put on Diana Ross again: *You see, my love is alive . . .* We danced entwined, shivering in our soaked bathing suits, and no embrace was enough to satisfy us.

And it's the force of that thigh between my legs, I don't know, shivers going down my spine. His "gluteous" form through the wet bathing suit, I don't know, my rough breathing and the sighs that escape me and that I try to hide. His kisses on my neck, his hands on my back, pressing me against him, and me sustaining the pressure, and the threat of that insistent mass that was unmistakable to me now. *Ain't no river wide enough / To keep me from you . . .* I felt a tug at my back, and in no hurry, gently, he unclasped the top of my bikini, which fell to the floorboards like the skin of a lifeless fish. I put my arms around him. I didn't dare let him look at me. Shame intermingled with desire made my lips tremble. I felt flushed spots burning on my cheeks. He held me tight, my breasts against his firm body, and now I could tell he was breathing hard too, and that disarmed me.

He moved away from me and held me by the waist, he put one knee on the floor and let his eyes move over my breasts. He stayed there a moment, kneeling, motionless, looking at me. For a few seconds I knew what it felt like to be a goddess. His lips moved a little, almost imperceptibly. I sunk my hands into his hair. When I saw that yes, it was true, a tear was sliding down his cheek, I pulled his head closer and he let me, I held it against my stomach. I felt the tip of his tongue in my belly button and we burst out laughing.

I never loved anyone again the way I loved Rodrigo. You only love that way once. I felt him next to me all day. Everything that happened to me happened only so I could tell him about it later. I fell asleep imagining his eyes upon me. He liked me, he thought I was pretty, he cared about me. And I felt I was, then, a beautiful woman. I looked at myself in the mirror and I liked how I looked. When I got dressed up, people thought I was gorgeous. I knew it. I felt the way men looked at me. And I liked that they looked, of course, but far and away what I liked the most was for Rodrigo to look at me. The mere idea of kissing another man someday made me nauseous. I was so sure that no one and nothing would ever come between us . . . He used to steal flowers for me, jumping over garden walls. More than once he was charged by a boxer or Doberman when he went into someone's yard like a thief to cut the first red camellia of that winter or the first flowering white almond branch of spring. "My love," I wrote him on a restaurant napkin or a sky blue card that I paid too much for at the bookstore or on a simple sheet of notebook paper. "My love" . . . *Mon amour*, and those two words had urgency, intimacy, an incomprehensible ardor: *Je t'aime*. Anything more was unnecessary. *Je t'aime*. To be able to say "my love" to Rodrigo and for it to be the truth, that I was, for him, "my love," was a flight, a state of suspension, a miracle of fire. Nothing bad mattered as long as the two of us loved each other as we loved each other, as long as we could love each other a little more every day. That kind of love doesn't happen twice.

But little by little, in some imperceptible way, my romance was transformed by his demands for rough sex, for surrender, passion and punishment, possession and loss, by incomprehension. And Rodrigo ran when he found out I was pregnant. This was when we had been together almost three years: he had fallen in love with someone else.

This is the raw truth, and I repeat it, trying to convince myself: Rodrigo wants to leave me for her. But he doesn't acknowledge it. He needs it to be my fault. He needs me to believe it in order to truly believe it himself. He has to persuade me that I was the one who ruined everything. Not him. And so he makes up stories.

And this was the same man who in El Quisco, kneeling down with tears in his eyes, gazed at my goddess breasts while I melted for him . . . Who would have thought he would abandon me like that? It's my own fault. Me, who got pregnant and didn't want an abortion and sacrificed his future, of course, Rodrigo's, no less. And on top of that, my own and ours together. I made him into a victim. That was it. Rodrigo didn't want to be tied down. No. That was the point. And the other? And me? *In the morning my eyes were so vacant and my face so dead, that the people I met may not even have seen me.* It wasn't, then, that he'd stopped loving me. It was that he *couldn't* love me anymore and was suffering by attempting the impossible. I smashed the vessel. He felt sorry for himself. And I was three months pregnant. I had wounded him permanently. It was beyond repair. He had the right to go on being young, he told me. That's what he told me. And he split. And I was split in two.

ELEVEN

I stopped seeing the few high-school girlfriends I still met up with on occasional afternoons. I was ashamed to tell them. A friend from university materialized, Rafa, with his big belly, his candid laugh and friendly gaze, and he took me with him to a demonstration. I walked along beside him, jostled and confused and with that ridiculous ball where another being, an abusive invader, was growing at my body's expense. I felt lost in the mass of workers with their overpowering smell, and I repeated to myself that a hand on the plow was worth as much as a hand on the pen. Then, one of those days I felt myself suddenly caught up in something big, an enormous collective body; we sang together and I was part of the hope harbored by those who suffered, the poor of the earth. The men and women who were Rafa's friends accepted me. I met Teruca during that time, and we became inseparable. She had a three-year-old son: Francisco. A chubby boy with enormous eyes, mild and dark. She was studying history. She had a long, black braid that hung down to her waist, and she was thin with very small breasts. Her wide, full-lipped smile could win you over completely.

Was Rafa interested in me? He never said so. He thought I was pretty. He did tell me that, and I loved that he told me, but I didn't believe him. I didn't feel pretty. And to me, Rafa was a great friend and nothing more. If he'd taken one wrong step . . . Several times I thought he was about to. It would have ruined our friendship. During that time, I pulled down the posters of Mick Jagger, Robert Redford, Peter Fonda, Julio Iglesias, and Led Zeppelin from the walls of my room. Now the faces looking down on me were Violeta

Parra, "La Negra" Mercedes Sosa, and two great bearded men, Karl Marx and Che Guevara.

We were a guild of students who studied almost nothing but the Sacred Scriptures of Marx (those of the young Marx more than the older) and Engels (I remember soporific afternoons trying to get through the *Anti-Dühring*) and, of course, our church fathers: Lenin, Trotsky, Rosa Luxemburg, Gramsci, Althusser, Sartre, Debray, speeches and articles by Mao, by Che . . . The job was harder because we knew so little of the history that most of these works presupposed. I don't know how much we understood, but the thing was to carry those huge volumes under our arms and quote them every chance we got. We did political and organizational—now I would call it "evangelical"—work among the peasants and workers who, armed with red banners, knives, shovels, chains, and a few sawed-off shotguns, forcibly seized urban terrain and agricultural fields. But Rafa would rant and rave against the "extremists" who, with their "military apparatus," as he said in an ironic tone, with their bank heists and Vietnamese IEDs, were just playing into the hands of the reactionaries who wanted a military coup. In the evenings we drank red wine and sang along to songs by Violeta, Mercedes, Ángel, Isabel, by Víctor Jara, Quilapayún . . . To sing is to wait. And we were living in a time of Advent.

Months later the presidential palace, La Moneda, was in flames. I'll never forget that image framed by the television: the strength of its walls resisting the fire, the structure's sheer will to survive. I was tormented by thoughts of those who died, but above all by thoughts of Rafa, Teruca, and the other comrades, men and women, friends I didn't dare call. I shut myself in, fell into bed, and wasted away. When Anita was born, it was an unimaginable joy that was, moreover, egalitarian. Almost any woman, I thought recklessly, has this happiness within her reach. My mother, always so cold, welcomed Anita like her own child. She was more loving with Anita than with me, I think.

Then one day Rafa showed up at my house and he was fine, which disappointed me a little. Teruca was safe, too. He'd be calling me soon, he told me. He hadn't called before for reasons of security. Some weeks later we met up with Teruca at Rafa's mother's house, which was on Calle Los Gladiolos. I brought my Anita with me wrapped in layers of shawls. Teruca, who had cut off her thick, black braid, made such a fuss over her you would have thought she was my older sister. Francisco, her son, watched her with his big, dark eyes. She told me in private that Rafa had been arrested. He'd been held in the Ritoque concentration camp. Of course, he'd taken a bad beating. He didn't talk about that. Didn't want to.

It was Rafa who put me in touch—years later, of course—with Canelo. Rafa had changed by then. Now he believed only in armed resistance. We met at Tavelli for a coffee. It was a dangerous meeting, he told me, and I was pleased.

Well . . . Canelo had entered Chile secretly. Toward the end of the seventies he had been one of the founders of the Red Ax movement, which gradually absorbed groups from the Elenos,[1] from Organa,[2] from Bandera Roja, from Espartaco and other far left groups. They were all convinced that an unarmed revolution would never be a revolution. They were part of what was known as the "revolutionary pole," the ones Rafa used to criticize, the ones who wanted *to create one, two, three Vietnams* . . . There aren't many who want to remember the infighting of those days. Canelo didn't avoid the issue that first day.

For the brothers and sisters of Red Ax, Allende's "legal path" had only been the opening act. You said you wanted historical facts, here's one, the kind people don't like to hear anymore: Fidel, Ho Chi Minh, they were also ambivalent in the beginning. Shortly after the military coup, Canelo left Chile and headed for Cuba. One of his teachers was the legendary Benigno, who fought in Bolivia until the end at Quebrada del Yuro, where they captured Che. Benigno escaped into Chile, wounded, with a fever of 104 degrees. The

---

1. Members of the National Liberation Army (ELN in Spanish) formed by Che Guevera in Bolivia.

2. Splinter group of the Socialist Party of Chile that tended toward armed struggle.

bullet had entered his shoulder and lodged near his spinal column; they extracted it in Santiago.

Later, Canelo would fight as one more Cuban soldier under the orders of General Ochoa in Ogaden, Africa. His unit, made up of Ethiopians and Cubans, crossed undetected through the mountains and took up a position behind the Somali troops who were defending the Mardas Pass, in order to attack them in a cunning pincer movement. Jijiga fell within two days, and all the other towns fell quickly one after another like dominos. In a month, Siad Barr, who was receiving support from the Yankees—this was, don't forget, the middle of the Cold War—ordered his troops to retreat to Somalia. Ethiopia won. The eighteen thousand Cuban soldiers with their six hundred Soviet tanks turned out to be decisive in the war. And Canelo was there. Later he joined the FMLN. He fought for three years in the guerrilla war in El Salvador.

I'm telling you about ancient, epic times, times of war aristocracies that live for death and honor. Nothing that would make any sense to you today, right? Che Guevara was an "international partisan," a man with a Bolivarian vocation, a knight errant. The stuff of legend. Everywhere you looked in Latin America back then there was another fabulous Amadís of Gaul, a Palmerín, a Tirant lo Blanc or Florismarte, who all wandered the earth in search of adventure with their swords at the ready, to set right every wrong, to succor the needy and destitute, redress iniquity, and amend injustice. But, of course, this time there were also ladies errant, and they did not lag behind the knights in courage or derring-do. We all wanted to recover *that happy age to which the ancients gave the name of golden*, because *they that lived in it knew not the two words "mine" and "thine"! In that blessed age all things were common . . .* It wasn't only happening in Latin America, either. Here in Europe, for example, you had the Brigate Rosse and the Rote Armee Fraktion, or Baader-Meinhof Komplex. Back then we lived confidently, auguring and weaving the future. And all the while at our backs, history, tight-fisted, dirty, vulgar history, was preparing to wash right over us like the giant wave of a tsunami.

He had short, light-colored hair, small, alert eyes, lips that were too thin. He wore a tie and a light gray suit. No long, sloppy hair or beard; no pipe or Cuban cigar, no poncho or leather jacket. Nothing that would suggest the combatant who had fought so bravely in the Ogaden desert or on Guazapa hill in El Salvador, where he slept in a dugout. He could have been a lawyer or an insurance agent. He told us about our commander, about his story.

Joel Ulloa was a simple teacher of history and geography at a high school in Valdivia. At that time Che was moving deeper into the jungle in the mountains along the Ñancahuazú River in Bolivia. Joel Ulloa abandoned his routine of blackboards and test correcting. He was disgusted, he said, by the hypocrisy of Chile's staid, bourgeois democracy. *To make the Andes into the Sierra Maestra of the Americas:* that was the goal. Canelo showed us a photo: glasses and black hair combed away from his face. Shaved beard, Asiatic eyes, ample nose and mouth. His mission was to lift up the Mapuche people and take back their land. Canelo told us how the Mapuches, who were used to revolutionaries with long hair and a shaggy, bohemian look, were impressed by this schoolteacher who showed such great practical sense when it came to organizing a battle, and later, too, with the work in the fields they occupied by force. They said he had never known *lincanquén,* fear.

And his triumphs began. At first, there were bank robberies to gather funds. This taciturn people subjected to the *huinca,* the white man, turned overnight into ferocious *aucayes,* into rebels. Commander Joel and his Mapuche peasants managed in a couple of years to gain control of almost all the forest ranches and livestock farms in that valley. *We must plunder the plunderers.* The ministers of that shoddy democracy, as he called it, vacillated between negotiation, turning a deaf ear, and reprimanding them. There were beatings and shootings and some injured Mapuches and police. Sometime later, during Salvador Allende's presidency, the organization grew stronger and more professional. "The criticisms came from the conventional left then, from inside the house of government, from Allende himself, who looked at us sympathetically but did not agree with our methods."

"They called us 'ultras,'" said Canelo, "they called us extremists, they called us 'pistol heads'" . . . Commander Joel's answer was: armed conflict is inevitable. His contact in Santiago was Bone. And that was the first time I heard his name, Bone, a nickname he'd been given by the Cubans, I found out later. Sometimes, in the Mapuche *nguillatune* celebrations, frenetic natives swollen with corn *chicha* liquor and galvanized by the mournful sound of the *trutruca* horn, the threatening rhythm of the *cultrún* drum, devoured their bosses' Hereford bulls. These things happen in a revolution. Commander Joel's fame grew quickly.

And then, one September day in the year of the Devil, at daybreak, the military came for him. It was never learned what went wrong with their defense, because the soldiers should have been fired down on at the entrance to the canyon in Panguicui, which means "Lion's Bridge," and which was closed off by a barricade of enormous, centuries-old coihue tree trunks. There were a lot of those military bastards. Commander Joel hid out in the old storehouses on the Pucatrihue ranch. There was a shootout among the piles of sawn planks, and some twenty peasants died. When he realized he was lost, Joel jumped out a window and threw himself into the Pillanleufú River. The military gave him up for dead. No one knows how he managed to float down in the Pillanleufú's current, escape through the mountains, reach Santiago, find Bone, and reorganize the armed resistance.

"Ours is a risky bet," Canelo explained to us, with his particular blend of confidence and serenity that dispelled all doubt and fear. "Allende's government didn't have a majority in Parliament to approve the laws that structured his program. Simple arithmetic. A revolution on paper wasn't possible. Unless," he said, "unless it was just an initial phase. That's what his adversaries quickly figured out, with that ruthless realism they have on the right. 'It would be extremely stupid and absurdly utopian,' as Vladimir Ilyich Lenin said, 'to suppose the transition from capitalism to socialism is possible without coercion and without dictatorship.' A Franciscan illusion is dead," he said. "Legal revolution—which President Allende put an end to with his heroic death—leaves us in the vanguard."

"A revolution," Canelo went on to say, "is paid for with gallons and gallons of young blood. Everything else was and will always be mere deception, cajolery. That's why we asked for weapons, but when the day came that we needed them, what we had in troops, infrastructure, weapons, and ammunition was clearly insufficient. And what happened, happened, and they got us how they got us . . . That was the end of *unarmed prophets*. The cauldron of the class struggle is turning red hot. We can't wait for the revolution. We have to provoke it. Víctor Jara: *Now is the time / for what tomorrow can be* . . . Our armed missions are symbols. Our writing of fire will incite the common masses to rise up. Then we will be able to dream of a society like none that has ever existed before, a society of equals that will allow us to leap *from the kingdom of necessity to the kingdom of freedom*. This is the vision of the brotherhood of Red Ax. When the people see that we're defying the established order, detonating bombs here and there—and the police look for us but can't find us—they will join us. Pyotr Tkachev, one of the greatest of the Russian revolutionaries, said: *We cannot allow ourselves any delay. It is now, or perhaps very soon, or never.*"

I believed him. He brought us the fierce truth of war and broke through the sweet lie of peace and of law. He didn't give us time to reflect or reason. It was a forceful jolt of hope in its purest state. My destiny was to seek vengeance. The silence of the dead hummed in my ears. Canelo said our armed actions would set off a repressive overreaction and then the people's angry rebellion. Rafa and I told him yes, we were ready to start as soon as he gave the word.

Two weeks later I went to my first camp in the mountains of Nahuelbuta. Our story or alibi: hikers. We studied the *Mini-Manual of the Urban Guerrilla*, by the Brazilian Carlos Marighella: "The urban guerrilla's reason for existence, the basic condition in which he acts and survives, is to shoot." And: "To prevent his own extinction, the urban guerrilla has to shoot first, and he cannot err in his shot." But we didn't have target practice, not yet. I was left with the desire. There were long walks in the hills, self-defense practice, basic notions of surveillance and countersurveillance. The indoctrination sessions were long. Our forces, the instructor repeated, would always be inferior in number and weapons compared to the enemy's might, but our advantages were surprise and the moral superiority of our fight. At nightfall, we stood and listened to a cassette recording of Commander Joel's voice. It was a greeting of no more than four minutes. It was the first of many more that we would hear in the future, sunk into reverential silence. One of those rituals that demonstrates inclusion in a community. His voice was slow, solid, well-pitched, midrange, with a rural southern accent. None of that "is he or isn't he Caribbean" that was common with our leaders. Above all, it was a voice I felt was trustworthy.

Then a couple guitars appeared and there were songs around the bonfire. The most important thing to forge ties: the song and the *fire woven into coiled tongues.* War has always been like that, atavistic. *¿Qué culpa tiene el tomate? . . . What fault has the tomato / peaceful on its vine / and then along comes the son of a bitch / who puts it in a can / and sends it to Caracas!* The song was from the Spanish civil war, but we knew the version by Quilapayún. *Cuando querrá el Dios del cielo . . . When will God in heaven decide / it's time for the omelet to flip / the omelet to flip / and the poor will eat bread / and the rich will eat shit, shit.* My eyes filled with tears. We were singing again. The time of Advent had returned.

And that's where I met the Gringo, a tall, very thin guy with long, blond hair and a moustache. He had a pleasant tenor voice. *Levántate. Stand up / and look at your hands, / reach out to your brother / so you can grow / . . . blow like the wind / on the flower in the valley / cleanse like fire / the barrel of my gun.* A German from Puerto Varas, he told me. We talked for a while. I don't remember what about. We laughed. I don't remember what about. The last night, he was on the other side of the bonfire and his eyes held mine with a gentle insistence. I was expecting something to happen, but in the morning he was gone. I was sorry.

That was my rite of initiation, and how I began the difficult process of self-elaboration that is necessary in order to embrace a moral asceticism. And understand that in those dark years, belonging to that family, that secret and forbidden family that I had chosen, was to be born again, and to be prepared for the sacrifice, anytime, anywhere.

TWELVE

Someone had opened my curtains, and in among the apricot flowers, I could see the first green buds that were opening to the sun. I closed the curtains and waited in the dark. I called my father at his office. He answered right away. I told him I was calling to apologize and that I hadn't meant to act the way I had. He choked up, searching for a way to thank me for my gesture, he said, for the generosity of my call, he said, the incommensurable—I remember that word, so unusual for him—happiness of that call . . . Then I told him: "If something happens to me, if I do something selfish, it's not your fault, Dad. Understand? I'm in bad shape. This anguish is eating me up. There's nothing you can do, understand? I wanted you to be prepared." And I hung up.

My first outing was to go to the metro station Universidad de Chile. Before I left the house I wrote on a greeting card the same thing I had told my father. Only I added: "Mom, I'm sorry, but you'll have to explain it to Anita. Hopefully someday she'll be able to forgive me."

I had to go out to a public phone to make two more calls that were in order. I knew my brothers must have had someone following me to find out if I had a tail, but I never saw who was watching me. Finally, the rendezvous: El Refugio restaurant, on Gran Avenida about a block south of Carlos Valdovinos. I was to wait, reading the newspaper *Las Últimas Noticias* with the front page facing the door until I was approached. Someone would say to me, "Hi, there, I've got a terrible hangover," and I would answer, "You should have a coffee with milk." When that person arrived, I was startled. It wasn't easy for me to keep calm. I didn't know the young woman, and I was very tense. But everything went according to plan. She ordered a coffee and I ordered another and we drank them quickly. She commented on an interview of a television celebrity that was in the paper. Nothing else. We went out to take a bus that left us on Alameda. We ducked down into the metro and reemerged at the station Unión Latinoamericana, where an old woman appeared out of nowhere—I had the vague feeling I had seen her face before—and the young woman disappeared. The old woman and I climbed the stairs at her slow pace, and outside we took a taxi that dropped us off on Calle Puente, which we followed until we reached the Central Market. The old woman took a couple of turns around it, bought some vegetables, and left me at a fish stall. The next instant there was the Spartan, no less, the Spartan in person, and we went into a restaurant.

It was hard to control my emotions when I saw him, and I was glad I was wearing sunglasses. How could he not have been captured? At that moment I felt I stood wholeheartedly with my brothers and sisters in the struggle, I was resolved to never fall into temptation again, resolved to give my life. The Spartan seemed shorter and wider than I remembered. He was wearing an ordinary jacket of blue cloth, a white shirt and no tie, and gray pants with pockets at the knees. Common, everyday clothes. The Spartan blended in. An average Chilean. He could be a vendor in the market, or a cab-driver. That was his cover, in fact: taxi driver. I shouldn't have known that, but as you see, I did. We sat down and ordered two bowls of a mouthwatering conger soup. We drank a Semillon wine from San Pedro. He was, as I've said, a truly respected combatant. His military training had begun in Cuba, under Camilo Cienfuegos. Later, already an officer, he was sent to Bulgaria as an instructor in courses of sabotage and intelligence at the Military Academy G. S. Rakovski. At the end of the seventies he was sent as an officer to fight with the *nicas*. He entered Costa Rica illegally and then crossed over to Nicaragua to join the Sandinistas of the Southern

Front, commanded by Edén Pastora. The National Guard was concentrated there, the most elite of Somoza's army. "I lived through that battle with the artillery stuck in the mud, and grenades that would sometimes explode from the humidity," he told us. "I lived through it as a practice run for what would someday happen in the south of Chile, in the Araucanía region." That's where he learned that "a dictator is only overthrown with bullets." Many Chileans died in that war. The worst, he told us, was on the hillside of Palos Quemados, close to Lake Nicaragua with its freshwater sharks. But then came the happy march to Managua and the entrance into Somoza's luxurious palace. The Spartan remembered drinking a Chilean wine there that the tyrant stored in his cellars.

"Cómo que tú andas, Irene? How're you doing?"

I felt pride at hearing my combatant name. I looked at him and shrugged my shoulders, not knowing how to begin. It was so like him to mix in Cuban expressions and turns of phrase when he talked. He did it with a trace of humor, sometimes, and other times out of habit, without realizing.

"I have an assignment," he told me with no preliminaries, taking on his curt tone of voice. "To pass on to you the Directorate's congratulations. You didn't give up any names during the required number of hours."

"I held out much longer than five hours," I protested. "Women can be very brave . . ."

He nodded silently and looked at his plate.

"And you were inside for twenty-nine days. That's a long time. You know what? It wasn't easy for us, either. In cases like this we have to hope the combatant dies in the fight, and if they're captured, that they're killed as soon as possible. I caught myself many times hoping you were alive and that they would let you go."

I tried to meet his eyes, but he didn't lift them from his plate.

"Canelo!" I said and my voice broke. I took a sip of wine.

He nodded again, in silence and without looking away from the plate.

"Did your ID hold up?"

"They never questioned the validity of my identity card."

"Strange. Unusual. Very unusual. Did you know your name was never mentioned in the press? The official communication didn't mention any arrests, it only talked about three dead 'extremists' and two more who got away. How was your questioning with the military prosecutor?" And when he saw the surprise on my face: "You know, there should have been a military tribunal. They caught you red-handed, you had the money in your purse . . . All of that falls completely under the 'Anti-Terrorist Law.' But according to the official information, the money was found in a bag one of the 'terrorists' was carrying. No one ever formally questioned you?"

"No. So I'm not named in the investigation?"

"As far as we've been able to find out, no."

"Then my case doesn't exist."

"Exactly."

"When I left, they made me sign a provisional liberty . . ."

"A fake document, obviously. Did you get to see anyone?"

"See, what you could call see, almost no one. But I'm sure they got Chico Escobar, I heard shouts one night and I have no doubt it was him. They also picked up Vladimir Briceño. I passed him in the jail's corridor, limping along with two guards on him. They'd broken his nose and his shirt was soaked in blood."

"So you did see something, and in detail: broken nose, limping, bloody shirt . . . Why did they fall?"

"I don't have information about that."

The Spartan nodded his head again and he stared into his soup.

"They didn't ask you about them?"

"No."

"Anyone else?"

"Tomasa. She says she was already a socialist in grade school, that her father was an 'entrista,'[1] that she had a boyfriend who was 'el-

---

1. Faction of the Socialist Party of Chile.

eno,' and that she got to meet Elmo Catalán himself when she was just a kid. Could that be true? I don't know when she joined the Red Ax movement. She must be thirty-something. They did bring her face to face with Briceño and Escobar. I don't know what cell she belongs to."

"Anyone else?"

His eyes looked me up and down. I thought: he's measuring the chain of denunciations; he's calculating, like the good chess player he is, which pieces he has to give up for lost.

"No."

He nodded again in silence and looked at me again with intense curiosity. He was a dark, broad-shouldered man; I've already told you that, right?

"And yet you seem fine," he finally commented. "Thinner though, yes. Tell me, why did they keep you locked up for so long, what did they want from you?"

"They wanted me to sing, at first."

"Obviously. And then?"

"They wanted to know where Commander Joel was, what he looks like, how he communicates with Bone, what our structure is. They fear and respect us a lot, I'd say. There's a lot of paranoia about us."

A burst of cold, absurd laughter escaped me. The Spartan furrowed his brow.

"And then?" he asked after a pause.

"They thought I could still be hiding something," I said, ashamed of my laughter. And I added: "Those pigs want to get at Bone. That's it. And they want him alive."

"Obviously. But they won't get to him."

"They want to know about the weapons and the cash. They asked about that over and over."

He didn't say anything. It was trivial, and I felt silly.

"They never brought you face to face with any of our people?"

I shook my head.

"I passed Briceño in the hallway, as I told you, and of course, we acted like we'd never seen each other before."

"Strange," he muttered. "Very strange. And those shouts you heard that were Chico Escobar, you say, why did you hear them? Did they want you to hear them?"

"Possibly."

"And you didn't take the bait?"

"Of course not!"

The Spartan swallowed a spoonful of broth.

"There are some evil guys inside there. They mess with you for a while just to punish you, and you end up like a scalded cat, you know?"

He didn't smile with me.

"Anything in particular to tell me?"

"Well, it was just like they'd told us it'd be."

He smiled slightly. It took a lot for the Spartan to laugh. When a smile did escape, his eyes turned sad and defeated.

"Nothing else? Any experience or reflection? You were a teacher, an intellectual, always spouting some quotation or other."

I let out another peal of strange, out-of-place laughter.

"Only something which never ceases to cause pain remains in the memory," I managed to say after a moment, serious again. "Those thugs don't need to read Nietzsche. They just know that's how it is. Order, their order, just like the transparent stages they create to show off their fetishes, those public spaces they design in order to usurp—their famous *malls*—it's all held together by cruelty. Underneath the banks and the stock exchange, the twenty-story buildings and the factories with huge, smoking chimneys, under the stadiums full of people cheering for goals, beneath the serpent television, there's the *promise of blood.*"

I make air quotation marks with my fingers. I wasn't lying, not in the slightest; at that moment it was what I felt, what welled up in me; it was the truth.

"Everything—understand me, anything—the most horrible things, chopping off their legs and arms with an ax—it's all justified."

And I really felt that to be true, as well.

"As long as it's effective," he tells me in a cold, firm voice. "Our hate, sister Irene, is also subordinated to our collective goal. Everything we do or don't do is justified by the cause. Otherwise, it's better not to fight. To resign ourselves to peace and endless negotiation. Which means tolerating the world's abuse and injustice. It means having endless patience and getting used to misery and the disgrace of inequality. It would mean adapting, reconciling ourselves to evil. No! We are at war, but it's not a conventional one. Any armed mission of ours is always a message. The formal retaining walls of the 'democratic bourgeois' have given way and class domination is exposed for what it is. The seed is germinating underground. The hour of the great vengeance is approaching. We're going to win, sister Irene," he says with a trace of softness, and immediately he hardens his brow. "And if we can't win we have no right to live."

He fell silent, sunk into his thoughts. That's how the Spartan was. He'd turn somber all of a sudden. He lived completely absorbed, I think now, in his task of revenge. He was disdainful of politicians because they all made concessions, because they were all dirty. He, on the other hand, was going against the current, and he knew himself to be tough and alone and superior.

"Why were they waiting for us at the currency exchange? What went wrong?"

"One must lose, sister, if one wants to someday win. This episode has been investigated. Your version of events will be requested and then you will be given a report."

I looked at him, but he was stirring sugar into his coffee.

"You know the procedure," he concluded after a long pause. "You'll have to write a report about what happened. It will be processed and then you will be called in to clear up any questions. Remember this number." And he made me repeat it three times from memory. "Call from a public phone, of course, on Tuesday at 12:10. Understood?"

"Understood."

"Sister Irene ends here, right? As you know, you'll be disconnected for a while. That means: no stipend. What do you plan to do?"

"Whatever you, my brothers and sisters, assign me to do. I'm at your disposal."

"I'm asking what you would like to do, compañera."

"I want revenge, a just revenge. That's what I want. I want a dangerous mission. This time I won't fail. I want to show what I'm capable of. I ask you, brother, for that chance. It's a formal request."

"I'll deliver this request at the appropriate time. The question was, what do you plan to do now?" he said, relaxing his tone.

"Go back to teaching French, I guess."

"And not leave Chile? You'll stay here and go on giving private French lessons?"

He looked at me approvingly.

"Teruca, as you know, sent her son, Francisco, out of Chile. He's in a children's home in Havana. There's a group of kids, the children of militants, living together there. As you know, it's an indispensable security measure. To avoid blackmail and to protect the children. You already said no once. You wanted to keep your daughter here, you said she was safe in your mother's house. We respect your decision, sister, though we don't agree with it. It's a very serious matter. Serious for you, as the responsible mother that you are, and serious for all your brothers. The time has come for you to send your daughter to that home on the island. Don't you think?" I lowered my eyes. "It's a tremendous sacrifice, I know. But it's necessary. Your safety is at risk, your daughter's safety, all of ours."

I nodded my assent. He took my chin in his hand and met my eyes.

"Everything for the cause, Irene. Everything."

I nodded again.

The Spartan, when we separated, gave me a Lonsdale Fonseca no. 1 that came wrapped in fine, transparent rice paper. That night, I went out alone in my mother's yard, and I contemplated its wrapper, as the Spartan called it, like someone staring at the skin of the person they love; I lit it from below, turning it around, slowly, as he had taught me, and I smoked it unhurriedly. Then I went barefoot into Ana's room. She was asleep. She slept with such trust. The air passed through her half-open lips so serenely. She looked so beautiful to me. With one finger I traced her profile. "Everything for the cause, Irene. Everything." I didn't shed a tear.

THIRTEEN

Some days later I went to a "meet" on Calle Placer. Evening was falling and the storekeepers were starting to close up shop. I spent a few minutes looking at tennis shoes outside the Danny and Robert shoe stores, until I saw the sign of recognition, heard the question we had prearranged, and I got into a Fiat with a couple in the front seat. He was muscular and very dark. The woman, a red-head, was driving. They asked me to lie down on the floor. I figure it was on Gran Avenida, around stop number 9, more or less, that we turned west, turned around, and crossed Gran Avenida again, heading eastward. After a couple of turns to disorient me, we stopped at a house that must have been on Calle Curinanca, or around there, maybe actually on Olavarrieta, which is what I thought then. The bell sounded twice in short bursts, and four big boxer dogs came out, plus a small mutt, black with a curved tail, which seemed to be the fiercest. The door was opened by a scrawny, jumpy, big-nosed kid they greeted with the name "Piscola Face." He calmed his dogs with a whistle and let us in. After walking a stretch along some paving stones in disrepair, we went into a garage next to an old, two-story mansion. It was a large space, cold, with unpainted brick walls and high ceilings, closed off at one end with chicken wire that had ivy growing on it. There was a carpenter's bench with tools, cans of paint on the floor, boxes, bottles of gas, paraffin drums. We were lit by a single bulb hanging from the ceiling. We sat down in mismatched chairs. On the cement floor, old oil spots.

They listened to my story in silence and then began to ask about details. They weren't too interested in why I had crawled under the truck but rather in what I knew about Tomasa, about Chico Escobar and Vladimir Briceño, about their functions. They also wanted to find out exactly what the brothers who made the plan had told us about the woman with glasses and the Bic pen, the one who'd put the money in my purse. I told them. Just that she was fixed, that she would cooperate. Nothing more. They asked me to describe her.

Half an hour later Puma came into the garage, and just behind him was Rafa. My eyes filled with tears when I saw him and I ran to hug him. He seemed distant. So, the next day I went to his mother's house on Calle Los Gladiolos and left a message with her: "I want to see you. It's been too long." My mother's phone number was below in invisible ink. He never called.

They accepted my version with a certain reticence, I think, but they didn't accuse me of anything. I was left in peace and disconnected. I hoped to be reincorporated after a few days. Above all, I needed a new identity. I requested one. I needed it for security reasons, I said. And I waited.

The red chalk mark I saw on the corner two weeks later meant I should call the number they'd given me. I did, and I met up with the Spartan in a dive bar on Prince of Wales Avenue. I told him I wanted to infiltrate Central Intelligence, to pass on firsthand information, to climb the ladder in Central; I wanted to plan with him a master stroke that would lift Red Ax to new heights and light the fuse of the revolution. I'm thinking of the Red Orchestra. I believe that every intellectual learns to split in two by interpreting texts that throw them into an arcane world full of trompe l'oeils and mirages. When they're thirsting for action, they want to be a double agent. Rimbaud: *Je est un autre*, I am an Other.

"I want to be a Kim Philby," I tell him, "a John Cairncross. You should be my Arnold Deutsch," I laughed. He listened to me attentively while we ate some Spanish omelets. He told me, "I'm not some intellectual recruiting students at Cambridge, like Deutsch. Even less if we're talking about sexual matters . . ."

But we agreed he would explore my idea. "Nothing else?" he

asked as we said good-bye. "Nothing else?" I never found out what happened to my infiltration plan. It became clear to me, little by little, that my brothers and sisters were starting to phase me out. They didn't trust me. It happened sometimes with people who'd been detained. It hurt me more than I realized at the time. Inside, deep inside, I felt wronged. Canelo had died protecting me, I had withstood my hours, and I wanted revenge. I wanted action. I deserved another chance. I couldn't quit. But the Spartan had decreed distance.

FOURTEEN

I rented an apartment in the Carlos Antúnez Towers. Just one room, plenty of light, and thin walls that let the constant murmur of my neighbor's TV filter in. Without my stipend I had no other choice. My daughter went on living as before, with my mother. I went to pick her up early in the morning to bring her to school. And I often brought her to stay with me on weekends. "I have to send her to Havana," I told myself sometimes, and my heart would skip a beat and the sweat would run down my back and soak my blouse. The Spartan leaving the restaurant on Prince of Wales: "Nothing else?" I had to do it; there wasn't the slightest doubt. I had to get in touch with him to make it happen. And the sooner the better. I promised myself I would talk to her on Friday night at my apartment. Friday, without fail. It wasn't easy, of course. But hell, it was my duty. In the long run she would understand. I resumed my classes and I recon- nected with my friend Clementina. Like me, she taught classes at the Chilean-French Cultural Institute. She also wrote catalogs for art installations. She showed me the latest one she was working on— a text that emphasized, of course, the politics of the work. My life returned to its course, only now at the sidelines of any real mission.

Clementina let me read the essays she wrote for conceptual artists and art actions. Clementina inhabited a world of gestures and words and metaphorical objects, a world I used as camouflage. I was always well aware, though, of the abyss that separated her form of "political activism" from filthy reality. I never lost my mental re- serve. "The only interesting artists," Clementina would repeat, "are those whose gestures call power into question. That's our parti pris,"

she'd say. "Our starting point. It's not about content, of course. No."
She took me to see works that, according to her commentary, infiltrated the official media culture to counteract it from within using
the logic of "hunger for novelty"—an art-news that accused the
circuits of production and reproduction of power. "News understood as poiesis," said Clementina, "as creation."

Clementina, with her black hair dye, purple lips, and schoolgirl's
black lace-up shoes, was an intellectual leader. A group of dissident
artists and critics circulated around her. At one of their openings I
met the *attaché culturel* of the French embassy. It was she who
introduced me to her Swedish counterpart, Gustav Kjellin, a big,
friendly man with long, white hair, who imparted calm from the
moment you met him. A couple of times Clementina and I went to
lunch at his house. His wife was pretty, cordial, and silent.

"The artist," Clementina was explaining to them in her whispery
voice, a glass of Veuve Clicquot between her purple-tipped fingers,
"is the inventor of destabilizing spectacles." That's what she wrote
about in her texts, positing that, once they were decoded, of course,
they would allow the observer to transform the observed. Gustav
saw it all as very political, but at the same time very much in the
province of elites. Of course, I agreed with him.

"Fassbinder's films won't overthrow capitalism in Germany," he
said. "It could very well be the opposite that happens: capitalism
could leave Fassbinder with no audience . . ." and he started to
laugh.

"But the critic," she went on, with stubborn missionary conviction, "discerns and creates at the same time; he's an inventor of
inventors. It would be bragging to drop names . . ." she tossed back a
good swallow of Veuve Clicquot. "But those who know, know. And
the day and the hour will come when we are recognized," said
Clementina. That "we" included her and no more than three critics
who followed in her wake. Artists believed themselves to be creators,
but really they were mere actors in a film directed by a handful of
critics and some gallerists, Clementina maintained with a conviction that I found attractive. Because the power of that select group

determined what was art at any moment. "Nothing is natural," said Clementina. "There is no essential art that we contemplated in our beginnings in the Platonic cave, and that we later recognize in the real world. No."

For my brothers and sisters, that world was my cover. Sometimes they congratulated me on it. Because through all this I continued to receive, on occasional afternoons, messages from the Spartan. Coded, of course. And I attended some unimportant meetings, and they gave me some unimportant tasks. I wanted to join a cell, take up arms once again . . .

Days and weeks passed. I thought nostalgically about the old times. I remembered nights spent in groups in some safe house listening to tapes played with the volume turned low, Quilapayún, Silvio Rodriguez, Los Jaivas, Inti, Serrat, Violeta, while we drank a well-steeped mate, a habit a brother from Cuyo had introduced us to—Pelao Cuyano, we called him—and talking and talking in order to escape our fear, to forget about what we would do as soon as dawn came and the patrol cars watching over the night disappeared from the streets. Then Pelao Cuyano would start telling us stories about the Bolivian ELN; about the Tupamaros' glory days in Uruguay, details about what the escape from Punta Carretas was really like; about the FMLN in El Salvador; about the great Santucho and the ERP's heroic fight in Argentina, his collaboration with the Chilean MIR, his attempt to join forces with the Montoneros, and the building custodian who, under threat, knocked on Santucho's door and told him to open up, about how Santucho, who didn't have time to get his weapons out of their hiding place, seized the gun the enemy was pointing at his head and killed him with it, and then killed one more enemy before they got him; and then he would talk about the growing forces of the Shining Path in the mountains of Peru; and of FARC in Colombia . . .

In November of '73 in Buenos Aires, when he was very young, and later, in '76, he went to Lisbon for meetings of the Revolutionary Coordinating Junta with representatives from MIR, ELN, the

Tupas, and ERP. He had been part of an ELN containment team that never saw action. But he had heard stories, and we listened to them eagerly. He gave us a blow-by-blow account of the kidnapping of the Exxon executives in Buenos Aires. Exxon paid $14.2 million as ransom, which came from New York in six suitcases filled with bundles of hundred-dollar bills. And also about the managers of Firestone and Swissair, and how the ERP distributed the money in a spirit of Bolivarian solidarity. The ELN, MIR, and the Tupamaros got $2 million each. He knew a lot of stories, Cuyano. He told us, told us more than was necessary, more than we should have known, maybe . . . He knew the details, he assured us, of some $100 million —others said it was $300 million—that Pepe, the Montonero commander, passed on to the Cubans for them to launder, after two of his men had been arrested in Switzerland trying to do it. And he told us that he had it on good authority that Tony de la Guardia and a Chilean managed to launder it in a complicated and risky operation in Libya and Switzerland. Do you think it's true?

Cuyano talked to us with shining eyes about contacts with the ETA and the IRA, about combatants trained in Libya and Vietnam, about secret meetings in Algeria with Palestinians from the PLO. Once, he told us about the assassination of Roque Dalton, the revolutionary poet. Remember? *What should revolutionary poetry be for? / To make poets / or to make the revolution?* . . . On May 10, 1975, his comrades (or was it his commander?) finished him off with a gunshot to the head in the safe house where he was hiding. Rivalry? wondered Cuyano. Fear that Dalton would become the movement's caudillo, its strongman? Internal divisions? That time the Spartan got furious. He cut Cuyano off short. His eyes shone with rage. He grabbed Cuyano roughly by the arm and dragged him into the next room. The punishment was for all of us. He left us locked in that safe house for a week and we weren't allowed outside. As if we were little children. On the second day the food stores ran out and we had to ration the rice, the only thing left. One would have to write the story of our morality, of our constant state of vigilance, both external and internal.

Later, Pelao told me that the Spartan's anger had entirely passed. The Spartan, he told me, is in love with the cause, and love forgives all, see? He'd been annoyed that Pelao would tell those kinds of stories in front of us, when they would just weaken our conviction. Those kinds of things should be brought to him, to the Spartan, in private. Not in front of us. It wasn't good to sow doubt, he told him. Those fits of rage weren't unusual in the Spartan. There was another time when Kid of the Day forgot to put glue on his fingertips before a mission. Kid was a Mapuche; he'd been born in Santiago, in La Pintana. His father had a stall in the market. He could say some really funny things, and we all loved him a lot. But the Spartan, trembling with rage, jumped on him shouting: "Asshole! What are you think-ing? You think it's a game, leaving fingerprints behind? You want us all to be fucked?" And he got the kid in a hold and threw him in the air. Something cracked: he'd broken his finger. He was ferocious, the Spartan. Of course, he apologized immediately and personally made sure that a reliable doctor put a cast on it.

They asked me, sometimes, to recite a poem. I didn't want to, but they always asked me for Neruda. And I, yet again, would give them: "Dwarfs concocted like pills / In the traitor's drugstore . . . they're not, they don't exist, they lie and / rationalize in order to continue, nonexistent, to collect." And I would repeat: "He poured forth promises, / embraced and kissed the children who now / scour the trace of his pustule with sand . . . / Wretched clown, miserable / mixture of monkey and rat, whose tail / is combed with a gold pomade on Wall Street." And also: "Then I became . . . order of combatant fists." It was our motto: "Order of combatant fists."

What I remember most from that time is the waiting. It's a perma-nent spiritual state, because the revolution is always situated in the future, it's always the second coming that lies ahead. Sometimes, many times, our orders were literally to simply wait. The action would be delayed. Then we would escape to my apartment and bottles of red wine would appear, and we would play the same cassettes over and over in the darkness broken by the red circle of a forbidden cigarette, and I would feel on my half-asleep lips kisses that held the force of fear and hope. Canelo would be with me, Kid Díaz or Kid of the Day was with Teruca for a few weeks, but that was incidental, because most nights Pelao Cuyano was with Teruca . . . These were loves without promises or exclusions. We loved each other with ardor and the terror of losing each other tomorrow. We lived with the mantle always on the verge of falling and revealing the hidden combatant lying in ambush; we lived on the lam, fleeing from fear. Not the kind of fear that grabs hold of you suddenly, no. Our fear was our daily sustenance, tensing our jawbones, gnawing tirelessly at our insides, a bat that sneaks into your dreams. It was also food for the rage that drives revenge.

FIFTEEN

Our cell—I told you this, right?—reported to the Spartan. I never met anyone like him. I'd like to give you a picture of his soul. If only I could. I want to tell you about him. His character was constructed from books, you know? From certain books, of course. Something clearly incomprehensible amid the promiscuity of ideas that exists today. A Quixote, maybe, or a Bovary. He would say to us: "We must be professionals, *revolutionary monks*, as Lenin demands." And he lived it day and night. "Everything else is a lie," he would say. "Our example is Rajmetov, the main character in Chernyshevsky's novel, a novel that Lenin"—he never tired of repeating it—"read five times." None of us ever read Chernyshevsky's novel. I started it twice . . . I finally finished it here in Ersta, surrounded by these medicinal smells that they use in this place to hide the stench of age and its incontinence. I liked it. Pure metafiction, avant la lettre: it was published in 1862! *What to do?* It's extraordinary . . . The critics haven't paid attention enough to its self-conscious narrator. It takes you from mise en abyme to mise en abyme. Did you know Lenin never wanted to read *Demons?* Neither did the Spartan. "I have no patience for reactionary books," he explained to me. The truth is, he read very few books, but the few he read he was passionate about. Canelo was the same way. Men of action.

Let me tell you, the Spartan was a true ascetic. He deprived himself of all pleasures, including intellectual ones. He was ashamed to allow himself pleasures that the poor were excluded from. Today it's hard for me to imagine being like that. Today it's hard for me to imagine how I could admire him precisely for being like that. I've lost that

purity. Maybe you'll never be able to imagine someone like him . . .
Today's atmosphere of complacency makes it difficult. We were so
sure that the corrupt, cruel, and miserable world we knew was about
to go all to hell. But it wasn't a prediction that came from the laws of
"historical materialism," which we studied with apostolic devotion.
It was much more than a theory. We felt it in our skin. We smelled
it like someone who smells smoke in the house before they know
where the flames are coming from. And there would be no *stone on
top of stone* left. We hated everything that existed. Nothing would
survive. Nothing had the right to. Only us, only us. But who were we?
Not the wife of an everyday worker chosen at random leaving a market in Renca. No. So, who were the New Man and the New Woman?
Wasn't it Paul and his messianic Christianity all over again?

The Spartan lived his life in wait for the great day, the Apocalypse,
the Revolution. Do you think there are any men like him left, mis-
sionaries and dreamers? Will there be any tomorrow? Always? His
name was Jonathan, Jonathan Ríos, I think. Or Jonathan González, I
never found out. But Jonathan. His father was a math teacher in a
primary school. He had been a labor leader, an anarcho-syndicalist,
but alcohol fucked him up. His mother was an evangelist, a member
of the Dorcas, and his younger brother became an evangelical
preacher in Valparaíso. I found all this out later, of course, from
Canelo. The Spartan was single. He didn't touch alcohol. He didn't
touch women. He wasn't tied to anyone. The cause made it inconve-
nient. He repeated Bakunin's famous definition to us insistently:
"The revolutionary is a dedicated man. He has no interests of his
own, no affairs, no feelings," he'd stop to breathe and then would
continue: "no attachments, no belongings, not even a name." This
last part, about the name, he emphasized more. "Everything in him
is absorbed by a single exclusive interest, a single thought, a single
passion—the revolution." Then he'd smile, and there would be
something childlike about his eyes. And he would say we were "the
salt of the earth."

The Spartan avoided music. He wasn't very Cuban that way. It made him mushy, he said. His logic, though crude, was steely. "More than anything else, I despise," he'd say with his lower lip sticking out, "those sissies and whiners who still believe in the *Milky Way toward socialism*." He loved that ironic phrase of Trotsky's. *"The substitution of the bourgeois state by the proletarian state is impossible without an armed revolution,"* he'd say. "Lenin," he'd say. The growing violence of the repression gave him hope. "The greater the repression, the greater the resistance. The process is dialectic," he'd say. *"The worse it is, the better,"* he'd say. "Chernyshevsky," he'd say. *"Insurrection is an art,"* he'd say. "Karl Marx," he'd say. *"To your axes! Anyone who's not with us is against us."* Zaichnevsky, he'd say. Like all revolutionaries, he was a tireless pedagogue. His instructions and interpretations deciphering our path forward from that ferocious present, supported with the usual citations, sometimes reached us in code and written in a script we had to read with a magnifying glass, on cigarette papers which we then rolled again with tobacco.

Cuyano and I used to get tangled up in long, theoretical discussions —peppered with quotations we recited from memory, since we couldn't always consult books—about the *Manuscripts* of 44, fetishism, and labor as a commodity, about the Incan empire and the Asian mode of production or about Che's focalism. We were troubled, as we shared the straw of a mate that Cuyano had brewed himself, by the tendency to tie the actions of a vanguard of professional revolutionaries to the proletariat, and the party to the apparatus, issues that were tackled in famous discussions by Rosa Luxemburg, Plekhanov, Lenin, and Trotsky—his thesis of the "permanent revolution"—and that were complicated even more by the function of the peasants in Maoism.

The Spartan would put a stop to these discussions, which he called "scholastic" and "paralyzing," challenging us to games of chess on two or three boards, which he would always win. Or he would quote Martí: *Today, when the verb is brought low before the putrefaction, the best way to speak is to act.* He never missed a chance to incite us to action. He liked, he would tell us, cold and calculating courage, not the harebrained improvisation of the pistol-heads or the disguised lack of resolve that went by the name of political wisdom.

As I say, we didn't have the books at hand, it wasn't like before. We had to work more often by memory. Some safe houses had a few books hidden away as if they were weapons. They were, of course. I remember a little library hidden behind some kitchen shelves. That time, the Spartan himself showed us the hiding place and gave us permission to read them. They were wrapped in plastic bags. Moments like that you don't forget. I held in my hands, as if it were a holy relic, a sky blue volume with the letters "M" and "E" in white. The selected works of Marx and Engels published by Política Press, in Havana, 1963. Then I thumbed the pages of the *Selected Works of V. I. Lenin*. Three fat volumes. Hardcovers with light green dust jackets. Progreso Publisher, Moscow, 1970. Of course, I used to have that edition. In the first volume there's a photo of Lenin that I looked at for a long time. What did I feel? It was Lenin. That's it. Canelo showed me Trotsky's *History of the Russian Revolution*, *The Basic Concepts of Historical Materialism* by Marta Harnecker, with a prologue by Althusser, and a selection of works by Marx and Engels edited by Daniel Riazanov, the director of the Marx-Engels Institute in Moscow. That book had been published in Chile, during Allende's time, by the state publisher Quimantú. I also remember a few issues of the magazine *Soviet Literature*, published by the writers' union in the USSR. I have a good memory, I'm telling you, it's like a stage actress's; we were diligent students, and more than anything, we had great powers of recall. For a combatant like me, life was a script in the Great Theater of the World, a work in which I, as a character, was looking for my authors among the bearded saints looking back at us from the book covers. I read a note in the "Literary Report" section. In the House of Writers in Moscow, there had been a soirée to celebrate the seventieth birthday of Julius Janonis, the first proletarian poet of Lithuania. It told how Eduardas Miezelaitis, winner of the Lenin Prize, had given an inspiring speech about Janonis . . . In another journal, an essay by the writer Nikolai Tikhonov: "Soviet literature, herald of the new morality." I'm seeing a photo of a painting by I don't know who. An enormous crane lifting a block of steel. The solderer's flame could have been the halo of one of Fra Angelico's saints. It certainly wasn't the kind of work that would have interested Clementina.

They were books that the military police had burned. "Salvaged remains from the shipwreck," Canelo said. "A treasure," he said. We spent all day and much of the night thumbing through those pages rescued from the barbarians: "Hey, let me read you this paragraph . . ." Or "I think it's put more clearly here, I'll read it to you"—and searching at random for yet another passage that would confirm us in our faith with its light.

The Spartan was almost friendly toward us, though too formal. His suggestions and advice were, really, orders. But he gave them to us with the utmost respect. He talked to us about chemistry and explosives. That's what he was interested in. His great love was his 9mm SIG-Sauer P-230 with a silencer on the barrel. He loved that gun and he showed it to us proudly. "The best gun in the world," he'd say. "It's already had its baptism of blood. It was up to the test, let me tell you." Once, we were in a safe house waiting for a mission, and a kitten fell off the roof. The Spartan turned into a mother. He gave it milk every six hours. When we left, he set out a bowl full of milk and a blanket for it to keep warm in.

He was extremely important to us, the Spartan. On dangerous missions, like placing a bomb or holding up a bank, he conducted himself with machinelike precision. He was obsessive about details. "The devil's in the details," he would tell us over and over. After any armed mission, he made us throw away our used sneakers and buy new ones of a different brand.

But still and all, the ascetic allowed himself one luxury: Cuban cigars. A taste he'd picked up from officials at the Military Academy G. S. Rakovski in Sofia; not in Havana, certainly, where his brothers smoked Populares or, if they dared smoke blond tobacco and be seen as queers, Aromas. And if the scarcity was really bad, they would content themselves with tearing out a page from a soviet book and rolling themselves a "tupamaro" with the tobacco gathered from the butts they'd collected at hotels. He, on the other hand, would offer us a Partagás, or a Romeo y Julieta. Sometimes, a real Cohiba. All of them, tobacco for export. No one ever asked him how he got them. But the fact that he had them was a sign.

In those long periods of waiting that fill, like I've said, a good part of a combatant's actual life, he talked to us about cigars, and he lingered over explanations that were more detailed than necessary. "A Flor de Cano cigar," he'd say for example, "is a cigar with short filler, made with tobacco trimmings. That's why it's cheaper. Though it's not bad." His eyes shone and he went on talking with a fascination that we didn't understand: "The binder tobacco is every maestro's recipe," he'd say. "You have to combine a light tobacco, which comes from high leaves and gives the cigar its strength, with dry tobacco from the center of the plant, which gives it its aroma, and the flammable tobacco, which comes from the lower leaves and determines the cigar's combustibility. The cigar roller braids the leaves in a fan so the air can pass through, which facilitates the draw and allows each puff to incorporate all the blended flavors. This," he'd say, "is the crucial moment, the most delicate moment. Technique isn't enough, experience isn't enough. Sweet Mother of God! It takes love . . . A cigar of the highest distinction is born of an act of love."

He would get caught up in his lecture, giving us more and more connoisseur's details. He didn't care that we got bored. Or he didn't notice, who knows?

"A Cohiba Lancero," he'd say, "has a wrapper with a fine, smooth, and light texture." He touched the air, seeming to feel that smoothness. "The famous Eduardo Rivero, who came from Por Larrañaga, started making them. He and Avalino Lara created the Cohiba that was produced in El Laguito. Che was Minister of Industry then. Great chess player, Che. Didn't you know? It's a high-caliber cigar, and it'll last me about an hour. It's smoother at first, it's filtered, see? That's why it lasts so long."

He convinced me to try them when he brought a cigar that was smooth and light—the best of the light cigars, he insisted—a Le Hoyo du Prince petit corona. I loved it. And like that, by his hand, I started to become an aficionado myself, gaining in tolerance. And Cuyano stuck his nose in and shouted, "Coño! How I love a woman with a Havana between her lips. The smoke billowing around her, the aroma . . ." I tried a Ramón Allones, a Partagás, a Montecristo, a Rey del Mundo. The Spartan loved to smoke a Rey del Mundo. He promised me that one day he would get a Sancho Panza gran corona, a Sanchos, which had a rough texture, and would last him over two hours. That promise was never kept.

For us, who didn't understand anything, like I say, the smoke from each cigar the Spartan lit was an invisible thread connecting us to Pinar del Río, to the meadows of Vuelta Abajo, and its aroma had us smelling with our own noses the omnipresent power of the revolution, of Havana, and of the Spartan within the apparatus. Faith is transmitted by witnesses. That smoke was our incense rising up to the heavens. That's why I didn't like something Canelo told me in sworn secrecy—it lodged a doubt in my head. The Spartan had left a lover in Cuba, Canelo told me, a girl who worked as a cigar roller in the gallery of the Fonseca cigar factory in Quivicán. What if she was the one who arranged things so she could send him those export-quality cigars, the kind a common Cuban would get only, maybe, if he was invited to the Convention Palace? But the question didn't last long in my mind: even if it were true that they came from Quivicán to Santiago de Chile, into his clandestine hands with their alibi and legend, it was proof that he possessed some truly influential friends within the apparatus.

I'm telling you about him because without him, you can't understand what we were. In these times of skeptical hypocrisy it's hard for someone to believe me. But the Spartan really was as I'm describing. His mold is incomprehensible to the weaklings and egotists of today. His complete devotion to the cause, his abnegation, gave him an unquestioned moral authority over us. "We are violent Christs," he repeated. But he didn't remind you of Christ. He was too machinelike for that. Maybe Canelo did. And Canelo was his brother. That's what he always called him as soon as he saw him: Brother, in English. An old friendship, from their time in Cuba. I know how much Canelo's death hurt him. Even though when we met at the restaurant in the Central Market he stayed cold, almost.

SIXTEEN

I always wanted a Paris love. I'm talking now about some years before that fateful day I was captured. I was twenty-four. When I had landed for the third time at Charles de Gaulle, I'd told myself: this is it, third time's the charm. Nothing happened. I completed the mission I'd been given, returned to Chile, and that was it. And now, as I said, I was twenty-four and I was in Paris again, at a table at the back of La Closerie des Lilas, telling Pelao Cuyano: "I always wanted a Paris love." And he almost died laughing at my petit bourgeois romanticism, my bovarism. He had devoured over a hundred pages of Sartre's essay about Flaubert before reading a line of Flaubert himself. He told me that while we were killing time in that café. We talked about Hemingway—we saw his bronze plaque—who came here to write in a notebook with a pencil. He brought a sharpener with him. Zola, I told him, was a habitué, as well as Cézanne, and, in the twenties of the twentieth century, Tristan Tzara, André Breton, Picasso, Modigliani . . . He knew all that. What he didn't know was that Lenin used to play chess here. We guessed at whether, among the people around us, so comme il faut, there could be some Tzara, some Hemingway, some contemporary Picasso. We decided not.

"Lots of them must be tourists," said Pelao.

"Maybe there's a future Lenin," I said, laughing.

We had left Santiago traveling over land to Buenos Aires, and we entered France as husband and wife, which obliged us to sleep in the same hotel room though not in the same bed, of course. Even so, our compartmentalization kept me from knowing what Pelao's task was in Paris, and him from knowing mine. The two-star hotel we'd been recommended was close to the Lafayette Galleries. Most important, there were two public telephones in the lobby. There were no phones in the room. A fat woman who was surely Moroccan checked us in. She handed Cuyano the key with what seemed like disgust. She demanded payment up front. The bathroom was at the end of the hall, she said. We squeezed into a wooden elevator. We had to put one suitcase on top of the other. On the way up, the machinery let out an exasperated noise as it trembled from the effort like an old, worn-out horse. The bedspread didn't look clean. I pulled down the covers: used sheets. Cuyano went down and came back with the fat Moroccan. She didn't show the slightest surprise and she changed the sheets and the bedspread. At least the shared bathroom looked clean. After a shower I eagerly persuaded Cuyano that we should go out to eat at a nice restaurant.

I don't know why, as we were drinking a Sancerre de Bué that seemed marvelous to me—although for us, very expensive—we started to talk about the famous preface to the *Critique of Political Economy*, about its idea that was central to our "historical materialism"—the idea that ethics and aesthetics, religion and rights, culture and politics, are all just expressions of the reigning mode of production in any historical moment, and they are consequences of that basic material, economics. They make up, then, merely the "ideological superstructure" of the system. Cuyano was intrigued by the role of technology within the "infrastructure," that's to say, the economic base. He wondered about its exact function in the assemblage of productive forces and production relationships that configured, *magister dixit*, every one of the modes of production—feudalism, for example, or capitalism. I lost the thread of the conversation, but regained it when I saw Cuyano's shining eyes. We were young and committed and we took ourselves so seriously . . . "It's a complicated issue, don't you think?" Cuyano was saying to me, animatedly, talking quickly. And it sure was. But he dove zealously into those complexities. He moved in those deep waters not with the weight and scrupulousness of an academic but with the natural agility of a swift and nimble fish.

On the Closerie's piano, "Good Morning Heartache." On the plate, an exquisitely delicate house pâté. The travel allowance, of course, didn't cover a meal in that brasserie. Cuyano asked me if, in my opinion, technology might actually be part of the "superstructure," and not the "economic infrastructure," as the *Preface* had taught us. "Because technology," Cuyano conjectured, venturing out into the mined terrain of heresy, "depends on science, and on practices that are tied to ethics, and it emerges from a framework of a group of institutions, among them the protection of the right to intellectual and industrial property."

If so, Cuyano maintained, it would dilute the primacy of the material base in respect to supposedly "superstructural" or "ideological" elements like ethics and rights. Because a mere right—the institution of industrial property—would then become a determining factor for the development of productive power. This posed thorny and disturbing questions of doctrine for us. To doubt "historical materialism" was to doubt everything. There was silence: "The Spartan would have had us playing chess a long time ago," I said, and we burst out laughing.

The streetlights of Paris had come on and the streets were calling to me.

It was strange to get into bed and see Cuyano's head beside me. I had trouble falling asleep.

It had rained and the dead leaves in the streets were wet. I wasn't nervous. There was no danger in Paris. My first "meet" was at nine thirty at the Medici Fountain in the Luxembourg Gardens, next to *Leda and the Swan*. A young man with a Chilean accent and the look of a college student gave the countersign. While we walked along the rue de Médicis he offered me a cigarette, which, as instructed, I put into my pocket. I opened it in the hotel and read my next "meet," which was written in invisible ink.

I got out one metro station early, took the rue de la Gaîté, turned right along boulevard Edgar Quinet and went into the Montparnasse cemetery through the main entrance. It was ten to twelve on that cold, gray morning when I stopped in front of Brancusi's sculpture. The stone lovers kiss with their entire bodies. The legs are bent and they touch from the knee down. Their intermingled feet moved me, their tenderness. As if they wanted to belong to the other's body, I thought to myself.

Someone coughed close by. A short young woman, with dark hair, moved decisively toward me. She gave the countersign, and in a Chilean accent she asked me if I could tell her how to get to Baudelaire's grave. I answered as planned: "Avenue du Nord until you get to avenue de L'Ouest and there you turn left." She took a package from her backpack that I immediately shoved into my leather bag. She said good-bye and left. I looked at the time: two minutes past twelve.

On the hotel bed I opened the package and went through the ten blank Chilean passports—they were impeccable—and hid them among the clothes in my suitcase, which I secured with a lock. Where were they forged? My nose told me: Berlin, GDR.

Pauline, the journalist from *Le Monde*, arranged to meet me at the Café Hugo in the Place des Vosges. It's going to be full of tourists, I thought. I arrived half an hour early. I sat down at a table and ordered a cafè au lait. An Argentine accent made me turn my head toward the table to my right. Cortázar! I recognized him immediately. His beard, his giant body, his youthful face. He was gesticulating with outstretched arms as he talked. There were two women—one of them very attractive in whom I wanted to see la Maga—and the rest were mature men in their forties or maybe fifties, with long hair and casual, stylish clothes.

I thought about running to a bookstore to buy *Hopscotch* and asking him to sign it. And what if they were gone when I got back? I thought about going over, introducing myself, and asking him to sign a napkin. I thought I should let him know I was a clandestine combatant fighting the military dictatorship. That would get him interested. I looked down at my coffee. I imagined myself in a spacious apartment overflowing with books, his friends scattered on chairs and armchairs and me seated among them on a cushion, on the floor, listening to old jazz records and talking with him.

Just then I glanced at the table: it was empty.

I paid as fast as I could and went out to the square. They were walking slowly and their conversation was still animated. I checked the time. Six minutes until my appointment. I was bringing a dossier for Pauline with documentation of the repression. She was a person of great political importance for Red Ax, I'd been told. They didn't explain why. Apparently she'd been in contact with our apparatus for years, but she only knew that we wanted to bring down the military. She was very anti-Soviet, I'd been warned, and didn't care too much for Cuba, either. A "Menshevik," they told me. I had to be careful answering her questions. A tremendously intelligent and well-informed woman, I'd been told. In the photo they gave me she looked attractive and severe.

But however important Pauline was, I still had six minutes. Without thinking, I started to follow them. They went into an art gallery where there was an exhibition of Japanese prints. They stopped in front of one with a wave in the foreground that curved over and seemed to trap a boat, allowing a glimpse, far away, of Mount Fuji. Horacio Oliveira lit a Gauloises. He said something enthusiastically—or *whenthusiastically*, to continue with *Hopscotch*—about those "images of the floating world." La Maga looked on disinterestedly, as if the charm of his intelligence was foreign to her. One of his friends—presumably Etienne, who was a painter—pointed to the trunk of a flowering cherry tree up above, said that this print had greatly influenced Van Gogh. Horacio then set off on a speculation about the close-up, the perspective of those Japanese prints, photography, impressionism, the fiction of representation. "It's painting," he said, "that has taught us how to photograph; never the other way around, never ever."

And they left. I followed close behind. It was raining, so I couldn't hear what they were saying. They went into another shop and I followed them in. It was an antique shop full of musical instruments. They spent a good while examining clarinets, bassoons, a tuba . . . Until all of a sudden Horacio started playing an old trumpet. A second later, they were gone. When I stepped back over the threshold, they weren't there. I looked disconsolately to the right, then left—nothing. I considered taking a taxi to scour the rue du Cherche-Midi, where Horacio's apartment was.

I went running back to the Café Hugo. When I went in, an elegant woman of some thirty-five years, alone at a table, was looking anxiously at the time. It could only be Pauline. I was twenty minutes late.

To excuse my lateness I told her the truth. She enjoyed my story about Cortázar, and we became friends immediately. She was a woman with sharp features, distant when she was serious, warm when she laughed and showed her large teeth, and seductive when she only smiled. A few errant grays shone in her light brown hair. She was wearing a simple, navy blue silk blouse and a Cartier watch. She accepted my documents and asked general, cautious questions. She didn't want to pressure me. I started to suspect, though, that her interest in Chile was perhaps instrumental. Maybe her heart needed to attack a monster of the right in order to make her attack on the monsters of the left credible. What was really important to her, I think, was to unmask those who gave orders from "behind the Wall" and who, with their tanks, had put an end to the "Prague Spring." She was interested in the uprising of the unions that was starting in Poland. "It's our greatest hope," she told me.

I tried to get back to my subject, my mission: to convince her to come to Chile and write a report on the situation there. We had to show the world that the resistance was real; that, for example, Red Ax was in full operation. We had to increase international solidarity. That could be very meaningful for us. She agreed, but quickly went back to talking about Europe. "You know," she said, "the Pope being Polish helps. Even though he's a tireless reactionary when he pontificates about sex. What can you do?" she exclaimed, "Voilà l'homme providential," that's a providential man for you.

I turned on the light and went up the four flights of stairs. When I got there, the light went out. I started knocking blindly at doors. Suddenly, one opened up behind me, and I saw Pauline smiling in a stream of warm light. Now, at night, the silk blouse was raw and natural, dense, with a tasteful cut. A golden ring hung around her neck. She wasn't wearing a bra, and her breasts made their weight and presence known. Her jeans were black and her high-heeled shoes showed her long toes with their rounded nails. I felt small. My green T-shirt . . . I felt ugly, boring and provincial next to that sophisticated woman and her apartment in the rue de Bourgogne. What the hell was I doing there? I heard voices, peals of laughter. I left my umbrella dripping in the porcelain umbrella stand, smoothed my hair, and went in. The smell of pipe smoke.

After a quick introduction, I sat down on a big Chesterfield sofa with somewhat worn-out springs, next to Dorel, a Romanian sculptor who was smoking a pipe. Its smell was inviting. His wife, Clarisse, was enthralled as she listened to Giuseppe. Whatever he was telling her must have been very entertaining. His accent was Italian. "My fiancé," Pauline told me. "Giuseppe is a documentarian," she said. Dorel lived in Paris and considered himself an exile, though no one had forced him to leave Romania.

"It was a necessity of the soul," he explained, blowing smoke toward the ceiling. "The truth is," he told me, "an artist can't breathe there." I myself was feeling a certain agitation that, against my will, turned into a sigh. Not for anything in the world did I want Dorel to think I was bored. Giuseppe's gaze had me perplexed; that's what was troubling me. I didn't notice anything else.

Dorel got up to change the music. He wanted to hear Brassens, "because there hasn't been anything better than him in France in decades," he said in a challenging tone. No one rose to the bait. Pauline had gone to the kitchen. I hid my eyes in the depths of the Bordeaux wine in my glass. I thought I felt her fiancé's eyes on me: Giuseppe. I looked up and sought him out: he was laughing with Clarisse, who rested one bare foot on top of the other. The room we were in had high ceilings and the lighting was low and intimate. The Chesterfield sofa with beat-up leather went well with the brand-new Wassily chairs that reminded me of herons. Behind me a white beech shelf full of pocket edition paperbacks went up to the ceiling.

Brassens: *Le singe, en sortant de sa cage / Dit: "C'est aujourd'hui que je le perds!" / Il parlait de son pucelage, / Vous avez deviné, j'espère! / Gare au goril . . . le!*[1] Giuseppe was looking at me with a half smile. Brassens: *Bah! soupirait la centenaire, / Qu'on puisse encore me désirer, / Ce serait extraordinaire, / Et, pour tout dire, inespéré! / Le juge pensait, impassible: / "Qu'on me prenn' pour une guenon, / C'est complètement impossible . . ." / La suite lui prouva que non! / Gare au gorille!*[2]

I couldn't help but laugh, and I covered my mouth with my hand. Giuseppe pointed at me. We all moved to the greenish provincial-style dining table that was at one end of the room. Brassens in another song, sung in a grave and ironic voice: *Mourir pour des idées, l'idée est excellente . . .*[3] Giuseppe, across from me, refills my glass without asking. He doesn't look at me. I observe his black velvet jacket, his abundant white hair falling over his ears, his forehead that wrinkles as he concentrates on my glass, the fine lines radiating from his eyes, his small mouth with full lips that rest one on top of the other, the protruding nose, audacious, thin, lively—a nose that differentiated itself from the apes billions of years ago. I return to the slight, elegant curvature of that nose that divides into two halves, the same as his chin. I'm twenty-four years old, I think to myself. He must be forty-three. He's an old man, I think. Brassens: *Mourrons pour des idées, d'accord, mais de mort lente . . .*[4]

Pauline, in one of her comings and goings from the kitchen,

---

1. "The ape, leaving his cage / says: "Today I will lose it!" / He meant his virginity / you will have guessed, I hope! / Beware the goril . . . la!"

2. "Bah, sighed the ancient lady, / no one could still want me, / that would really be extraordinary, / and to be honest, unexpected! / The judge thought impassibly: / to be taken for a floozy, me! / it's entirely impossible . . . / Later, he was proven wrong! / Beware the gorilla!"

3. "To die for ideas, the idea is excellent . . ."

4. "We shall die for ideas, all right, but let it be a slow death . . ."

invited me to talk about Chile. The *soupe à l'oignon* burned my tongue. I don't remember what I said. I do remember that Giuseppe proposed an idea to me: I should invite Lech Walesa, the Polish labor leader, to speak in Chile about Solidarity. Everyone loved the idea, including me. But I loved even more Giuseppe's Italian-accented French and, more than anything, the fact that he'd had the idea for me. Pauline assured me that the European press would all follow behind Walesa, and that of course she wouldn't miss it. Would the dictatorship let him into the country? Everyone talked at once and I didn't understand anything. In the hubbub I could only distinguish the *donc*'s, *bon*'s, *quant meme*'s, and *voilà*'s. Giuseppe let more Bordeaux fall into my glass. His gray eyes flitted around and came to rest on mine like a bird on a branch. The branch trembled, but held him.

Dorel clears away the plates but doesn't stop talking. He's telling us about *Broken Kilometer* by Walter de Maria. He'd seen it before in photos, of course, but to have those rows of bronze rods lined up in front of you is another matter. "The purity," he says, "of that folded distance." Afterward he went with Walter, he told us, to a Chinese bar that you had to pass through a sushi restaurant to get to. "Trés New York, tu sais."

Giuseppe disappears to make coffee. "Brassens is boring!" shouts Clarisse.

"Dorel loves this junk left over from the fifties!" laughs Giuseppe from the other room. Clarisse puts on Paco de Lucía. She starts to dance flamenco. She's not bad, to tell the truth. You can tell she's taken classes, but it's not just that. She has grace. She pulls Giuseppe up by the hand. Giuseppe resists, and finally feints a dance to that *soleá*, his feet hint at a tapping, it's just a glimpse and the flame is lit, the stance of his torso, the attitude of his arms and face are exact, the passion and intensity are there, but he practically doesn't move, it's just the possibility, the insinuation of a dance. He breaks off, laughing hard, and goes back to serving coffee.

"Giuseppe," I tell him, "you've danced an imaginary dance for us."

"Did you like it?" he asks me, his mouth full of laughter. The scent of his woody cologne reaches me. He's just returned from making a documentary in South Africa. "There's a protest in the streets," he tells me, "the police come with enclosures that they put up quickly to cage the protestors right there, as if they were animals." We're talking now, as we eat a practically liquid Camembert on thin slices of apple. Giuseppe prepares them and hands them to me. Impossible for anything to pair better with the Bordeaux cabernet. No one interrupts us now. He talks to me about Kruger Park, about a lion couple he saw making love like lions, he tells me how he saw gay lions, *pour tout dire inattendu*, and yes, he tells me laughing, *anche tra i leoni ci stanno i culatoni*, even among lions there are fags, and he tells me about a program he's seen on TV, about a she-lion who lives among the rocks with her mate and two cubs. Another male comes along. They fight. The female comes to her mate's defense. The recently arrived one kills the other male and defeats the female. At some point, she gives in to him. Then he attacks the cubs—the mother gets up and defends them, but in the end she gives up again. The winning lion kills the other's babies and stays with the mother. She accepts it. He says with perplexed eyes, the eyes of a child: "A drama from Sophocles, n'est-ce pas? Excuse me, I'll be right back," he says. "I'm going to the bathroom to have . . . a lovely piss." We laugh.

I look attentively at the Bordeaux in my glass. Giuseppe, who's returned, asks me what I see in there. I shrug my shoulders. "I don't know," I say. "I like it," I say. His smile makes me hide my gaze in the depths of the wine.

Suddenly, I'm the only one at the dining room table. I look around in alarm. Dorel and Clarisse are leaving, I say to myself. Yes. Did I say good-bye to them? Yes. Giuseppe and Pauline are seeing them to the doorway. I hear Giuseppe's full, confident laughter. Pauline makes a silly face at me and goes into the kitchen. "Voilà la plus belle!" Giuseppe says and he sits down next to me. He leans in very close. Pauline is in the next room, I think to myself. Giuseppe's hand on my face, his hand on my hip. I tremble like a child. Pauline will appear any second, I tell myself, and she'll catch us. But with two fingers I follow his calf upward until his pants stop me. His hand grabs my head and we kiss.

"Why did you take so long?" I murmur in his ear. His smile enters through my eyes and reaches down into my stomach. It's a vertigo I can't resist. We kiss again. I jerk away from him roughly.

Pauline comes over to clear the table. Did she see us? I go help her. "Call me a taxi," I tell him.

"Yes," he says, "it's raining and windy." It comes right away. I pick up my umbrella. Giuseppe, behind me, is saying to Pauline that no, better not, he has things to do early tomorrow, it's very late, and he'll share the taxi with me. They're in the doorway now and I see them kiss tenderly on the mouth. She closes the door, and he kisses me. We run down the stairs holding hands. We get into the taxi laughing like naughty children. The white hairs of his chest peek from under his shirt and he looks at me with smiling eyes. His happiness, I don't know why, it moves me. Madam Bovary's stagecoach, I think to myself, as we kiss and kiss again, borne along by a quick passion.

The light from outside the fogged window of his apartment was enough. The streetlight among the chestnut trees that were losing their leaves in the rain. I left my shoes on the rug. We kissed standing up, we bit each other gently on the ears, we looked into each other's eyes for a long time. He was almost my height.

"Sei come una pantera," he said to me, caressing my hair. "What makes you so attractive," he told me, "is that you don't realize how attractive you are." He kissed me. He held me and kissed me lovingly, and I felt his lips playing with my nipples, and I fell backward with him holding my waist and I lost my balance, which was, I suppose, what he wanted, since the bed was right there, and I fell onto it and he fell hungrily on top of me, and I struggled beneath him to take off my pants and also his shirt, and I rolled over and once on top I managed to do it and I felt his muscles that were still firm and I felt his hands on my thighs and more and I felt him and I felt him slide a hand under my elastic and I practically felt a splash, and I was ashamed and I held his hand in mine and still I pushed him in and I was above him and I moved pressing myself tightly to him so I could feel him more, more, and then I came, like an idiot, I came suddenly, I couldn't stand it anymore, I came, I swear, and I couldn't hide it, because I came with everything I had.

Then we drank some water, and I took off all his clothes and kissed him from head to foot and he kissed me, and I stopped to kiss him where I thought he would like it most, but I kept changing my mind where that was; he sighed and at times he maybe groaned, or maybe I imagined that. And I got on top of him and I wanted him to come, and I started to feel again and I thought he had come and I got off but he hadn't, and we went on loving like that until, sticky with sweat, he finally came and we fell asleep and it was already starting to dawn by then.

I got back to my hotel room a little after seven in the morning. Cuyano was waiting up for me and was very worried about me, he said. He asked for an explanation. I started to laugh and he understood. A couple of hours later I flew to Marseille, birthplace of Antonin Artaud. In the doorway of a café I met with an ETA contact. I brought a box with five cigarettes that carried a message. Of course, I never found out what they said. I only knew that there were always Mapuche comrades among us—like Kid of the Day. Many of them also participated in organizations of their people. The contact was close. That was what interested the ETA. And the ETA interested our Mapuches.

I went back to Paris that same day and went straight to Giuseppe's apartment. "Voilà la plus belle!" He exclaimed when he opened the door. He uncorked a bottle of Moët et Chandon and in his miniscule kitchen he made an omelet with mushrooms that was delicious. "Je n'ai jamais aimé que vous," he told me.

"You liar!" I shouted.

"It's a line from that old guy Brassens you liked so much," he protested, laughing. And as proof he put on the song "Il suffit de passer le pont."

Let me tell you, that night was the best of my life. We parted at eight in the morning. It hurt my skin to pull my body away from his. And his eyes were full of tears.

Pelao and I flew back to Buenos Aires and traveled by land to Chile. It was safer that way. I never found out what Pelao did during those five days in France. Pauline never wrote her report and contact with her was cut off. I knew nothing more of Giuseppe until many years later.

SEVENTEEN

Our organization functioned as a body fed by "ties" or "meet points." If the "meet" was with our cell, the Spartan would arrive last of all, and he would always sit with his back to the wall in the spot with the greatest visibility in case of attack. He took orders from Max, his immediate superior, by means of a liaison. Who were they, these intermediaries? Where did they come from? Who recruited them? I never knew. The ones I saw were fragile women between sixty and seventy years old, who wore clothes that were neither luxurious nor poor, and who moved through the streets of Santiago with a dignified slowness. They almost always carried a purse on one arm and a bag with some vegetables, a wedge of cheese, a bottle of oil, a couple of apples, whatever. Many times I had to take from that bag a book or notebook that held an envelope with a coded message from the Spartan. The public telephone was used only in extreme cases. The old women gave the sign of recognition and then they would give the password. Of course, they never gave a name. They were the circulatory system. Most of them had belonged to the old forbidden party, they were retired, widows . . . One might want to avenge her husband, another her brother, or a daughter who had been raped or murdered, another her own defeated dreams.

Who was above Commander Max? I don't know. There was also Commander Iñaqui. He was important. That's all I ever knew. At the top of the pyramid, Commander Joel. There was also a man who, as you know, had the job of "general liaison" and whom everyone called "Bone."

We had instruction and indoctrination meetings, which we went to compartmentalized, for safety. They put us in a car with blindfolds over our eyes and they brought us to a house that we wouldn't know how to find again. Sometimes, the entire meeting would take place with us blindfolded. In that case, when we came in, the brother who would talk to us was already waiting there. The opposite happened with our other leaders. They would say: Commander Iñaqui is here in the room waiting for you. And he would start talking very quietly, you could barely hear him, and little by little, he raised his voice without ever reaching a full-blown shout. His voice was insinuating, serene, intimate, and full of silence. An intensely personal voice. It had a hypnotic power. After a while it was impossible not to feel complicit. You were caught up and bowled over.

One afternoon he talked to us about the color red. I'll never forget it. In Saint Petersburg, at the start of the revolution in February 1917, he told us, when people were going out into the streets to protest, the Cossacks were sent to restore the tsarist order. In Nevsky Prospect, not far from the Kazan Cathedral, a squadron held back the fevered crowd. Everyone thought a massacre was about to start. Then a young girl stepped out from the crowd and, dignified, slowly approached the Cossacks. Amid a silence full of expectation, the girl pulled out from under her shawl a stem of red roses, and she offered it to the official. The people looked on, stupefied. The official bent down from his horse and took the flowers. The crowd shouted enthusiastically. For the first time shouts were heard in favor of the "Cossack brothers." Then they let the protestors pass into the center of Saint Petersburg. It was a decisive moment. That's how the October Revolution began, with the red color of that bunch of roses, he said. Later, the red of spilled blood would come. The word "red" (*krasnyi*, in Russian), he told us, is related to the word "beautiful" (*krasivyi*). The place for icons in a Russian house, the place for sacred objects, was red. "The red-beautiful," he told us, "has power. Red will always be the color of the revolution: 'krasnyi.'"

EIGHTEEN

The woman with glasses and the Bic pen examined the fake Argentine passport I handed her. Through the bars and without speaking, she showed me on her calculator the number of pesos I could buy with the two hundred dollars I'd given her. I nodded. She hit the buttons with fingers tipped with blunt, purple-painted nails, and she passed me the receipt through the drawer so I could sign it. Canelo was behind me; I could hear him breathing. I stared at my fingertips, at their transparent layers of dried adhesive, and I checked the time: one thirty. According to our information, every day at that exact time, a man with white hair and dark suit and a halting walk opened the heavy door that led to the two registers and protected them from the public, left the currency exchange with a faux-leather briefcase, and went straight to the Bank of Chile to deposit traveler's checks and other documents.

At the other register, to my left, an elderly couple with German accents. They were calmly changing their money. A bald clerk about fifty years old was helping them. There were no other customers. The place had been well chosen by those who did the planning.

The German man coughed. "Smoker's cough," I thought to myself, and then Canelo's harsh shout paralyzed me along with everyone else. I saw his ski mask covering his face and I put mine on, too; I imagined my sketch spread out on the kitchen table of the safe house, my bars, my pencil drawing of the door; I saw the white-haired employee drawn with a real pallor now in that real door, and he was looking at the drawn revolver with frightened eyes, eyes that no one would be able to sketch. He wavered for a second with the door shut before opening it and surrendering to Canelo, backing up with his hands raised and never taking his eyes from the barrel of the Smith and Wesson. The cashier followed his example without hesitation.

I felt like I was taking too long and I tried to hurry, but I couldn't, I kept lagging behind like I was in a slow-motion movie, and there was a deceptive silence and I knew I needed to draw my gun right away but I couldn't because my hand would not obey me. But finally I went in, I went in through the aisle behind the registers, following Canelo, and I found in my hand a trembling Beretta that was already threatening the cashier. She was watching in astonishment, without dropping her Bic pen. The silence was suddenly full of unbearable noise. The out-of-step orders from Canelo and Kid of the Day. And Kid of the Day came past shoving the German couple in front of him. But it wasn't just that. Everything sounded too loud. The white-haired employee and the bald cashier and the German couple disappeared through the interior hallway, with Canelo pointing his gun at them. The plan was for him to lock them in the bathroom and stand guard. That must be what he was doing, I guessed. That's what that brutal slam of the door must have been. I looked at my watch: I couldn't read the time. I looked at the cameras sweeping the place, the red light always on. Kid of the Day passed by me and I saw the horrible scar they'd given him on his forehead as camouflage, and he seemed to jump suddenly. I was in a cloud, with no up or down. What was he doing? Oh, I remember, he was going back to keep watch at the entrance and to lock the front door. That was all according to plan.

And me? I was pointing my gun at the cashier with the Bic pen. Following the orders I barked in a hoarse voice from a throat with no saliva, she was patiently turning the dials of the Bash safe. In those years, that's the kind of safes they used in Chilean banks. And I looked and saw the clock on the wall, a big, round clock with a restless, jumpy second hand. Its relentless tick tock was unbearable. We had to hurry. When it opened, the metal door of the Bash safe must have been some twelve centimeters thick. The woman with the Bic was about to empty the bills into my purse. But she was unresolved. In spite of my Beretta, which was still shaking a bit, not a lot, as I tried to keep it steady. Ridiculous, I told myself, a well-trained combatant like me. The layers of adhesive were coming off my fingertips. I must be sweating a lot, I thought. The butt of the gun was sticky. My makeup must be getting smeared, I thought.

"There's thirty thousand," she whispered, and she pointed at the rolls of bills. I saw them so clearly. The colors shone, the letters and numbers were of astonishing precision. Those old bills, encircled by their elastic bands, vibrated with a new intensity. But the woman, in spite of my orders, was too slow. She picked up one roll. I suffered through every millisecond of the imprecise journey her chubby hand with its purple nails made to my purse. It was a long and clumsy trip, let me tell you. And there was still another to come. The thought was exasperating, with her sluggishness. And another. And then, the pesos. Several million. More than four, she said. When I heard the sound of my purse's clasp, I felt my heart beating and beating, marking time with the rhythm of a solitary drum.

But now she was telling me that no, she didn't have the keys to the closet. And I repeated the order and she was shaking her head and telling me no, that the keys to the closet were only handled by the manager and the manager, of course, wasn't there. This wasn't in the plan. She was "fixed." That's what we had been told. I looked at the camera on the wall above the door with its red light. We knew what we had to do. There was a reason this place had been chosen. We had to bring the tape with us no matter what. Just as planned. And it had to be done before some customer tried to come in, got suspicious, and called the police. We were in the manager's office. I hit the woman in the teeth with the butt of my Beretta. It made a loud noise. The sound of teeth. I repeated the order to open up, open it any way she could. The closet door had a small opening where the cable passed through. She had me get a nail file from her purse and she started to pick the lock, holding it with nervous fingers. I leaned over to look at the clock on the wall: the second hand was still moving with fidgety jumps. "Hurry up, shit!" I said. I heard a shout and a thud: the closet was open. Canelo had opened it with a single kick. Now the alarm, we knew, would go off in twenty seconds. And then the police would come. They would be here in six minutes, they would block off the streets and start searching for us. By that time I had already to be in a taxi speeding west on Moneda. She knelt down. I looked at those buttons and the little blue and yellow lights in the darkness of the closet. I searched anxiously for the one that said "Eject." I was thinking: the seconds are going by even though I don't feel them, they're going by and she can't find the "Eject" button and I can't find the "Eject" button either. I was thinking: there can't be more than ten seconds before the alarm goes off, there can't be more than nine, and I still can't find the button. I heard the sound of inner gears, dull, tight, and short. A pause. Then another sound, open and dry. I waited. I felt my heart pounding like a second hand. I heard a rough, dragging sound. She made a sudden movement and I brought my Beretta to her head. She turned slowly to face me with her hands up. In her left hand she had the tape, which she gave to me. I held in my hand everything the cameras had filmed. Suddenly, I was discombobulated. Something yanked me out of my head. The howl of the alarm had destroyed that sliver of time we inhabited. It became the only thing happening. It bore into our skulls like a jackhammer. The police. The police would spread out through the city behind us.

We put the woman with the others in the bathroom. Canelo shouted at them, saying anyone who followed us would get a bullet between the eyes. We threw our ski masks on the floor and ran out. Canelo first, then me, and further back Kid of the Day, covering our retreat. Before crossing the threshold I looked at my watch. We'd been inside a little over three minutes.

And Canelo saw something I had not when he shouted at me: "Run! Run!" Because when I started running toward Calle Moneda, zigzagging through the people, as we'd been taught, I heard, like I told you, his Smith and Wesson .44 and, afterward, the 9mm CZs, but not the machine-gun fire of our AK. And one brother, Samuel, he was called, had been posted outside the currency exchange to cover

Canelo, Kid of the Day, and me with a Kalashnikov hidden beneath his ample coat. *It was the only long gun,* the report would say in its analysis of the situation: *Never again only one man with a long gun. The struggle has passed to another phase.* While I was zigzagging though the pedestrian street I managed to think that Samuel's AK-47 must be silent because he had given us up. I was wrong. I found out much later that Canelo had seen Samuel fall. It was right at the moment we were coming out of the currency exchange. Samuel went down without ever making a sound.

The street was full of people at that hour. A woman and a young man gave their versions to the police. And we had two lookouts. One was Rafa, across from the currency exchange, who was watching the exits to Alameda and north to Calle Moneda, which was the emergency route. And the other lookout, Puma, was watching the southern route leading to the subway station that, according to the plan, we would go through to get to the taxi. Rafa and Puma, who both escaped, wrote a report for the Directorate. The report gave the names of the heroes who had died in battle, Canelo, Samuel, and Kid Díaz, and of the survivors, Rafa and Puma. It also stated that I had been captured by the enemy.

Samuel, according to the report, was attacked from behind at the exact moment he approached the door of the currency exchange to cover us. He had to check with our two lookouts, who would give him a signal that meant "all's well" or "danger." Samuel had to repeat the signal to Canelo and cover us with his Kalashnikov, which was easily capable of reaching a human target three hundred yards away. It's dependable, that gun. For rapid fire, it's the best. It's so easy to use. I know that gun by heart. The Polish AKMS, too, the one that has a folding stock and is a little lighter. The one Samuel was carrying that day weighs a little over nine pounds, seven ounces when loaded. It has thirty rounds in its clip. But Samuel, as Rafa remembered, bent backward violently over the back of a man who turned around and knelt down. His AK fell to the ground as his legs flailed desperately. Several people dressed as civilians and indistinguishable from the pedestrians—agents, of course—surrounded the spot, and no one could see when Samuel's body fell to the ground.

"Garrote" is what they call that maneuver in the intelligence manuals. The victim is taken by surprise and a short, very thin wire is put around the neck and pulled hard. The man goes backward, falls heavily over the bent back that his assassin offers him, and he's strangled. A silent way to kill. I never managed to find out who the assassin was. They finished Samuel off with a silenced shot as soon as he hit the pavement. Two days later, his body appeared in one of our safe houses that stood empty. Suicide, they said. No one believed it.

In the meantime, Canelo had opened fire on the man coming at him head-on, and people scattered, shouting and running. In the curve of the street, the protuberance of a building served as cover. At first he didn't know where to fire, because all he saw was Samuel's body bent roughly and a man underneath shielding himself with it. He fell back, covering me. Another agent shot at him from the side leading to Ahumada. That's where he aimed his next shot.

After that the report of the skirmish gets hazier. Bone, they say, got personally involved in reconstructing the battle. He wanted to extract lessons. Our training was based, in part, on the stories of different confrontations. The idea was for the combatant to imagine the kinds of situations he or she could possibly face. The problem was, of course, that no encounter was the same as any other. Even so, the study of these cases, of past failures and successes, prepared us for the day of combat. Most of our fighters—as was my case until that morning—spent years and years without meeting the enemy in a firefight, without hearing the whistle of a bullet seeking their bodies; in other words, without being subjected to the test of reality. Shooting at a flesh-and-blood person who's also armed is different from target practice on a bottle hanging from a tree branch, you understand.

I used to wonder how true to life these kinds of reconstructions really were. We'll never know. The Spartan grew impatient when someone like me raised epistemological objections. He'd gotten used to acting quickly and taking risks without waiting for certainties. To me it seemed like the stories we were given left out and censored doubts or alternative hypotheses. It was a polished and carefully selected version of what memory was capable of restoring. I would have preferred an interpretation that was more open and contradictory to the facts. I was suspicious of so much precision. Because, they warned us from the start that a shootout in the streets is a confusing, fleeting event, and you remember it in fragments. No one was watching it all from outside in order to give a complete, unified view. In spite of that warning, they inevitably put forth, borne on a fallacious and inviolable voluntarism, an ordered chain of events, with a beginning, a middle, and an end. But I always held onto the doubts appropriate to a graduate in French literature.

The only answer I ever got from the Spartan was something like: "We have to try for a coherent, complete, and objective story of what happened. It's an unattainable ideal, we know. But as an ideal it's inalienable. We see its usefulness in practice." And then, considering the matter closed, he took a Havana from his jacket pocket. The Spartan gazed placidly at its wrapper, he sniffed it and then smelled the tobacco itself, and then he started to palpate the cigar, enjoying its corklike consistency. "It's an Upmann," he told me. "A Sir Winston, maybe the most balanced cigar I've ever had in terms of smell, taste, and strength. It has a very wide pull. When you draw on it—not the first puffs, of course, which are for lighting it more than anything—you can taste notes of coffee and cocoa. It should be smoked with utmost respect, let me tell you." He offered me the other one.

"Some other time," I said. He lit it serenely with a cedar match and then cut it. A thick smoke with an inviting aroma enveloped him.

According to Puma, it was our own Kid of the Day who hit the agent threatening Canelo from in front. The man fell face-first onto the pavement. Then a skinny, well-dressed woman, who emerged all of a sudden from among the terrified, fleeing pedestrians, a woman who could have passed for a young secretary, took a pistol from her briefcase and opened fire. Canelo and the Kid retreated toward Moneda. They withdrew little by little, firing, each one glued to his piece of wall. And they discovered that the walls of those buildings were full of protrusions and hiding places that allowed them to maneuver. It was that skinny woman who hit Kid of the Day. According to information in the press, a bullet went through his left eye. Another two perforated his abdomen. Rafa and Puma, our lookouts, fought until Canelo fell. The street had emptied out, and only agents and machine-gun fire were left. They had set a trap.

The shots came now from up above. They had to protect themselves. Rafa says in his report that he remembers a man with a casual suit and dark glasses, glued to the wall, looking for Canelo. Puma says he didn't see the man, he was focused on the roofs, where he could make out one or another jockey hat and pair of dark glasses that appeared and disappeared with each gunshot. The man in the dark suit hid behind a protruding entrance to an office building, and, pressed close to the wall, was trying to reach the next doorway. He says Canelo shot at him twice. The man kept coming. Suddenly, he was already too close; and he was holding his gun with both hands. He shot Canelo in the chest. Impossible to miss at such close range.

Canelo fell. He tried to get up. Rafa and Puma—because they both saw this final scene—say that he managed to get on one knee when another burst of fire hit him point-blank. Was it an unnecessary death after all? The story in Commander Joel's monthly letter ended more or less like this: "After a bullet perforated his artery, a stream of hot, living blood poured forth. The enemy agent sprang back. Canelo fell, secure in the knowledge that he was a hero, secure that he would go on living forever in us. According to the Mapuches, Canelo is now an *am*, which means he lives and eats and celebrates and fights with us as long as we keep his memory with us. A hero who gives his life lives forever."

NINETEEN

Of course, I didn't read that reconstruction until months later. I read it alone in my sweltering apartment on Carlos Antúnez. The walls, I think I've mentioned, were very thin, and I could hear the constant murmur of my neighbor's TV. I hadn't finished moving in yet. There were still suitcases and boxes to open. I got into bed and I couldn't cry for Canelo. I spent the whole day between the sheets, not eating, my face turned to the wall.

Canelo was thin and lanky, with straight, blond hair cut short like a soldier's. I loved to run my hand over that short, wiry hair, toothbrush hair. I liked his eyes, very light green. We were friends, and we slept together purely as friends. We didn't love each other with the madness and faith of lovers. It was more a way of keeping each other company while the passion of fear pursued us. I still feel the shape of his bony shoulders in my hands sometimes, his ribs where I would pretend to play the piano until it tickled him. His smile was a little shy. We kissed a lot, but there was no savage hunger in our kisses; they were tender. He was a tender man. I've never felt a tenderness toward anyone like the one Canelo awoke in me. I trusted in him. I've never trusted anyone more than Canelo. Although sometimes I tried to ward off my feelings. I didn't want to be just a pawn in Canelo's plan.

Like I said, I wasn't even in love. We were comrades in arms. But something resonated in me, and I told myself that if it weren't for him I wouldn't do it, I stuck to him and his fight like ivy to the wall. Just listen to the sexist cliché I use! Without him, what I was just evaporated.

That's why I agonized so much when I couldn't take comfort in our leader's words in the report. I couldn't stand his rhetoric. My antipathy opened a rift. His words made me grit my teeth like I would at the sound of nails on a blackboard. I felt my ears burning red when I remembered swallowing that kind of drivel before. And I did as I was told like a little girl, and I felt put upon and I blamed myself the same way I did in school when the nuns punished me, when it filled me with peace to accept my blame and it brought me happiness to repent. What the fuck! . . . Canelo wouldn't live among us forever, because we, too, were going to die without shame or glory. *And that hot, living blood* . . . No. They'd wipe us out like fumigated ants.

I knew, I had been in their dungeons. Instead of heroes, our destiny was to be misguided extremists half-invented by the military, idealists who inspired pity. The vanguard of combatants that was to inaugurate a new world would become a herd of victims; the spear point of warriors and heroes would turn into a flock of sacrificial lambs. And after all, maybe it wasn't power that we wanted but rather to oppose all power—maybe we wouldn't have known how to do anything with power except lose it. And that was, perhaps, what we wanted: to be the lambs of a great sacrifice and for its memory to remain on the altar of history so that others who came after us would identify with us and resurrect us.

And when President Salvador Allende fired the AK—the one Fidel gave him—into his own mouth, what if he had wanted precisely to avoid our sacrifice, to sacrifice himself for all of us? A Christ, then, revolutionary, Masonic, then, and atheist, a disciple of "historical materialism"? Do you think I'm off base, that I'm being disrespectful, that I'm moving away from the stubborn and inexorable facts? Allow me some imprecision, some imaginative improvisation, which can be more illuminating than the *fetishism of facts*. Sometimes interpretation is better than the data. For better or worse, you've told me you want to get a novel out of this. Or have you been convinced it's better if you don't? In any case, there's another hypothesis, one that sticks closer to actual history. You know, he sent a message to Miguel Enríquez, the head of MIR, the leader of those who thought armed struggle was inevitable and were preparing for it. He sent it just moments before he died. "Now it's your turn," he said. Miguel's turn, he meant, and the turn of all those who thought the way he did.

Nevertheless, in the end victory belongs to the crucified one, and the opiate of his church of poor souls bereft on the earth. A taboo against armed struggle has been instituted. *The incapacity for revenge is called lack of desire for revenge*. And meanwhile, in the vale of tears, the rich hoard more and more treasure. And, well, *for the lambs to be upset at the great predatory birds is no strange thing*. Of course they know, poor little rich boys, that it's easier for a camel to pass through the eye of a needle than for a rich man to enter the kingdom of heaven. Oh, how scary! They had taught us that power came *from the mouth of a gun* . . . In a few years, *weakness was falsified into something of merit* and the sanctimonious were asking, as you are, with widened eyes: But what war, what revolution, what insurrection are you talking about, pray tell? We were caught up in the *vengeance of the powerless*, their *imaginary vengeance*.

The police report informed of an "armed confrontation" in which "two extremists and one officer of the intelligence service were gunned down." Two others "were shot and injured, and are recuperating in the Military Hospital." The place was cordoned off for some forty minutes, after which not a drop of blood was left on the ground. The broken windows of the currency exchange and the offices on the corner of Ahumada were replaced that same afternoon. When they took the cordon down, office workers flooded back in. From the moment when a thin wire fell around Samuel's neck and strangled him until I was taken prisoner, four and a half minutes went by. That was what our lookouts estimated. According to more experienced combatants the encounter had been a long one. People don't realize: normally a shootout in an urban area doesn't last even two minutes.

TWENTY

And there was neither war nor guerrillas, you say now; there was nothing, so many say today. Just a few isolated acts of sabotage and erratic attacks. Insignificant factions that were, moreover, ineffective. And that's what you've been told and what you've read, I know. There was nothing, you repeat, that could pose a threat to the terror of the established order. So the sacrifice of our comrades was in vain.

And how do you want me to answer, from my bed in this Ersta home? What would the Spartan have thrown back in your face? What did the reports say back then? I have one here that I saved. I have it at hand because I knew you were going to ask me that. I want to answer you with the facts. I want to be meticulous with you about this. Ha! As you can see, I prepared for this interview. Well, as I told you, you can have five hours. You can take notes, if you want. I have a raspberry juice for you. I like how they make it here, it's natural, they don't add sugar or anything. Not bad, right? So listen, while you sip your raspberry juice:

"The armed conflict is intensifying: in the past months there have been twelve attacks on high-voltage towers and electrical substations belonging to Endesa in Talca, Osorno, Quilpué, Renca, La Reina, Río Negro, Santiago, Concepción, and Valparaíso, which each time left a large part of the surrounding territory in darkness for some six to eight hours; nine explosions on the rail lines in Osorno, Chiguayante, Río Negro, Concepción, Valparaíso, and San Miguel; fourteen attacks with explosives or incendiary bombs on municipal grounds in San Miguel, Quinta Normal, Quilicura, Pudahuel; five bank expropriations, three of them simultaneous, with the goal of collecting funds for revolutionary activities; attacks with incendiary bombs on supermarkets in Pudahuel and Conchalí; two explosives in gas valves in front of factories in Santiago; Radio Revolución blocked the signal of the national channel, interrupting transmission of the Festival of Viña del Mar to nine countries, and for four minutes the rebel, antidictatorial voice reached millions of Chileans who were listening to that channel; ambush and machine-gunning of a police patrol in Pudahuel; the resistance assaulted and set fire to a bus belonging to police; seven confrontations with agents of the repression in which the capture of members of the militia was attempted by raiding their houses, and in several of these instances the combatants gave their lives rather than fall prisoner; a combat group met for two hours with the people in the village of La Mora and explained to them that in order to overthrow the tyrant there is no other choice than to take up arms . . . It was suggested to them that one of the current tasks is to unmask the reformists and social democrats. Just as with Somoza in Nicaragua or the Shah in Iran, the wheeler-dealers are doomed to fail. Electoral conjuring entails collaboration in the subordination of class, and dialogue leads to capitulation. . . ."

That's what the reports that reached us were like. I could tell you about some spectacular missions of unquestionable veracity; the execution of General Urzúa, the mayor of Santiago, for example, or of Colonel Vergara, head of the Military Intelligence School, and the failed guerrilla war in Neltume, all missions that MIR carried out. And, later, the tyrannicide attempted by the Patriotic Front on the road to Melocotón: it failed by a hair. And, already in the phony democracy that came later, they kidnapped the son of the owner of the newspaper *El Mercurio* (they had previously kidnapped Colonel Carreño and the Cruzat boy, son of another magnate); then there were the executions of "Wally," the head *asesino* during the darkest years of the dictatorship, of General Leigh, one of the coup leaders —he lived, miraculously, but lost an eye—and of Senator Guzmán, the right-wing leader who was murdered coming out of the Catholic

University. And there are more. Like when several combatants escaped from Chile's highest security prison, dodging bullets as they were raised up in a basket hanging from a helicopter . . .

It's true: we took some hits, even some hard ones that were possibly devastating. The Spartan took it especially hard when Arturo Vilavella, head of MIR's military apparatus, died in combat. The Spartan really admired him. Also, of course, when the Front's arsenal was discovered hidden away in the caves at Carrizal Bajo.

I want, I need to be precise: those seventy tons of weapons could have altered the course of history. You know? The famous general of Special Troops in Cuba, Patricio de la Guardia, personally negotiated their acquisition. They traveled from Vietnam to Cuba, from Cuba to Nicaragua and from Nicaragua to the north of Chile aboard the Cuban ship *Río Najasa*. I don't want to bore you with numbers, but a writer like you would have no reason to know this and I, like I said, must be exact. They found, I remember it well, 3,383 M-16 rifles with ammunition, 2,393 TNT explosives, over three hundred LAW and RPG-7 missile launchers, two thousand hand grenades . . . A respectable arsenal for any revolutionary movement anywhere in the world.

Later, the sinister Operation "Albania" wiped out several leaders of the Front, depriving it of their best and most experienced officers. Canelo would have been furious if he'd seen how, in the news reports, they depicted Juan Waldemar Henríquez and Wilson Henríquez as mere rebellious citizens killed by the dictatorship and not as combatants who fell defending the school of urban warfare on Calle Varas Mena. Those two fought back. It was thanks to them the other ten combatants escaped. You see what I mean? Heroes made into victims; instead of honor, there was regret and compassion; instead of lions, lambs . . . Tyrannicide and rebellion, which even some priests thought warranted based on ancient scholarly theories, lost their moral and political legitimacy. I'm being too literal, I'm being pedestrian. This doesn't help you, it's not part of the book you want to write, it's just documentary context. Fine.

But then there was armed resistance, and there wasn't. The uprising never took hold. Light the fuse that would enable the poor of the earth to free themselves from fear and rise up—that was the idea. But when it actually happens, the soldiers start killing and nothing is accomplished. *And beauty, where was it? Ah Beauty, do you come from the deep heavens or have you sprung from the abyss?*

If the ambush on the way to Melocotón had killed the tyrant . . . Listen, can you imagine how José Valenzuela Levy must have felt when he had the dictator in the crosshairs of his LAW rocket-launcher, for those tenths of a second when the idling Mercedes was a sure target? There were, I've been told, two previous failed attempts. But no one except José Valenzuela Levy had quite that experience. Having him right there, just a few yards away, in the sights of his antitank missile launcher. He was saved by the bulletproofing on the Mercedes-Benz, he was saved by the shouts of "Back! Back!" that the head of the escort repeated over the radio, and by the chauffer's agility and quick reactions; he was saved by the LAW rocket that didn't explode: Click. Click. Why didn't it explode? It was the last chance. And it is what it is: there was no triumphant overthrow, only transition; the epic revolution never came, just a tired and pedestrian reform.

Though maybe I'm being too harsh. Maybe we just didn't get it. Years and years of pain and hate and terror had sown a longing for brotherhood and reconciliation and democracy and peace and agreement. Because, as the entire world knows, that was what they ended up prioritizing in my country: the search for a new civic accord. Even if it meant swallowing shit. We were excluded from that process, you see?

Listen well: don't be constrained by this historical anecdote I'm telling you, or by Chile's narrow geography, either. You're looking at me with intelligent eyes. You know I'm giving you more information, more political and social context than you need in order to understand the situation, right? I'm too long-winded, I'm obsessed with detail. Because ultimately, all of this is happening all the time. I don't want to seem presumptuous. What would Clementina be saying if she were here with you? This is just raw material that you'll have to shape into fiction. And, please . . . I'm talking to you from a moral place. Do you understand? I'm talking to you about the truth that lives in collective mythologies. When I read about the prisoners in Guantánamo, held for months and months without trial or due process, when I see the photographs on TV of the people they tortured in Abu Ghraib, in Iraq, I think I know what that's about, I think I recognize patterns and procedures. Déjà vu. What they did to us in that miserable back alley called Chile, the Yankees had done before in Vietnam, and the military did in Brazil, in Uruguay. Later, it would be repeated in Argentina, in Peru. Now it's the Iraqis' turn . . . The mujahideen know it.

Look, these days no one's going to buy a pig in a poke. You have to tell your reader: you are reading a novel, these are pure lies. That's what Clementina would demand. And you keep going from there and you do it in such a way, with such magic, that the reader gives himself over and goes along with you. And then, you destroy his innocence again. The texture gives way, it breaks like a torn sack, you've betrayed him. It was just one more ingenious lie built on top of the other one, you tell him. And the reader gets dizzy and nothing seems real or unreal and he's a prisoner among your amazements and inventions, he has no way out, he can only go on cooperating in this other thing, the new texture of the new sack, the new mantle that masks the combatant . . . That's what you are if you are a writer: a liar who tells the truth in order to lie once more. It's the power, *mon chéri*, the thankless power that always shows itself in disguise. Or no?

So, greed won. Exactly what we wanted to prevent with our complicated clockwork of sympathizers, militants, collaborators, and the hundreds of combatants who entered the country with meticulously falsified passports and their corresponding alibis, with their military training in Cuba, Bulgaria, Vietnam, Moscow, or East Germany, and our charges of explosives and coded messages on cigarette paper, and our AK-47s and our martyrs and our stipends paid with the dollars or pesos taken from banks and currency exchanges, like we were doing when they killed Canelo, Samuel, Kid Díaz, and they captured me. *You walk upon the dead with scornful glances, Beauty, / Among your gems horror is not least fair.*

It wasn't enough. The poor were too suspicious or cowardly or wise. A *humanity of cowardly monkeys and wet dogs.* They were too realistic, a frightening realism just like the one that grabbed hold of me the instant I should have crossed Calle Moneda and instead I threw myself to the ground and waited, in surrender, for my captor. That quick and irreversible decision imposed itself on me as the truth of my very being. It was a betrayal, but a sincere betrayal. I mean to say: my betrayal sprang from the truth. Now I think that, deep down, I didn't want to go on living the life of a clandestine combatant, I didn't want to go on living on the run, always on the verge of being caught; I had no hope because I'd lost my faith in the people, in their revolutionary heart. Although I denied it, of course. Notice that phrase, "the people," I choke on it now. Brassens's irony, as I looked at Giuseppe and focused on his long, lively nose in Pauline's apartment: *Mourrons pour des idées, d'accord, mais de mort lent* . . . I wanted to live. I wanted to go peacefully to the super-market and the beauty parlor, to fix my hair and paint my nails, to buy new clothes and go to the movies. I wanted to spend more time with Anita. Of course, that's what I say now.

Hearts with a single purpose. That's why I admired them, and for that same reason I would hate them later, and myself as well. That society of equals we believed in would never exist. The nation of before was dead. They killed it. You can murder a country, too. You only had to look at the workers. Before, happily crowded into trucks, fists raised on the way to the march, waving their red banners. Now, coming out of the mall, fists lowered, carrying shopping bags and frustration back home. What did they want? To recognize them-selves when they looked in the store windows overflowing with objects they could never buy? That's something in itself, a piece of the dream. Ours isn't the only utopia. But there always is a utopia, you know?

The master's gaze is burned into the slave's forehead. And the slave sees himself in that gaze, he begins to exist within it. How to break away from it, if it's the very thing that creates him and sustains him? We hang over an abyss, and the thread that holds us and keeps us from falling is the gaze of our masters. But then, the wound that splits your face and gives it shape also gives you the right to the ax, understand? It gives you the right to turn your fire on them, understand? You wanted me to talk to you about politics, right? You wanted to understand how we thought back then, right?

We paid dearly for our attempt. We paid with our lives. Or, as in my case, with a perversion of life. That day I threw myself to the ground instead of fleeing, I knew more than I would have been able to admit.

I knew that divisions were growing among our people. The virus had entered. We didn't know how to believe anymore. The very idea of our communion of equals was being diluted. What was it about now? The solution of the compromisers, who were gaining ground, was *to shake hands with the party leaders of the repressive regime— trying all the while, of course, not to be spattered by the fresh blood— and to negotiate in their salons with tails between their legs.* That's what our newsletter said. They became *objective allies* of Washington money. The victory went to the bigwigs of the big business of "peaceful" negotiation, the scam that the press worldwide was to applaud with hands and feet, and that would allow the tyrant to die in his home, peacefully in his bed. Do they think that without us, without our attacks, bombings, our injuries, torture sessions, and deaths without coffins or funerals or graves, do they think there would have been any room for their filthy negotiation? Don't those cowards realize that without our sticks of dynamite affixed under cover of night five or six yards up on the high-voltage towers to blow them up, cables snapping; without the sudden, tremendous, and terrifying darkness that covered Santiago, or half of Chile; don't they realize that without us, there would never have been any massive protests? Don't they remember that anonymous blackness that brought the people out into the streets and terrified the bourgeois, terrified the soldiers themselves, who couldn't contain the barricades and the looting? It was then, only then, that the profiteering gentlemen decided they had to change horses, and they and their lackeys started looking for a "democratic exit." There were overreaches, stampeding lumpen, you say?

Of course! The revolution frees people's instincts. Cruelty blossoms along with free love, song blooms along with the garbage in the streets, hate along with poetry. Revolution is chaos. It's a torrent that, if it doesn't swallow you, lifts you up.

We called those nights of barricades *aucaye* nights, rebel nights. Because in that darkness that we created, equality existed for a few hours, and the city once again belonged to everyone. The bonfires transformed the impersonal, estranged city of Santiago into our *quitrahue*, our hearth, our home. From the dark depths of the race awoke the primordial fascination with fire, and we recognized each other's faces and genotypes in the light of the flames; in the shrill whistles we could hear the fateful wail of the *pifilca* flutes made from the tibias of dead Spanish conquistadors, calling out for an ancestral, murderous war. That's what people forget now. The military bastards didn't dare stop us. On those nights, carnival and combat intermingled. The blackout created a situation of objective risk. And over our heads flew the rattling helicopters shredding the air with their sharp blades, shaking the windows, deafening us with the unbearable, dirty roar of their rotors; they filmed us with their infrared lenses, but didn't dare to get out or to use their machine guns for fear of a massacre, for fear of the *aucayes*, fear of the rebels. Our instructions were not to look at the helicopters so we wouldn't be photographed and identified. The same went for the press photographers' cameras that multiplied on those blackout nights. We were careful. We disguised ourselves, we used hoods. *Aucaye* nights, those were really our nights. The lords of the commerce of concession have forgotten all that now.

So then the attack from our cowardly and pragmatic branch came at us. Many of our own went over to their side, the majority. For them, we now represented the "maximalist temptation." Our acts of "sabotage and recovery of funds legitimized the repression." We only wanted to bear witness. We were prophets, we were nostalgic, we were not politicians with a future. And, of course, our armed approach was "unviable." We'd heard it all before. Their knees didn't bend out of fear, oh, no; it was because they were "realists." As if it were human to renounce hope, as if reality were not precisely that which waits to be shaped by human beings. What they proposed meant: now there is no place for the beauty of the hero. But as it happens, history always leaves room for heroes. *We know their dream; enough / to know they dreamed and are dead.* Heroes are the ones who carve out that space. Allende's death is proof. At the last second, he, alone, transformed a political and military defeat into a moral victory. He made himself into a hero when it seemed that there was no time or place left for it. *Because he had to die before seeing the tyrant's face.*

When Canelo fought back, covering my escape as he had been ordered to do, he went toward death instead of letting it catch him. *And what if excess of love / bewildered them till they died?* He fell with a Smith and Wesson .44 Magnum in hand. That revolver, shot from a few yards away, will lift a man off the ground. It has a tremendous stopping power. They got Canelo, but he was already an inert mass, not a living combatant. *Angels of fire and ice.* He was equal to our oath and to what was repeated in the monthly communications that each cell had to decode and read out loud. *One who allows himself to be taken prisoner puts the entire apparatus at risk; one who lets himself be captured will face torture and will merely postpone his death, which will come as the enemy wishes, without dignity or historical significance; one who lets himself be captured breaks our vow and concedes a moral victory to the enemy. Conversely, one who dies in combat will claim a moral victory that can never be taken from him; his blood will be the fount of history.*

Did Canelo believe that? He fulfilled it, there's no doubt about that. But hadn't he been, for a long time, courting death as if it were the solution? Sometimes, when I looked at his face, I sensed that he wouldn't last long; a dullness in his eyes, I don't know.

Then, as Canelo said we would, as he warned us sometimes in our meetings, we ended up with the odious outcome, the one we would get if we came up short, if our revolutionary violence wasn't enough to incite the masses beyond the level of protest, nocturnal barricades, and vandalism. Canelo intuited that, and in fact, he mentioned it sadly to me just a few days before he was killed. In the end we were useless idiots, we were involuntary accessories of exploitation. The meanness of the petite bourgeoisie won. Their miserliness won, the hard and cold selfishness that petrifies the hearts of the rich and makes them feel themselves to be good. It's unfair to judge us only by the outcome. We lost, no doubt about it, but we came so close to winning. You have to understand *ex ante* the ambiguity of the situation. There was a moment when history opened a door to us. The invisible, our dream, for a while was there, pulsating in the visible. *Now is the time / for what tomorrow can be* . . . It wasn't an illusion. Though it seems like one now. We thought: we are what we haven't yet become. The low drum of Quilapayún marked time for our invincible march . . . *La luz, de un rojo amanecer, / The light of a red dawn / announces now the life to come.* The omelet was about to flip . . . the rich would, finally, eat shit. But just like that, dawn turned into twilight. And when I think about it, the rage still rises up like foam within me. We paved the way for the treacherous and filthy pact of the hogs with their slaughterers. The Great Whore of capitalism won, we were fucked by the Great Slut. And I wonder: Did Canelo let himself be killed the same as I let myself be caught? And wasn't it because of that?

TWENTY-ONE

His death was his life's work. That's what being a hero is. The combination of doubt and the desire to believe was resolved in action. He told me, "It doesn't hurt to not exist, only the bullets hurt." He wasn't a sensual man, Canelo, as I've said. He was tender in love, but not passionate. He preferred the idea of love to flesh-and-blood women. But he had loved a beautiful woman—*tiposa*, as a Cuban would say. This was in El Salvador. She was the daughter of the pharmacist in Laguna. One night he arrived at her house with its thick adobe walls, unannounced as always—a guerrilla never announces he's coming—and when they didn't open the door for him, he jumped over the wall into the yard: she was in the hammock with another man. The betrayal reached to his soul.

We're holed up in a safe house, it's nighttime. We've eaten a plate of pasta with tomato sauce and, for dessert, canned peaches. We're talking about what might happen to us. The atmosphere is tense. We're speaking very seriously. Kid of the Day asks what a person can do when he's afraid: "What do you do to overcome fear?" Canelo talks about a mission he carried out some time back: to set off a bomb in a bank. In a dull voice he says that, sadly, a boy died there, an eleven-year-old boy, and a nine-year-old girl was left mutilated. One of the bank's windows exploded outward just at the moment the children were going by with their grandmother. The old lady was untouched. The boy's name was José, he says, and the girl's was Karina. It's the thought of the mutilated girl that eats away at him most. There is silence. Pelao repeats a quotation from our violent

Christ. The Spartan had reminded us of it when he gave us the mission that awaits us tomorrow: hold up a currency exchange. *"This is going to be a long war,* says Che. *And, we repeat once again, a cruel war. Let no one fool himself . . .* They are collateral damage, see? It's unfortunate," says Pelao Cuyano. "It can't be avoided . . . *For us*—and it's Lenin himself who says it—*morality is subordinated to the interests of the class struggle of the proletariat.* And that's it."

Canelo, who has fallen very quiet, straightens up. "I think," he goes on talking, paying no attention to Pelao, "about what that girl's life must be like, Karina's, without half of her left leg, and sometimes I see the boy José's body torn to pieces. I feel guilty, and even so . . . and even so it's necessary to act, it's necessary to face the greatest risk out of love of justice," he says. "It's the only thing that can redeem my guilt for those innocent children: the danger of dying. We are not murderers. If I die tomorrow I'll be the same as that boy José. If we aren't capable of doing it, it means that God exists, brother. If we're unable to make that sacrifice, it means that in order to be able to give your life for something, you have to believe in God. But we don't believe in God, and we will give our lives for justice. We'll prove that God is unnecessary. Once, I went to the Metropolitan Cemetery to see the boy José's grave. There's a little angel carved into his headstone. I promised myself that day that I would be capable of dying. For him, you know? And for that little girl, Karina . . ."

He goes on saying something else, but I just look at his clear eyes, his hair that makes you want to caress it. Kid of the Day looks at him in surprise, "And the fear?"

Canelo tells him: "You can't think so much. If they get you, they get you. Coño, you just have to give them hell, that's it."

And the next day, well, you know what happened the next day.

For us, "History"—that word had a lot of weight back then—gave direction to our lives, and History was something like a long, collective pilgrimage for redemption, a long and torturous Purgatory that led to Paradise. Belonging to that brotherhood, I think now, gave shape and direction to my scattered life, it incorporated my life into a chorus of pilgrims, changing my whims and impulses and trivialities into destiny and salvation. The drop of my miniscule life was transfigured when it became part of a river. Ours was a Sacred History. The revolutionary—but who understands today what that was?—sacrificed happiness. His death justified him and opened the way to the New Society. That's what it was to believe. The way Canelo did. That he knew how to die was proof of his conviction. He needed it. And it equated him, as he had promised himself beside the boy José's grave, with his victims. I wish he could have lived to contemplate his death, like an artist does his masterpiece.

TWENTY-TWO

After exactly seventy days of freedom, a white Mazda pulled up next to me in the street, a block away from my mother's house. I was coming back from teaching a French class. The door opened, an arm yanked me inside, the car took off, and the blindfold went over my eyes. I recognized Ronco's shouts and I caught a glimpse of, yes, Rat's matted red hair. He was looking at me with the same mocking smile. My mission of revenge crumbled. I obeyed like a worn-out ox. They put handcuffs on me. Now, don't imagine these were two big, burly men. Quite the opposite—they were a couple of buffoons, the kind you don't even see when you pass them on the street. Ronco, like Rat, was fairly short. He had a giant head, small, narrow eyes, big hands, and squat legs. When he smiled, which he only did halfway, as if hiding, a gold tooth peeked out on one side. But in that Mazda, as I said, my eyes were blindfolded. I felt an unbearable exhaustion. I hadn't forgotten.

We crossed a yard and I entered a space whose contours I couldn't picture. It wasn't Central. They pushed me forward. I took a few steps and fell and hit my head, and I kept on falling and banging my head with my hands trapped behind me. The fuckers didn't warn me there were stairs. As I fell, the handcuffs bit into my wrists. Those scars stayed with me for weeks. Rat shouted at me. "Dirty whore!" A boot kept my nose pressed into a puddle on the floor. "Like a little bitch!" laughed Rat. "You're a little fucking bitch, stinking whore!" A kick in my kidneys and the order to stand up.

I went stumbling into a room that seemed dark and narrow and smelled of dampness. I was thrown onto a metal cot. My head hurt and I was dizzy. Nausea came and went. In spite of my confusion I understood very quickly that Gato wasn't here, that I was truly a secret prisoner, that I'd been kidnapped and taken to an underground storage space who knows where, that here there was no structure or command or doctors or anything else, that my life was in Ronco's hands, and he would do with me as he wished . . . My hopes were minimal then, the hopes of a dimwit, of a snail. I was consumed by the terror of dying. It's the uncertainty that causes fear. That's what they want: for everything to be unpredictable. It wasn't just my own story that made me afraid; more than anything it was other women's stories, the ones I'd heard or read about, the ones that poisoned my memory. I remembered we had been advised to defend ourselves, to kick, shout insults, scream . . .

I took my clothes off in silent obedience and it was cold, the wet cold of a closed-off space. And no one knows you're here, you catching on now, you little cocksucker? And I was a little bitch shivering from the cold and the fear. You stupid dyke, don't fuck with us, and they tied me up and how much longer you goin' to fuck with us, you dirty whore, and they tied me up and put the thick, stinking rag in my mouth again, and you get it now, motherfucker, you get what this is about, or are you a stupid little cocksucker? You want us to break your ass with the end of a broken bottle? And they shaved me and delved their fingers into me without desire, and on top of that the fleabag's dry, and laughing with hard, mocking peals of laughter, she can't be any good for a fuck, this skinny bitch is bland as hell, I couldn't even get it up she's fucking ruined and ugly the fucked-up bitch, and like someone examining a horse's teeth to guess its age, what'd they do to your tits, dyke? More cackling. And wasn't this the one they said was so hot, good for a fuck and all that, huh? It was a rough friction, harsh and painful, as if ripping something out of me, it was a suffocating appropriation to which I didn't put up the least resistance. Afterward came a punch in the stomach with the butt of a pistol. There you go, little shit. At least you'll like the air, you little bitch. I couldn't breathe for a long time. The rest was passing through a tunnel of quick, sharp, unbearable pains, a horrific and dark crossing.

How the hell do they find animals like those? How do they round them up? The answer I'd give you today: it's not that they go out looking for them. Once the space of delimited impunity is there—because there *are* limits, there is a system, it's not just pure chaos—the monster we carry within us, the beast that grows fat on human flesh, is unleashed within the good father or the daughter of a good family. But for that to happen there has to be an order that you follow and that keeps you innocent. This, belonging to an institution carefully elaborated over time, the discipline, is what allows the transfer of blame to whoever is above you, your superior in the hierarchy. That's what I think. Sometime later, Macha would tell me: It's not the man who is evil; it's what he does that turns him evil.

My head falls and bounces against the metal bed frame. The bed acts like it doesn't know you. As if your own guard dog is attacking you in your home. The torment makes your body into a foreign object, and at the same time, the one suffering is you—you, incapable of obeying your brain's instructions. If you could at least control your mouth, if you could stop one jawbone from clattering against the other.

Ronco shouts something about my daughter, "Ana," he says. Now it's an unmitigated pain. "Anita, that's the kid's name," shouts Ronco. "I'm going to go grab her when she comes out of the French Alliance, in Calle Louis Pasteur. There, that's the school your kid goes to, right?" I hear Ronco's words in my memory, words he surely uttered on his way out. Gato tells me my first duty is to protect my daughter . . . When did Gato get here? I am devastated.

"My daughter?" I ask, lifting my head with a wavering, little girl voice. And suddenly: "Nooo, pleeeease . . . noooo," I plead, struggling, or I try to; I'm on the verge of fainting.

Suddenly I lift my head up: How do they know about my daughter? Canelo would have thought about her. He would have fixed things to hide her for a while. I'm terrified: the Spartan was right. I should have sent her to Havana. I knew I had to. It was my duty. I put it off and put it off... I cry out in rage at myself. I see her coming out of school in all her innocence, playing around with her friends, never imagining that those men coming closer are going to kidnap her. No! How did they get to her? My alibi has fallen, I think. When that happens, it's as if they've killed you. A combatant without an alibi isn't worth anything. You are no longer the ghost you were, and now you're consumed by a new fear.

I give a start and I ask Gato to please, run after Ronco, order him to leave my daughter alone, Anita is only five years old . . .

"All right," he says. "I'll go see if I can catch up with him," he says. I hear him get up slowly and leave the room with heavy steps. The door shuts with a dry sound.

Ronco's cold laughter wakes me up. I must have been out for a second. They're sitting down. "Gato stopped me. Let's see what you have to say, you stupid dyke . . ." Rat frees my hands and feet. I hear him breathing. I ask for water and he says no, it's not allowed. Holding on to him I manage to sit up on the frame. I sit there, naked.

What's happened is simple. They photographed me. When I was arrested the first time, they sat me in a chair, handcuffed, and they took my picture. I don't remember it, but it happened. Later, they gave me the prisoner's uniform. Investigative Police received that photo. Gray and methodical functionaries searched long and patiently—in those years the system wasn't computerized—in the Cabinet of Identification's registry until they found a photograph that looked like me, and with luck on their side, they came upon my real name and ID. And my alibi falls. I'm cooked: they find my parents, their addresses, where I work. In Central they quickly find out I have a daughter and that she goes to school at the French Alliance, located on Calle Louis Pasteur and, obviously, that the identity I had given them was false. I put all this together later, of course.

You see, I was prepared for torture—or I thought I was, more like it—and my duty, I repeat, was to last five hours. After that I could talk and it didn't matter anymore. My comrades would have vanished. Then one of two things would happen: they would release me or kill me. But now I was inside for the second time, my alibi had fallen, my cover had fallen. When that happens, I don't know, it's an awful feeling of helplessness, like nothing else. There's no possible defense. Because then they have a way to blackmail me, starting with my daughter and moving on to my parents. And I don't want them to bring Anita; I don't want her to see me here naked among these clothed animals, naked among them, shaved for my torment. They have no right to make my daughter see me like this, no, they have no right to do that. But what is a right? In the meantime, they ask for names and more names, alibis, descriptions, houses, addresses . . . But in the end the questions all lead to Bone.

Moments open only to the future or the past. In that state of anguish you can find no refuge within yourself or in anything you've been taught. Nothing makes sense. All that's left are your cries half muffled by the gag. It gnaws at me like guilt, my daughter.

Ronco stops. The miserable Gato then grows enormous before my blindfolded eyes. His voice calms me. His memory. I've already told you, I've never met anyone with such an ability to remember every detail of a story, to make someone tell it over and over until he found those raised bridges between two truths, the inconsistency, the lie that accuses and bites you. And as frightening as he is, it becomes more and more tempting to see him as one who is, deep down, good, or at least beautiful and cruel. It's harder to accept that unlimited power could be in the hands of an abject being. The evil ones are his subordinates, like Ronco, not him. That assumption helps me resign myself. In the depths of that basement there is someone good, the invisible Gato on whom I depend, my *deus absconditus*. Hidden desires well up, I want to save him so that he can save me. The distressing thing is that he's gone. Once again I'm at Ronco's mercy.

I surprise myself by searching for the fault in myself. He's an implacable but fair god whose anger I myself must have unleashed. And so guilt sets in, and with it comes the will to sacrifice something as expiation. The attraction of collaborating with him will grow. It's fear, of course, but fear transformed into remorse. The omnipotent father cannot be that evil, it must be possible to redeem my sin.

When I heard, hours later, Gato's feigned voice again, it was a relief, a happiness, a hope, and I gave myself over to him, sobbing and cursing what I had been. I was the guilty one now, putting my own daughter in danger. That's what I shouted at him, out of control. And then I talked. I talked as if I were already one of them. The person I'd been was gone. She abandoned me the way someone I once loved and have stopped loving would leave. It was a change of skin, of language. And that is not innocent. One is never the same in another language. There had been pain, but it was before. Not anymore. My confession flowed out as a vomit of hate toward my brothers, toward myself, my previous self. Everything happened faster and at the same time much more slowly than what I'm telling you.

Later, when they removed my blindfold and someone wearing a hood, I think it was Ronco, or maybe Rat, I don't remember, I don't really know, showed me the photo of my daughter, they finished breaking me. No one said anything. First it was the photo, and then a video, a couple of minutes of video shown on a small video camera that one of them plugged in and placed on the floor: her, Anita, coming out of school in her little blue skirt. She was talking to a friend and I heard her laugh. That was it. I need for her to go on laughing, I said to myself. And I surrendered. And I became one of them.

TWENTY-THREE

When I came out of there, shivering from cold and shivering from fear, and filthy, thirsty, fetid, and suffering, under the edge of my blindfold I could see where they'd held me: two red trucks, shiny and at the ready, waiting for the alarm. It was a fire station. Where was it? I never found out. At Central they took my clothes, which were disgusting, and they handed me the grimy prison uniform.

Tomasa squeezes me in a hug. "How can you possibly still be here?" I ask. She tells me that no, they had let her go, too, and then picked her up again. I lie down at one end of the cell's cold cement floor. I wake up: the same cell, the same stinking clothes, the same sweaty grime on my skin, the same greasy hair. The same woman in jeans who brings us the same watery broth.

Tomasa quietly hums "Te recuerdo Amanda" as she lays out the cards for solitaire. She tells me about an official in charge of the department of analysis. She thinks he's attractive, different from the rest of them. "Flaco Artaza is a real intelligence agent," she tells me. "Not like the others, who are just full-time gangsters."

Suddenly she tells me: "They've broken my spine and I need to be recognized as someone, at least as the whore with . . . It doesn't matter who."

"You told me before," I say. She doesn't hear me, or she pretends not to hear . . .

"As long as I have someone taking care of me," she says. "Without a pimp you can't even be a whore. If I could just find some way to get one of these thugs to soften, to warm up. I'd have to get something in return, of course. A hot shower and new underwear, maybe." We're back to the same thing.

The noise of the lock turning startled me. I was sleeping. Several nights had passed, I don't know how many, interrupted only by the arrival of the day's glass of water and the watered-down broth. The same fat guardian in jeans brought me, in handcuffs and with the end of her baton sticking into my back, up to the second floor. "You're going to see the famous Flaco," she told me. Tomasa liked him, I think to myself. I had only seen him pass by once, from far away. He walked down the hallway with long strides, graceful and indifferent, with the elegance of authority.

When he saw me come in like that, he shouted an order for the woman to remove my handcuffs. He took off my blindfold himself, and a sob escaped me. He took a can of Coca-Cola from the small refrigerator that was camouflaged in a cabinet, opened it, and handed it to me. I kept crying. The soda tasted so good to me. But I went on crying, and I felt I was disgusting. My chest hurt so much with every moan, it was as if the sobs were fighting their way out with a knife blade.

Flaco was a man with an aquiline nose and enormous liquid eyes, blue and melancholy. He moved with lethargic ease. He struck me as attractive when I saw him from behind, one hand on his hip, the other writing on the chalkboard. Long legs. Well-shaped, he was. I noticed his wedding ring. A serious man, I thought. He'd gone bald. He couldn't be over thirty-four, I thought, and already bald as a father—a father with youthful skin and no potbelly. He offered me a cigarette. We talked. I felt his eyes on me. No one inside there had looked at me. He did. You can't know what that means, it's the warmth of a nest. He told me he'd been born in Valdivia. He missed the Calle-Calle River. He hated the Mapocho River, he told me. "We can agree there," I said, and he laughed with me.

On the whiteboard, a flowchart. In the box at the top, our Commander Joel. It was the same image that appeared in our internal newsletters: his glasses, behind which you could see his serene Asiatic eyes; his abundant black hair combed away from his face; his nose and mouth, wide; his beard, trimmed. It was an image that we carried with us burned into our memories. Flaco noticed my unease. A vertical line connected Joel to "Bone," who didn't have a photo. From there three lines radiated out and opened up into boxes with names and photos—almost all very blurry—from which other lines led to other boxes. Over time I learned that it was copies of these blurry photos that Macha had been given. In one of the boxes I recognized Tomasa.

He asked me in a smooth, respectful, and convincing tone to help him fill in the boxes with our pseudonyms. They had christened my brothers and sisters with the names of the streets where they had been located for the first time. "We put him to bed there and got him up there in the morning." That's how, he told me, the agents in charge of surveillance gave their reports. I never found out who it was they called "Antonio Varas" after they saw him stay overnight the first time in a building on that street. The photo was too blurry. The tail sometimes allowed them to see a "meet." Surveillance was the thing those bastards did best. But there were also brothers and sisters who had turned. And Flaco wanted me to understand that very well. Tomasa? Briceño? Escobar? How many had flipped? Whoever arrived last to a "meet" and sat in the safest place was the most senior in the hierarchy, they did know that. That's how they recognized the leaders. The intermediaries confused them, I noticed; those sainted women threw them off the trail. And, looking at things from a distance, I must have been the one who gave Flaco a precise explanation of their function. Accordingly, he perfected their system of tailing and location of leaders. Because it was easy to figure out that they came to few group "meets" but had many meetings with intermediaries.

The box at the top of my cell had a name: "Prince of Wales." I had met once with the Spartan in a restaurant on that avenue to eat

Spanish omelets. Next to our cell, a series of new nicknames were waiting for me to sort through them. "Gladiolo" was obviously Rafa, because his mother lived on Calle Los Gladiolos, where—remember?—I had left him a note he never answered. Others were "Redhead Curinanca," "Plaid Curinanca," and "Big-Nose Curinanca."

"What a way of guarding me," I said. And with tears still in my eyes I started to laugh, disconsolate, understanding that this would be forever.

At Flaco's instruction I called my mother and explained to her that I had to leave right away for Paris—for Paris, which for me meant Giuseppe's love—as an interpreter for a delegation of businesspeople. The interpreter who was supposed to go was sick. It was urgent, it was a good opportunity, I was packing as fast as I could. One week, I lied; I would be gone for one week. My voice shook a little. I said good-bye to her and to Anita.

"Relax," Flaco said to me, "Relax." He took hold of my jaw and turned it roughly to the left. A vertebra cracked and I cried out. Then he did the same thing toward the right. A vertebra cracked again. I felt better. "Relax," he repeated, "Relax." He got behind me, took me by the legs, and launched me toward the ceiling. In the middle of my flight, my spinal column cracked violently. I shrieked. But it was a good pain. He caught me, placing me gently back on the floor. And that's how my first conversation with Flaco ended. They gave me a bar of soap and let me shower. If you could only know how marvelous it was to feel the hot water and soap suds sliding all over the skin of my poor body.

The next day, Flaco called me into his office again. He had a surprise for me: a Lancôme *palette de maquillage.* That's what he called it, and I was delighted with his gesture and the effort he put into his badly pronounced French. It fascinated me: to be able to wear makeup again. We had lunch together. It was a bit late and the cafeteria was almost empty. I looked at him, trying not to. His smile made my knees weak. I was invaded by a sweet languor, and a few yawns escaped me. My mouth was dry. He'd left his cigarettes in his office. We went to get them after lunch, and I kissed him there. It was an impulse. I kissed him with an exquisite calm, and it was as if he knew intuitively that if he rushed, it would ruin everything.

TWENTY-FOUR

Would you believe me if I told you that more than one prisoner came out of her cell at night to kiss and dance with her jailers in some club, and that was part of the horror? Would you believe Tomasa and I did it, that sometimes, like a couple of Cinderellas, we went happily into Oliver to toss back one Chivas Regal after another, and that we also went to that mansion with adobe walls and high ceilings on a plot of land in Malloco?

Flaco took me out in his brand-new Volvo and—I almost forgot! —he took me first to Calle General Holley. There were many fine boutiques on that street back then. He gave me a lot of gifts. I had looked down on those clothes, those mirrors, those boutiques designed to flatter the skin and eyes. They didn't mesh with the steely spirit our struggle demanded. But now I wanted to look pretty, I wanted to feel like a woman who could drive those fool men crazy. In Privilege, I chose, without doubting for a second, a pair of black pants with a matching velvet jacket and a leopard print Lycra shirt that hugged my body (the original, the saleswoman told me, was Versace). We bought a pair of dark glasses. From there we went to Mingo and found a pair of boots made of soft, shiny leather. I was delighted. I felt like a little girl getting presents from Santa Claus. Never in my years as a clandestine fighter would I have worn clothes like that. All that austerity of ours, I'm telling you, I threw it out the window. Was I turning into a whore? Me? The timid girl who'd been educated by nuns? I trembled when I felt the sensuality of those fabrics. And later, looking at the way the stockings evened out my skin, leaving only the essential geometry of my legs. The stockings made me into a Cézanne painting, I thought then. And in the Lycra shirt I looked at my breasts in the mirror as if they were my very being. I thought: if my soul existed, it would be in my breasts.

It was Flaco, as I said, who took me to Oliver. Great Dane was at a table in the back. I'd caught a glimpse of him at Central once, wearing workout clothes. Tomasa thought he was the best looking. Though, as I've already said she thought Flaco was more attractive, maybe, for that elegance that was so unique to him. Great Dane was with a young woman with intense, light blue eyes and brand-name clothes who smiled at him like a Siamese cat, caressing his three-day-old beard and his long, blond hair. He signaled to Flaco and left, his kitten draped over him and, enormous as he was, moving nimbly between the pub's tightly arranged tables. He noticed me and right there, at that moment, I realized that Flaco was looking at me anxiously, and that my leopard print shirt was driving him crazy. His eyes flickered every so often to exactly where you would imagine. And it pleased me to please him and it made me move and laugh with much more grace than I actually have. I think I'm pretty ordinary, but not that night, no. That night I shone.

As we were leaving Oliver, Flaco wanted to buy a bottle of Chivas for the road. The waiter told him no. Flaco, annoyed, got up from the table and went to talk to someone. Two minutes later, a man who introduced himself very solicitously as "the manager" saw us to the door. We had with us as a gift from the house, a recently opened bottle of Chivas that we drank in the car, with no glass or ice, straight from the mouth of the bottle. We took small sips, and my tongue lapped up every drop of the golden liquor in fascination.

The first time he brought me to a dance club—it had three floors and was all the rage, on Calle Recoleta, I think—I let myself go as I had never done before. Dancing slowly to fast songs in the middle of the dance floor, taking advantage of the darkness and the closeness, I put a hand into his pocket and then lowered his zipper a little, and I slid a hand in and took hold of him right there, still dancing. "That killed me," he would tell me later. And that swollen, thick, and firm thing was my doing, and I liked that he wanted me, and I liked him because I liked that he wanted me so much and that he was looking at me with his big eyes, tense and shining. That thing of his wanted me. And he wanted me like that, with that tremendous and always strange thing that rose up, curving at the end, for me. I was capable of making that happen. So, of course, was any other woman. That's how men are, I know that. But at that moment it was me, and that hard thing with taut and demanding and soft skin was for me and no one else. And it was him and it wasn't him, and it was mine and it wasn't mine.

And later, in his Volvo, I was as I was not and he was as he was not, and I liked the feeling of being someone else and of Flaco being someone else, with those great blue eyes that shone on me and that slight smile, happy and tense at the same time, another who was him, another who was me, impassioned, with an urgent need to envelop inside me that intimate and secret Flaco that was now emerging into the light with a clumsiness that amused and gratified me and made me wait and tremble. And when he was lying on his back and I was above him, given over, and I felt him as I moved on top of him, it was agonizing that he was there and also that he wouldn't go on being there or that he hadn't been there before, always, and the air became thin and then living meant always wanting more air that would always be lacking.

TWENTY-FIVE

Flaco paid my cover charge. Several bills. "Some expensive place," I thought. They gave him a key that he put in his pocket. He handed me a mask that was Zorro-style, only red, and a top hat. That made him laugh a lot. "Put all your hair up under the hat," he told me, laughing. "I like you better with short hair," he told me. And he kissed the nape of my neck. He wore the same disguise as I did.

Tomasa was with a friend of Flaco's, Mauricio. He was a big man, with a blunt nose and small eyes, bald, with a big belly, a shiny, black leather jacket, and gray jeans held up by a thick belt with a buckle shaped like a horseshoe. I never really found out where he worked. We were in an old landowner's house that had been made into a dance club, and there was darkness and champagne and, well, young boys dancing with macho men and women and girly men and manly girls embracing manly men and womanly women, and uppers and poppers, yes, and the white stuff, of course, just a few lines, and lights flashing on for a second and off again, fragmenting the bodies, music at full blast.

The men I can see around me are vigorous, self-assured, warm, and masculine; but, I don't know why, they are also vulnerable. They prefer tight jeans, boots and black leather vests with sleeveless shirts, or nothing, underneath. A lot of them have their hair short or shaved, or long, very long, and there are masks and caps and hats. Are they truck drivers, military men, traffickers, dancers, motorcycle riders, pimps, artists? What are they playing at with such aplomb, such tenderness? The myth of the macho falls like a shadow over them. It lets them invent a role on that stage we all occupy. Because that party—I notice right away in my body that as I walk is already dancing—is happening, if it is happening, in a time that will be brief, an open and shut of the eyes, and in a space that is closed, metaphorical, dreamlike, and fleeting.

I can tell you whatever I want. Like with everything that happened in that club in Malloco. I can be someone else. That was the fascinating thing. Because there, I discovered I was not who I thought I was. Flaco Artaza took me there, as I told you. He took me, soaring in his silver Volvo with its new-car smell. Why? Why did he need to go, and with me? And can you see me there, amazed, at the black marble bar that was frankly louche, with all its liquor bottles shining and lit up in front of me, drinking a pisco sour with Flaco, who smiles as I laugh for no reason, Flaco, who is transfixed by my perfume, transfixed by my breasts that press against the Triumph bra—which we bought together, of course—and overflow, and that I look at from above? At that moment I like them so much I want to take them in my hands and caress them gently as if they were two turtledoves, two baby rabbits, two newborn fawns.

When we came out of that imaginary house the dawn sky was made of salt. Tomasa and I went back exhausted, and I felt my anguish rising into my esophagus: What would happen today? And we returned to our prison. When we went in we saw Chico Escobar and Vladimir Briceño. They were handcuffed and blindfolded. They had also been picked up again.

Over the gates of Dante's *Inferno* is written: *Abandon all hope those who enter here.* That's how I lived. I'd lost all hope and I still wasn't dead. I would see many others in that state of despondency. They were eaten up by desperation in those dungeons. Because they had sworn to fight unto death before giving up and they'd been captured alive; they had sworn not to falter and they'd faltered. The enemy's cruelty had ensnared them and driven them mad from fear. What did they have before them? If they were released they would never again be what they had been. Their brothers would look at them suspiciously. They would have to give a statement. They could be punished and disgraced. No matter what, for reasons of security and for a long time, as in my case, they would be excluded from any risky missions. Hadn't they been warned that it was better to die than to fall into enemy hands? The ancient Christians' baptism of blood washes away all stains and allows direct entrance into Paradise. The mujahideen—didn't they know it! The miseries of an entire life are erased in an instant, forever. *All changed, changed utterly: A terrible beauty is born.* But they hadn't been up to it.

So they vegetated, lacking a purpose and sick in their souls. They suffered—we suffered—without relief. Even though the guards and interrogators didn't do anything to them anymore. They'd finished with them, and one of these nights they'd kill them or throw them out in the street like ownerless dogs. We had trained to be heroes and now we had bodies made of jelly and we longed for a death that we hadn't be able to consummate.

Along with the first light of day, the pain in my head started to invade my sleep. My mouth was dry and I swallowed saliva and it was still just as dry. When I opened my eyes in the semidarkness of my cell I let out a scream like a wild animal. My heart was in my throat and I went on screaming. I tried to stop but I couldn't: Tomasa was hanging from one of the bars in the window. Her fixed eyes bulged as if they would come out of her swollen face. She was swinging slowly. A trickle of blood flowed from her ear. When they opened the door and took her down I saw she had hung herself with a thick black belt with a metal buckle shaped like a horseshoe. Mauricio's. I said nothing.

TWENTY-SIX

I give them the address of a safe house. We met there the night before the mission when I was taken prisoner. Calle Zenteno, between Sargento Aldea and Pedro Lagos, I told them, and when I did it, a tremor passed over my face. A crack was opening up. The vessel had broken.

We parked some fifty yards from the house—Rat in the driver's seat, Ronco in the back next to me in my ski mask. A Fiat taxi and a blue Toyota four-door pulled up. A man with narrow shoulders and a crooked nose, a woman with a black shirt that hugged her breasts tightly, and another guy who looked Indian climbed up onto the neighboring roofs. A huge, agile, brawny man leaped, his blond bangs flying, and the door flew open under his kick. It was Great Dane, the man I'd seen in Oliver with the girl with Siamese eyes. A woman, skinny as a mouse, went in with her CZ drawn, and behind her went Great Dane, his blond hair grazing his shoulders. From the van, wearing my ski mask, I was just starting to recognize this group. Then, silence. It seemed that a long time went by.

They made me get out and go through the house. Ronco asked me how I could prove that this was a safe house. I hadn't thought about that. Except for an old woman who was half deaf, no one was there. "You lyin' to us again, you little bitch? You want us to start all over again? Lemme tell you, Great Dane's not here to waste his time . . . You saw what that guy's kicks can do . . ."

I didn't answer. I went straight to the closet in a small room at the back, I knelt on the floor, and, trembling, I removed a board. I wanted to say: here. My voice wouldn't come. "What's she got?" asked Ronco.

The man with narrow shoulders and crooked nose looked at me anxiously with his deep-set eyes. Mono Lepe. The woman with the tight black shirt, Pancha, Pancha Ortiz, came over fearlessly, though she took precautions. Her sure, agile hands, her meaty fingers with their manicured nails and no rings, opened the black plastic bag that was sealed with a zipper: there were two long, black, brand-new 7.62 caliber AKMSs with collapsible stocks, made in Poland.

"I'd like to pet them," Pancha told me with a deliberately sensual smile. "But I can't, not before they're examined for fingerprints. There are some guns that are beautiful, don't you think? And is it possible to separate their beauty from their function?"

I saw them shove outside the poor old deaf woman who gave the house its cover, as she protested, handcuffed and blindfolded. I watched from behind my ski mask, in that dirty war up to my neck.

I would have liked to be Scheherazade. I should have been. But once my alibi fell I didn't know how to keep inventing stories.

And that's how I started collaborating, and collaborating meant informing on my brothers, handing over—contritely—their names to my confessor, Flaco or Gato. Mostly Gato. There's a vertigo that comes with informing. You turn completely. And you confess and cry and talk and cry names, dates, faded places. And in doing so, the fear of pain disappears, and for a moment, you're reconciled with that terrible god who demanded that sacrifice. Because that disastrous god, you discover later, asked you to give him an argument for your life and your future. It was a Faustian bargain. And still you have no inkling of what that phrase really means: "to sell your soul to the Devil." A *deus absconditus* took for himself all you could ever be, he's a jealous Mephistopheles whose desire is violent and all-encompassing. There's something cannily attractive in that death. I have to be born again for Flaco, for Gato; I'm a new woman, I'm "la Cubanita," Consuelo Frías Zaldívar, native of Matanzas, who is interrogating Chico Escobar and Briceño.

My loss of respect for myself will make my job ever easier. In my betrayed brothers' faces—though of course they don't recognize me, they will never see me—you can read the hate mixed with fear. They're stupefied. Little by little it will spread through Red Ax. A death sentence has been communicated and hangs over an informer —they don't know who it is, but I do—and there's no turning back, the cards have been dealt.

And when, a month and a half later, they let me go again—earlier, I'd had to call my mother from "Paris" to justify the unforeseen extension of my trip—an urgent and concrete problem occurred to me, one that "inexplicably" no one seemed to have thought of before: What happened to la Cubanita? How to explain her disappearance, which coincided with my freedom? My situation was extremely dangerous. There was a death sentence hanging over this "Cubanita," I'm telling you. *A spy who is caught in our organization will be punished unto death. The same is true for one who deserts or informs to the police.* The solution fell by its own weight: I had to go back to headquarters and interrogate. People had to know that la Cubanita was still in action. As for me, I had already given up. I didn't need incentives. So the circumstances—did I really say "circumstances"?—obliged me to return, hooded and using a fake Caribbean voice. I now had this job in addition to my private French classes. I started earning exactly 35 percent more each month. I was no longer receiving, as you know, the stipend from Red Ax. I had to educate and support my daughter. I didn't want her to suffer because of me, I didn't want her to lack anything because of me. The prose of life is like that, prosaic and hackneyed.

And I didn't give myself halfway, let me tell you. Once I'd taken the step, I did it all the way. I took courses in intelligence. I was a diligent student. I learned quickly. I came prepared. And at the swearing-in ceremony I intoned the hymn of Central Intelligence: "We are children of silence. . ." No sooner had I received my new general ID card, my Central ID card, and my CZ, I swore I would use it. I hated my brothers.

I thought about the thousands and thousands and thousands of innocent lives martyred as they searched for us, the clandestine fighters. We behaved, I told myself, as if we had already done what we hoped to eventually do; we believed that the magnitude of our hope was enough to make us right. Now it irritated me that I had listened, enthralled, to Pelao Cuyano, who had done a course in military instruction at Punto Cero and I hadn't, and who told us in an accent that reminded us of Che: "Mirá, look, Giap had never fought before when he took over as the leader of the Armed Propaganda Brigade, and with only thirty-three men, think about it, Che, with only thirty-three men, Giap started the revolutionary war in Vietnam. Ten years later, in Dien Bien Phu, four divisions entered into combat, some eighty thousand men. What do you have to say about a thing like that, girl?" And he looked at us with fevered eyes.

Our political analyses were hermeneutic exercises. They were about recognizing in our profane present the repetition of archetypal events from our sacred history. That's how the crusader lives. The truth is, our story was much more modest than Giap's: a miniscule number of trained combatants had unleashed the military's paranoia and its politics of extermination. Everything was out of proportion: our rhetoric of armed struggle and the implacable cruelty of the military response. I came to think all this much later, certainly, when betrayal and treachery had become a habitual form of revenge against my brothers and against myself. Against my brothers because they refused to acknowledge that we were going to be grabbed by the eyelashes, for making me believe in a utopia whose only possible future was failure, and against myself for being duped by a religion that, like all religions, was no more than a cult of death.

A collaborator, to be used by that Moloch to facilitate his plans. And also to quell the remorse and self-hate that come when you feel yourself to be a traitor. A person needs to believe herself to be good, and to justify her actions. *They* are the guilty ones, not I, and I must denounce them. What sense does it make, what they're doing? It's a thanatotic sickness, I tell myself. The truth is they don't even believe anymore that their sacrificial death will bring about a new world. They go through life clinging to a dream that's long gone. The "revolution," as they remember it, is over. They're tied to something dead. They identify with something that has vanished. They can't bury their dead and resign themselves to the idea that their dreams are buried, because it's as if they were burying themselves.

So they take some ammunition by force from the Aquageles plant, they lay their cables, set their watches, and oil their Brownings, their Kalashnikovs. They're being summoned by the defunct. They are few. They are ancestral voices demanding blood, revenge, and sacrifice. Though there is no hope, and perhaps *because* there is no hope. That's the great thing, I tell myself, the noble thing, I tell myself and contradict myself. The idea is to sacrifice yourself. A symbol, a moral testament.

And so their fight against inequality, their scientifically blind trust in victory and life, gets confused with the death that patiently waits for them and ties them up and leaves them with no tomorrow. Otherwise, there would be only the futility of a life given over drop by drop to a cause that wasn't worth the trouble. Then, to live is to die along with your dead. My death is fidelity; it is a solution. To give everything in order to detonate some bomb, to do damage of any kind and not acknowledge that in the meantime they've switched the movie. To change is to betray myself, sell out, and dilute myself. That's how I came to think when I was one with my brothers: I am what I was, and what I was, I will be always. What we were, or nothing! What we were, or death! Yes. And hope, where was that?

And now that same woman had the job of asking questions in a Cuban voice. The weapon of my spite. I wasn't bad at it. Gato was beside me. The stench of garlic and accumulated sweat. I'm sure he wore his shirts more than once. He had a slightly crooked nose. Every so often he would pull his lapel tighter with a small, clenched hand, showing his pointed knuckles and the protruding veins that ran from them to his too-thin wrist. That was when he wasn't interrogating, because he used gloves for that. A flap of fat and skin hung down over the neck of his shirt.

In the meantime, I diligently went on giving my private French classes, I continued going with Clementina to art openings, and I brought Anita to school every morning. I went to pick her up at my mother's house at a quarter to eight. I left my apartment wearing a sweat suit at 7:20. She would be waiting for me in her little blue skirt with her backpack ready. She was never late, always there waiting for me. When I returned home, I showered, got dressed, and ate breakfast. I remember that my showers were endless. A sudden memory, like rays of sunlight filtering in between Persian blinds: I would see myself in Pauline's apartment in the rue de Bourgogne, listening to songs by Brassens, eating Camembert cheese melted over thin slices of apple. I tried to imagine Giuseppe's long, thin, lively nose, his embrace, his laugh: *Anche tra i leoni ci stanno i culatoni,* Even among lions there are fags . . . I tried uselessly to reconstruct the expression on his face when he opened the door for me: *Voilà la plus belle!* It was no use. Faces, even the ones we love, fade away.

I would emerge from the shower with my fingertips wrinkled. I remember that often, the room full of steam, I would shake my head and say to myself in a loud voice, as if to someone else: "I'm really tired, too tired. I can't do it anymore." Sometimes, as I was drying myself with my thick towel, white and heavy, I would stop for no reason. I would stand there looking at the ceiling or the bathroom tiles and think about nothing until the cold made me snap out of it. "I'm exhausted," I would repeat. "I'm really exhausted." It was hard for me not to get back in bed. Some mornings, I did.

TWENTY-SEVEN

Though it was hard for me to admit, I had started to fall in love with Flaco. He infected me. I thought about his gestures, and I felt myself copying them. Without consciously trying, I imitated his way of walking and moving. He hypnotized me. I wanted to help him. Why? He was the strong one, after all. I was a submissive lover, as if my submission would allow me to participate in his power. I felt that his hands, when they touched me, shaped me anew as if my flesh were soft clay, that old image that my feminist "self" hated and thought she'd overcome. My humiliation had undone me, and only another human being could re-create me. Does what I'm saying make sense to you, or do you think I just wanted to survive, or that I'd whored myself out, period? Because I knew he could kill me with those same hands, with one single, silent blow. That frightened me. He would know how to make all the evidence disappear. A faint and dangerous excitement ran through my body.

I see myself in the half-light, my heart pounding as my tongue explores his strong muscles. He wasn't what he seemed to be, either. No one is. That's why that house existed, hidden away on a plot of land in Malloco. And I can skip over details and imagine the situation all over again for you. I don't even know anymore. They left me irremediably broken and disguised. You know? I can't stop thinking, as I talk to you, about what you'll do with what I tell you. Maybe your book will be a barely disguised report. I see a problem with that: the weight of the real could suffocate your novel. And this story, as you've seen, is plenty unpleasant. It couldn't be any other way. A novel should be constructed as the dream of a poet, don't you think?

Maybe no one will know. But in any case, what happened, happened. You can be sure of that. I'm not talking just to talk. My story continues to be a testimony—of course, it's a testimony without innocence. I shape myself in words for you, I lift myself up on my own air, and that's what I am, then, a flow of sound that emanates from the chords in my throat and that I put within your reach, nothing more. For you, there's nothing external with which you can contrast me. I'm Narcissus, constructing my mirror of water and looking at myself, and you watch me do it.

With an old-fashioned flourish of his arm, Flaco introduces me to Jerónimo, a tall guy, very young, younger than me, with sleepy eyes. We're in the club in Malloco. WILD CAT, I managed to read on a discreet neon sign over the entrance. Jerónimo is wearing a purple shirt, untucked and unbuttoned, over a white T-shirt. He looks me in the eyes, he looks at my breasts, he looks me in the eyes, he looks at my lips, he looks at my breasts. He can't stop looking at me. He smiles, timid, or intimidated, maybe. I like that. He offers me a sip of his drink and starts to laugh. I don't like it at all. That vulgar mixture of red wine and Coca-Cola makes me choke. He tastes my pisco sour and praises it, amusement in his eyes. I like him already. He hands me his joint, which is almost out. I draw in deeply. It's strong. Flaco's turn. It goes around again. On the dance floor there are people dancing in pairs, in threes and fours. Jerónimo tells me that the fat guy dancing with the pretty dark-skinned girl is a fag, that the pretty, dark girl is jealous, she's trying to seduce him but nothing happens. He laughs with his sleepy eyes. I take another hit on his joint.

I want to dance. The three of us are already laughing a lot. And laughing, Flaco introduces me to Rabbit, who has a long face and a laugh that shows his cheerful rabbit's teeth. Jerónimo's joint goes out and I say I'm going to cry and he lights another one. His hand with its short, thick fingers. He passes it to me. It's Colombian herb, he tells me. We're dancing pressed close together. I rest my head trustingly on his shoulder. Jerónimo takes the spliff from me, takes a hit, and puts it in my mouth again. Rabbit is shorter than me. Flaco runs his index finger along my lips, taking his time, as if he wanted his finger to memorize them. And I'm dancing with three men, Jerónimo's rough beard sometimes scratching against my chin.

You know what? If I had been a man, I would have wanted to visit whorehouses, lots of whorehouses. I would have been a whoring motherfucker . . . That kind of woman has always intrigued me. Flaco hands me a piscola and leaves me dancing with Jerónimo and Rabbit. But I grab his arm as he passes, I'm afraid of him leaving, and I'm with three men again. We dance in an embrace. A slow song comes on and I kiss Flaco and I stay with him, almost not dancing, and we kiss. I stand on tiptoe to kiss him. A hand on my back that isn't his. I feel different hands touching me, but I go on kissing Flaco. He takes my arm and leads me away.

We cross the gallery, go up a staircase, and Flaco takes out the key they gave him at the entrance. He opens the door of a private room, a small salon with a vulgar and decadent elegance. At the back, a canopied bed and a bathroom. All four of us are there. The music doesn't pound as much here, but it's the same music as downstairs and it doesn't lose its hypnotizing power. We go on kissing, barely dancing, pressed tight, and Flaco's hand unclasps my bra. Jerónimo and Rabbit are watching us now, sitting—sprawled, more like it—on frayed embroidered armchairs that could have been Louis XV— cheap copies, of course. Between them, a black table, lacquered, and a faded black velvet sofa. Flaco takes a blue bag and an oval mirror from his pocket. He makes lines using his MasterCard Gold. I see the enormous orifices of my powdery nose in the mirror. Flaco tells me to take off my blouse. I tell him OK, as long as he takes his shirt off first. He snorts a line and complies. Knowing I'm being watched is tantalizing. Those red-rimmed eyes. Will I do it? I bite one of Flaco's nipples. I have my eyes closed. We move as if to a lullaby.

I open my eyes. Who are these men looking at me? Am I still the same person if I like that they want me? But I do like it. That's why I'm looking back at them. I look at them without shame. Like you look over a new car or a purebred bull. I'm excited by the imminence of a dangerous threshold. I'm excited by a magnetic force pulling me in an unknown direction. Flaco takes my blouse off. My bra is held up only by the lift of my firm breasts. Flaco bites it and lets it fall to the ground. We go on dancing like that, so close, skin against skin. I'm not hearing with my ears, now. It's something inside me. The strings of the bass run through me, and I vibrate as if my body's depths were a guitar. I sink my hands into the back pockets of Flaco's jeans.

"You have to do something for them," he whispers in my ear. "Look at them, they're going crazy, you've got them hypnotized," and he laughs.

Jerónimo looks back at me with such languid eyes. The rest of his body is completely in shadow.

"Tell them to come over here," Flaco says to me. "Tell them."

I waver. I hesitate.

"Tell them," Flaco gently insists.

I hesitate. I reach out an uncertain hand toward them.

"Tell them: come and dance."

I obey. And when I do, a levee breaks. It was a matter of beginning, of crossing the threshold. I'm breathing hard from nervousness, agitation, from damned and wretched pleasure: their desire drives me crazy. Look, I think to myself, I'm trembling.

"Come and dance," I repeat in a muted little voice. I'm looking at them without daring to take my arms from over my breasts. "Come."

They surround me, they embrace me, men's skin on my back. The four of us dance slowly and the anticipation of I don't know what suffocates me. Am I still myself?

"Show yourself," Flaco tells me with a hard exhale. "Let them see you. It's what I want, for them to see you."

It's what I want, too, though I didn't know it before. It's exactly what I want. Then I get on the sofa and stand up and my breasts fulminate them. I see it in their faltering eyes, in their suddenly dry lips that their tongues cannot moisten. Flaco undoes my belt with his mouth. I help him. My skirt falls to the floor.

"Make them happy, girl," he tells me. "Yes, make them happy. Now," he orders me with an excitement rooted in pain.

I'm staring into Jerónimo's eyes. And he looks back but then lowers his gaze to my breasts and returns to my eyes. I have him, I feel it. They're going to be dreaming of me. I get down from the sofa and go over to Rabbit, his rabbit teeth behind a trembling smile. I brush his chest with my nipples, I kneel down, open his belt, and slowly, very slowly I lower his zipper. His pants come off. I look at Flaco, at Jerónimo, his feverish eyes, his half-open mouth. "I have them," I think to myself. Rabbit, in only his black underpants, is at a precise distance from me. I put out my tongue, stretch it out, I feel it vibrate in the air like a viper's. Flaco's gaze rests on me. My pointed tongue is getting closer. I know what I want. My tongue gets longer still. I look at Flaco and at Jerónimo. I've got these fuckers now! And my tongue reaches its mark. One touch only, one touch, and it retreats.

And then, obeying Flaco, who orders me in a whisper that is gentle but also urgent and controlled, I lie down, languid, on the black velvet sofa, and I hear Flaco's whisper and those two unknown men come closer, obeying Flaco, those two strangers with young, firm bodies, Rabbit and Jerónimo, they take turns and trade places. And he gives me orders and I submit; "Yes, let him do it," Flaco murmurs, "yes, go on," and they say yes silently and I want to obey him and please him and them, to please them all until there's nothing left of me, just a stain, and I submit with a frenzied heart, with fear and desire, and something breaks inside me and I cross an invisible barrier and I do it and I welcome them and embrace them, I'm made of water and I see Flaco's eyes and I see his tongue on his lips. But I'm always with those firm bodies and I feel them everywhere, and my body is never alone and I wish I had more mouths and arms and legs because I don't want to miss anything of either of them and I go from one to the other and we try to come together and it's difficult and Flaco can't stand it anymore and joins the group and in the end it's wonderful.

Kissing a stranger is a quick and abrupt pleasure, absolute. I had never done it before. I never thought I would, not until Flaco ordered me to, and I overcame myself and vanquished myself and I found myself doing it, and I swear, I liked it.

I spent that night with them, and I writhed and bristled with the pleasure of passing from one man's smell and skin texture to another's, with Flaco's intense gaze always upon us, and to feel that if one of them was worn out then the other was waiting for me, ardent and tenacious and full, it drove me crazy. I liked to see, in that darkness overflowing with the insidious rhythm of the bass, bodies connected like the arms of a starfish or intertwined like giant flowers with many petals. And you know what else? It set me on fire inside to think that they were our enemies, the very same gangsters who had defeated us and captured and debased us, the same killers who tomorrow or the next day could be crouched on a roof shooting to kill us.

TWENTY-EIGHT

I saw combatants go to pieces. Not from the torture itself but because they weren't able to withstand it. Not because they were afraid of being arrested and tied up again, that the whole ordeal would start over, but because they'd collaborated. All of this pursued me, eating away at my conscience; it stayed with me like a persistent bad odor. For weeks and months and years I felt disgusted at myself. I still do. I'm contradicting myself. I'll never be able to understand myself. Or forget. No. Never. But I don't want to remember. Nor do I want to forget.

I know there were many others like me. We only know about some of them; we know because they've bravely confessed in writing. They repented and collaborated with the authorities. Good for them. I'm not judging. I speak only for myself. What I want to make very clear to you is that I didn't inform under duress and only after screams of pain, no. That's normal, anyone would understand that. Lorena, though, she's on a mission to annihilate. So that when this is all over and she comes out of it alive, there will be no one left to hold her accountable. I collaborated with the repression and I swear, I kept them buzzing. Collaborating means, for example, going out "fishing." We would arrive at the specified time to that plaza, or station, the window of that shop, that diner, the usual church, and I would point out the brothers coming into the "meet zone" or the ones who were already there, handing off a package or a single cigarette with a coded message written on its paper, passed surreptitiously from one pair of hands to another, allowing them to be photographed or followed, or else the gorillas fell on top of them and overpowered them right there.

That moment had a terrifying tension. The combatants of Red Ax were courageous and well trained; they were professionals. Sometimes there were shootouts, in which it was difficult to follow what was happening. I would tremble with emotion. I wanted to see one of their faces right at the moment of surrender. Later on it wasn't the same: pale and blindfolded, dirty, handcuffed and limping, half dead, their faces broken. I remember one night in particular, the long wait in front of a safe house. Some shots rang out and my soul froze. Suddenly, I saw them dragging someone out in handcuffs. My heart started pounding like it wanted to rip itself from my body. They brought him to me in handcuffs, with Mono Lepe and Indio Ramírez holding him up. They pressed his face to the truck window. He was panting, his jacket was torn, and blood flowed from his upper lip. His eyes, his terrible, wide, and imploring eyes searched for mine behind my mask. His jaw was trembling. I told Rat in a whisper: Pelao Cuyano. That night and all the next day, in Central, I heard his screams. Later I found out he'd died on them.

Did I feel real regret for Cuyano? And if I didn't, why not? Did it affect me, and I just managed to bottle up my emotions? Maybe. Shit! *This existence is immoral . . . And this life depends on immoral preconditions: and all morality denies life.* I was a ruthless agent. I know that. I had a ferocious rage. No one will ever know how many people I fucked over. I was the ultimate traitor, the whore queen sucking those scumbags off . . .

Because the interrogation would come and yes, I did know what that was, and they still didn't. "We got a package," they'd say, we'd say. I would go in wearing a mask. I sat next to Gato, who from behind his metallic desk observed every movement, every sign of vacillation with his lifeless green eyes. Sometimes there would be breadcrumbs or drops of the Pepsi he'd had delivered left on his mouth. He wore a mask, too. "Sometimes their blindfolds slip," he told me, and he put on his rubber gloves. No one would recognize his little hands and their dainty fingers. *Disciplinary power is exercised in its invisibility.* He used plugs in his ears to muffle the screams and keep his calm.

"I'm a professional," he says to me with the insidious little voice he's cultivated, "and I have to keep myself lucid and serene. A person in this job develops a certain ability to numb his senses. Well, it's the same for doctors . . . It's not easy, Cubanita, to control those moral emotions or to keep them in check so the investigation can go forward. Or to hold back the instinct to attack the man once he's been broken. It's discipline. A man who loses control is only fattening himself to be slaughtered like a butchered animal. It happens. Many men have had to be relieved of duty. They weren't useful anymore as investigators. You know, before they created Central, things happened that were so horrible a person defames himself just by talking about them, he blasphemes—what can I call it—the bare minimum of humanity that we all share. Anyway, that's how I feel, but I wasn't ever there, I wasn't around during that time. You know I've only been in Central, I've never killed anyone, I've only worked in Analysis."

The detainee would be on his back, tied up and stark naked with his eyes blindfolded. *In discipline, it is the subjects who have to be seen.* They still wanted to be brave. I liked it that way. That was the joy of it, to break them. That *glissement*. Gato and I worked very well together. It was a roller coaster of terror and seduction, a game in which anything was permitted, except the unnecessary. Supposedly, "la Cubanita" had met these comrades in Punto Cero, and she had worked in Cuban intelligence. I don't know how many people believed it. In any case my name, as I've told you, was Consuelo Frías Zaldívar, native of Matanzas. My "false history," my "F.H.," as they called it in Central; my "mantle," my "legend," in Red Ax.

I was there. Yes. I was part of the horror. I lived in the heart of evil. I traveled through the belly of the Beast.

You know what it is that breaks a man, a woman, the toughest ones? It's not pain or fear. Though all of that helps, of course. What will finally break a person in the end, though, is the knowledge that the interrogator possesses information that concerns him and he doesn't know what it is. Above all, he breaks when the interrogator catches him in a lie. After that nothing will be the same. There's a before and an after to that moment.

"I like the tough ones," Gato tells me, "I like the challenge, how you can ride it out to the climax, to the breaking point, and get all the information out of them. It's better than the whining of the soft, apologetic ones." There are things that have become blurry for me. It's better that way. There are things, feelings, that I wouldn't know how to describe without adulterating them. Let me tell you, there's a powerful and mysterious bond that forms with the interrogator. There's a purpose to that pain that gradually passes from the body to the soul, and you perceive it and anticipate the surrender. "You have to grab hold of those two or three seconds of weakness as they pass, because they might not return for hours," Gato told me. Sometimes it happens as a moment of intense, though brief, spiritual communion. Finally, he gives you the intelligence that you need right now: the next "meet," the time and place, names, the cell, its leader, the latest mission. And you give him the peace his body craves.

TWENTY-NINE

I remember a man with hairless skin and small, black eyes. His teeth were even and square, he had short, strong arms, and legs that were also short and muscular. He was like a little tank. "Lechón," they called him, "Piglet." His hair was sparse. You could see the skin of his head between the thick, separate strands. I remember that hair well, and his arms, so thick and so short, and the enormous Adam's apple in his throat. Supposedly, he had headed a combat cell that blew up a bridge over the Tinguiririca River. But I knew little about him, and my questions didn't get anywhere. The guy would hardly answer anything. His Asiatic eyes would narrow and he'd go into a kind of trance; and when the jolts of electricity came he would scream loudly and regularly like he was following a rhythm, and he gave off that repellent smell of shit that gets stuck in your nostrils. Afterward, he would take a breath, filling himself slowly with air from the pit of his stomach upward, and he closed his mouth and his jaw fastened shut. They showed him photos of Rafa, the Spartan, Max. There was no way to get him to talk.

Why is it so hard for me to imagine him today? Didn't I recognize myself in that determined man's body lying there, abused and contorting, his skin suddenly pale, his brow wrinkled, eyebrows distorted, his hair on end, eyes spinning wildly and unable to focus on anything, his cries muffled by a rag? Who was I looking at, if not myself? Who did I hate, then, and vilify?

I'm telling you, at a certain point the person lying there starts to seem like he's no longer a man. His moans are irritating and they enrage you, and the desire to punish him more grows stronger. *I found I could extinguish all human hope from my soul. I made the wild beast's silent leap to strangle every joy.* We must break through his legend, we must make him bear fruit, it's a question of pride now, there's no going back and he has to surrender, he must vomit out the truth, his resistance insults me, it is spit in my face; then I approach him, I get very close and I spit on him, I spit on him because I hate him and I must get revenge for his insult.

That he still dares to maintain his legend forces us to keep going, he's an imbecile who leaves us no choice. I tell him precisely this in my Cuban accent, and still he sits there like someone listening to the rain; we've got to give him more. He's so disfigured he looks like an obscene monster, a revolting being whose revolting nature offends me. Why should I put up with that smell of acid sweat? It makes me nauseous. We have to give him more, give him more until he breaks, we can't let him beat us, he smells, he goes on stinking; it's the repugnant smell of fear, I'm sure you've never smelled that stench, it's like no other in the world. I'm indignant. Why does he subject us to this repugnance? Of course he is doing it on purpose, he's provoking us, seeking out our hate, he doesn't want to give his arm to be twisted though he's nothing but a human rag, a rag that humiliates me with its resistance, and goes on shuddering and flopping like a fish out of water that never reaches the end of its death throes. If he dies, it doesn't matter—fuck him!—but it does matter, the fucker would take it all with him, he's no good to us dead, he has to be broken first. Gato's calm voice stops me.

I went on feeling a strange vibration. Ronco brought in Rat Osorio to give him a beating, but nothing. Ronco took out his knife, trembling with rage, and he stuck the blade in between the man's teeth. Ronco's tightened face, his fury turning his face and neck red, his mouth half-open and panting, the shine of saliva on his gold tooth. But he could do nothing, and he had to put away his knife when Gato, in his calm, nasal voice, warned him to be careful not to cut the man's tongue. Something happened to me with "Lechón" when

I saw the blade shining between his teeth. There was a terrible determination in that closed jaw as it bit down on the knife blade.

Then they tied him up and he was left there hanging like a chicken. The *pau de arara*, learned in La Rinconada in Maipú from some Uruguayan instructors who had fought against the Tupamaros, Gato explained to me with a medical coldness. They learned it from the Brazilians, who had learned it, according to Gato, from the French paratroopers who fought in Algeria. That's where all the techniques they used in Vietnam came from, he told me. And he gave me names of French military men—Colonel Roger Trinquier, General Paul Aussaresses—who had taught in the Special Forces schools in Fort Bragg and Fort Benning. One of them had been in Brazil. Gato had spent some time taking a class at Fort Benning, and more time in Panama, where the instructors were gringos who taught them to kill and eat monkeys in the jungle. Flaco Artaza was there, too. And Macha? He tells me: "No, not Macha. Purely a South American product, that one." And he laughs under his breath.

When they called me in, "Lechón" had his eyes half shut, and his jaw fastened in silence.

Some hours later the guard let me into his cell. The door opened and I smelled that prisoner stench that suffuses the walls of the cells. He looked like he was sleeping. I tiptoed over to him and I lay down beside him on the mattress on the concrete bed. He must have been very thirsty, and it was only now time to give him water. He thanked me with a slight movement. I massaged his arms, his legs, his back. The guy just let me do it and we didn't say a word. I felt his tight skin and firm muscles. I liked that feeling of a compact, dense body. It was nice to touch him. I imagined the meat under the skin and I thought it must be delicious to eat. In other times, when we were cannibals, I would have devoured that meat by the mouthful. I noticed a flicker of light in his eyes: he was looking at me. All at once I took off my shirt and freed my breasts from my bra. I was squatting down beside him and there was a glitter in his eyes and I heard him swallow. Not moving.

"You're a brave one," I told him.

The words slipped out of me. The flicker of a smile went over his lips and vanished without ever taking shape. I caught a glimpse of his square teeth. He didn't touch me, and I had an urgent need to feel the contact of his skin. I brushed against his face with a nipple. He didn't move. With one hand I squeezed his shoulder, round and hard. I kissed an impassive mouth and, despairing, I grabbed at his pants. And I knelt down and took hold of his buttocks and pulled him toward me. His heart was pounding. I had my eyes closed. "Your sense of touch is delicate as a blind person's," he told me softly.

"Hit me," I begged him. "Kick me." And I curled up on the floor and waited. And he did nothing to me. "Spit on me, please, piss on my face." And he did nothing to me. Now he was breathing slowly and rhythmically, and neither my fingers nor my lips or tongue could break through his willful indifference. Then I cried and I lay down on my back and opened myself. "Fuck me," I told him. "You're scared," I told him. He sat down calmly on the floor. "You're afraid you'll like it and your revolutionary zeal will all go to shit," I told him. "Look at me at least, you faggot." I was putting on my pants, I was tying my shoes. "You're scared to be a man and you hide behind the 'solidarity' of your gang." I kicked him in the mouth. It bled a little, but he didn't move or say anything. I kicked him again and I left. Who was that man and what had he done? Did he finally break? What ever became of him?

THIRTY

I spend hours alone in the apartment, in my room in the dark with the door closed. I don't want to see anyone. I throw myself onto the bed. I don't even take my shoes off. I don't know what I'm thinking about, if I'm thinking about anything. Sometimes I wake up at dawn with my guts twisted in anguish, and I realize I never even put my pajamas on. I didn't feel like it and I just stayed there, still dressed and stretched out on the bed. Cold. Morning comes and it's so hard for me to get up.

I'm writhing. The earth opens up beneath my feet. I sink into the same bottomless swamp as always. This thing is stronger than I am. The handcuffs return, squeezing my wrists, the slave of memory returns. The mental torment takes my breath away. If only I knew how to howl like a wolf. If I just had more air. My stomach wrenches.

If I could only rest. I'm not complaining about the world. *I'm* the one who doesn't belong here. I'm not interested in the question of the meaning of life. It's obvious that life has meaning. How could it not? This isn't just about a theory. I do not want to go on living. Period.

Keep in mind that Dante puts traitors in the last circle of the *Inferno*. Their tears freeze like a visor over their eyes and it keeps them from crying, and their anguish grows and accumulates without end. Their souls go to Hell even when their bodies are still alive in the world. A demon guards them on earth for as long as they live. But for them, hell begins not the day they die but the day they commit their betrayal.

THIRTY-ONE

I would lose it suddenly, I would seek it out and yearn for it, for his gaze close by me, covering me, and later I would find it again, contemplating me. Because what attracted me were those masculine backs and arms and legs and chins, and of course the mocking and tender smiles of some and the staring, intense eyes of others, but I enjoyed them most of all if I felt Flaco's great, shining eyes on me. His peremptory orders in that cavernous voice, the release, the sweetness of fulfilling them, humiliating myself; and his forehead in concentration, his dilated pupils, and the trembling of his lips, it all made me throb. I didn't know who the others were, nor would I ever know.

One of them told me, "My name is Phoebus," just like that, like Apollo, and he was what you call an *homme beau*. He put his arms around me and pressed me against him and I felt it against my belly, against my thigh. After that night I found myself with him a few more times. An *homme beau*. There were thugs in that place, as you know, men and women of the repression who frequented the club, despicable and disgraceful—monsters, if you like. They hid themselves among slender whores and rent boys and gorgeous transvestites that you'd only recognize as transvestites, if you even did, by their muscular backs, and stupendous fags and horrible fags and maybe one or another prisoner who would return under the salt sky of dawn to the underground cell that I knew well, and pimps and young men with piercing eyes and old men who weren't so old, well-heeled, gray-haired aficionados of these games, and simple mafiosos who put on airs and felt at ease here. Once I thought I recognized two actors I'd seen not long before in a play by Heiner Müller. I'm not sure.

There, inside that mansion cum club and hotel, sliding in the restless dark with those sharp guitar rhythms and provocative drums, we melted into a single high-voltage sea, and the hate coincided with attraction and the rage dovetailed with compassion and the fear with laugher and the violence with tenderness and the desertion with intimacy. Nothing is true, believe me, nothing of what they teach us is true.

In the bathrooms you could always find some upper or a line of white powder. In one of the bathrooms, there was always someone naked in the sunken bathtub, and bodies would go up to it with their kidneys full of beer, and they would unzip, draw, swords would cross for a moment, and they would empty themselves in a fountain spray. I liked to see that those repugnant things, it made me laugh to see those manly men clashing their swords and then forming, euphoric, a proud yellow arc of triumph. And someone received that golden water as a blessing. You wanted details, didn't you? There's a baptism for you.

THIRTY-TWO

I watch Macha in the cafeteria. Gato never sets foot in here. I watch Macha at his table eating his *charquicán* beef stew or his beans with noodles with a bottle of Cristal beer. His agents surround him, the women and men of his horde. I remember the scene exactly. Great Dane is there. I've already mentioned him to you: he was at Oliver with the girl with Siamese cat eyes, he's the one who kicked in the door of the safe house I gave them. He's a handsome and simple blond, with a huge body and a big head and long, well-tended hair. Sometimes I see him in a karate *gi*. Great Dane is a black belt and he smashes bricks obsessively on the patio with the calloused edges of his giant hands. There's Iris Molina, skinny and gaunt, with a mysterious voice and an oily, astute gaze. She's the one who went first into the safe house. She's an expert in pistol shooting and she hopes to make the Olympic team. (She never will.) There's Mono Lepe, with his rebellious hair, dark circles under his eyes, his flat nose crooked from some ugly punch, his narrow little shoulders. There's Chico Marín, his lips always livid, his eyes always darting, abrupt and nervous like a lizard, his head shaved. He's wide and thick like a cube. There's Pancha Ortiz, whose anxious eyes follow Macha constantly; she has haughty, high breasts and is the mother, she confessed to me once, of a pair of fraternal twins. She was the one who talked to me about the beauty of guns. There's Indio Galdámez, in a gray sweatshirt with dark spots of old perspiration. Indio is attractive, proud, and reticent. His hair is greasy and he has a green boa tattooed on his left forearm. And then there are the other men, coarse and forgettable, and women who are rougher and more common, with indiscreetly dyed blond hair and whose names I never learned. Am I exaggerating? From this home in Ersta, Stockholm, do I see things in black and white? Obviously, none of them had the words "I am a monster" written on their faces. Mono Lepe hovers at the bedside when his little Carmen has a fever. He makes her hot lemonade and won't go to bed until the fever breaks and the girl falls asleep. He takes her to day care every day in the Nissan 4×4 that Central gives him to use. I know all this from Gato.

But they're surrounded by an imaginary circle of silence, enigma, and risk. They share in the true mysteries of Central. Every one of them is a trunk full of secrets in the shape of a body. A *brotherhood of blood.* The others in the cafeteria treat them carefully, look at them with admiration: they've been chosen for this. They are the workers of death. And death inspires respect, even here. Macha has told Flaco: "In my team, a person who has killed no one *is* no one. Around here, Flaco, it's a corpse that baptizes you."

But Macha hardly speaks. He's shy, he's stony. But, you know, the others talk to him. His difference. His distance. His contained sadness. Once in a great while, the surprise of a smile under his bushy moustache. Then the row of large, even teeth. His conspicuous cheekbones, his cleft chin, the sharp lines of his face, and his dangerous eyes, his eyelashes long like a foal's: all this intrigues me. I'd like to sit at his table, look at him from close up, smell him. And at the same time there is this, my hate: he killed Canelo. The gang he commands loves him with a doglike loyalty. Is it jealousy, damned jealousy, this bitterness I feel when I see the way Pancha looks at him? And what of it?

THIRTY-THREE

One Friday, I don't know why but I remember it was a Friday, Flaco took me out to lunch. He brought me to the Giratorio, the rotating restaurant on the top floor of a building on Avenida Lyon. From up there you could see a good portion of Santiago. San Cristó-bal Hill was in front of us as we started lunch and we turned, we turned without noticing it while we ate an exquisite sole and drank a Santa Rita white wine. I felt happy up there. Everything was left behind, down below. The snow-covered mountains paraded in front of us and Flaco showed me the Plomo, the Provincia, the Punta de Damas, the San Ramón, mountain names I'd never heard and that seemed to me mysterious, poetic, evocative. He described the way to climb up the sheer cliff of El Altar—anchors, ice ax—or the La Paloma glacier, the hanging glacier of San Francisco wedged into the Morales canyon. Two days it had taken them to go up, bivouacking only once. They'd slept hanging from the rock. During the night a sudden jerking and a collision woke Flaco up. A bolt had come loose, and he was left hanging by only the other one.

"You never feel as free as in the mountains," he told me, and it seemed incredibly profound and true to me. Then he asked if I would dare go climbing with him up a peak that wasn't very diffi-cult. I loved the idea. "The air," he said, "what I like most is to feel on my face that cold air, biting and pure, which at that height has touched nothing but the ice." At that moment, the only thing I wanted was to feel the freedom of that cold air, biting and pure; I wanted to leave with Flaco right away and go there. When the check came we were in front of San Cristóbal Hill again. I leaned over the table and kissed him. Flaco gave me another kiss as we got into his silver Volvo, then he got onto the Costanera highway. We drove fast.

I was picturing myself standing in the wind of a glacier. Then I thought of the house in Malloco. I saw myself in my mind's eye disfigured in the little mirror, anxiously inhaling what was left of a line he'd shaped with his MasterCard Gold, the same one that just paid for lunch, and I felt my body swept up by the loud guitars and the powerful, tireless motor of the electric bass. I told him we should go that very night. He smiled. We shared that powerful secret. The complicity was exquisite. I believe in that: the attraction you feel when you share a dangerous secret. Don't you? I always loved that exclusion that separates those who are in on the secret from those who aren't. It's the drug of co-conspirators, and without it there wouldn't be secret societies or networks in clandestine life, or loyalties among secret agents like the one who was beside me in the driver's seat then. He turned suddenly and parked in front of the Tajamar Towers. "Where are we going?" I asked.

"You'll see, my dear," he smiled mischievously.

We went into an eleventh-floor apartment, with big windows looking out over the river and San Cristóbal Hill. It had a light beige carpet, almost white, wall-to-wall. A bedroom and a living-dining room. The walls were white. There wasn't a stick of furniture. "Do you like it?" he asked me. Everything was luminous. "Would you like to live here?" And in a voice that was too serious to be serious: "For security purposes, the time has come for you to change your residence, don't you think?"

In that moment I loved him with a furious, urgent passion. That silent, empty apartment, those windows high over the San Cristóbal Hill, I don't know, I was flooded by an acute sense of helplessness just at the moment when Flaco was protecting me. I pulled off my clothes and we made love frantically, standing up, and then again on that recently carpeted floor. I'm seeing him lying there on his back with me astride him, his clear eyes and his bald, youthful head, the dark hair on his chest, the almost white beige of the rug. Me? Could this be happening to me?

To rest my head on his chest brings me a perfect peace. The cedar scent of Flaco's soap brings me back to my father's workshop. He's a big man, Flaco. The muscles of his chest are my pillow. I'm protected there, almost merging into him. I press closer. I'm happy like that.

When he left, I was still naked. I kissed his bald head. I always did that when I said good-bye to him. He left a ring of keys in my hand and a folded paper between my breasts. When I straightened up it slid to the floor: it was a fat check. Enough to pay my move from the little apartment with thin walls I rented on Carlos Antúnez and to furnish the new one. I installed a little safe in the closet, built into the wall. I hid my documents and the CZ in there when Anita or my mother or the cleaning lady came.

And it was that apartment where he would drop in without warning, where I waited for him always just in case, in case he could get away from his wife, from his two small daughters whom he adored, I knew, and we could lose ourselves for the night in the disco music and among the rooms of the house in Malloco. I'd been holding back for such a long time. One of those nights, I let myself be carried away by the voluptuousness of the forbidden. I shouldn't have. But the secret was burning my lips. I shouldn't have. But I loved Flaco, I wanted to keep him with me, I wanted his complete intimacy; I longed for that communion, to open the door for him to a secret he didn't know. It was vertiginous. So I told him something I shouldn't have.

I told him tremblingly that the "Prince of Wales" smoked Havana cigars. He looked at me with widened eyes, surprised. "I want to punish," I told him, "the irresponsible people who've gotten us into this imaginary fight that has very real deaths." I said it firmly, and I believed it; I needed to believe it, just as Rodrigo, when he left me, had needed to convince me that I was the one to blame. The Spartan shouldn't have smoked. It was forbidden. And yet, he did. The perfect combatant had that one defect, that trace of rebellion against an absolute and unequivocal order of the organization. He let the ashes fall onto a saucer using the utmost caution, and then he flushed them down the toilet. I knew it was a valuable clue. Some of the ashes must fly off and be left behind.

That detail would be important for Flaco, for his career. And of course, the information was duly processed. From then on, as soon as a safe house came up, they headed over there with magnifying lenses to look for cigar ash. The Spartan ("Prince of Wales," to Central) would fall because of that, he would fall because of me.

THIRTY-FOUR

Gato wanted "Gladiolo" and he wanted him alive. That's it. In Flaco's flow chart, "Gladiolo" appeared now as the leader of one of the cells under "Prince of Wales." Where had that information come from? They had watched the house on Calle Los Gladiolos, but the man never turned up there. The tone of that terrible order was peremptory. I understood very well. What could I do? Those were the rules of the game. I asked for time. How much? They gave me a month. There were three weeks until Teruca's birthday, and I'd heard she was going to celebrate at her mother's house in Ñuñoa, a few blocks from Irarrázaval. Through Teruca, maybe I could get close to poor Rafa.

I dropped in that day with a tray of Chilean pastries that I knew she loved and a light blue blouse that would look good on her. Her mother let me in very solicitously, but said she wasn't sure if her daughter was coming. At around 6:30, Teruca arrived. "You've let your braid grow again," I said. "I love it like that." She was surprised to see me. I'd even say she hugged me with a trace of distrust. Her mother came in with a *mil hojas* cake, and after singing, blowing out the candles, and eating our slices, the two of us went out onto the terrace. Then she loosened up. She told me, enraptured, that she was engaged to Rafa now. Her mother knew. Not Francisco, no, it wasn't worth telling him. Because, how do you explain something like that to your son in a letter? Francisco was still living in a group home in Cuba. In spite of her efforts, Teruca couldn't keep in regular contact with him. Of course it didn't make any sense to tell him. So why was she telling me she just didn't know how to break the news to him? I knew Teruca bore that pain every day: having abandoned her son to avoid putting him in danger, so she could have more freedom and fight without being tied down. And I knew, too, that the few times they had met, in Mexico City, it hadn't turned out well: "I try to understand you, Mom, I try because I love you and that's exactly why I can't understand. Why can't you stay here with me?" That's what Francisco said to her.

That's where we were when Rafa came in carrying a gift. He let out a great bellow of laughter when he saw me, and he hugged me with the frank affection of earlier days. "What's up, sweetie?" he said. He kissed Teruca effusively on the mouth and he sat down next to her on the sofa, holding her thick black braid in one hand. "This way I can control who she looks at," he laughed. "I guess you already know, right? This little gossip must have told you, I'm sure." The three of us hugged.

I offered to go buy a bottle of champagne, and in the end all of us went to the liquor store. I insisted on paying. Back at the house, when the champagne had run out and we had started in on pisco and Coke, I steered the conversation to mention that I was finding more and more frequent red chalk marks on the edge of the sidewalk on the corner. I was lying. "So you're being reincorporated," said Teruca.

"It's about time," Rafa stated roundly, his tongue loosened from the pisco. And he added with no prompting from me: "Two red lines, parallel?"

"Exactly," I said.

"Unmistakable." He gulped down a big swallow and laughed: "My cell, on the other hand, uses gum." He laughed again, a laugh that was strange in him. He threw back another swallow. It's fear, I thought to myself, fear. "They leave a piece of gum on the leg of a bench in Plaza Manuel Rodríguez. The Spartan's idea, I'm sure," he laughed, looking at me with glassy eyes. Teruca furrowed her brow and stayed quiet. Then she told me that Cuyano had fallen, that since Canelo's death Rafa had been in charge of his cell, the one that used to be mine, too, and that this had left her shocked and very sad; frightened, too. I covered my face with my hands.

"I worry about serial arrests like that," she said to me. Teruca had been disconnected as a precaution. A thick silence fell over us.

"An angel went by," joked Rafael.

The doorbell rang and a tall, thin, very blond man came in wearing jeans and cowboy boots. "The Gringo!" exclaimed Rafa. He and Teruca got up to welcome him. He handed Teruca her gift and hugged me. "It's been so many moons!" he told me. "So long since Nahuelbuta! Right? . . . you haven't changed a bit." We toasted. He and Rafa seemed to be good friends. I liked the way his gray eyes turned toward me, left, and came back. He clinked his glass against mine and laughed for no reason, with something of the child who laughs from pure joy. Then he started talking to Rafa. Teruca asked me about my French classes, the latest art openings. The bottle of pisco went quickly, and Teruca and I went to get another from the pantry.

"Handsome, isn't he?" she said as soon as we were alone.

"Mm," I said.

"Mm," she replied, smiling. "He remembered you from Nahuel-buta, at the camp . . ."

"Mm."

When I was ready to go, the Gringo looked at his watch and exclaimed in surprise over how late it was. We left together, walking toward Irarrázaval. I don't remember what we talked about. When we got to the bus stop I felt his gaze holding mine again. "I want to see you again," he told me. "Give me that chance. The last time we saw each other was years ago and there was a fire between us . . ." My mouth filled with laughter and I trembled a little. My bus pulled up and from the landing I said: "All right, let's talk soon." I gave him a wave and the bus pulled away.

THIRTY-FIVE

Plaza Manuel Rodríguez was empty and all the shops had closed. It was eleven thirty at night. Plenty afraid, I circled around checking the plaza's benches, in search of a piece of gum. I kept thinking I heard Rafa's steps behind me, and the sweat was rolling down my back. When I had only two left to check, on the bench under a big, bluish cedar tree I saw a little white-tinged spot on the green-painted iron leg. I didn't touch it.

Plaza Manuel Rodríguez is small and secluded. It's bordered by four streets: Calle Plaza Manuel Rodríguez to the north, Grajales to the south, Almirante Latorre to the east, and Abdón Cifuentes to the west. And I have to mention a fifth, Teresa Clark, a short alleyway that runs north to south between Almirante Latorre and Abdón Cifuentes and ends at the plaza. Before dawn, twelve men and six vehicles distributed themselves on those streets, blocking off the plaza. Only the old Peugeot taxi parked on Teresa Clark had a direct view of the benches. We were in that taxi: Indio driving, Iris as copilot, and me, wearing a mask. The day passed in vain. "Gladiolo" didn't show. Macha ordered sandwiches and drinks, but he didn't change the stakeout team.

At a quarter past one in the morning, the silence was broken by the motor of a car stopping, the slam of a door, and then footsteps coming closer. I ducked down in the back seat as Indio and Iris embraced like lovers. The man was walking on Calle Grajales. On the southeast corner of the plaza, he stopped and observed the solitude of the place and the calm of the adjacent streets. From that corner, close to the palm tree, he had the best view of the scene. But because of the curve of the street that bordered the plaza, the Dai-hatsu on Abdón Cifuentes was out of his visual field. The same was true of a Toyota parked south of the plaza on Almirante Latorre. None of them could see him, either. As I said: only we, in the old Peugeot taxi in the alleyway Teresa Clark, were in a position to observe the "illicit activity" that the man in the plaza was about to initiate. Did he notice our Peugeot?

Iris said to me: "If that's really him, he's having trouble making up his mind." And a second later: "OK, he's walking through the plaza, make sure it's him." I sat up just enough to see, and I recognized him. I didn't need binoculars. That way of walking, of leaning back and dragging his feet a little, was Rafa's and no one else's. He walked along the gravel walkway toward the cedar tree, which must have been no more than fifty yards from us. He sat down on the bench with the gum, looked at the stars for a while, turned to scan the plaza, and then languidly let a hand fall, feeling his way along the iron leg. From that position he could have noticed our Peugeot. He would have had to turn his head to his left. He didn't. He looked at the stars again, pensive; he got up slowly and headed back at a relaxed pace toward the southeast corner.

Iris communicated over the radio that the Subject was headed toward his car parked on Calle Grajales. A motor started up, and a white Chevy moved at a normal speed eastward along Grajales, along the south edge of the plaza. The Toyota on Almirante Latorre started up, turned right on Grajales, eastward, and casually began to tail the Chevy. At night, the small amount of traffic made it difficult to tail without being noticed. The Toyota, which Pancha was driving with Great Dane beside her, let Rafa get ahead. Great Dane communicated that the Toyota had the Subject under control. Was that when Rafa noticed the headlights of the Toyota behind him and the Nissan parked to the right, close to the corner of Almirante Latorre? Who knows. Rafa's Chevy continued eastward on Calle Grajales, and three blocks past Almirante Latorre, when he reached Ejército, he turned suddenly and sped southward. Great Dane reported that they had lost the control, and they kept going straight to avoid raising suspicion. Mono Lepe's Nissan, which was farther back on Grajales, took Ejército southward and became the control car. Rafa's Chevy sped some five blocks farther, crossed Blanco Encalada, and turned, wheels skidding, onto Tupper. He went straight along O'Higgins Park, crossed the highway, and catapulted onto Avenida Matta, heading east. Mono Lepe informed us of these movements and assured us that the Subject remained under control, that his Nissan was keeping up though the Subject was performing countersurveillance maneuvers. Then Macha gave the order for the blue Daihatsu to take the lead as the control car. But Rafa had already turned right again onto San Ignacio, and then he wrenched the car eastward to double back on Rondizzoni, where it dovetailed with the highway going southward, and he floored it. The Daihatsu was left behind, and it lost the control. Macha gave the order to disperse. Rafa had detected the tail. Nothing could be done . . .

A couple days later I went back alone to Plaza Manuel Rodríguez. It was cold and the night was very dark. I took a couple of turns around the adjacent streets to be sure that there were no suspicious people or vehicles. My steps echoed on the pavement. I started at the sound of my own footsteps. Just as Rafa had, I arrived on Grajales and stopped on the southwest corner of the plaza, next to the palm tree; I made sure the place was empty and then I set off down the gravel path toward the bench under the bluish cedar tree. I could smell the dampness of the grass. The sound of leaves in a thicket startled me, and I stood there paralyzed. I touched my gun. A pigeon darted out and flew away. Once I was under the roof of the enormous cedar, I sat down on the bench just as I had seen Rafa do. I looked at the dark sky, across which even darker clouds were gliding. The plaza was intimate, secret. I reached my hand down until I touched the leg of the bench, and I made sure to affix the paper firmly with the gum.

THIRTY-SIX

He called me right on time at my student's house, interrupting my class as I'd wanted. I arranged to meet him without giving any explanations. My tone, firm and decisive, was enough. Address, day, time. Nothing else. I don't know why I was so sure he would listen to me, in spite of the irregular way I went about it. The "meet point," the shadowy Plaza Concha y Toro in the old part of downtown Santiago, had escape routes on three narrow streets: Erasmo de Escala, Maturana, and Concha y Toro. That, I thought, would give him confidence. At one thirty on the dot I heard his footsteps on the cobblestones, breaking the silence of the night. And then he was there. He'd entered from the south on Concha y Toro. His way of walking was the same as always: hesitant and slightly tilted backward. His open parka couldn't hide his belly. His right hand in his pocket made me think he had a small weapon. He was suspicious.

He made no sign when he saw me. Close to the fountain, as soon as he could check the little street that ends at Maturana, he stopped. Rafa looked and listened carefully. I didn't move. I watched his legs. I didn't dare look at his face. Then he rounded the fountain and came closer to me with short, measured steps. When he was very close I reached out my arms to hug him, but he didn't take his right hand from his pocket. I kissed a cold cheek. Right then, I wavered. I was afraid to do it. I felt a wrenching in my guts. Could I still save him? Yes, I thought, it's still possible. And in that fleeting moment I wanted to, I swear I wanted to. "They're following me," I told him anxiously.

He looked at me with an attentive, cold intensity. I was desperate,

I withdrew into myself. "Inform the Spartan that they're following me," I told him, dazed. "He won't answer my messages. I need help." He looked at me, disconcerted and annoyed. "I'm sorry," I told him. "I didn't know who else to turn to."

"Why don't you get in touch with your contact?" he reproached me. "Why don't you follow procedure?"

Something, a flash, passed over his tense eyes. I wavered then, just barely, but I wavered. I couldn't stand the situation one second more. I still wanted to save him, still . . . I looked over his shoulder. "They're coming!" I told him. "Run, run!" And without waiting for his reaction I took off running desperately toward Maturana. He ran northward to Erasmo de Escala.

I swear, of all that I did, that was the worst.

I fell to the ground. I was running, I heard footsteps and gunfire, a Browning, I thought, and I fell, and then I heard more gunfire. Rafa? Then I heard the first CZ. Now there was machine-gun fire. The narrow streets made the noise echo. I didn't feel any pain, but when I brought my hand to my calf I felt something warm. I brought my fingers to my mouth: blood. Shouts, but far off. Now there was Macha's grave voice. He was telling me no, don't move. The light from a flashlight, a penknife or pocket knife, something cutting my pant leg. "It's not serious," Macha was saying to me. "It's not serious. This will hurt a little." He lifted me in his arms and carried me as he walked. Pancha supported my leg, which was starting to hurt. Macha laid me in the back seat of a car. He took off his belt and made a tourniquet that almost strangled my leg. "Let's go," he said to Pancha. "Let's go."

I wanted to know if Rafa had shot me. But no, it hadn't been him, Pancha explained to me as I was rolled on a cot through the hallways of the Military Hospital. "He had someone with him," she told me. "Rafa ran toward Erasmo de Escala, with his bodyguard following. He was the one who shot you. When he got to the plaza, he shot toward Erasmo de Escala to cover Rafa's retreat, but he saw you running to his left, toward Maturana, and he fired. I'm sure he wanted to protect you from me, because he must have seen me next to the car, waiting for you on Calle Maturana. He was aiming at me or at Macha, and he hit you. That's what I think."

"And what happened to him, Pancha? What happened to him?" She tightens her mouth.

"He was eliminated."

I ask: "And what did he look like?"

She tells me: "There wasn't much left of his face. Macha and I emptied our cartridges. He was, how to put it, all over the paving stones. He was a big guy, I can tell you that. I noticed a piece of skull that was left and his hair was really blond. He was wearing cowboy boots. Great Dane took those off him. He wanted to save them from the blood, he said, and he kept them. He said they'd fit him well."

As if in a bad dream, I saw then what was left of the Gringo, who had wanted to save me, I saw him emptied out over the cobble-stones. All that had lain behind his eyes, all that was inside him, I saw spread out now over the ground. I felt nauseous, and I vomited in the cot.

When I woke up from the anesthesia, they'd removed the bullet and given me stitches. That was it. I would have a small scar. And, of course, the indelible and burning memory of Rafa next to the fountain, looking at me with those eyes that were suddenly suspicious. He had managed to make it almost to the corner of Erasmo Escala, I found out later. There, after the curve, Mono Lepe and Iris blocked his path. They aimed their guns at him and ordered him to stop. He fired and missed. Great Dane appeared behind him and with one kick to his head knocked him down and overpowered him. Three seconds later he was in cuffs. They lifted him up and brought him struggling to the van.

They made me interrogate Rafa. My Cuban voice. And he, Rafa, with his eyes blindfolded . . . Don't ask me for details.

We don't know what we want to talk about when we want to talk about this. I still rebel. I know it's a rebellion that's doomed from the start, just like the Devil's. And nonetheless I rebel. I'm an apostate. They broke my being and I apostatized. But I can't change or erase my past; I *can* hate it. The past is what I am, though I cannot live it. It hurts. You see, I'm crying now. I don't want to trivialize what happened to me. But you, you've convinced me to talk. What for? Now I think the sadistic part of you has been unleashed. I didn't want to talk. You are morbid, you're sick. That's why you're interested in me. Admit it! You convinced me, little by little. But I was right: I'm sinking, alone, down into the same pit as before.

THIRTY-SEVEN

Laughing, he repeated: "My Malinche, thanks to you the empire will fall, my Malinche." And he laughed, smelling of garlic. Gato never made any advances toward me, but he created an atmosphere of intimacy between us. And I listened to him, bound up in my impossibilities with my insides contorting. And he talked to me in his viscous, sticky voice.

He told me about his trips three times a week to the sauna, about the massages he got from a woman there, she was skinny but her hands and fingers were strong enough for all the different maneuvers—the pinching, drumming, the sweeping—and how the smell of camphor in the paraffin cream relaxed him, of the osmotic film they wrapped his belly in to dissolve the accumulated fat under the heat of the electric blanket, the massage for his always-tired feet, of the cranial draining, which always put him to sleep . . . Or he would talk about some show on TV. Or about his darling mother who loved him so, so much, about his father and the tangos he used to sing in the shower, about the highway accident on a curve close to San Fernando in which the two had died together, about the few friends he'd had as a child and whom he had stopped seeing and now could never see again, about a tall girlfriend, almost a head taller than him, thin and blond, of Polish parents, whom he'd loved and lost. "Because of the schedule of this damned job," he said, "because of this shitty schedule." And then he would yawn, and the mouthful of garlic breath would wash over me. And putting one elbow on the table, he'd rest his head on his hand. He was nostalgic, that damned Gato.

He told me once about an infection he'd had not long before. I don't know what it was, some kind of venereal disease, obviously. He didn't say which one. The nurse had led him to a bathroom and explained how to give himself the test. He couldn't believe it. She left him alone with two rods in his hand. He lowered his pants and underwear. He looked at the cotton-covered end of the metal rod. "The whole cotton part has to go in," she had told him. "It's only an inch," she said, and she closed the door. His eyes found his face in the mirror. He looked very pale. He thought about asking for a cot. He looked at his member and it had shrunk to almost nothing. He was ashamed, then. He imagined the nurse's disdainful gesture if she were to help him. He took hold of his little-boy member and started to force the rod into it. It bent completely, poor thing, to escape that penetration that went against nature; it hurt terribly and the little devil slipped away like a worm feeling the hook. He panted desperately. It was impossible to get it in; it was a basic problem of circumference and diameter.

"Do you need help?" it was the nurse.

"No," he answered, trying to seem calm. "No, thanks very much."

And she, coldly: "I'm only asking because you're taking so long. There are people waiting." He managed to get the rod in a quarter of an inch. A howl escaped him. "Remember you have to get the whole cotton part in. Otherwise you'll have to repeat the test," she told him. Now his little turkey waddle was hanging there pierced through by an arrow. But it wasn't in far enough, if it didn't go in farther he would have to repeat the whole torture all over again. That's the word he used. So he pushed it in and he heard an animal-like whine, he told me. He was feeling unwell. He sat on the lid of the toilet, grabbed his slippery little creature with his left hand, took a deep breath and closed his eyes, and, with his right hand, pushed that cruel arrow farther in. He thought he could feel his innermost, most sensitive fibers being shredded. His heart gave a leap that surely saved him from fainting. There was knocking at the door: "Don't forget there are two, we need two samples." When he came out he was so white that the nurse made him lie down on a cot.

That atmosphere of closeness with him made me laugh, it disgusted me and it intrigued me. But once I emerged from that basement of damp odors and into the wind of the street, it weighed on me like a poncho soaked in dirty water.

THIRTY-EIGHT

I found out that a detainee from Red Ax, one I hadn't seen, had given up an address. By this time I was completely recovered from my injury. They sent a team to check out the information. They went through the garbage and found cigar ash and the end of a smoked cigar. The tobacco was still fresh. It's hard for me to believe that someone of the Spartan's caliber could make such a big mistake. It's enough to make you think he wanted them to catch him.

Once, an urgent mission had come down to our cell: clear out a safe house that had been marked. Two cells met at the house. Ours was in charge of collecting all compromising objects. The other cell was security. They came with small weapons and one large one. Agents of the repression were en route. It could be necessary to shoot. And this very Lorena was there. So you'll see.

It was a two-story house with a high fence, white, I remember, with a gated driveway and a garage. An old married couple lived there, acting as cover to normalize the house. There was a storage shed in the backyard. I don't know where the house was because they brought us there on the floor of a car, but from something I heard in passing I think we were in Quinta Normal. We had just a few minutes. If you'd only seen the Spartan's attention to detail, his precision and speed. The Spartan took care of us. To start with, he made us wear plastic gloves he had brought for us. We went around throwing things into big black plastic trash bags: clocks, rolls of insulating tape, nails and screws and steel bolts, cables, pliers, screwdrivers, a hammer, and some sticks of dynamite. And of course, the ammunition. Then we went over everything with a cloth to erase fingerprints. The agents could arrive at any second. Oh right, I forgot, the first thing we took out was the TNT being stored at the house. It was rare for us to have military-grade explosives at our disposal. I don't remember an order to use it. All this went away immediately in a car with Canelo at the wheel. Then the Spartan looked over everything again with a flashlight to be sure there was no trace left behind. Then he had Teruca and me go over it again. So how he could forget that incriminating cigar butt is something I just can't understand.

Macha asked me to go with them. I went in disguise, and carrying my service weapon, my 9mm CZ. He asked me, when we were already in the truck, to identify the "Prince of Wales"; the photo was blurry, he said, he didn't want to make a mistake. It had happened before, more than once. When we were leaving, while we waited for the heavy door that led to Central's lot to open, I saw Gato—his slow walk, tired and downcast, his hands in his coat pockets—on his way home.

I went with Macha, feeling a fascination that I reproached myself for; there was something in him that attracted and frightened me, moved and terrified me. His brusque sentences. His guttural voice. The innate authority with which he imposed his will. His lonely animal silence. His black eyes in which I saw death.

It was close to midnight when the white Toyota double cab 4×4 parked in Calle Juan Moya, behind a run-down Ford truck with no one in it. Iris was next to Macha. I was in the back seat with the binoculars. I saw them check their cartridges and stuff bits of cloth into their ears. I was pleased to feel my heart pounding again in anticipation of action. I was alive. It was an intense moment. I was consumed by *a thirst for enemies and opposition and triumph.*

The Spartan lived there as a lodger. The problem was that there were other lodgers, two students, and, of course, the widow who owned the house and who knew nothing about the clandestine activities of the "Prince of Wales." That's all they had managed to find out. We had to avoid innocent deaths, and we had to take him alive.

He came serenely around the corner. He was three blocks away from us and he was coming closer, wearing the same blue jacket, common and worn, as he had in the restaurant at the market. I recognized him right away: his physical solidity, the poise of a man who walks with confidence through the world. "That's him!" I exclaimed. I passed the binoculars to Macha and he sat watching the Spartan as he walked closer to us. Then he gave them to Iris, and she watched him for a while, too. The Spartan stopped in the doorway of the house, inapprehensive, and took a key from his pants pocket; he looked mechanically to the right and left, and went in. He did not act like the professional I expected. He didn't check his surroundings the way he should have. He did not attentively note the presence of the old Ford truck and the Toyota parked behind it. That carelessness kept him from sensing the threat.

Then we got out of the Toyota, walked to an alley and climbed up onto a roof that didn't have a steep incline. The terrain had been studied. Iris and I went up. Macha helped us, but he stayed below. We crawled, Iris ahead of me, until we were on the house next to the Spartan's. I don't know how no one woke up. The zinc roof made noise. From our position we could see the yard, lit up by two streetlights, and a wing of the L-shaped house. We saw a light on at the back. Iris was very attentive. "The bathroom," she told me in a tiny voice I could barely hear. "The pension's shared bathroom," she said.

Do you want another glass of raspberry juice? It's good, go on, have another one. Now, as I tell you this, one thing stands out to me: the Spartan had to share a bathroom. And what did I feel at the moment? Nothing. Except I was nervous, except I was shaking. That light went out and another one came on next door. "The bedroom," Iris told me. The second light went out. Iris looked at her watch. We waited for a long minute to go by. Iris stood up without making a sound and flashed a small flashlight to signal. She looked at her watch. And the wait continued. "Now, thirty minutes," she whispered to me. "Until he's asleep." We couldn't talk or move. In situations like that my back starts to itch, a leg will go to sleep, I yawn or start sneezing. All of that happened to me on that damned roof. Not to Iris, of course, who chastised me with the disdain in her oily eyes.

Suddenly, she checked the time, stretched out her neck, and slowly stood up, flexible and silent as a panther, until she was crouched behind the cornice. I imitated her. From her new position, she drew her CZ and removed the safety. At that same instant, a footstep scraped the sidewalk. After another silence, a slight metallic groan sounded. Iris didn't take her eyes from the room with the light turned out. You couldn't see anything. The house was silent. But any experienced ear could clearly hear the sound of a lock pick searching for the combination. Until the lock gave way and the door opened. Light, very soft steps barely sounded on the wooden floor. A single, small circle of intense light flickered, advancing through the interior of the house. It was getting closer to the room where the light had been extinguished minutes earlier. Iris stretched out her neck and took her weapon in both hands, her nose sniffing at the night, her eyes scrutinizing the movements of that solitary beam of light.

A thud, a kick to the door suddenly broke the calm of the night. Then we heard a revolver fire, a window was smashed to smithereens, shouts; the circle of light turned, searching, and there was another shot. There was a tense pause during which I heard only my heart reverberating in its cage. And then, machine-gun fire from an AKM.

"They fucked us!" Iris shouted without looking at me.

Another burst of fire.

THIRTY-NINE

Iris raised her arms unhurriedly, aiming her gun with both hands, and waited. I saw a shadow run through the yard toward the back. It knelt down and covered the others who were following, shooting. Then it was relieved by another shadow and it took off running. They weren't just students, those two students. They knew how to fight. Iris calmly took aim. There, with her sharp face, she looked like a fox. I think I've told you she was an expert shot. The best of the team. When it reached the wall, one of the shadows seemed to take a wrong step, stopped short, faltering close to a streetlight, and slammed onto the pavement: Iris. I wanted to imitate her.

Just as we'd been taught, I didn't put my sights on the precise spot of the other figure, but rather a little ahead; I fired, but my shadow kept running. I had missed. In the middle of the noise and confusion I recognized the Spartan from his way of moving. He had already climbed the wall and he was getting away over the roof of the house behind. It was him. I didn't feel any guilt, none, not even when I pointed him out to Iris. My heart was pounding as I imagined what would happen next. The other shadow let itself fall, sliding down over the zinc roofing. And the Spartan kept going; unstable, taking hesitant steps, he kept moving over the treacherous roofs. I wanted to see how they got him alive. I laughed, a peal of uncontrollable laughter I couldn't suppress. Then he disappeared, followed by a burst of gunfire. We slid down from the roof and took off running. A red Datsun passed us at full speed toward Avenida

Dublé Almeyda. "I'm sure he stole that Datsun," Iris told me. The Spartan had broken through the cordon.

Macha was waiting for us in the Toyota with its motor running. He was dirty, his hair was disheveled, and he had a cut on his forehead. The traffic on Dublé Almeyda, though scarce at that hour, protected the Spartan. He was alone. We chased him southward down Vespucio. As he drove, blood dripped down from Macha's eyebrow and into his eye. Iris tied a handkerchief around his head. The cars we passed seemed to be standing still. That's how fast we were going. The Spartan seemed to be about to turn east, but then he broke fast to the west, tires squealing, and took off down Avenida Grecia. We couldn't shoot at him because of the other cars. We couldn't. I would have liked to get him with my still-virgin CZ. My heart was in my throat. I was someone else; I was unhinged, blinded. Before we reached Vicuña Mackenna, the Spartan threw a hand grenade out the window, and it exploded just a few yards from our Toyota. The splinters smashed our windshield. At the corner, he turned left, tires screeching, across four lanes of cars going in the opposite direction on Grecia, and he headed south on Vicuña Mackenna. He left a swarm of horns, brakes, and tangled cars behind him. Smoke and the smell of burnt rubber.

We lost him, and that's where he made a mistake: he should have turned onto a different street. For some reason he kept going full speed down Vicuña Mackenna. As soon as we managed to get free of the tangle of cars, Macha floored the accelerator of that beefed-up 4×4 with its big pistons and augmented carburetor, and soon we saw the tail of the Datsun again. We were gaining ground. Iris drew her gun, looking for the right angle with half her body out the window. We got close to the Datsun, and on his second try, Macha managed to bump it close to the rear wheel. It was a technique they'd taught us at the training camp in La Rinconada, though I never thought it would be useful in action. But it worked.

The Datsun went up onto the sidewalk, sped a few yards farther, barely missing a tree, scraped loudly against a wall, veering side to side. Just then we heard a peremptory voice on the car's radio that startled me: "You are under orders from your superiors to stop the Toyota immediately and cease the chase. Do you copy? You are under orders from your superiors . . ." it repeated. The Spartan's Datsun made it back onto the street and lost us, fleeing southward.

A silver Volvo pulled up in front of us. Macha got out and went over to it, his black leather jacket half open. Iris turned off the motor. Macha slammed the Volvo's windshield with the butt of his CZ. The door opened very slowly and a slender, distinguished, serene form appeared—Flaco. I had recognized his voice, of course. Macha tucked his gun behind him, under his belt. We could hear his dark voice as he looked up at Flaco: "We've got some fucking scared shitless, fat-ass generals around here. And you, Flaco, you're one of them now? Are you listening to me?" Flaco was looking over Macha's head with a vague, indefinite expression and a cold, steady smile that I didn't recognize. But his gestures had the same calm as always as he began explaining something to Macha.

"I'm telling you . . ." Iris was saying to me. "Let's see, how many times has this happened to us? Macha always does this shit. He goes off on his own, and then they de-authorize him from above. Why did we go in with so few people? . . ."

Then the figure of Gato came into my mind, downcast, his hands in his coat pockets, dragging his feet while we waited for the heavy door to open.

FORTY

The Volvo left and the operation was considered terminated. Macha took out the first aid kit, cut a piece of gauze with his Swiss army knife, opened the bottle of peroxide, and, looking at himself in the Toyota's mirror, cleaned his wound. It was a superficial cut, but there were little shards of glass in it. Iris helped him get them out with the tweezers on the same pocketknife. One splinter had gone in sideways and when it was forced out, it tore the flesh with its irregular rhombus shape. Iris, who was shining a flashlight on it, had trouble getting it out. Macha put a few drops of iodine on it, applied a bandage, straightened his clothes, combed his hair, and happily invited us for beers at a nearby dive that he knew would be open at that hour. It was on the same avenue to the south, near stop number 20 at Calle Santa Amalia, he told us, right across from a phone booth. He would have to go back to Central later on to file a report on what had happened. Then, Lisandro Pérez Olmedo would have to appear, like so many times before, in the appropriate police station, number 18, and make the required declaration: "In circumstances that the individual XX, identity number such-and-such, ignoring the order to freeze, fled through the back yard shooting an AKM, it was necessary to neutralize him, for which I used my service weapon . . ." He started to laugh.

Lisandro Pérez Olmedo still had time for a beer. He didn't seem worried about the declaration he would later stamp with his signature and that would then be archived in the case files in the Tenth Third Criminal Court of Santiago. Iris offered to go herself, since any ballistic study would show that the shot came from the roof and not the ground. Lisandro Pérez Olmedo rejected the argument with another laugh. "Who says I didn't go up on the roof? You, off to bed after this," he told her. "That's an order," he told her.

We were drinking a few beers, as I said, in a diner on Calle Santa Amalia. Through the window I could see a forsaken phone booth next to a broken streetlight that offered no light. When Iris asked him: why the order from above, and what had happened with Flaco? Macha made a disdainful gesture, wrinkling his brow, and took a long swallow of beer. "They're going to put a citation on your service record," Iris told him. "It's really bad for your career." Macha twisted his mouth in the same disdainful scowl. A drop of beer shone in his black moustache. The first round of beers was gone in no time, and I was in the middle of my second when Iris stood up to go to the bathroom. I got up to let her pass. In that exact second I recognized the Spartan. He was approaching the phone booth, his hair disheveled and his jacket dirty. Coincidences happen. Not always, of course, but sometimes, and they are decisive.

Could I keep quiet? My heart was in my throat. I realized that no one was paying any particular attention to me. Why did I do what I did? Squeezing my glass hard with both hands and looking at the table with its flowered plastic tablecloth, I said it in a voice that I remember as sounding terrified. "There's the 'Prince of Wales,'" I said. "There, in the phone booth." I expected Macha to go running out with guns blazing, but he didn't. He didn't bat an eye. We went right on drinking beer as if nothing was happening, until Iris came back. Then he handed her the keys to the Toyota and gave her the order to follow the Spartan.

"Don't use the radio," he told her. "Got it? Do not use Central's radio. Call me from a public phone when you can. I'll send you another car for support." As soon as the Spartan hung up, she went out to follow him. Macha and I calmly finished our beers.

Only then did I dare to ask him if he had really thought he'd be able to take down the "Prince of Wales" alone at the pension and bring him out in cuffs. He nodded.

"But he wasn't sleeping. He wasn't even in bed," Macha said.

And looking at a distant, indefinite point: "The man was dressed, pacing in the dark with his gun in his hand. The others were dressed too, in their rooms, each one with his AKM at the ready. Strange, right?"

The tail stayed on him day and night for more than two months. They put him "to bed" at night and "woke him" in the morning. They used three cars and nine agents in rotation. He never left their sight. This allowed them to sketch a complete web of contacts. They followed a person who once, at a "meet," arrived last and placed himself in the most protected spot, revealing his superiority to the "Prince of Wales"; he went into an apartment on Calle Viollier. In the photo of "Viollier" I recognized Max: his small eyes, his dark, wiry hair. Twice, the "Prince of Wales" lost them, both times in the Vega market on the way to a "meet." He got away from them among so many people and fruit and vegetable stands. But they found him again in the same market. It was a tail Macha organized behind Flaco Artaza's back.

FORTY-ONE

In the meantime, Clementina had a book published that compiled her reviews and catalog copy. She was invited to Paris to give a series of lectures. I thought of Giuseppe. I bought him a gift—a book of photographs of Patagonia—and I wrote him a card. Clementina happily agreed to deliver it. When I went to say good-bye to her, I brought the gift in my bag. At the last minute I thought better of it, and I didn't want to give it to her. I chickened out. Clementina's lectures were a roaring success. One publisher was interested in putting out a book of her articles. When she got back, we got together with three other girlfriends to celebrate and talk about her trip, her triumph. I felt uncomfortable having lunch with them. I was used to pretending, but that day, as I raised my glass with them, it was difficult, it hurt, I felt sorry for myself. I was sad when I left them.

That night—another of the many nights in Malloco when I lost sight of Flaco—I felt sad again, and I found myself dancing, pretty drunk, with two women I'd never seen and who I thought were pretty. My "mixed race," you know—my "hybridity," as Clementina would say—was born of the original sin of violence. And they moved gracefully, and we laughed together and embraced and I think we kissed a little. My memory is cloudy. Then we went up to a private room—the novelty of the house—and laughing and touching each other tenderly, we fell onto a waterbed. "I'm Josefina," one told me; "I'm Josefa," the other said. "I'm María José," I said. We were all lying.

One of us closed the door, and we floated there in the sweetness and the thickness, and in the darkness we were touching each other the way you palpate a chirimoya or a pear to see if it's ripe. Our movements were slow and persistent; we were enveloped in a net of tenderness and silence. A high-heeled shoe or a stocking that had captivated me while we were dancing now became a barrier, a wall to climb over. Each bit of bared skin was a discovery, as if that profile, those breasts, that waist were the silent starting point of a piece of music being played for the first time. It was the hour of my beauty, my very own, and I was proud of having taken it for myself.

It's easy to kiss a woman; the hand can imagine with such ease a shoulder or a thigh that turns into *her* shoulder or thigh, and the hand protects it, as if the permanence of her skin depended on my hands moving over it, as if, without the soft and insistent touch of another's skin, she would wither and fall to pieces. And it was as if the constant caress of those hands were reconstituting an invisible shell, an egg that incubated a metamorphosing body. We felt each other, letting ourselves go without hurry, purpose, or fear. The next moment trembled like the flame of a candle in darkness, and all was anticipation and surprise.

At some point I cried and Josefina cradled me and Josefa licked my tears, and I cried some more and the three of us cried in each other's arms, each one hiding in the other. And later we started laughing and nothing existed apart from the three of us laughing, intertwined on that waterbed. Until the kisses returned, and a slow loving. Then I focused on Josefina and Josefa's eyes, their serene and emptied gaze.

A person is not a "lesbian" or "fag" or "sadist" or "straight" or "masochist" or "loyal" or "deceitful" or "hero" or "villain." We must *break through language in order to touch life*. A person simply does certain things. *We never step into the same river twice.* There, in that house of Dionysian lights and shadows, I encountered phalluses that were big and long, others that were narrow and short, and straight ones and curved ones—the thousand and one shapes those little devils can possibly take. That man, Phoebus's, was pointed. I remember another one with a fold covering it, so thick and noticeable. Every phallus is different, you know, and it has a personality of its own, expressive and individual like the nose on a face.

Energized by amphetamines or seeing, thanks to the amyl, the violent power of the light and the palpitations of my heart beating full speed, I could endure all, embrace all, accept all, desire all, and the skin of my soul, of the omnivorous beast that we usually suppress, was captivated and threw itself headlong into the frenzy. It was the night of the great "Yes." *Nothing is true, everything is permitted.* Because we are disguised barbarians; that's what we are. Why do I say "barbarians"? The Scythians, says Herodotus (wasn't it Herodotus?), shared their women and fornicated in public like animals. That's why they were barbaric. Let me correct myself, then: we are carnivorous animals, badly disguised and without innocence. That's what we lost with Paradise: animal innocence. We looked at ourselves naked and shame was born. Hell is a mirror that we can't look away from.

FORTY-TWO

I got a call from Central. I was summoned to appear in Macha's office right away. Indio Galdámez greets me, in his sleeveless shirt, sweaty and foul smelling, that shows off his cretin's muscles with their green boa. I sit on the brown plastic imitation leather sofa in the waiting room. He goes back to his game of foosball with Chico Marín, who, wide as a cube, waits for him scratching his shaved head. Over the chessboard, Iris is motionless. Across from her, Mono Lepe. He's lost three pawns and a knight. He looks on, alarmed, and leans down until he's almost touching one of his rooks with his crooked, sunken nose. Pancha is watching TV. She knows very well she's looking good in that black shirt. An everyday, coarse woman, but with the kind of good tits that make the men like her. There are several chairs scattered about, a table in the middle of the room with two copper ashtrays, the butts twisted inside them, and a vase holding artificial flowers. I hear Macha's voice. He's barking into the phone.

"I repeat: this is fucked. No," he bellows after a silence. "To blow the operation now doesn't make sense." Silence. "No. I don't want to throw away a tracking operation that's taken months." Silence. Angrily: "And what did you want me to do? Sit on my ass and wait for the order? Sure! And now it's all fine and dandy and you want to come in and take advantage of the situation." Long silence. "And why did you go in person to abort the arrest?" Silence. "Of course! Are you threatening me? What? I was shitting all over procedure? Oh, please . . ." Silence. "The situation has changed. That's why. Now it would be premature. We're getting very valuable intelligence, Flaco. We're on the verge of . . ." Silence. More calmly: "I repeat: it would really fuck things up. They're getting to the bottom." Silence. "Yes. That's not the point. We're ready. I've just called my people in . . ." Silence. "Then I'm receiving an order. It's definitive. An order." Silence. "All right." Silence. "Yes. I'll go. Fine. The order will be carried out immediately." Silence. "Yes. All right. Let me say one thing: you all upstairs, you're some bloodsucking bastards. But the mission will be carried out immediately."

Indio Galdámez ushers me into the office. Behind his desk, Macha greets me indifferently. The room is small, and the grayish linoleum floor smells of wax. A single neon tube lights the room. I sit down. His desk is between us. I look around for any personal object. There's no photo, no picture or paperweight, nothing that would tell me anything about him. The ink pen I see in the desk is an everyday yellow Bic that rests on a block notebook. To one side, a coat hanger holding no coats and a metal shelf with some file folders. Behind him, the radio and a solid safe built into the wall. Over the corner of the safe are his shoulder holster and his service weapon, his 9mm CZ Parabellum, and a magazine with no clips in it.

"I need you," he says in that grave voice of his. "We're going to blow the tracking operation we've been doing on the 'Prince of Wales' and 'Viollier.' Orders from above. We can't make any mistakes. I need you there. I repeat: we can't make any mistakes. I want them alive. Are you willing?"

"Of course," I say. "Of course. When?"

He looks at his Rolex.

"It's eleven thirty. We leave within ten minutes. Go have them disguise you. You have your weapon with you, right?"

"Yes," I say, pointing to my purse.

And as I'm about to open the door:

"Did you tell Flaco or Gato that we had a tail on the 'Prince of Wales'?"

I shake my head.

"I believe you," he tells me somberly. "But it doesn't matter now. Don't talk to anyone. We'll meet in the parking lot in ten minutes. Clear?"

In the hallway I ran into Gato. He was walking with his head down as always, moving with slow and heavy steps. I noticed his worn-out gray pants, his old tennis shoes that he wore without socks. Chico Marín passed next to me and tugged my hair, laughing with his jumpy eyes, and walked on as if he didn't see Gato. When I could smell his garlic stench, he looked at me, grabbed my shoulders, and shoved me up against the wall.

FORTY-THREE

"Where you headed, Malinche?"

"To Makeup."

"And? Why? Are they taking you on a mission?"

I smiled enigmatically.

"I don't like it one bit. It's dangerous. Your place is here, with me. Anyone can do that other thing. Macha's bringing you, right?"

I smiled.

"Are you sure the operation is authorized?"

I nodded. He made a sudden, unexpectedly quick movement. Now I didn't have my purse and my arm hurt terribly, twisted behind my back. He manipulated it from my wrist that was bent painfully. He did it all with an agility and skill that were unthinkable in such a fat man.

"You're coming with me," he whispered. "You belong to my department. Let's go. Let's see if this order really exists." And he let out a laugh.

My wrist doesn't slacken, but the pain does. We go down to the basement. I can smell the bleach from the floor. They must have mopped recently. He turns on the light and makes me sit down. He puts my purse away in the drawer of his desk, tosses an empty Pepsi can and a sandwich wrapper into the garbage, and lets himself fall puffing onto his chair. Finally, he makes an internal call.

"We're just going to make sure," he says. "And don't look at me with that put-upon little face of yours . . . I'm protecting you, Cubanita."

He asked to be put through to C3.1. I knew that number was Flaco. They told him his call would be returned shortly. I explained that the operation was about to start, that I couldn't be late, that I had no way to justify my absence.

"Are we going after big fish, here?"

"I don't know."

"Even if they're not big fish, it's good for these operations to happen, you know? It's important to maintain contact with the enemy. The terrorist network is designed to avoid contact, except when they hit us with a surprise attack and can get away. And, of course, we have to decapitate the movement. We know that. The subversives scatter when their leaders fall. 'If you want to kill a snake, cut off its head.' But *you* shouldn't have to take part in these things, Cubanita. You're just looking for adventure, aren't you? The drug of danger. I know you too well, kiddo . . . But no. It's not wise and it's not convenient."

Gato was convinced that my comrades were about to bring me back in completely, that they had been testing me and would be giving me important missions any day now, and he wanted me to be his informant. He was expecting great things, I thought . . . And then, out of nowhere, after a short silence, he put one elbow on the table and held his chin in his hand and he started talking.

"It's like I don't even exist," he said, as he picked up some bread-crumbs that had fallen from the paper wrapper onto the metal top of his desk. "Even the agents I work with look down on me. They avoid me in the hallways, they look the other way if they see me crossing the lot. You just saw that asshole Chico Marín, man . . . You saw how that little jerk turned away from me." He didn't want to make any-one uncomfortable, he told me. That's why he didn't go to the cafeteria. He had his Pepsis and sandwiches—steak with tomato, avocado, lettuce, and mayo—sent in from the shop on the corner. He devoured it all here in his office, in the same basement room where we carried out interrogations. So he wouldn't bother anyone . . . "And some of them I've known since we were kids . . . But it's not the bullets that'll decide this filthy war, you know? They know it. It's these bits of information, these dirty little jobs. This work is like being an executioner."

He goes back to collecting crumbs with a fingernail that's a little long and not very clean. His stomach spills in a wave over the metal surface of the desk. No one trusts anyone else around here. Is that why Gato is confiding in an outsider like me?

"Everyone knows it. Without the evil executioner," he tells me, "society wouldn't exist, but no one wants to see him in society. Am I wrong? Maybe it's the little angels who create the social order? Wouldn't that be nice! Unfortunately, you have to use terror, you have to use evil, you have to use the most vile and fucked-up parts hidden inside a human being. Later, of course, those methods are condemned and the cruelties that made it possible to move beyond cruelty are punished. Or no? They're left behind, forgotten, not necessary anymore. Like the journalist in that old cowboy movie says, I can't think of the name, 'When the legend becomes fact, print the legend.' What do you think?" He smiled at me, his eyes narrowing with a feline air. "Do you think, Cubanita, that the owners of the planes and ships and banks and copper mines and the pasta and ice cream factories know that someone like me exists? Do you think they know that their power would all go to shit without us, the ones down here in this damp, dark dungeon, like sewer rats? Do you think the housewife who goes out in the morning to do the shopping has any inkling that we're protecting the long chain that makes it possible for her to find her noodles, her rice, her bottle of oil in the store? Do you think that pretty young girl in the morning light, at the lake in her bikini, sliding along on fiberglass skis in the wake of a boat with a 150hp outboard motor, you think she knows about me? Do you think she has any idea that her daddy's gold card hangs from a thin and invisible thread that connects it to an 'abject' being like me? Not to mention the intellectuals who analyze the 'political situation,' as they call it. What do you have to say about those fuckers?"

Has my past been erased, or does he think that by talking to me this way I'll erase it myself? I feel his breath on my neck, and that obscene closeness revolts me.

"So many intelligent reports for us to read! They know everything, they're 'political analysts' and they write about power. Makes sense, since they're smart and they've studied everything at the best universities in Europe and the United States. Sure, they understand everything, except for one thing: the power of fear. The intellectuals don't know a thing about that. And we do. I'm plenty professional, you know me. The thing that traps a man who is naked, tied up, and blindfolded isn't what will happen to his body. Although he imagines it, or believes he imagines it, he still has no idea what it means to have a jolt of electricity turn his body into tongues of fire. But with the tough ones, the well-trained ones, that only softens them, it only softens them up."

A shiver runs down my spine. I can't get air, I'm starting to gasp. He asks what's wrong with me. "Nothing," I say. He goes on:

"Interrogation is an art. I know how to bring anyone, anyone at all, to a place of desperation. There, he gives up, surrenders. Am I offending you?"

He goes quiet. My anxiety recedes. He takes a sandwich from the drawer, calmly unwraps the paper, peers at it, and sinks his teeth into it deliberately. A dribble of mayonnaise slides out of the corner of his mouth. He chews energetically, concentrated. He softens his tone:

"And no one escapes. No one. It's a fact. It's normal, human. That's why they shouldn't feel guilty."

"I have to go, they must be looking for me," I say.

"I have to protect you. It's my duty."

"Gato: I know this operation is authorized. Not only that: the order comes from above."

"That's the story Macha gave you, right?"

"I heard the conversation on the phone."

He furrowed his brow.

"What's that?"

"While I was waiting, I could hear the conversation."

"Macha does shout on the phone. I'll give you that."

"Yes. I heard it loud and clear."

He calls again on the internal phone. I hear the secretary's voice on the other end. It's taking a while, she asks him to be patient, C3.1 is on the phone with someone else and he'll call back in a minute. He looks at me, lowers his eyes to the sandwich, and plants another precise and determined bite.

"No one escapes, or as Ronco would say, 'ain't no one.' It's a fact, a fact." And he goes on as if we had all the time in the world. "I had one, maybe two, who didn't. I remember a doctor from the FPMR. We'd just gotten started on him when he had an epileptic fit. Two of our doctors checked him and rechecked him. There was nothing wrong with him. A hysterical reaction, they said. Nothing we could do. That one didn't talk at all. Exception that proves the rule. Every person has his weak point. It's just a matter of finding it. Macha, for example, has Cristóbal. He lives for that kid. Since he split up with his wife, he's had women but never a woman, you get me? Cristóbal is his unconditional. That kid Cristóbal's best friend is his father. Sometimes he brings him here and takes him shooting at the firing range. Real bullets, you can hear them. He loves that damned kid a lot. He takes him out on his Harley, on long trips, you know; he takes him camping, or fishing down south, at Yelcho. Fly fishing. Macha really likes that. He loves to fish, Macha does."

He delves into his left ear with his pinky finger and then observes the extracted wax with great attention. He goes on chewing zealously.

"What do you have to say? I feel like our adversaries are respectable. That's what I think, and I've seen them at their worst, human garbage, the mother giving up her son or the son giving up his mother, all dignity lost. But even so, I consider them respectable. But the feeling is not reciprocated, you know? That hurts. I don't like to walk around this neighborhood. I come here by bus every day. I don't have a car. If there's an emergency they send someone to pick me up. But normally, I come in and leave through these filthy streets that are a boiling cauldron of foul-smelling cars all squeezing in together and thousands of pedestrians who look like beggars. What my mother would say if she saw me go by on my way home from work! This godforsaken lot, the pigeon shit on the ground and on the bodywork of the cars, fucking up the paint on the undercover cars and taxis they use when they follow people . . ." The mayonnaise slides down his chin. "And outside, in the honking horns and squealing breaks," he goes on. "The litter, the leftover food in wet and stinking cardboard containers, the scraps of fruits and vegetables that fall from crates and rot in the streets, the vulgarity, you know? The crushed beer cans that no one picks up, the oil spots on the pavement with its tar patches, the walls with curse words scrawled on them and shredded posters stuck on top of other shredded posters, the kiosk where they sell cigarettes, peanuts, sweets, and chocolates in the middle of the machine racket, the evil whine of the pigeons and the piss left by skinny, sleepy cats, those skin-and-bone cats that are always stretching, and the dirty roofs, the black smoke from the bus engines, their breaks that screech and squeal and hurt your ears, the same tired little shop on the corner, with its television always on full volume, where they sell *mote con huesillo* and where for safety reasons I never set foot, though that's where these sandwiches and my Pepsi come from, the worn-out noise of the old trucks, the air heavy and stinging from the nitrogen oxide and carbon monoxide and the ozone and the cancerous soot from the diesel engines . . ."

"Gato! I have to go. They're waiting for me. It's urgent . . ."

He falls silent. He takes another bite of the sandwich. I can't avoid seeing in his open mouth the results of his back molars' indefatigable chewing. As for him, he seems to be squinting at something far away.

"What would my mother say if she saw me in the middle of the muck of this neighborhood!" And he looks at the ceiling. He wants me to feel sorry for him. At the same time, he's being sincere. "She, who was such a lady; she made such delicate embroideries that my aunts, who were both older than her, were jealous, and they competed with her but were never able to match the lace on her immaculate tablecloths. If she were alive, could I stand this job? What could I tell her? Listen, Central owes so much to me. I wasn't here before, you know that, I've already told you that; I wasn't here when the worst things, the most gruesome, were happening, the things that were so horrible that lots of people can't even believe they happened. And that's what they expected back then, that no one or almost no one would believe the victims. And the ones closest to them, the ones who actually would believe, well, even better, because they were exactly the ones who had to be taught a lesson. That was before they created Central. I started this shitty job here. And they owe me a lot, hear? Even though I just follow orders same as everyone else on the chain of command, same as Flaco Artaza, who gives orders to me and to Macha, who started working here after I did. He hasn't been in this for very long, when it comes down to it. And here, no one answers to himself. If they did it would be pure chaos, we'd all be fucked, tearing at each other's throats. Get it? Chain of command. Sure. The Chain of Command gives us orders that we'd rather not get, right? I wasn't made for this. I mean: I am not what I do. Because, what the fuck, these are our fellow countrymen, it's really hard, see?" He drags his little voice, inviting my commiseration; he thinks it's possible, he wants to be thought of as a victim. "But," he says with a dignified gesture, "I've done my duty, I've obeyed. That's my honor. I'm right where they've ordered me to be, down here in this sewer, no judgment. Responsibility lies with the ones who give us orders. I just have to carry them out. Verticality of command. Compartmenting. As it should be. As I was taught. Though of course, I still manage to find out what goes on around here. But I haven't invented anything new, no new techniques or procedures. It's not like I enjoy what I do, and I go around thinking up new shit, you get me? You've seen it. You have to hold back the nausea sometimes . . . But this is what I have to do, and if it wasn't me it would be someone else. The order is there, it has to be carried out. Even so, when it comes to me, no one wants to see me. No one here inside, I mean.

"Macha is different, you know? He's the only one who looks me in the eye. I wonder: Is he afraid of me? Macha, who they tell me is so courageous? . . . Some afternoons he invites me out for a cold one at a bar around here, close to the market. We talk in a way we can't talk with people who work directly with us. Because of compartmenting, you understand. I don't know who Rat is. I know his pseudonym. I don't know who his wife is or anything about his kids. I'm not supposed to know. Although, don't ask me why but I get the feeling he's fuzz. He doesn't know anything about me either. It's for good reason our anthem says 'We are children of solitude.' No one is more solitary than us, man," and he looks at me with emptied eyes. "With so much distrust, you end up not trusting yourself. You start to think of the enemy as an equal, almost like a brother. He must be all alone, too, in some miserable room in a boardinghouse out there, living his lousy clandestine life. His presence, which is always alive in your imagination, accompanies you from afar. If it were possible . . . You know: hate and love can change places. Later, you tell yourself that no, obviously it's not like that, he is, truly and completely, your enemy. And still . . .

Macha doesn't know who Iris really is, or Chico Marín. He doesn't know . . . On the other hand, since we're in different departments, Macha Carrasco and I can talk. Not a lot, but some. Even though we only know each other by our fake names. But I know who his son is, I do know that. We talk about soccer, we talk about his father, who was a truck driver. He drove a Ford with a trailer on it, and Macha hardly ever saw him. He carried cargo to the south, Macha's dad did, and he was hardly ever home. They didn't get along well. 'My old man,' he told me, 'put me in military school to straighten me out.' That way, they'd see each other less. 'My old man didn't take me into account,' he says. His old man wasn't there for Macha. Maybe that's why he turned out so macho. That's what I think.

"We don't talk about work much. A little, though. He looks down on it. He looks down on our 'fat-ass bosses,' he looks down on the decorations, the circular commands; he doesn't trust anyone. . . If there was ever a solitary man, it's him. I think he can't even imagine how far his 'fat-ass bosses' would be willing to go. The day he least expects it, they'll get sick of looking the other way when he ignores procedure, they'll get tired of his habit of going off, out of an excess of 'professional pride,' as they say, to arrest the "Prince of Wales," for example, on his own and with no one's authorization—not no one's, as Ronco would say—I don't think a thing like that even crosses his mind. Or Iris's, or Great Dane's, or any of the other people who blindly follow him. Command has hardened feelings, you know. To Command, we're all disposable, hear? Not just the terrorists. Everyone. And above all, the ones who do this job."

He goes on chewing and chewing, concentrated. He examines the bit of sandwich he has left and he takes a giant bite right in the center.

"Macha lives with no yesterday or tomorrow. Those acts of blood and guts he's so wrapped up in happen and they swallow him up. It's like he dreamed them. He's isolated in a present that's separate, I'm telling you, from what happened before and what will happen after. Maybe he lives like he's dead. He thinks: this has to be done; it has to be done, period. Tomorrow no one will understand us. He and I understand each other, you know? 'Someone,' he says to me, 'gives the order: clean out the building's plumbing, it's stopped up. And someone else has to go and open it up and look at the plumbing, shine a light into the pipes and watch the shit go by in that thick and stinking water, someone has to stick the metallic tubes in there and unclog the pipe. And the hands that are feeding out the electric snake end up stinking like that sewage. Gato, we are nobody, and we always will be,' he tells me.

"You know what he was telling me about the other day, last Thursday, I think it was? 'The bad thing about these CZs, Gato, the down side is that they're too fast. You shoot, and the bullets go through the man so fast he keeps on moving, right? It seems like he's still alive, he won't die, he goes on opening and closing his mouth, poor fucker, and so you go on shooting him. When the guy finally stops moving, you've already emptied a clip into him . . . ' As for me, Cubanita, you know I've never shot at anyone. God willing, I won't. Macha suspects that someone higher up is protecting the terrorists, he thinks they don't want to finish them off once and for all so we can maintain the threat, the justification, he tells me, he asks me. And he watches me. Like he's trying to get in my head. That's how it feels, I don't know . . . Did you know Macha has terrible aim? But he gets up close to the target, he holds the gun at eye height and shoots at the man between his belly button and his neck. He gets really close to him and that, of course, makes all the difference."

The phone rang. Gato repeated the order I had received. Silence. "I wanted to be sure the operation was authorized," he said.

"Understood," he answered, submissive. "It's just that with Macha Carrasco, you never know . . . Right away," he adds, resigned. "Right away!"

He hangs up, chastened, and he squats down to take my purse out of the drawer.

"Go on. They're waiting for you." And when he handed it to me: "Of course, he would do it now. I forgot: they're doing evaluations this month. That Flaco doesn't miss a trick!" he exclaimed.

He licked the mayonnaise off his lips, though a smear remained on his chin; he smiled at me, sphinxlike, and waved his thin little fingers in the air.

FORTY-FOUR

They intercepted him at eight in the morning coming out of a house that was being watched. He walked calmly, an ordinary man. He didn't worry about checking for a tail. Once again, no attempt at checking his surroundings. Nothing. I watched what happened second by second through my binoculars from a fake taxi parked a block and a half away. As soon as I recognized him walking toward me, I gave the signal. Macha got out of another car parked closer, got right on top of him, and aimed at his forehead. No more than four yards between them. I would have liked to see that exchange of power in their eyes. The Spartan tried to take his gun out. But Great Dane came out of nowhere, leaped into the air, and planted a foot in his face. The Spartan fell but he got up, blood streaming down his face, and ran toward a pickup truck, ignoring Macha's bullets as they whistled past. As I told you, they wanted him alive. He put the key in the lock. Macha shot holes in the tires and the Spartan's truck started to lean to the side. He managed to get the door open. When he saw he was lost, he put the barrel of his SIG-Sauer in his mouth and fired.

I liked it. The guy had balls. The Spartan didn't want to surrender: "Talking isn't the sin, the sin is letting yourself be taken alive." That thick paste, mixed with viscous liquids—it was hard to believe that repugnant pulp was all that was left of the head that used to lean over a chessboard and could divine moves none of the rest of us could see. And if he was only that, then so was my daughter, so was I, so was anyone. He was left shamelessly exposed, turned inside out like an animal destroyed. And I remembered the Fonseca no. 1 wrapped in rice paper that he'd given me at the restaurant in the Central Market. And I remembered the girl who was waiting for him in Quivicán, rolling tobacco leaves.

That same night, three leaders of Red Ax fell, including "Viollier." They made me identify him after he was already dead: it was Max, no doubt about it. He was almost intact. It happened at the corner of Argomedo and Raulí. He was on his way in to the "meet." He didn't obey the order to stop, they said. Lies. They shot him point-blank. He never even fired. It wasn't like with Rafa or the Spartan. They didn't even try to take him alive. Macha crossed in front of him, aiming at him and cutting off his escape. Iris, from the sidewalk across the street, hit him with a single 9mm bullet in his temple. An old woman who'd just arrived heard the bullets and started walking down Raulí; they let her escape and put a tail on her.

FORTY-FIVE

"Let's go to Wild Cat," he says, "Come on." And in the Volvo he gives me a bottle of Christian Dior perfume—a small bottle so I can carry it in my purse—and then he hands me a line on his gold credit card. Flaco is attractive, but you know, the fire of the beginning has cooled over time. But not if we go to the den in Malloco. There, my whole body starts to vibrate again. Sometimes, I go with Flaco to the private room with Louis XV chairs and the faded black velvet sofa. And after a little of the white powder, I start to smolder again, burning up my desperation, my resentment, my twisted sadness. Then, to receive Jerónimo and Rabbit under Flaco's gaze is to kill them and resuscitate myself. And Flaco loves me then with a re-newed passion.

So we went, and I lost him soon after we got there. I went to the bar and drank two pisco and Cokes. I looked for him until I got tired of looking for him. I danced with a big, slightly pudgy guy who squeezed me and whom I didn't like. He gave me a black mask, soft and flexible. "It's Italian," he told me. He gave me a couple of lines. A boy with a shaved head embraced us, a friend of his, and we danced like that, the three of us. Then the two of them were kissing. I went back to the bar and I was drinking another piscola when Flaco appeared; he was laughing with a younger guy, dark, not very tall, thin, with dark glasses. There was a lot of complicity in the laughter of those two. We went into the room with imitation Louis XV chairs, and Flaco took out his little mirror. The other guy fol-lowed the rhythm of the music, and he inhaled and looked at me seriously and went on dancing.

"You've got white on the nose of your mask," laughed Flaco. He knew what he wanted from me. The other guy came closer. Flaco told me yes, yes, with his somber voice that conquered me. The other man laughed. I had already given myself over.

Then I recognized him, suddenly and without a doubt. I recognized his smell. He was wearing a T-shirt again, sleeveless this time, and his arms were more muscular than I remembered. He looked at me in the darkness, but he didn't remember me. My heart jumped when I felt my captor's arm around me, and Flaco's clinging gaze. Now it was me who was nervous. I whispered into his ear. "I remember you," I told him. "I saw you once and you were wearing a green shirt." He didn't answer. I don't think he heard me. He was licking my nipples and he caressed them tenderly and in the darkness he gaped at them and then went back to biting them gently. He was concentrated there. His body was hairless. I like hairless men. Rodrigo was hairless. The Greeks didn't sculpt men's hair, except for where it should be: on their heads and down below. Their shapes emphasize a smooth and continuous surface. Hair interrupts the beauty of the muscles. At that moment, I was enjoying his chest, too, I liked that it was bare now and free of hair that would impede my tongue.

And so I understood him, I understood his fascination because I was also kissing his masculine breasts. "Your nipples are big and round like coins, like monedas." That was the only thing he said to me.

"It was on Calle Moneda," I told him. "Remember? You pointed your gun at me." I don't think he heard me. He seemed really high. He was panting in my ear the same way he had on that frightful day. It was him, no doubt about it. But that day on Calle Moneda he'd been very nervous, he could have fired accidentally. And I felt the cold of the gun barrel on my temple. I'd been more serene than he was. He entered me, his phallus long and thin like a bull's, reaching deep inside me. I shuddered. Like a good bull, he came in no time. And that was it.

When I came back from the bathroom, they weren't there anymore. The two of them had left. I went to the bar. I ordered a tequila.

And then, wandering around, I found a shadowy room full of cells, like a gym with weight machines, or like a torture chamber with black leather beds with straps, and handcuffs, masks, nipple clamps, rings to put around a phallus, whips, of course, and crops and various chains: in short, the classic paraphernalia of that particular tribe.

I went into another room, small and dark. In it there was a cross that you could be tied to, whipped, and spit on. And I saw a man wearing a mask, one of those men of indefinite age, short, double chin, long hair, muscles that had once been defined and were now soft waves, a potbellied man, with a fevered and broken spirit—I saw him seek out that place of transformation, of death and resurrection, and place himself up there in the role of a slave. I recognized him by his garlic smell. He was there. He had that high voice, as if he were faking it. My confessor, my all-powerful, my unseen one, my ally, my accomplice, my boss, my corruptor, he was there, a few droplets of sweat shining on his weak lips. At first I didn't dare look at him for fear that he would recognize me in spite of my mask. My heart sped up, I felt anxiety tightening in my stomach. I should have left, I wanted to and I didn't want to; I stood there turned to stone before that mortified figure. Behind his mask his eyes were hollow and red; he didn't notice I was there.

I moved backward and circled around until I was looking at his back. In that place he was so much shorter and fatter and more insignificant . . . I saw myself lying down, tied up, naked, and blindfolded, imagining that the one who was pressuring me with his questions and punishments was a beast both beautiful and cruel. I lost myself among the people surrounding the crucified man. It was him, no doubt about it. There's a memory that remains in the flesh. He was my *deus absconditus* to whom I had sacrificed myself trying to imagine he was good. At that moment I started to retch, but I held it back.

It was contagious; there was a woman and a strapping, strong boy and a skinny, ugly man with long hair tied in a ponytail. They took turns punishing him with a crop. After a while even I laughed with pleasure, like an idiot, and I spit on his back and I wanted to whip him. In truth, at that moment I wasn't out for revenge. Real revenge, when it came, if it came, would be something quite different. But I didn't know that art, and they turned me away.

Now another youth with sunken eyes and gaunt face whom I hadn't noticed before takes the whip. The crucified man looks at him with imploring tenderness. The other looks back with distant severity. Do they know each other? Is he a detainee? Could he be an informer like me, though he's the master now? I've seen him, it seems to me I've even talked with him. A prisoner. But I can't be sure. Maybe he was an agent, or a whore, who knows.

"More, harder," the whipped man begs confidently.

The other doesn't change his rhythm. They search in each other's eyes. After a while the skin has started to relax and the man with the whip gives it to him harder but keeps a steady rhythm. I watch in fascination. His muscles contract. The other man shouts in pain; it seems like he wants to stop the game. Why doesn't he? *To be like victims burned at the stake, signaling through the flames.* The man with the whip is sweating and he goes on whipping, perhaps a little harder still. He yanks off his leather jacket and throws it to the floor, and he's left in a sleeveless black shirt, sweaty and tight against the muscles of his chest. I like his collarbone, thin and feminine. He starts up the whipping again at a slower, more violent rhythm. His sweet, reddened face shines with sweat. This is not a genital orgasm; it's a voyage into unknown territories of the mind. They look at each other like they're hypnotized. There are no shouts now, just a giving in to the love in each lash of the whip.

"More, yes, yes, more," the victim says, "that's it, keep going, more, more."

On his back red dots have sprung up that lengthen into drops.

The eye contact resumes and it's like a tense thread about to break; they see something in each other that I can't see, a phosphorescence, an apparition.

At some point everything stopped. Gato was untied. He was trembling and swaying, panting. He took off his mask and tears were falling down his cheeks and blood down his shoulders, his back and ribs. The young man helped him sit down on the floor. "Cover yourself," he told him, solicitous, "cover yourself." And he put a damp towel over Gato's shoulders and sat down next to him. I left the two of them shivering in an embrace on the floor under that towel, and I rushed off to the bathroom to find a line I desperately needed.

That inversion was a cruel game, but it was consensual. Completely different from the unilateral horror, from the power imposed by one body on another. We are taught to be ashamed of our instincts. Our hypocritical education, a gag. There's a tyrannical pleasure in the degradation of oneself. We are that, too. In the underworld of that dark, bewitched house, I lived it frenetically, like one returning to a lost Paradise—not the sterilized and anodyne paradise of Genesis, but a cruel and delicious unleashing, a plunge into the burning and confused sea of our origins, a sudden fusion with the savage animal that inhabits us and that we deny ourselves. In that pit I touched the bottom of the truth that we deny ourselves, the truth that we invent. Not "The Truth" but rather instants of vehemence, vertiginous truths like bites or burns, momentary passions that I lived deeply and free of doubt.

FORTY-SIX

I say to Flaco: I'm going to leave you, I'll retire and start my own security business. Don't you think I'd be able to start a security business and make money?

And he says: Of course. You could start a business and make a lot of money. I have no doubt.

And me: And you know what I'm going to do with all that money?

And he looks at me with questioning eyes, and waits.

And me, smiling: I'm going to buy myself a penthouse, or, more like it, a penis-house.

And he: Oh! Really? That's what you want?

And me: It's not what I want; I need it.

And he: A penis-house . . .

And me, very seriously, holding back the laughter: Exactly. So I can have lots of penises in my house.

And he, laughing: So you need lots of penises . . .

And me: Yes. One night with one, another night with another. To miss out on all of them, except yours, shows a serious lack of consideration.

And he: You're unfaithful to the core. You can't help it.

And me: Who told you? The thing is, I'm a different person with every man I like. That's why I don't feel guilty. It's just that I'm a different person.

And he: You like to change men, then.

And me: Change penises.

And he: Ah, really?

And me: Sure, we're living in the era of diversity. The same thing every day gets boring, even if it's Iranian caviar.

And he: Have you tried Iranian caviar?

And me: Never. But I read in some magazine that it was the best caviar. Iranian beluga. And you know something else?

And he: What?

And me: I want them with money. I'm tired of these poverty-stricken guys; I'm past the stage of hot, handsome guys, boys who are strong but who are ultimately pretty poor, like you. Let's see, what's the most an intelligence official can make? That's that! Now I want hard, big, thick penises and you know what else? I want them stuffed with money. That's what I want.

And he: But who wants that? Do you, really? Or is it just that you want to get married and you're thinking about your kids, so they'll have a good life?

And me: Maybe yes, maybe no. But above all the one who wants that penis-house is the one you're imagining and you keep quiet about. Above all, her.

And Flaco bursts out laughing and gives me a kiss that his own laughter interrupts. He pulls off my dress and kisses my nipples and I fall onto the bed and he penetrates me without even removing my underwear.

I'm not going to deny it: I loved Flaco Artaza. If I didn't, I wouldn't have been able to stand doing what I did, I think now. Can anyone understand that? He was a man who pleased me, I was a person to him, and he took care of me. He had problems with his wife, she suspected there was another woman. So many times he came home at dawn, or just he didn't come home at all. Work, he said. She had her doubts. But divorce was unthinkable. Their two little girls came first. I knew that very well, and I had no illusions. Or at least, I had them but I denied it.

FORTY-SEVEN

Suddenly, Flaco is tormented by the future. He tells me: "We have to wipe out the terrorists. We're in the process of exterminating the rats in this country." That's what Central's director had told him that morning. He'd asked for an audience so he could "expound on" a few things, as he put it. Flaco did not agree with what was happening. It's impossible for me to connect the person talking to me now with the one who goes with me to the Malloco house. Of course, the same happens with me and with everyone else who goes there. Images of Wild Cat cross my mind, and I wish I were there with him now. But he's talking to me about his problems, sitting on the worn black leather sofa in the apartment at Tajamar Towers. The sky over San Cristóbal Hill is gradually losing its light.

It's a conversation that he would never have with his faithful wife or with women like his faithful wife. Part of the attraction I have for him is that with me, he can talk about these things as if I wasn't a woman and, at the same time, not as though I were a man. It's a small hollow where a warm intimacy is born, one that is novel for him. Because he's never encountered women like me before. Because for him—for all of them, really—a woman doesn't participate in this open and cruel world, she is outside of "History" and completely absorbed in the *petite histoire* of the family. He goes on talking in a tired voice, and I think about my long, tedious Saturdays and Sundays spent alone and thinking about him, imagining him going to the supermarket and the cinema with his faithful wife. Does he still sleep with her? He showed me a photo once. I asked him to. I needed to have an image to anchor my imaginings. She wasn't a bit ugly, the bitch. I was furious.

"Just to capture one single enemy combatant," he is saying, his forehead wrinkled and his voice contrite, "too many people are martyred: people who are mere dissenters, lefty kids who are treated like full-blown terrorists. And they're not, they're just members of the opposition, they are not military enemies. Poor kids. They get treated like shit. We're confusing the Opposing Front with the Subversive Front . . . In the inspections, the assault teams swoop in at night on a house and grab everyone in sight. Well, I put my balls on the line, I told the director what was what, I called a spade a spade."

Did he really put them on the line? I wonder . . .

"The director didn't like what he heard. What we're sowing here, I told him, is terror, of course, and then hate and more hate. In the end no one will believe us about anything. Not even that there ever were groups of trained terrorists . . . Because they kill in cold blood, they kill people who were never terrorists . . . I don't deny that fear brings about a military 'victory,' but it's a pyrrhic victory. It's achieved at the price of political failure and moral shame.

"I don't know what the director answered. Chain of Command, Chain of Command . . . 'But what does Command want?' I asked him. There was nothing concrete in his answer. Our job isn't to conquer a territory but rather the people in it. In this conflict, the main thing is to win the war of images. You know?" Flaco goes on saying to me. "We live in a world of pure interpretation." And he opens his long arms, inviting me to understand him. Because that's what he wants from me, he wants me to think he's good. In the midst of the filth and disgust, here is a just man who loves me. I take advantage of the situation to ask him why he fights. It's something that intrigues me in him, in all of them. What really drives them? Are the sacred rites of "order" and "Command" enough?

My question irritates him. I've taken him out of his noble deliberations. His answer is rote, fast, machinelike, he launches his entire demonology at me: that they are fighting so our country won't be taken over by people who defend a system that builds a wall in Berlin so the populace can't get out; the same people who in '39 supported the pact between Hitler and Stalin, the same ones who wrote panegyrics for Stalin and later for Brezhnev, who in '56 supported the Soviet Union's invasion of Hungary, who in '68 supported the Soviet Union's invasion of Prague and—incredibly—here in Santiago came to defend the Soviet embassy against the people who went there to protest the invasion; the ones who trained in Cuba, in Vietnam, in Bulgaria, and who received and were still receiving AK-47 rifles, and M-16s and FALs and RPG 7 rocket launchers . . . Didn't they catch MIR, at the very start, with something like two hundred AKs hidden in gas cylinders? Meanwhile, in Europe, they think these people are social democratic doves . . . Idiots! They'll never understand the double dealing these con artists are capable of. They just sit there sucking their thumbs! Castro fooled them already, but they didn't learn. Idiots! Because this irregular war is against Fidel Castro's Cuba. Because it's Cuba that wants to destabilize Chile and it's Cuba that sends trained men and the weapons we find in arsenals and hideouts. From Cuba and the USSR. He tells me: "Behind it all, the big Russian bear is always lying in wait . . . No, not here," he boasts, "here they're not going to do what they did in Nicaragua; in Iran, in Vietnam. No, no. Here, we're going to tear them a new asshole . . . Our freedom is at stake. And democracy?" he asks himself. "It will come, not yet, but it will come."

I tell him that such an attitude, so reactionary, is lacking in poetry. He smiles with the simplicity of the simple and literal man that he is, a smile that inspires in me a certain disdain and, at the same time, an uncertain tenderness. Then he talks to me again about the purity and freedom of the mountaintop. "If you only knew the beauty of Alto de Los Leones. A true obelisk that's 18,570 feet high. Huge walls of smooth rock, vertical cliffs of over 3,000 feet. One of them is 7,200 feet! The famous German alpinist Federico Reichert, who explored the Alps, the Caucasus, and the Andes, said in his book in 1929 that the Alto de Los Leones 'will never lose its virginity, since its inaccessible summit seems beyond the limit of all possibility.' Can you imagine? Even so, after the Italians Gabriele Boccalatte and Piero Zanetti went up in 1934, there are several of us who have reached the summit. Believe me: that's what poetry is," he tells me. "Unadulterated poetry."

But after that moment of exultation the furrowed brow returns, and the same aggrieved tone as before.

He's bored with what he does, he tells me. He's disgusted, he tells me. "My work is 'intelligence,'" he tells me. "My work is secret recordings, tracking over the course of months, photos taken from fake ambulances and false taxis, fingerprints, duly verified confessions, microphones hidden behind the plate of a power socket, recordings from a tapped phone, weapons found in secret compartments, documents that I turn into classified information . . . But, of course, the evidence is never more than the tip of the iceberg. You have to imagine the reality. But where the imagination creates, reason prunes. That's what we're here for, that's what we train for, to investigate. But here there has been bad intelligence, there's been shooting into the flock, lack of professionalism, and simple barbarity. The cruelty of wolves in a cage.

"I don't mean to say they're all tame doves. No. And I know that Mossad eliminates terrorists and, sometimes, they make mistakes, too. I know it very well. We've had instructors from Mossad in Central who spoke perfect Spanish. Smart guys, let me tell you. And the English do the same. You don't believe me? For example, in 1978, on the way to Gibraltar, I'm telling you, gunmen from SAS and MI5 murdered three terrorists from the IRA. Three. They didn't even give them a chance to surrender. Well, and then there's the United States . . . Not only in Vietnam. Later, in Libya . . . But here, there's no sense of proportion. Macha's people fight just to fight, because why not, you understand?"

I answer, quoting Violeta Parra: "Pero no es culpa del chancho . . . But it's not the pig who's at fault, it's the one who feeds it the mash."

He looks at me with a disdainful sneer on his lips.

"I know what you're thinking. . . And yes, you're right," he explains, showing the white palms of his hands. I had hurt him. "A lot of missions go straight to Macha from C-1," he says. "They skip over me because they know what I think, did you know that?" And his tone gets softer to win me over. "And Macha thinks he's the Macho of all machos, right?" Now his tone is mocking. "The little boss of that mafia only obeys macho orders and he only gives macho orders, right? He goes first into the most dangerous safe house. He wants to take risks. And you know why? To assuage his guilt. It balances things out, he figures. He ignores procedure so he can attack with few people, he's even gone into a house alone, and then he makes mistakes, like what happened when the 'Prince of Wales' got away from him. And then the ones he wants to catch or blow the whistle on get away from him, poor fucker . . . It's so he can avoid leaks, he says, to avoid accidents, because in small houses there's a big risk of friendly fire, he says, he only trusts his own people, no one else, he says, there's a mole here, someone warns the enemy; he says he had to investigate Colonel Vergara's assassination and found it would have been impossible without information from inside . . . That's what he says. I've asked him for proof and he doesn't have any. But of course, you know, they shot at him point-blank and the bullet stayed in him. Too close to the femoral to extract it. So it hurts him. So he limps a little. They could have killed him, but they didn't kill him. Friendly fire? Betrayal? We'll never know. That's it. The truth is that when it comes to Macha, one more death won't keep him up at night."

He takes his knees in his hands. He's dejected. "This shit comes from above," he tells me in a barely audible voice. "That's why no one puts a stop to it. My complaint went into a vacuum. The director wants more power, so he needs a bigger budget, so he needs to increase the danger posed by the enemy. And the boss above him, you think he's not doing exactly the same thing?"

He shakes his bald head, with its smooth, soft, and shining skin that I like to kiss when we say good-bye. He's already regretting what he's going to tell me.

And you, writer who wasn't there, does my telling you this help you see the situation, the ambiguity of that moment of mine with Flaco?

"Listen to me," he says, and he lowers his voice until it's nothing but a thread. "Listen to me well. This is a secret for you and no one else. A couple of weeks ago, Macha got the order to organize an operation to deal with an ugly situation. The order wasn't to arrest the subject, the terrorist, you understand? They were about to leave. They were in the cafeteria having sodas: Great Dane, Iris, Chico Marín, Pancha Ortiz, Indio . . . Macha didn't know who the victim was, nothing, not the slightest idea. He had a photo, an address, and an order, that's it. You know how these things are done. And he was listening, surrounded by his people, and he was quiet as always.

"I asked him: 'And you, Macha, what do you think of having to carry out an order like this?' There was a silence. 'Answer me,' I pressed him. Macha leaned back, balancing calmly on the back legs of the chair. After a long pause he looked me straight in the eyes and said:

"'Flaco, tell me, old man: What does one more fuck matter to an old whore?'

"Everyone started laughing. But I didn't laugh at all.

"And he said: 'Let me be the one to live with this, old man. Other people can't do it. They have a future to think of. Me, I've got nothing.'"

Flaco rolled his eyes upward and he laughed, then, a cold laugh.

Macha is a murderer. That's what Flaco is telling me. So that's what it was that drew me to him. He was a killer. I thought: Flaco envies him. Because Macha is an animal with no conscience. He's more primitive and pure.

And then he came out with it. Just like that, no preamble: "I'm separated," he told me. "I left my wife." And I, like an idiot, thought he was pulling my leg, and I laughed.

"Don't laugh," he reproached me. "There are two little girls and a woman who are suffering, their hearts are broken. Have some respect for that, at least."

"I'm sorry," I say. "I'm sorry, Flaco, it's just . . ."

"They cry when I come to pick them up, they want to stay at their mother's house . . . She's brainwashed them," he goes on telling me. "They used to love me so much. It's unthinkable that they don't . . . I only see them two hours a week, and sometimes not even that. They don't feel like it, they say, or they have homework. They can't forgive me. Should I go to court? She tells me: You're the one who left home, aren't you? My lawyer tells me that this gets fixed with money. But, where the fuck do I get the money? From a promotion; it's the only way."

He sighed sorrowfully . . . Then I embraced him and cradled him in my arms. In that moment, there on the black leather sofa, I truly loved him and I thought I would live with him, and I imagined myself in his Volvo coming back from the beach at El Quisco, and then I saw myself on a mountaintop, and we were laughing and happy in that pure, cold air he loved so much. No more Saturdays and Sundays alone, I thought. We kissed softly, intensely. The tears slid down my cheeks. And the tears that I imagined welling in his eyes, if they existed, never fell.

FORTY-EIGHT

Pancha Ortiz was putting on makeup. She barely greeted me. With the lipstick still in her hand, she pursed her lips in the mirror, spreading out the color until it was even. Her lips were much fuller and more sensuous than I had noticed before. Her black blouse, open, left bare that fissure that men like so much, and part of those insolent breasts of hers. She took a little bottle of perfume from her purse and she sprayed her neck and I watched her, turning her breasts, contemplating herself in the mirror as if she were alone in the bathroom. Alone, or seducing a man. She said good-bye to me, kissing the air by my cheek, and off she went, leaving me confused in a cloud of perfume. Only then did I realize what was causing my confusion: the perfume was Christian Dior and the bottle was the same as the ones Flaco always gave me.

I went out, walking quickly to the darkened lot. I got there in time to see her get into her Nissan. The offices upstairs where Flaco worked were dark. I looked for his silver Volvo, but I didn't see it. I took a taxi and tried to follow the Nissan, but I lost it after three blocks. When I went into my apartment in the Tajamar Towers I went straight to the bathroom. There was a sharp pain gouging my insides.

"Why are you in such a bad mood?" Flaco says the next day. "Chewing your fingernail is not an answer," he said, with laughing eyes. A few days later, very early, I saw him kissing Pancha in his silver Volvo. They came in together and he was looking at her. I swore I would break it off with him. And I waited for him. The fucker didn't even come to my apartment that afternoon.

Then, without thinking about it, the next afternoon I went up to the second floor and presented myself in his office. He ushered me in with that friendly, affectionate manner of his. I sat in the chair facing his desk. As soon as I had him in front of me and felt him looking into my eyes with that faint, shy smile, I despaired. I imagined him looking at Pancha that way and it drove me crazy. Tears came to my eyes, I brought my hands to my face; I fell, tears streaming, from the chair onto the rough carpet that covered the floor of his office. I lay there face down and he came over, murmuring in my ear, telling me the same things, I was sure, that he said to Pancha. He tried to kiss me, to get me to turn my face to him, but I wouldn't let him, I wouldn't, not for anything.

Suddenly I felt his strong fingers on my spine; he pressed on it and it cracked, and he pushed on it again, higher up, and it cracked again. They were the same hands, I thought once again, that could kill me with a single, silent blow. It was still a reassuring feeling. I got up and he kissed me on the mouth. I returned the kiss, but when I felt his hand moving up my thigh I pushed him away and left his office.

He didn't call me. I waited, though. I spent so many afternoons, and entire Saturdays and Sundays, in my apartment in case he showed up. Weeks went by.

Her eyes full of excitement, Anita told me about Leila, her friend from school, whose mother had a room full of doors and those doors were closets where she kept all her clothes. It was one of those languid Saturdays during that time of my life. Anita, if she was with me, could turn those days into something wonderful or disastrous. Because if she had a tantrum for some reason, there was nothing I could do except bring her back to my mother's house.

Leila's mother, she told me that day, is the Moroccan ambassador. And Leila, when her mother isn't home, takes some little keys out from where she hides them among her gloves, and with those little keys she opens the safe. And the safe is in another closet, the shoe closet. Leila's mother has thousands of shoes, and she keeps them in their boxes and behind the boxes is the safe. Anita helped her move the shoeboxes very carefully. Leila opened the safe and took out mountains of rings, necklaces, bracelets, and earrings that belonged to her mother. "It's like a princess's treasure," she says smiling, her face radiant with happiness.

"Like a chest in Ali Baba's cave," I say.

"Yes," she says. "And Leila," she says, "puts them on and looks at herself in the mirror." And with her hands she draws pictures in the air of those jewels that shone on her friend's hands, her neck, her ears. "She looks like a real live princess, Mama!" Sometimes, she let Anita wear a pearl necklace.

"Mama," she said, filled with enthusiasm. "When are you going to show me your rings and earrings and bracelets?" I looked at her, surprised. "Because you have all those things hidden away, too. And I know where." She ran to my room, opened the closet, and showed me the little safe built into the wall. "Come on, open it, Mama. I want to see your rings and bracelets." I put my hands on her shoulders. I thought about the darkness of my CZ at rest. As always, minutes before Anita arrived, I had put it in there with my documents from Central.

"No," I told her. "I don't have jewels, Anita."

"But Mama, what do you keep in there, then?"

"Letters," I told her. "Documents."

"Love letters, Mama? Letters my father wrote to you?" And Anita looked at me with rounded eyes. "Let me see them, Mama. Mama . . . Let me see what my dad's handwriting looked like."

"Another time, Anita."

"Mama, please!" I closed the closet door.

The night when Flaco finally came, without warning as always, I had my plan ready and decided on: I would flirt like a crazy person and then, nothing. So he'd be left high and dry, so he'd be left longing for me. He brought a bottle of Absolut vodka and a little jar of Iranian beluga caviar. He was one of those who said the Russians couldn't even get vodka right; only guns. Hence the Absolut. We sat down, and by the second Swedish vodka we were kissing and kissing, and he was frantically pulling off my shirt and jeans and everything else. I couldn't bear the idea that Pancha had slept with him. How was it possible, when I was so much better than her?

I was lying on the sofa, on my back. He knelt down in front of me. He placed me there, and I knew what for. And I let him do it. And I opened myself and turned my hips in search of his thirsty tongue. And he sunk his fingers in. And I touched my breasts. And he returned with an insatiable tongue. I brought my hands down. And suddenly the rhythm of my body seized hold of me, it broke away from my control and I came, I came suddenly and completely. Afterward I started to cry.

He doesn't understand. He wants me to stop crying. Why? Why doesn't he let me cry if I want to cry? He gets mad. He won't leave me alone. There's nothing to explain. I give up. I say to him: "Why do you have this power over me? You do something like that to me, and I come like an idiot. That power I've given you is humiliating." He starts to laugh, and he pulls my hair away from my face.

"You're pretty," he tells me, after inspecting me with his playful, tender, ironic gaze. That's it: You're pretty. That damned son of a bitch knows that when he gives me that look, I melt.

"I know," I tell him. "I'm going to find another man who will make me forget about you."

He says: "You'll wish the sex was as good with him as it is with me."

I tell him: "I'm the one who knows how to fuck, I'll teach him everything." He laughs. "Also, as you know, he'll be rich," I tell him. "He'll have tons of cash." He laughs less loudly, now. I say: "There comes a time when a man's money becomes almost the only thing that matters to a woman." He's not laughing anymore.

FORTY-NINE

A week later Flaco Artaza had already been promoted. The positive evaluation after the "elimination"—the term they used—of the Spartan and Max got him that. Two very hard blows for Red Ax. They took him out of Central and installed him in Military Intelligence. It was what he wanted. Flaco left Central behind and he vanished from my life without even saying good-bye. Do I need to tell you how I felt?

But after about four months he called and invited me to lunch. I got into my red Nissan in the parking lot, and when I started it up, I saw . . . What? But, it's Macha! He was a few yards away from me walking with his slight limp, without his Ray Bans and escorted by six armed men. Two of them carried long guns. They stopped next to a black Chevrolet four-door with tinted windows that I'd never seen in the parking lot before.

The one in front went over to Macha and spoke to him. He was a dark, thick guy with a short moustache. I had my windows rolled up so I couldn't hear, but I saw. What I mean is, I saw Macha put his hand behind him, to his belt under his dark leather jacket. I watched with my own eyes as he handed over his CZ. He did it without any ceremony, like a person returning the keys to a car. Then I saw how he let himself be cuffed, his hands tamely behind him, putting up no resistance. The black Chevrolet with tinted windows sped off with him in it, followed by a Peugeot fake taxi.

Flaco took me that day to eat oysters at Azócar. I arrived still trembling a bit from what I had just seen, but I didn't want to mention it to him. We laughed, we had a good time in that old

Chilean mansion illuminated by a skylight above us. The oysters were marvelous. When, after several glasses of sauvignon blanc, I dared to tell him what I had seen, how they'd taken Macha away in handcuffs, he wrinkled his forehead and assured me that he wasn't up-to-date on counterintelligence matters, that his new job had to do with strictly military intelligence in neighboring countries; countries to the north, he added with a smile, to make it very clear to me. And he changed the subject.

We kissed in his Volvo, and he invited me on a trip, a short and intense trip, he said, just three or four days in the pure mountain air. He told me about a unique place in the mountains close to Torres del Paine, full of stalactites; a place no one has photographed yet, he told me, ice sculptures carved by the wind. I ached to go. Even so, I told him no. Looking at me with sad, languid eyes, he told me that I was very pretty, that we deserved a real good-bye. I told him that too much time had passed for me to care about being pretty, that when I was younger, sure, I would have been grateful for the flattery. Lies. I didn't want to suffer, I told him, I begged him. That trip, when it ended, would leave me worse off than before. And that was true. He insisted, but I didn't give in.

He went with me to my apartment. I didn't invite him in. The slam of the door when it closed. I jumped. As if an enormous window had shattered. I closed my eyes. When I heard his footsteps moving away down the hall, I burst out crying. For months and months I waited for his call. It never came.

FIFTY

I'm feeling tired . . . You know, during that time it never even crossed my mind that my life would end like this, alone in a Swedish home, or even abroad . . . One of my students helped me out of pure kindness. There are good people out there, too. She got in touch with Teruca's mother and gave her my message: I was being followed and had decided to go into exile for safety reasons. It wasn't the bravest thing to do, but what the hell, the decision was made. She would pass along the information to her daughter Teruca, who would communicate it to my brothers and sisters, the ones who were left, and so a curtain of smoke would extend over me. And while that was happening in Chile, I was on a plane flying out of there.

As soon as I got to Stockholm, I got a job at Berlitz. Every morning I dropped my daughter off at school, took the subway, got off at the Gamla Stan stop, emerged onto Gamla Brogatan, and in a few steps I reached number 29. That was my routine for years. I taught French to advanced students and studied Swedish on a grant. They helped me a lot here. It's not true that the Swedish are cold. I'm thinking of my friend Agda Lindstrom, who took us into her house for our entire first month here. She was a lawyer. She was killed. Car accident, a year and a half after I arrived. Horrible. She was a thin woman, not very tall, with very white skin, dark brown hair, and gray eyes. She was an older sister to me. Frank, direct, serious, at first she seemed a little distant to me, perhaps a bit hard. But after a few days, I discovered a person of exceptional generosity and gentleness. She knew only as much about me as I wanted her to. She introduced me to her friends, all of them professionals. I talked to them in French. After two years, I had learned Swedish. Of course, I'll never have Anita's accent.

I remember my first walk along the docks. Agda wanted to come with me, but I wanted to go alone: the calm of that ocean, the clearness of the air, the sharp colors, the rolling ships. I walked to the bridge that crosses to Skeppsholmen and the beauty stopped me short. My nose touched the uncertainty of my future, as if uncertainty were a wind carrying the scent of the sea and pushing me onward. I wanted to keep that island for later. I saw a mother running a brush through her daughter's hair. With what care, with what sensitive slowness, what infinite love. And the little girl's long, blond, almost white hair takes on life and brilliance. Did my mother ever brush my hair like that?

I arrived in September, and the weather was often good. At lunchtime I took my sandwich to Kungsträdgården Square, and the yellow leaves from the oaks softly grazed my hair or my shoulders as they fell. I picked them up from the grass and they were damp, and I sat looking at their veins, persisting still.

FIFTY-ONE

Roberto was six years younger than me. A tall, handsome Brazilian. We met in the Berlitz cafeteria. It turned out he was friends with Agda and that made things easier. You know, I actually can't remember when we started dating. How odd. That says something. I remember his first gift to me: an amber perfume. Of course, I'd already told him about how that mysterious substance had fascinated me since I was a little girl and how it was linked in my imagination to the Vikings and the Baltic Sea. Later, he would give me a beautiful necklace with stones that shone with an internal light. Roberto . . . with his Portuguese-accented Spanish, so full of tender *eñes*, such soft, kind sounds.

I brought him to the Kungsträdgården and talked to him about the yellow oak leaves that kept me company during the solitary lunches of my first weeks, and how they healed me when, as they fell, they brushed against me for a moment. Now those leaves were light, luminous green, and in the grass wild blue and white anemones were growing. His voice warmed and protected me. What more could I want than to love him and for him to love me? We liked to walk, to lose ourselves in the streets, talking and laughing. I like men with a sense of humor. I think it's more important than looks, you know? When you have a man you can laugh with, the doors open by themselves.

And with Roberto I crossed over the Skeppsholmen Bridge for the first time, clattering over its wooden slats. That's where we first kissed. We were walking along, our arms around each other, toward the Moderna Museet. Roberto was talking to me, and he would suddenly interrupt himself to kiss me. He was telling me about what we were going to see, about the brilliance of the *Brillo Boxes* by Warhol and about the incredible power of the color orange in his electric chair; no one, he said, before Warhol had ever seen an orange like that, because the chair's mossy green made it into the orangest of all oranges; and about the feeling of movement in the face of Picasso's *La Femme à la collerette bleue*, about his drawings of birds—a running ostrich, a truly chickenlike chicken, a hawkish hawk, an unforgettable dove in flight—and about Rauschenberg's embalmed goat encircled by a tire, its look of primitive masculinity broken by civilization, the symbol of sexuality and tragedy, of Dionysus, god of abandon, transformed by the tire into a victim, the sense of unease conveyed by its suppressed instincts and the nostalgia of its paint-spattered head. We took a long time, because he would be in the middle of telling me about Picasso's unforgettable dove in flight or the tragedy of Rauschenberg's billy goat in modernity, and we would stop again and again to kiss with Dionysian passion. When we finally got to the museum it was already closed. We made do with more kisses, running and embracing and running again among the happy, colored sculptures, those round, restless, powerful women by Niki de Saint Phalle. I think they've removed them now. Someone told me that. I hope it's not true.

For months, we devoted a weekend each to the archipelago's islands. It was a wonderful period, that time with Roberto. He took me dancing, and I've never seen anyone dance like him. He danced to every rhythm with a spontaneous joy, graceful and contagious, that always made me want to dance with him. He danced standing up sometimes, almost without moving; he danced sitting down, moving only his head and shoulders. But the fact that he was younger than me made me nervous. Of course, he couldn't understand my past. I couldn't either, to tell the truth. He was a man with taut skin, mulatto. He loved me.

FIFTY-TWO

There were plenty of exiled Latin Americans in Stockholm, all victims of the horror. I made friends with some of them. Mireya, a survivor of the Tupas's struggle in Uruguay; Claudia, whose husband had been taken prisoner and never heard from again; and María Verónica. All three of them had been taken prisoner and gone through hell. We gave a wide berth to that subject. Instead we talked about our children, our latest pap tests, and Mireya talked about her menopause, which had started recently. The rest of us listened to her and tried to mask our dread. And, of course, we discussed politics. One approach, we said, was to join in the ecumenism of the human rights movement. The battle of stamped papers, of lawyers and their endless court cases.

"What other weapon do we have besides moral denunciation?" María Verónica said. And, turning red from passion mixed with a half-ashamed laughter that was very particular to her: "We were going to start the revolution in the only way possible: with blood and firing squads. You all, military bastards, got ahead of us and screwed us over. Now you have to pay. Because the blood you spilled, your cruelty, there's no pardon for that."

And Claudia, interrupting her laughter and looking at her seriously: "But no, it's not like that. We would never have done to them what they did to us. Anyway, for me it's not just about a weapon, it's about something higher: truth, justice."

Mireya objected, folding her hands together: "The price is to break with Che's example. His sacrifice doesn't die. Neither does Santucho's, Inti Peredo's, Miguel Enríquez's, so many others . . ."

And Claudia, frowning: "I don't think all that pain has made the poor any less poor. It hurts me, but the truth is I can't believe it anymore."

And Mireya: "For shit's sake! His gesture lives on; it lives on because of its moral generosity."

And Mario, a history professor who had been beaten to a pulp in ESMA: "Vos, Claudia, you want us to subscribe to the cause of universal and ahistorical human rights, no? And for real, not as a tactical position. Great! Who am I to argue . . . The problem is, you see, they are situated beyond the class struggle, in a metaphysical beyond. It's idealistic claptrap, my love . . ." And he put his hand to his black beard sprinkled with white. "Look, the first case of interrogation under threat that's recorded in literature is in Homer, in the *Iliad* itself. Don't believe me? It's a Trojan spy named Dolon. Ulysses and Diomedes capture him. Once Dolon has talked and is begging for mercy, Diomedes breaks his promise and thwack! *Dolon's head rolled in the dust as he was still speaking,* says Homer. That motherfucker, man, that's how power is, it's ruthless."

Still, Mario's wasn't the tendency that prevailed among us, but rather Claudia's more peaceful leanings. The truth is I listened to those conversations with very little interest. I was in love, and my love filled my days and nights.

News started to reach us about the demonstrations at Saint Nicholas Church in Leipzig, Mondays at five in the evening, processions of people with candles and banners: *Ohne Gewalt,* No Violence. Some of them dared to cross over from Germany into Hungary. No one shot at them. Then many more crossed over. Soon afterward, the Berlin Wall crumbled; I watched on TV as they pulled down a statue of Lenin. It collapsed like a big sandcastle—a grand castle that, like Kafka's, we never managed to reach. The truth is, we knew little about it. The world I'd been born into and grown up in just disappeared, that Cold War that divided Berlin in two and the planet in two, that damned war of empires that reached all the way to the ass of the world, all the way to Chile, and infected us and wounded us to the core. For someone like me, that conflict and that war *was* the world, not just one among many possible worlds, not one that could eventually disappear and be replaced by another, with other conflicts and other wars. It's hard to understand what that meant for people like me. It's incomprehensible. Everything I'm telling you is incomprehensible. I'm telling you about a way of life that is gone. I'm talking to you from a junkyard of broken, illusory, lost ideals.

You know what? All of us, on both sides, lived inside a language that's been forgotten now. The inscriptions are still there, but now no one knows how to read them. The truth is, those of us who remain from that time don't know how to recognize ourselves anymore. Though we claim otherwise . . . People like me don't exist anymore. Do I believe that? Am I contradicting myself? There will always be young people like the ones we were. Maybe. There will always be those who fight for equality. Yes. And against the Great Whore. Certainly. There will always be lives that death will transform into symbols of hope for humankind.

But our rhetoric, the language that was home to our utopia, the place of our no-place: it has ended. Because that rhetoric and the liturgy of the mountain—with its walks, its bonfires and guitars— that addictive language, I'm telling you, was the forge for our brotherhood of clandestine strangers who only knew—or should know— each other's aliases but who were prepared to die together the very next day. That's what people today don't believe in: the inner nobility that made our souls quiver as we felt ourselves to be among the vanguard, the chosen ones.

During that period, Claudia invited me to meet a boy, a Chilean college student who was coming from Cuba to study for a few months. (Who today could imagine the dream Cuba embodied for us back then?) "His name is Francisco," she told me. "His mother belonged to Red Ax, and he was raised in a home with a group of children whose parents had entered Chile clandestinely to join in the struggle." Claudia didn't know anything about that practice.

"It was a safety measure," I explain to her. "It helped to avoid moral extortion." She opens her eyes wide. And suddenly my hands are trembling and I shout at her: "It was indispensable! How else could they do it?! Don't you see? What world of little angels did you live in, you nitwit?" Claudia looks at me and falls silent.

"I'm sorry," she says, "I'm sorry." I say nothing, of course, about how I should have sent Anita to that home for combatants' children in Havana and I never did. I say nothing, of course, about the price I paid for it.

"The kid," says Claudia, hurt, "holds a grudge against his mother. He has these marvelous dark eyes, let me tell you. He understands her, he says, but he still doesn't want to see her again. He understands perfectly, he says, but at the same time he can't accept what she did. He's tried and tried again, but he just can't, he says. She wasn't my mother, he says, and now she can never become my mother. That's what she doesn't understand; she thinks she can, now. She says she needs me now, that at least she could be a kind of aunt. But that's impossible, too, he says, because she's not my aunt, she's the mother I never had, he says. For me, it's better not to see her. That's what he says."

Claudia asks me, as a Chilean, to talk to the boy, she wants me to tell him about our struggle, try to explain it to him, try to reconcile him with his mother. Could this Francisco be Teruca's son? I didn't want to meet that boy, I looked for any excuse not to meet with him. I didn't want to see his face. I was afraid. I wonder what ever became of him?

Claudia called me to cancel a lunch date. "Something came up last minute," was her excuse. "Let's get together next week," she said. "I'll call you to set a time." She never called. I called her, and she never answered. The same happened a few weeks later with Mireya. I went out for coffee with Mario. He was very nice. He said he would call me and he never did. It must have been around then, I think, when the rumors started about me, and people started to edge me out. I could never find out how much they knew or what exactly the rumors were. It didn't matter much to me. I was, finally, a free and happy woman. Roberto still loved with me and he got along well with Anita. That was enough for me.

FIFTY-THREE

Out of pure nosiness I find an envelope in her desk and my heart skips a beat. Nosiness? No. The truth is that she's been a different person for some time now. She is distant. I'd like to ask her: Why did you forget how to hug me? At what moment did my body become foreign to you? I want to put my arms around her, but I don't dare. Not like before, at least. She seems so indifferent.

And I know that handwriting. How could I not! It's Rodrigo's. That's how I find out that, after all these years, he's found my daughter and now he exchanges letters with her. I don't like it at all. Anita, under pressure from my questions, admits that she plans to go to Chile and live with her father. Just for a while, she tells me when she sees how my face falls in sorrow. I say a few silly things in an effort to dissuade her: education in Sweden is so much better, she's better off graduating here . . . She says she's leaving the following week: "My dad sent me the ticket." She says it so casually, as if her dad had always been her dad. I'm struck by her innocence. I hug her, barely holding back the flood of tears, and I tell her that I will always want the best for her and that she should live wherever she will be happiest. I pull her to me in a long, tight, terrible embrace, which I cut short suddenly to run to my room. I throw myself onto the bed, the feather pillow in my mouth. If only my rough sobs could suffocate me.

I break down. I have to learn how to live all over again. Without Anita. With this sadness. She calls me on the phone the day after she gets to Santiago. She's delighted. Her father has a house with a giant yard, he works as a real estate agent, his wife is charming, so are her brothers and sisters. "Hello, hello. Hello! Hello, Mom, are you there?" I can't talk. If I open my mouth I'll burst into tears.

Nostalgia gnaws at me. In the morning as I make breakfast, I can almost see her sitting at the table, eating her muesli with honey and cold milk, her hair falling forward over her sleepy face. In the afternoon, after work, I find myself going through photo albums, postcards, notebooks, school report cards. When I used to come home from work, she would run to me and hang around my neck before I even got my coat off, and she would press her warm little face against mine, cold from the wind and snow outside. Like before, it's hard for me to get out of bed. It's too much. I try to go on sleeping, but I can't do that either. Only silence awaits me, and in the evenings the same silence when I come home.

I think about my parents. All the times they must have been waiting for a letter from me . . . I write them rarely, if ever, to tell the truth. I don't want to. I'm not interested in reading their letters, either. There are envelopes I don't open for weeks. I imagine Anita peering at an envelope from me, full of distrust. I think: Maybe she'd rather not open it. In fact, she doesn't answer my letters. I think: How does she get along with Rodrigo? That sudden friendship that snatched her away from me fills me with rage. I don't like it. She looks like her father, her nose, her slender figure, her slightly curved legs, her unsettling smile, her tranquil eyes. Incestuous images come into my mind. My therapist is interested in those. She turns them around: it's me I'm imagining there with my own father. They are explanations. Understanding isn't enough to exorcise the ghost. Anita, she's the one who matters to me. And Anita isn't with me. She left me, just as her father did when as she was beginning to grow in my belly. I never could have imagined this. I started to love her right from that moment. He didn't. He never even wanted to meet her. Until now, until this sudden whim. It's not fair. My soul is torn away along with her.

When I dream about her—and now that happens a lot—she's always a little girl and we're in Stockholm. She never appears in my dreams as the woman she is now, always as she used to be. I wake up: Could it be true? I look into her room. Everything just as it was: the same bedspread, the curtains, the books, the clothes in her closet, her CDs. Her photos, photos of her as a little girl, cause me pain. She's the same little girl who visits me when I sleep. I try to convince myself that the little girl in those photos doesn't exist anymore, she's changed and it couldn't be any other way, and she'll never again be the person she was before. I have to resign myself to this new person. I put the photos away. I don't want to suffer. I put them all away except for one. It shows us here in Stockholm with a ship in the background, and we look so happy. So much time ahead for the two of us. Like never before, like never again. I'm suffering a lot, I say to myself. I try to forget her and I can't. Can a mother hate a daughter? I catch myself starting to hate her, and I'm horrified.

And if I dared to ask her: Are you still my daughter? What would happen if I asked her that over the phone? I have to accept her as she is. But it would be easier if she hadn't changed so much. I can't stop thinking that the real Anita is someone else, the one I lost, the one she let escape.

FIFTY-FOUR

And she's not here. The one who is with me is Roberto. Without him, I don't know what would have become of me. His accent caresses and numbs me. I don't want to make love, I want his voice to pacify me, I want him to sing into my ear: *Bésame, bésame mucho / como si fuera esta noche / la última vez* . . . And he smiles and starts to sing softly, almost in a whisper, and it lulls me to sleep. *Que tengo miedo a perderte, / perderte después.*

Could someone else accept me if I couldn't accept myself? "You're too suspicious, too susceptible," Roberto tells me. It's true. I know it. Thanks to therapy I understand it all. But understanding isn't enough. My therapist asks me if I think of myself as the daughter of a good-looking and absent father and an intelligent professional who wanted me to be the beauty she wasn't. My psychiatrist likes to ask questions. Too many. From his chair behind me, while I'm below, on the divan. Him above and me below. And he asks his questions in a neutral voice, as if it wasn't him I'm answering but God. I'm just a case. It isn't a conversation. He's giving me his professional services. That's what he's paid for, obviously, to listen to me.

He asks me if I feel as though my mother has failed me, if I feel guilty for not having been able to keep my father from leaving home and marrying someone else, if I feel resentful toward my father, if that's why I'm attracted to rough men and their guns . . . I let him ask. Even here in Stockholm you have to put up with those banalities. In exchange for a prescription for sleeping pills and antidepressants that otherwise I couldn't get in the pharmacy. My mind wanders somewhere else.

He tells me that "terrorists" suffer from "free-floating anxiety," that they suffer from "personality disorders," that in order to stabilize the "ego" they join the movement, that the collective cause becomes greater than the "ego." Now I'm the one who asks: And?

And Roberto is there. He goes on being there, he goes on taking me to visit islands on the weekends. One day he takes me to Gotland. A forty-minute flight. From there we go to Faro. Roberto wants me to see the stones with etchings left by the Vikings in Bunge. "You always loved the Vikings, right?" But I'm more impressed by the beauty of some cows with clean and shining hides, an old windmill made of stone, and, of course, the rocks. We walk along a pebble beach, and there are those strange, dark, rock sculptures rising up, chiseled by millinery winds. The sea is dark gray or very white. I'm startled by a ship's siren. They have the tonalities, I think, the spiritual atmosphere of *Persona*. It occurs to me that we should find out where Bergman's house is and go past it. But I discard the idea before suggesting it to Roberto, which is for the best. He would have been capable of ringing the doorbell once we got there.

"I know I'm not capable of inspiring love," I tell him out of the blue, and I lean against one of those bleak, forsaken rocks. "I always know I'll be abandoned and betrayed, it's what I deserve." But he caresses me in silence, he wants to redeem me. He thinks his love can save me. "I'd like to believe you," I tell him.

I know I'm lying to myself. I want someone to forgive me and love me unconditionally, exactly as I was and am and will be. But I'm afraid. I defend myself. I don't want to tie myself down. I care for Roberto a lot. I need him, but maybe because of that, it's difficult for me. I defend myself before the fact, in anticipation of rejection. I demand too much, I'm insatiable, I know it. I demand unconditional and absolute love in exchange for nothing. First I want to be loved just because. Then I can start to love. I want to put my misery on display and to be loved for it before anything else. I don't just want to be loved. Someone also has to pay, someone has to suffer for me, and it will fall to whoever wants to love me now. It falls, though it's not what I want, to Roberto.

I make the one who loves me submit to tests because I don't want to believe in his love, and I give little in return because I'm afraid of disappointing him, of boring him. I'm so insecure. I hide inside myself.

Roberto talks to me. He tells me I'm not well, he tells me I'm sick, I need to take my pills. Roberto is so naive sometimes . . . I ask him: "How do you know?" He says from my face. "And what is my face like?" I ask. He tells me I'm not going to like the answer. I insist. He says I look ravaged, sometimes: my jaw droops, I breathe roughly through my mouth, my gaze is emptied out as though I'm looking at the void. I say: "The void? Death?" I start to laugh and I look at myself in the mirror. I don't see what he sees. I'm skinny and gaunt with dark bags under my eyes; ugly, in a word. "That's what you're seeing," I tell him, "I'm ugly. That's my 'illness' you're so worried about." He denies it.

But I'm afraid that he won't find me attractive and I'll be punished. Roberto is attractive to other women. I realize that. More than to be with him myself, what I want is for him not to be with anyone else. Jealousy consumes me at the mere thought of him with another woman. So I punish him. He doesn't love me enough. That's how I feel and I tell him so. I would have liked for him to love me until my jealousy and my fears dissipated. We fought and made up. Obviously. Who doesn't?

One wretched night, out of pure rage, before he gets into bed, I dump a glass of water on Roberto's side. When he feels the cold wetness he's furious. I am forcing him to sleep on the sofa. From then on the fights happen more and more often. We can go weeks without speaking. And I manage it: Roberto, the only person I have, gets tired and leaves me. I am once again what I am . . .

I try to let my work as a teacher at Berlitz save me. Once again I walk under the oak trees at the Kungsträdgården. The virgin snow on the naked oaks. I need to be accepted by a human being so that I can be a human being. Some afternoons, Agda's old friends invite me out.

They're very kind, they take me to see a play at the Dramaten or the Folkoperan and out to eat, and I don't know why it tends to happen on Thursday and we eat crepes with blueberry jam and they give me good cognac to drink. I go back to my apartment seeing double.

This dull November light in Stockholm, these four hours of light. *And my past returns. And my sin is always before me.* And seen from the vantage of this wind and this fog, my past is incomprehensible to me. Pills? You want a list of the sleeping pills and antidepressants that I toss back every day? I'm not going to deny that I drank more vodka than I should, I drank Absolut vodka every day, and plenty of it, but I wasn't an alcoholic. Not that.

Suddenly, a burst of energy, and I go out shopping. At H&M I go into the dressing room and try on lots of clothes. Everything looks fantastic. At the register I have to put one dress back because my card has reached its limit. Then I go by a music store. I buy the *Nocturnes.* Piano by Arrau. "For when the sorrow comes back," I say to myself. But what's that? Georges Brassens: *La Mauvaise Réputation.* I leave with those two CDs. I drop the bags in the hall of my apartment and I run to put on Brassens. The eleventh song: *Il suffit de passer le pont, / C'est tout de suite l'aventure! / . . . Je n'ai jamais aimé que vous.* Giuseppe making omelets in his little kitchen. He stops all of a sudden and raises his glass of champagne with a mischievous smile. I sigh. I slowly gather up the bags from the floor and I start to try on one of the new dresses. No. Now I don't like it. I try on more. In the mirror in my room nothing looks good on me anymore. I was tricked by the lights in the dressing room, I tell myself. I look terrible. I yawn. I should go return all this. I'm exhausted. Tomorrow, I think, and I fall into bed.

I force myself to walk under the oaks at the Kungsträdgården. On their naked branches, a layer of snow has hardened. A piece of it comes off and falls with indifferent misfortune. February. The little light there is shines from underneath. There is beauty in those oaks lit up from below, and in the sea that in ancient times was a forest, and in those bees, the same as the ones today, that millions of years ago were trapped in amber. It's not that I don't perceive it. It's that the beauty doesn't move me anymore. I know it's there and it should touch my senses, but my senses are dulled now.

This malaise is like that, it's suffocating. There's no place for that ironic distance behind which elegant young men like to hide their fear of feeling with their guts. Here there are pathos and poor taste. It's *the brittle feeling of being made of glass*, of *the body being dragged on and on.* The feeling of disquiet eats away at me. And at night, the nightmares. And when I wake up shouting and sweating it's because I feel Ronco's breath in my ear. Then, insomnia. I see the color of the crows Van Gogh painted soaring over a wheat field, *that truffle black* . . . Then the black claw returns inside my stomach and the abyss sucks me in and old scenes of horror pile on top of me like black cars trying to run me over. And those old Furies return, as if those black events, so vivid, were happening now. The smell of fear returns: strong and sharp, decayed, old, repugnant. Voices come back to me, slamming doors. "We've got another 'package,'" shouts Rat, and Ronco laughs. And I see once again, as if it were happening that very moment, the gag, the foam . . . I can't stop my heart from pounding, and I sweat and sweat unable to turn away from what I don't want to see. I know, I'm in Stockholm, and I curse its skies. I'm the mangy bitch that no one wants as a friend, I tell myself. And in spite of everything, I'm proud. I've already told you: I contradict myself.

Why didn't I run from those claws? Why not one day before I gave Rafa up? The passage of time can't undo what I did. I'm the one I want to erase from my life. Forgive myself? How could I give myself something I don't deserve? *Unhappiness has been my god. I have lain down in the mud and dried myself off in the crime-infested air.* I distrust, and my distrust becomes acid in my guts. Don't I hate all things noble? Is my spite a lying form of consolation? Because now it hurts my eyes, the light that radiates from a good man like Roberto.

Then, do I still admire Canelo? Like every innocent, he didn't know he was innocent. Is it because he's the sacrifice? As if by defying death, he could kill it. His freedom made destiny. *Who speaks of victory? To endure is all.* And there were women who went through the same terrifying place I did, or even worse places, which of course existed. Today those women prevail with rocklike dignity because they remained in one piece. When they came out, testifying gave them a purpose. That was the case for my friend Claudia, to mention just one. And there were many others like her.

An instant, every instant of the present, is a scar made into a window. Here in Stockholm, I still sometimes wish someone would shoot me. It could happen. Maybe they're looking for me, to kill me. But no, no one is looking for me. I reproach myself. Then I feel an urge to kill someone, some stranger passing by me in the street. So I would matter to someone. If no one is to love me, may someone at least fear me. Frustration, I tell myself, I contradict myself. This lasts.

You don't understand this Lorena you're listening to: I drink from the chalice of my own abjection. It's sweet and bitter, my chalice, like a vice. A long resentment can protect and sustain. It can become a religion. Ha! I want to laugh, but the laughter dries up in my mouth.

I have to leave behind this thing that is freezing me. How? I will, but not yet. I will. Am I doing it already? Suffering has not purified me. I'm a prisoner. I'm a wretch. If only I could drag myself to the wretched door. If I could turn the lock on that door. If I could. If I had the key. I would have had to reach the door. There would have to be a door. But I survived. I became a worm, but I survived. I'm alive. I've become shit, I'm dying, but I'm still alive here in Stockholm.

FIFTY-FIVE

I've come only to see him, as a surprise. And as soon as I get to Charles de Gaulle Airport, my spirits rise. I call Giuseppe that same afternoon. I've kept his number for years and years, written in my personal code. I don't dare leave my name on the machine. What if he's not in Paris? The next day I call again. A sleepy voice that could belong to anyone answers. Suddenly, I recognize my name in his shout. He can't believe it's real, he tells me. He's tried to find me so many times, he tells me. We agree to meet at five in a café.

I got there early so I could see him go in. I waited for him, trembling, on the other side of the street. I recognized him and my heart gave a jump. His hair was completely white, but he still had a thick mane. He walked with resolve, but a little bent over. He sat at a table close to the entrance. I kept watching through the window. In no time, a bottle of white wine and two glasses appeared on the table. He had arrived early.

I decided to stay in the street a while. I was sweating. I remembered his smile as he opened the door to his apartment: *Voilà la plus belle!* I went into the bathroom of another café nearby, and I spritzed myself with perfume, touched up my makeup, and brushed my hair. I crossed the threshold five minutes late. My heart was in my throat. I stood for a moment with the revolving door behind me. Was I waiting for him to give a shout and run to embrace me? I passed slowly among the tables and I recognized his same cologne as always: Giuseppe, I thought. But I said nothing to him, and I sat down at the end of the bar on a stool. I ordered a whiskey. Then I looked at him: his elegant nose now held up a pair of glasses, and his face was a full net of wrinkles. Giuseppe was still a very attractive man. The glass shook in my hand. I started to feel the same fire as before, *l'antica fiamma.*

He picked up his glass and took a long sip. He smoothed his hair with his hand. He turned his white head, and his eyes took in the tables. They finally landed on the bar. There were three men and me sitting on the stools. I felt his eyes scanning my body. He lowered them and took another sip of wine. That was it.

As I passed very slowly by his table, I smelled his cologne again.

Sometimes I still ask myself: What if I had stayed a few seconds longer? And if I had spoken to him?

Anita's devotion to her father lasted some ten months. Then she announced in a letter that she'd gone to live with two friends from the university in an apartment in downtown Santiago. She insinuated in a phone conversation that his wife was too jealous. Now they saw each other every morning because he—the model father—went to pick her up to bring her to the university. And then December came and two days before Christmas, when I opened the door of my apartment, I heard music. I saw a shadow in the hallway and I heard a "Mom?" It was magical. In an instant I went from sadness to utter joy. I've never gotten or will get a better Christmas present. Those were wonderful days. We went to the movies, out to eat at our favorite restaurants from before. We went together to H&M to buy a sweater she wanted. She seemed so womanly, so pretty. We found ourselves together in front of the mirror.

"I'm looking gray," I say, when I see the surprise in her face.

"No," she tells me. "You *are* gray."

The aging process seems to come from outside of me. It's a disguise, a mask that disfigures me. Youth, on the other hand, sprang from within me. The old, gray-haired woman in the mirror isn't me. She's an invader who took over my body. I try to tell Anita something of that.

Anita went out at night with the friends she still has here. But she wanted to be Chilean, she told me. She goes to bed late, when I am already asleep. When I get up every morning I see her closed door. I know she is in there, sleeping. Then slowly, slowly, I run my fingers over her door, caressing the wood, not wanting to wake her.

And, just as she arrived, she left. On the fifteenth of January she took the plane back to Chile. Only then did I realize how little she had told me about herself, about her real life. She was studying business at a new university, a private one that I didn't know. And her father? Nothing. She never told me anything about him.

FIFTY-SIX

Returning: the old woman, the liaison who was waiting for "Viollier" the day they killed him, goes a few days later into a currency exchange in Calle Monjitas. She does it twice in the same month. Pancha, who is following her, has the temerity to follow her in the second time. She watches as they let the old woman into an interior office. She soon comes back out again. She looks tense. Pancha tries to find out which office she went into. It isn't possible. She goes back to Central to report.

I run into her in the hallway. She keeps walking almost without acknowledging me. Her black shirt that fits her so well. "They called me in," I say. She shrugs her shoulders. I follow her in. I see Chico Marín, who gives me a forced smile. His lizard eyes. He goes on talking at half volume with Mono Lepe. Only the television makes any noise. Iris goes over and turns it off.

The door to Macha's office opens and Great Dane appears. He's wearing a dark suit. His blond hair falls frothy and shining over his shoulders. I've never seen him in a tie before. He slowly takes off a pair of Ray-Bans that are just like Macha's. He looks at us one by one from left to right. No one says a word. When his eyes leave those of Indio Galdámez and fall on mine, they try to get inside me, to tell me, "I know you, kid," and then they go back. Suddenly, he looks at the ceiling and says: "Macha has been detained. Counterintelligence. I ask—I demand," he corrects himself, "absolute confidentiality. They've opened a case against him. I'm the one in charge of this team now. Until new orders come down. I'm the interim. Any questions?" Silence. "OK then, go on with your work."

He goes back into the office and closes the door. But he thinks better of it and calls to Pancha. He ushers her in. She throws me a look just before the door closes. We disperse without talking. Macha has fallen, fait accompli. The king is dead, long live the king.

Great Dane orders a tail put on everyone who works in that currency exchange. They take photos of people going in and out. They don't get much. Great Dane sends in two fake technicians from the phone company: Mono Lepe and Indio Galdámez. They go into the inner offices. They see an old woman come out of the manager's office. They report to Great Dane. He orders them to go in and check the lines. They're not allowed in. They wait. When they're finally let in no one is there. Seems like someone escaped, right? They report. Outside, agents are waiting to take a photo. No one shows.

Great Dane has them call me in. I'm summoned urgently to his new office, the one that used to be Macha's. Something smells off to me. I meet Gato in the hallway. He's just arriving. It's six in the evening. He doesn't know anything, he tells me, his head hanging down. The new C3.1 doesn't like him too much, he tells me. "He's not like Flaco," he tells me with a complicit little smile that I can't stand. "But soon he'll realize what I'm worth. It's always the same . . . Macha, they've got him fucked good," he tells me. "At night," he tells me mysteriously, "I hear sounds, like this building is creaking . . ." And in a whisper, mischievously, "Careful with Great Dane. That blondie has a really big one . . . If you don't believe me, ask Pancha. She told me herself." And he bursts out laughing.

I open the office door: it's not Great Dane, it's Macha. He's looking at me with his long-lashed eyes. He has me sit down. His desk is between us.

"*You're* here? But I saw you leave the parking lot with an escort and in cuffs," I tell him straight off, and I laugh.

He lets out a contemptuous sigh:

"It's just a disciplinary action. That's all. Another one . . ."

Often, as now, his eyes didn't shine, they were opaque. I felt it as a challenge, that tragic veil. He turns and opens the safe. Hanging on the corner, his holster and CZ.

"I received this file," he says in a short, brusque tone. "Classified information about the currency exchange on Monjitas. The owner and manager is named Juan Isidoro Zañartu Cortínez. But Juan Isidoro Zañartu Cortínez died fifty-nine years ago when he was five months old. They used that name to falsify his ID card and get a national tax number. Because the number is valid. Do you know anything about this?"

"No," I say.

"Nothing?"

"Absolutely nothing."

"You have to get to him. You have to find him."

"How?"

"Your problem," he tells me.

"You photographed everyone who came to work there in the morning, right?"

"Affirmative," he answers reluctantly.

"And also everyone who leaves at night?"

"What makes you think we're such stupid motherfuckers?" He laughs.

"It has to be one of them. Find the ID that corresponds with those photos. The one who doesn't have a registered ID, that's him."

"Already done, woman." And he laughs in short, low bursts. "The Department of Identification informed me that everyone there has a valid ID and none of them is Juan Isidoro Zañartu Cortínez. Look."

He shows me some pages with photocopied IDs and the photos that were taken of people going in and out of the currency exchange. "One of those women works for us," he says, bored. "She infiltrated a few days ago. She's a 'cleaning lady.' But she hasn't gotten anything." I look at the faces. I recognize the woman with glasses who lent me a black Bic pen to sign the receipt at the currency exchange we held up. She was "fixed," they told us then.

"What are you thinking about?"

"Do you have the blueprints of the building? There could be a private elevator and an underground parking lot."

He hits his forehead. In his smile, I see the shine of his white, even teeth.

"I'll call you."

The day they showed me the photo, I couldn't believe it.

"He's in a wheelchair," Macha told me. "You can just see the backrest there, see?"

"No, I don't know. It could be a spot, or a shadow on the wall . . ."

"Here, you can see it better in this enlargement."

And, now yes, I can make out the metal of a wheelchair. As for him, he's a distinguished gentleman with gray hair receding on the sides, a streamlined nose, fine lips. He must be some sixty years old.

Seeing the photo made a strong impression on me. I held back. Macha must have noticed. He looked at his Rolex.

"Come with me," he said, putting on his Ray-Bans and sliding the CZ under his belt.

A couple of minutes later we were going around seventy-five miles an hour on his '76 Harley-Davidson, under the oriental plane trees in Forestal Park. I smelled his scent and the scent of his black leather jacket, and I felt the hard triangle of his back against my breasts. I wasn't thinking about anything. The afternoon air blowing on my face, his smell and the smell of his jacket in my nostrils, and my breasts against his back. That was being alive, period. How old was I then? Twenty-seven? And him? Thirty-two, thirty-three? Does that explain anything? I see his CZ without its holster, held only by his belt. Vertigo: What if I grabbed it and pointed it at his head? If I made him stop the motorcycle and then I killed him and took off on it?

We stopped on Calle Agustinas. Macha offered me a cigarette. We each smoked two, and then he handed me a Minolta.

"You have a very pretty neck," he told me suddenly.

I laughed, surprised.

"Long and thin," he said.

A white Volkswagen van came out of the underground parking lot. I took my first picture. Macha stepped on the kick start lever and we followed it. The van went up one block, turned and went several blocks on Monjitas, and then turned right and we followed it up Compañía. Another two or three photos. The license. Half a block after Plaza Brasil it disappeared behind a metallic door. Compañía, street of old houses with a single continuous facade. We drove past it slowly. Another photo. A big, grayish house from the end of the nineteenth century, balconies, stucco ornamentation, thick bars on the windows, the door to the street in the middle of the house's front.

"There," Macha says to me. "Have you ever been there?"

"Never," I tell him. "Notice it has an alarm."

We shot away when the light turned green. We went fast. We went down the Costanera highway along the edge of the park, leaving the cars behind. The way the motorcycle leaned into the curves. The violent air in my mouth.

FIFTY-SEVEN

"What are you thinking about?" he says.

He's sitting on the floor, his back against my black leather sofa.

"Cheers," he says, raising his glass.

"Cheers," I say, and I feel his eyes looking for mine and I don't look at him.

I look at the foam on my beer. He wanders around the room. He looks out the windows. It's dark and he's looking out from the twelfth floor. Below, the restless lights of the cars and the immobile street-lights along the Costanera.

"You can see San Cristóbal Hill during the day, right?"

"Yes."

"Smell the pine trees?"

"Yes."

"The sun comes up over there, right?"

"Yes."

He sits down at the dining room table. It's small, for four people. He gets up and goes on pacing.

"I'd like to take pictures of you," he tells me.

His straight nose, his prominent eyebrows, bushy and intense. On his forehead, a small scar. Small, but ugly. That shard of glass the night he went into the Spartan's pension and tried to take him alive.

"It's not smart," I tell him. "In the life we lead it's not a good idea for photos to be floating around out there."

"Correct. We'll tear them up."

"I don't believe you."

"You don't trust me."

"Of course not."

He smiles under his moustache.

"You're used to this," I say.

"To what?"

"To this life where nothing is what it is."

"There are some things a person never gets used to."

"Like what?"

"Like the feeling of coagulated blood under the soles of your shoes when you take a step." And, as if that were nothing: "Years ago I saw a movie, it had a French agent who was taking pictures of a woman. It was an old movie, black and white. It was a video we found in a raid. It was in French. I didn't understand much. I don't remember what it was called. I remembered it when I came into this apartment. The woman was beautiful, beautiful, naturally beautiful."

"So you like movies about spies and detectives, then?"

"No. About naturally beautiful women."

We laughed.

"Why don't you like spy movies?"

"If they had a smell, no one would go see them." And, as if that were nothing: "Tomorrow, Saturday, at four o'clock, come meet me at number 86 Calle Libertad. It's an aikido academy. Go in and ask for Luis José Calvo. OK? We're going to take some pictures of you."

"I never knew you were a samurai," I laughed. "How long have you done aikido?"

"About eleven years."

"And? Are you any good?"

"That's the problem: no."

"Black belt?"

"No; I haven't been able to pass. But Cristóbal will be a sixth dan before he's out of school. I promise you that."

FIFTY-EIGHT

And there I was. AKIKAI–CHILE AIKIDO CULTURAL CENTER. The sign was small. The house, big, old, and run-down. I rang the bell, the door opened, and I went in through a dark hallway. At the end, a refrigerator with drinks, and beyond that, a spacious light well. I was greeted by a fat woman with round arms and her hair pulled back in a bun, who must have been over seventy years old. She was behind a big table, and she put down her knitting to come and talk to me. I explained I was looking for Luis José Calvo. She told me to go through the gallery, turn left, and go up the stairs. Señor Calvo was watching a competition that his son was in, she explained.

"He's one of the finalists," she told me with a smile. A moment later I was sitting next to Señor Calvo, who was in a big white shirt and wide black pants, watching two children fight.

Macha pointed out his son. Cristóbal was slight and dark. He couldn't have been over seven years old. He and his opponent were flying through the air, falling and rolling on the wooden floor, and then they were back up, uncomplaining, to attack again. They looked like birds or fighting cocks. I caught a glimpse of a hand on Macha's son's chin. His head went backward and I thought I saw the other boy grab Cristóbal's raised arm; a quick spinning motion and then Cristóbal was on the ground, immobilized, with his arm stretched out.

"Ryokatatori ikkyo," Macha exclaimed. "Impeccable execution."

"Your son lost . . ."

"Well, what can you do. He came in second. He fought well. His sensei is excellent."

After the recognition ceremony I saw a tide of children and teenagers go by in robes and wide white pants on the way to the changing rooms. Cristóbal ran to find his father, who lifted him up in a hug. He greeted me with forced indifference. He told Macha his mother was coming to pick him up. Macha congratulated him and gave him a good-bye hug before disappearing into the locker rooms. He came back five minutes later with wet hair, black jeans and shirt, bag over his shoulder and leather jacket in hand. "Let's go," he told me, and started walking quickly.

Cristóbal came running over and took his hand. Macha said good-bye to him again, but the boy wanted to walk him to the motorcycle. We went past the woman at the entrance and filed down the dark hallway, the two of them in front of me. The door to the street opened. Macha stopped. Against the outside light was the silhouette of a woman, who barely greeted Macha and hugged Cristóbal. Her Chanel perfume invaded my nostrils. Macha introduced me as "a colleague" and she reached out her fat hand to me almost with disgust.

She looked older than Macha. She had brown hair and green eyes. Cristóbal had inherited those big, light eyes. Other than that, starting with his eyelashes, he was purely his father. She must have once had good breasts, but wrinkles and sunspots had formed on them, and the eye could intuit their gelatinous consistency. Close to her belt there was a roll of flesh. The two-piece suit she was wearing didn't help her at all, of course. The pant legs, thick and very white, ended in a pair of low heels with severe lines. The two of them stayed there, silhouetted in the doorway. Cristóbal and I went back through the hallway. She was saying something to Macha about her mother's birthday, that it was already past two . . . The tone was of barely contained rage. I turned around and looked at them. Macha said something I couldn't make out. Her nostrils flared. She raised her chin and pointed an accusatory finger. Cristóbal gave me his hand and we went farther back along the hallway. Her shrill voice was getting louder. Macha answered her softly.

We sat down on a rat-colored sofa, between the refrigerator and the fat woman with the bun who watched over the entrance. I asked Cristóbal if he had plans for his vacation. He told me in a firm voice that he wanted to go with his father on the motorcycle to Yelcho.

"Something bad happened the last time we went camping. But it wasn't in Yelcho."

He says it after a pause and with that gravity children are capable of.

"What was it?"

"My dad and I went to the mountains. My dad took me there. We went with two mule drivers. We drank mate. Everyone from the same straw and you couldn't move it. I thought that was gross. One of the herders had a scab on his lip. That was really gross. The guy was dirty and he smelled bad. But my dad told me I had to grin and bear it, so I did. We went on horseback for lots of days. We went up the Cuesta de las Lágrimas and there was a huge, huge cliff. If the horse slips and you fall over the cliff, there's nothing left of you. That's what they told us. The little horse path was like this, this narrow."

"Dangerous, huh?"

"But that wasn't the bad thing. The bad part was when we came to a lake and there were some ducks."

"And? Were the ducks pretty?"

"The ducks were really pretty, they had green feathers in their wings. And they were all quiet in the water. They weren't afraid of us at all. I thought we should hunt them. I asked my dad for the rifle. I asked if we could try shooting for real. My dad didn't want to. Then the herder with the gross scab on his lip, said: 'Go on and let him, boss. Come on over here, I'll show you how.' And he went to grab the rifle from my dad. But when he tried to take it, my dad held on to it. 'Hey, OK, I'll teach him,' he said. He showed me how to aim. I'd already gone shooting at the firing range with my dad. Revolver and pistol. Never a rifle. It was really heavy. The trigger was hard to pull and the rifle moved and the duck I was aiming at was getting away. Then all of a sudden you heard the shot and the butt of the rifle hit me in the shoulder. The ducks flew away and disappeared in the sky. I looked at the lake and there was only one left. It was lifting up one wing, but not the other. It went on floating, like that, tilted over.

"'Dad! The duck. . .'

"My dad looked at me really serious.

"'We have to kill it, son.'

"I shouted 'No!' It was awful.

"'That duck is suffering. It's going to die anyway, Cristóbal. It won't be able to find food like that. Do you want to make it suffer? We have to kill it.'

"Then I threw myself on the ground and started to cry. The duck, tilted over, went on swimming in a circle. It didn't make noise. It kept swimming so calmly . . . He fired a shot. The duck fell over. My dad lowered the rifle. I jumped on him, kicking and punching him. I went crazy. I wanted to kill him. I was screaming and crying. Later that night when I was falling asleep, my dad came over to my sleeping bag. He told me again that it would have been worse to leave the poor duck in pain.

"'How do you know? Maybe it would have gotten better,' I told him, and I didn't talk to him again until we got back to Santiago."

Cristóbal looks at me, and I see all that he is right there in his eyes.

In the doorway the argument went on. We couldn't hear what they were saying very well, but she seemed beside herself. A red vein was pulsing in her forehead. Macha's head was bowed.

"Why do they argue so much?"

"It's 'cause my mom doesn't want to let me go to Yelcho with my dad over vacation. But don't worry. This always happens. I'm going to have to convince her myself, later on."

A friend of Cristóbal's came over and I took the opportunity to say good-bye. Macha and his ex-wife had moved away from the door and were still wrapped up in their argument. He was trembling like a rabbit. I didn't have any problems leaving without them seeing me. When I got to my apartment, I opened a can of beer, threw myself on the bed, and turned on the TV. A slow, boring movie. My mind wandered.

FIFTY-NINE

I thought the noise of the lock was coming from that bad movie, so I was terrified when I heard footsteps in the living room. The door to my room opened: Macha. While my heart was doing somersaults he showed me his lock pick and smiled. He made some delicious hot ham and cheese sandwiches that we devoured with a couple of beers, and I made Turkish coffee.

I asked him why he was so afraid of that witch. We were on the black leather sofa and I could smell his animal smell. He told me it was because of the boy, because of Cristóbal; his mother tried to keep them apart, she was furious at the poor kid for wanting to be with his father. So she punished him out of pure malice, and of course that only made Cristóbal want to be with his father more. But there was nothing to be done about it. The law gave custody to the mother.

He told me that she ran her house with "managerial" efficiency. Cristóbal was very lonely, he said. He had almost no friends. Macha was afraid of her power to do damage, even if she damaged herself in the process. She didn't give a shit. She was a vengeful and bitter woman. That's how he saw her. And Cristóbal had insomnia, he had terrifying nightmares. And Macha was never there with him. He had given him a short-wave radio and Cristóbal kept it on his bedside table. He loved that, being a radio ham. That way they could talk at any hour of the night. But when he had insomnia or nightmares or problems with his mother, Cristóbal didn't call him, he said. He didn't understand why.

He asked me for another beer and he drank it quickly. Then he started taking photos of me. I walked around the apartment pursued by the lens of his Minolta. I sat down, ran, looked out the window, I rested my head on the back of a chair, I knelt down, looked at myself in the bathroom mirror, I got up onto the sofa. Behind his Minolta, his beard cut even with the skin—a close, level, bluish beard—and his cleft chin. I touched his arm as I said something, or I said "you" with a pointed finger on his chest. A few long hairs were peeking out of the neck of his shirt. His smell welcomed me now. His intimacy. Like I'd entered into his cave. He gaze held mine. I knew what was going to happen. Maybe.

And he was following me and saying: "Hold up your hair, like that, pull it back." And he was saying: "What will make a face like yours pretty?" And: "What do you feel when you're on the motorcycle going full speed?" And: "Don't laugh." And I held back my laughter for an instant, fighting with it until I gave in. And as soon as the laughter escaped, again, in a soft and very low voice, coming from under his moustache black as coal: "Don't laugh." And those were, he would tell me later, the best pictures.

"I like your boots, that rough material . . ."

"Buffalo," he says. "From Argentina."

And suddenly:

"What do you know about Bone?"

"Maybe something, maybe nothing," I say. His hand is removing the lens. "I know he's the one who coordinates the organization."

"We all know that. Get me another beer," he says, leaving the camera on the table in the living room. We're face to face. We clink glasses. I feel that at that moment I matter to him.

"Tell me something," I say. "I'm still an intellectual, you know? A spectator of life. I've never killed anyone. What's it like? What happens to you inside?"

I actually dared to ask him that candid question. Macha Carrasco, you know, gave the impression that he was one of those people who doesn't ever doubt. His actions didn't arise from mental deliberation but from a throbbing, a dark compulsion. That's why I asked him that. I would never have asked it of a banal Eichmann-style bureaucrat of extermination—because of course, Central was full of those little gray ants in the service of terror.

"It depends," Macha tells me calmly. I'm looking at his eyelashes, the lashes of a pony. "The first time you kill, you kill two men with the same bullet. The one you kill and the one you were up until then. They don't teach you that at the Military Intelligence School."

"And afterward?"

"Afterward? Then nothing ever makes you feel more alive than killing again. At the same time: it's dirty, there's nothing romantic about it. Never. The enemy, once he's dead, was never your enemy. He looks like a pathetic accident victim."

He fixes his eyes on me. When he looks at you like that there's nothing else in the world but you and him.

"I heard a story once. Canelo told it to me."

And I know I shouldn't tell him what I'm going to tell him. Why? I contradict myself. I try to control myself. It's a familiar vertigo by now, the one that's taking hold of me. I can't resist the temptation to tell him something I know, something Canelo told me, something Canelo shouldn't have told me just as I shouldn't tell Macha this secret now. But revealing a secret is delicious.

"He talked to me one night about this extraordinary guy," I tell him. "Attractive and brilliant," I say. "A born leader. He'd just gotten his degree in medicine, Canelo told me, and he was chosen to go to Cuba. In the seventies. First in his class at Camilo Cienfuegos Military School. Everyone who knew him at that time agreed that he was destined for great things. His maturity in spite of how young he was, his theoretical and strategic knowledge, his specialization in clandestine struggle and sabotage, his physical dexterity, his political ability, his integrity, his innate intelligence, his kindness. He was the best of all of us, Canelo told me. Until the night of the accident. No one, they say, had his charisma.

"It was at a party, the graduation party for his class at the Havana

Libre Hotel. You know, the old Hilton hotel during the time of Batista, with its great hall, its gigantic dome lit up over the pool. He was headed for the Bolivian sierra. He would leave two days later to fight alongside Che. He was going as a military doctor, no less. He was talking animatedly—very animatedly—with a very beautiful woman. Then they were dancing. Then their arms were around each other and they were looking at each other and smiling for no reason, and then it seemed like they were about to kiss or maybe they were already kissing.

"A mahogany table went rolling across the floor, with its old tablecloth of good, mended cotton, and then everything was crashing plates and smashing glasses. There was a shot and a window shattered. A captain of the armed forces was aiming his gun at the Chilean. There was a movement too violent and fast to be described, a feint, a jump, and an expert kick, and the jealous man fell to the floor. His 9mm Makarov PMM slid across the floor.

"You could have chewed the silence. All the students focused on the steel that was waiting there on the floor. The young Chilean official moved slowly over to it. His adversary, behind him and to one side, was getting up with difficulty. You could hear his footsteps on the cream-colored ceramic tiles of the Havana Libre Hotel. He was going to pick up the Cuban captain's Makarov, his steps sure and calm. His new black boots of a recently graduated official creaked.

"Then the pistol skidded out of his path, sliding quickly over the gleaming ceramic. Someone had kicked it. Another shot rang out in the room and the Chilean bent double and collapsed to the floor. The bullet had shattered a vertebra. The Cuban doctors saved his life.

"I never found out his name. Canelo didn't tell me. I only know that he survived and spent two years hospitalized in Cuba, he was paralyzed, and he returned to Chile at the start of Allende's thousand days."

"He's our man," said Macha. And his black eyes shone the way black marble shines. And after a silence: "This has to stay between us. Is that clear? No one else. Clear? Tell no one."

I never saw the photos he took of me that day.

SIXTY

Mono Lepe looked at me with his dark-ringed eyes, then up at the post, measuring the distance. He clambered up easily and used pliers to cut the telephone lines. That disconnected the alarm, too. It was three thirty. Operation "Night of the Wild Boar" had commenced. Lepe also cut the electricity lines. They had gotten the blueprints to the house from City Hall. A couple of minutes later I made out a few pulses of light from a flashlight in the darkness of the night. They came from up above, on the other side of the house. Mono had already met up with Pancha, who had a radio. She had arrived a while earlier and gotten in position on the roof of a neighboring house. The siege was in place around the perimeter. That's what they were saying, those lights turning off and on from the roofs, which Macha answered with his own flashlight. Macha didn't put much trust in technology when he conducted operations. Indio Galdámez went up to the solid front door. It wasn't the kind you could just knock down with a kick. He tried his lock pick. It didn't work. He took out a second pick: no go. Great Dane let out a bellow of rage.

"How could you not try the picks first, Indio?"

Galdámez didn't answer. He tried a third.

"They're locks from that Spanish company, Azbe, with an HS-6 safety cylinder. The picks won't work," he said.

"Motherfucker!" growled Great Dane. "How the fuck did you not . . ."

"Let's move on to plan B," Macha interrupted: "Bring the jack."

He checked the time, got into his car, and picked up the radio. I was close by, and very excited.

"You woke me up, Dad," I managed to hear. "Is something wrong? Over."

"Are you asleep, son? Do you copy? Over."

"Yes, I copy. No, I'm waking up now. Did something bad happen? Tell me, Dad. Are you OK? Over."

"I'm great, how are you? How was your day at school? Did you win the game? Over."

"We tied one to one. And I almost scored a second goal. I headed a corner shot, dad. A header that hit the crossbar . . . We would've won, Dad. Over."

"Good man! In the rematch, that header will be a goal. Over."

"You think that could happen? Over."

"Sure, of course it could happen. Listen to me, Cristóbal: Do you copy? Over."

"Yes, Dad, I copy."

"I want to congratulate you. And now you need to go back to sleep, OK?"

"But do you really think that'll happen, Dad? Another corner shot the same way in the rematch, and I'll be right there, Dad, and I'll head the ball in?"

"Not likely, but yes, it could happen. The point is that in the next game you'll score a goal. I'm sure of it. Now, go to sleep."

"Hey, Dad, why'd you call me so late? Did something happen?"

"No. I just wanted to know how the game went, that's all. And now, go back to sleep. Over."

"Yeah, I'm going back to sleep now. Over."

"Good night. Over and out."

Great Dane was panting. His long, blond hair moved like ostrich feathers on a helmet. He snatched away the simple car jack that Indio Galdámez brought over, and with his giant hands he fitted it midway up between two bars in a window. When he turned the lever and put pressure on the bars, the jack let out a little metallic whine that was unsettling. Little by little the bars were buckling. Now Great Dane was smiling.

"Let's see, Chico, put your head in."

It didn't fit.

"Just four or five more turns and we're there," Chico said.

"You're sure you can get through there, Chico?" Great Dane asked him. "You sure?"

Chico Marín assented with his restless eyes, and Indio Galdámez put away the jack with the same calm with which he did everything. Chico traced a rectangle on the glass with the diamond-tipped glass cutter. Great Dane held up the suction cup. Macha and I watched, smoking. He pulled me farther away. He was serious and grim, even more than usual.

"You didn't say anything about this to anyone from Analysis, right?"

"No, of course not. Not to them or anyone else." I'm surprised. "Why do you ask?"

Great Dane removed the glass with the suction cup. Macha threw away the cigarette butt, which gleamed as it fell. He took hold of my shoulders.

"Don't fail me," he said, locking his terrible eyes on mine.

"Why?" I asked him. "Why are you trying to hurt me?"

"It's just that we can't fail. Not this time."

"Why?"

"Because I violated procedure," he said mockingly.

"When? Is this about the 'Prince of Wales'?"

"Yes, well, that was the straw that broke the camel's back." And, seriously: "This is my last mission. They demoted me. They fucked me. Fucking pencil-pushing, fat-ass, scared shitless generals!"

SIXTY-ONE

He didn't wait for me to react. Without looking at anyone he gave the order to go in through the window, and he jumped through. Great Dane tried to go behind him, but his corpulent body wouldn't fit. Chico Marín tried next. Great Dane let out another roar.

"Hurry up, shithead! Put your head and your ass through right away."

Chico Marín was more frightened than ever and all the color had gone out of his face. Though he was short, he was solid and had a big head—a cube, as I've told you.

"Motherfucker!" shouted Great Dane, containing the shout in a whisper. He tapped Chico's forehead with the calloused edge of his hand. Chico's big, shaved head bounced against the bars of the window. A few inches lower and unleashed with Great Dane's precision and strength, and that blow would be fatal.

"Come on, boss, don't be like that," Chico complained.

We heard a noise at the front door. According to plan B we would open it from inside. I slipped quickly between the bars behind Iris, who had drawn her formidable CZ. Outside, Great Dane, enraged, ordered Galdámez to put the car jack back in and widen the gap. The light of a streetlamp illuminated the living room of that old house. I stopped. I took cover behind the empire sofa, which was the closest thing to me. I made out some dark red plush armchairs, a big oval mirror with a gold frame hanging on the wall, which was papered in a light green color, I think; there were bronze lamps shaped like flowers affixed to the wall, a blurry painting of a hunting scene,

an immense crystal chandelier that hung from the molded ceiling . . .
Then we heard a shout. A woman's shout and a roar.

"Shit. Dogs."

It's Iris.

"Stupid motherfucker!"

It's Great Dane. He and Indio Galdámez are still in the street,
apparently.

"How could you possibly not mention the dog, you idiot?"

"There were no dogs here," Indio apologizes.

"I gave you the order, shithead, to check every detail."

"I carried out the order, but there weren't any dogs . . . At the
house next door, yes, but . . ."

"Dumbass! You didn't realize they had a dog, Indio, motherfucker. You didn't realize, right? What's in that head of yours? Saw-
dust and cat piss?"

Before we'd set out, Great Dane had explained to us that Bone
slept in that house, plus two trained and armed bodyguards. Their
alibis were driver and caretaker. The driver slept in the room next to
Bone's, at the end of the hall. The caretaker was in an exterior room,
attached to the garage in the courtyard. A door connected the courtyard with the hallway that led to Bone's room, and another door led
to the kitchen. We saw them in the blueprints. There were those
three and Bone's mother. Her room was on the second floor. Plus
the cook, who slept below in a room off the kitchen. Of dogs, no one
said a word.

Behind the empire sofa, I pressed my face, I pressed my entire body
to the floor. A gunshot rang out. Then another, then machine-gun
fire from an AK. I saw Iris running. Something flew from her hand
to the floor. A bright and violent light flashed and illuminated the
enormous crystal chandelier and reflected in the big, gold-framed
mirror of the living room. Then came the explosion with its deafening blast. The room filled with smoke. From that moment on everything was sudden, simultaneous, and impossible to follow. Every

tenth of a second is a minute, every minute, an hour. The gunshots filled my ears and blotted out the world. I heard machine-gun fire and bits of plaster and molding falling, leaving the brick walls exposed; tables, lamps—if they were in fact lamps—blown to pieces, all very close by. The thunder of the bullets filled my ears until they felt as if they would explode. There was no room in my brain for that maddening jackhammer.

Macha, it must have been Macha, went running past toward the bedroom at the back. Great Dane's blond mane was behind him. I seemed to sense a shadow moving near me, close to the wall. I looked at the shadow and then it jumped. It leaped off the ground. And it immediately sank down, leaving behind it a slight pink halo of pulverized tissue that floated in the air for a split second. Iris was coming toward me, firing. I was terrified. She jumped over the empire sofa and over me and she slid along that wall. The silence of a tomb. The gases burned my throat and nose. The smoke was clearing.

Chico Marín cut off the passage to the kitchen and the patio; Iris controlled the hallway that led to the bedroom at the back, Bone's room, and she was looking upward. No one moved. The shootout hadn't lasted more than three seconds. When the order came, I crawled out from my hiding place behind the sofa and over the floor, following the light from a flashlight. That was according to the plan. Then, by the light of the streetlight, I saw very clearly on the floor a Kalashnikov that I almost stepped on, and, no more than two yards away from me, a shape; spreading out over the parquet, a pasty and pinkish pulp dotted with white lumps.

At that moment, I tried to comprehend what was happening, to interpret reality according to the plan. I couldn't do it. And I knew why: the explosion of light up above, close to the ceiling, its tremendous crash, the cloud of smoke, the footsteps of several attackers shooting and running in rigorous accord in opposite directions, it all confounds the observer, leaves him bewildered. With his attention so fatally divided, the only thing he can do, if he manages to do anything, is to shoot at the shape. They had explained it to us many times in Rinconada de Maipú, we had practiced, but it was quite another thing to live it. I'll describe it now in order: Iris, whom I lost sight of in the noise and smoke of the explosion, neutralized the first of the defenders. The man emerged, as we had foreseen might happen, through the kitchen door. But Macha was already running past with his pistol held in both hands toward the hall at the back, Great Dane following. Chico Marín rushed over, firing, to take up the position Iris had left. And there I saw his shaved head now, next to the door to the kitchen. In the meantime Iris threw herself toward the wall at my back. An unexpected fighter had appeared, firing an AK. Iris unloaded her CZ into him. From there she dominated the entrance to Bone's room. Iris had saved my life.

I stopped next to the window. Iris approached the stairs, staying close to the wall as she moved. They ordered me to go up. At that moment I saw a loose, severed foot with its black Nike in a pool of thick blood, and a hand missing three fingers with a light blue shirt cuff still intact. The smell was unbearable. I forget a lot of what I saw. But I can't forget that smell. What could be in that stench I couldn't help but breathe? Shit, of course, and the sweat of fear, and dust and plaster and gunpowder and paint and smashed bricks and smoke and gases, I guess, and tiny particles of blood and human tissue suspended in the air. I breathed it all in, reeking as it filled the hollows of my body. At the end of the hall I could hear gunshots and silences. Nothing sounds louder than the silence between gunshots. A bullet whizzing past much closer paralyzed me. I thought it had grazed my arm. Chico Marín's shaved head bounced against the wall. He looked at me, moving his eyes that were terrifyingly wide-open. He opened his mouth to say something to me, but he suddenly fell silent and collapsed against the wall, smearing its blue-green wallpaper. What is left of a person killed in combat is impossible to align with what he was in life. Something had changed. By now it was clear that nothing corresponded to the plan. They'd been waiting for us and there were more fighters than we expected. They were shooting at us from the second floor and the shots from the end of the hallway were coming faster and faster.

"Cover me! Cover me!" shouted Iris.

I started to shoot while she climbed the stairs doubled over. A short gun fell to the floor. It came from upstairs. I waited. "Come up!" It was Iris. I recognized the Andean profile of Galdámez on the landing of the stairs. "Not yet! Don't come up yet!" Iris shouted. The noise was unbearable. Pieces of glass were falling and shattering as they hit the floor, fragments of stucco and plaster molding were returning to white dust. The enormous chandelier in the living room suddenly plummeted with a crash of metal and shattering crystal. With that crash, Indio Galdámez rushed upstairs, firing. I went up behind him. They were still shooting at us. I recognized the clatter of an AK-47. A body slid down the stairs past me, leaving a trail of blood. It was a woman. It wasn't Iris. Silence again. I waited. Nothing. "Now!" Iris shouted to me. Lit clearly by the streetlight, she was standing on the threshold. She was panting and her eyes were full of fear. There were bloodstains on her pants and her left running shoe. Galdámez was checking the second floor, slamming doors and pounding.

I went over a leg wearing blue Levi's that ended in a natural leather boot. There was beauty in that old contact of jeans with the leather of the Texan boot. I saw that, where my eyes fell. I remembered the Gringo dead in Plaza Concha y Toro the night I gave Rafa up, his cowboy boots. Half of that man's torso had ended up under a colored pane of glass. And in the skin of his anemic face, the encrusted shards shone like crushed ice. The skylight is destroyed, I thought. An idiotic thought, right? His fingers and arms were still moving. Sparks, electric reflexes.

It took no effort at all to overpower the poor old woman. She had practically fainted. "There's no one else on this floor," shouted Indio Galdámez. "Those three who were shooting at us must have come in from the house next door," he shouted, his voice high and uneven. "And they brought the dogs, I'm sure."

She was in bed but dressed in street clothes. Iris blindfolded her and tied her up with expert knots; I put a rag in her mouth, and a strip of plastic tape sealed her lips. We waited. No more shots were fired. I was still panting, and I had a crazy desire to smoke. Iris told me no, not a chance.

SIXTY-TWO

Do you want to believe me? Because we're here in this hospice home in Ersta, Stockholm, and if you don't want to, I'm not about to try to convince you. I have no way to. As for me, I don't give a shit about the truth. Am I telling the truth when I tell you I don't give a shit about the truth? It's my story, after all. But does such a thing exist? As I talk to you, I look at you and calibrate your reactions. Everything I'm telling you is formulated for you. I would be saying this in a different way to Roberto, in another tone, with other things emphasized and other omissions. Understand? What you want to do with my story, and above all your gestures—the way you suddenly raise your eyebrows or twist your mouth or interlace your fingers—I assimilate them, and it all gives shape and content to what I say and don't say. The same thing happens in an interrogation. Who is asking, what they ask, and how they do it all gives shape to what you say and what you hide.

I didn't find out about the attack itself, its objective, the date and time, until half an hour before we left. Macha summoned us that night to the lot at Central, he ordered us to come armed for a mission. I remember that Pancha, when she got there, took out her little bottle of Christian Dior and perfumed herself. I think she did it to piss me off, and it worked. I felt bad. Once we were all in the parking lot, Macha told us that Operation "Night of the Wild Boar" was about to commence, and he explained what we were going to do, spreading out the blueprints of the house. He took his precautions. Then? Do you want me to tell you the story, or should I simplify things and get to the point? You know, in reality all this happens very quickly and later it's told very slowly. You can't imagine everything that can fit in a minute.

I heard Indio Galdámez walking on the roof. Why Galdámez? Weren't Mono Lepe and Pancha Ortiz the ones who were supposed to cover the roof? He must have climbed up through the hole left by the shattered skylight. His steps resounded on the zinc shingles. The ancient old lady tried to say something. I knew from the movement of her head and the contortion of her mouth obstructed by the piece of black cloth. Iris kept her at gunpoint. A burst of machine-gun fire pierced my ears. There was a dull noise. I went over to the window and looked through the opening between the curtains. A motor running. Iris got close to the edge of the window. A white Volkswagen van that I recognized was backing up over the driveway at full speed. It fit its rear against a doorway to the house.

"Careful!" Iris shouted at me, "Careful!"

She pushed me back, opened the curtain, and with one burst of fire she shattered the window. She dragged the old woman over to the window, holding the gun to her head.

"Give me some light! Shine the flashlight on me!"

Bone's mother was struggling, she was desperate and moaning, but Iris, skinny as she was, had her hostage well under control. I obeyed. Iris was shouting that she was going to kill her, she was going to kill Bone's mother if they didn't throw down their weapons and surrender immediately. I think she gave them a time limit, I think she started counting to seven. A man ran across, hugging the wall of the yard, and opened the van doors. Iris counted louder and louder. No one heard her. You don't see that in movies, do you?

And of course, the gate was starting to open now. It obeyed a remote control order. You could see the light from the street. My heart gave a leap of joy: they were getting away. Why? I'm contradicting myself. But that was how I felt at that moment. I heard Pancha on the radio, requesting backup from Central. She must have been close to the broken skylight.

I thought: it's her. And I had no doubt about it. She arrived first, in time to warn someone as soon as she got there, some contact in

Red Ax. It was before Mono Lepe met up with her on the roof. Of course, they'd only had time to prepare their escape, not to carry it out. The mother they had to get dressed, was that what slowed them down? Because they didn't want to leave her behind? And who was Pancha's connection in Red Ax? Since when? Had it been Pancha, then, who had given us the address of Macha's lover, which turned out to be bad information and had cost the life of some unimportant agent? And was Pancha the source of the address—correct, this time—of the kindergarten Cristóbal went to? How much did they know about me? Was it her information, incomplete as it was, that had caused the Spartan's reticence with me? And how much had she wheedled out of Flaco about me? Did she have help in Central, another mole?

And then I thought: If there's anyone who's really suspicious here, who would have warned Bone about that night's attack, it's me. Not Pancha. Obviously: they all must be thinking it that very instant.

A crash made me turn around. A cornice of the building had fallen, bringing a gutter along with it, and it landed right in the space between the house and the Volkswagen. The van gave a jump and lurched forward, tires squealing, toward the half-open gate. But it got there too soon and collided with the black metal that still hadn't receded. Iris threw the old woman onto the bed, ordered me to guard her, changed her clip, and, crouching down, started to fire shot after shot. She wanted to hit a tire, but she didn't have the angle. The same thing must be happening to them on the roof. Was that Mono Lepe down there, those remains of a fallen human animal, the open and exposed flesh immobilized in an unnatural position?

"Why aren't reinforcements here yet?" Iris yelled.

Her bullets left cracks in the back windows of the van but didn't destroy them, or they rebounded, maybe, inside its bodywork.

"It's bulletproof, you stupid fucking idiot!" she told me when I asked.

The Volkswagen was still stopped and two shadows were approaching it, keeping close to the wall of the house. Finally, the gate was open. But the van didn't leave. The sudden silence surprised me. Iris lowered her CZ. The shadows stayed immobile against the walls. No one dared take a step. Then the driver's side door opened and an inert body was shoved out. The Volkswagen started moving. The bullets shattered that tense silence. They returned fire. I saw one, two men running. Iris shoved me away from the window.

"Watch her!" she ordered me and went on shooting, unhurriedly.

I made the woman as comfortable on her bed as possible without lowering my gun. I tried to think back. In my life as a clandestine fighter I'd had to maintain some M16A1 caliber 5.56 weapons. Since they were too long—986 millimeters—sometimes their stocks were shortened. They were kept in bags sealed with tape that we stuck into a drum of Motrex oil. We hid the drum in a hiding place in a wall, behind a bookshelf, in a safe house. It was an M16 like those that were now shredding the night. A fighter from Red Ax. I was sure of it. The clatter didn't let up, punctuated by those short, suctioning silences. And I kept trying to imagine what the hell was happening down there in the yard.

Iris, haggard, sat down on the bed without looking at me. We could hear the murmur of people talking. The bullets had stopped suddenly. We kept quiet. How good, how blessed that silence was.

"You know?" Iris says to me, suddenly calm. "There were two of them, two pit bulls. How could they not give us that information?"

"They had them in the house next door," I tell her. "That's what I heard Indio say. They had a backup team there."

"Those dogs attack without warning, silently. They were inches away from Macha." She looked at me with cold eyes and a vague, feline smile: "I took them down at the last second."

SIXTY-THREE

Voices. I peeked over the banister of the second-floor hallway. They were inside the house. Iris stayed in the room with the old woman. Downstairs in the living room was a man in a wheelchair. A gentleman with disheveled white hair and a distinguished nose who was wearing pajamas. His hands were cuffed behind him. In front of him, Macha, his CZ drawn and his head full of dirt and half white from fallen plaster, asking where was Commander Joel, was he in Chile or not, show him a current photograph . . . Macha wasn't shouting. The other man was shaking his head no.

In a piece of the gold-framed mirror that was inexplicably still hanging on the wall I could see, as if it were an insect squashed on the windshield of a car, what was left of one of the pit bulls. And I saw a piece of human head next to the leg of the sofa I had hidden behind. There was no blood in its hair. The rest was a vomit of body. Suddenly I understood that that poor white-haired gentleman handcuffed and in a wheelchair was Bone. None other. But was it really him? His pajama shirt was unbuttoned and open, and I could see the tangle of white hair on his chest. His stomach was swelling up. A dark pool was accumulating and spreading out under the wheelchair.

"You're going to die," Macha was telling him. "You're bleeding out. You're a doctor, so you know." He brought his hand to his waist, above his hip. "I can still take you to the hospital. Talk. Who is Commander Joel? Who? Who gives you your orders? Who do you give them to?"

"Let's go, Macha," said Great Dane, rushing over to push the wheelchair. "This is over."

His blond hair was turning red in the back from blood. He must have gotten cut on his head, I guess. As it flowed out it stained the back of his dusty jean jacket.

"Let's get him out of here now. They could come back for him. Let's not waste time!"

Macha didn't let go of the chair. The man went on shaking his head no.

"Macha!" A spot of dirt or a bruise, I wasn't sure which, prolonged Macha's eye downward over his cheek. "We have to stop this cocksucker's bleeding and turn him over to Gato! He'll give up everything then. His belly is swelling up from the blood, man. Let's go!"

The sound of a siren coming closer knifed through the night. It must have been less than a couple blocks away. I looked around. The others had come downstairs. All except Iris, who was guarding the gagged and bound mother. I heard the punch. Bone's face lurched. A thread of blood ran down from his nose to his lips. His head lolled backward, but he straightened it again. The man passed his tongue over his lips. He was pallid. He was in bad shape.

"Feeling pretty thirsty, huh?" Macha said to him, changing his tone. "That's because you're losing blood, man. Nothing matters now. Talk, and we'll save you. Does Commander Joel exist? He doesn't exist, fuck, he died in '73, drowned in the Pillanleufú River, and you lied and said he survived . . . Answer me, shit! Or you'd rather we bring you in to Central? We'll save your life. It was all theater, all a big set-up of yours, wasn't it? A cripple like you could never be the leader, isn't that right? And so . . . Tell me! Or they'll take care of you in Analysis and you'll end up singing just like they all do. You want that humiliation? You'll give us every last fucker left in the organization. You think we'll let you die here? No way. We're not that stupid . . . You're fucked. We got you alive. Talk. Better to do it here. In there, you know how it is . . ."

"You got me alive and I'm dying, fuck . . ." Bone said. "But I got a bullet in you, Macha. You're bleeding, too, you son of a bitch."

"OK. Let's get him out of here, Macha," Great Dane repeated. "This guy's gonna go before we hand him over to Gato, he's bleeding like a motherfucker."

Macha let go of the chair handle and he looked at his hand with its bloody Rolex. He lowered it to his side and then looked at it again. We heard the insistent siren of the ambulance. It was parked right there, apparently. Outside, voices.

"See? You're wounded, Macha. But it's not a serious wound, I'm afraid. I feel sorry for you, man. Nothing will be left of your brave deeds. They'll all be erased. You'll end up alone and you'll die alone. Your own bosses will toss you out on your ass. The moment will come when they'll wipe their asses with you, man, they'll pin everything on you for being a damn foolish asshole, you'll be up to your ears in shit for the rest of your life! That moment will come." The bag of his stomach continued to swell. "You'll understand then that you spent your life in the service of a cause that wasn't worth it and that didn't need you. It'll be the last mission they give you: act as the toilet where your big bosses can dump their shit and piss and stay clean themselves. Cristóbal, your son, will find out some day what you are. He'll distance himself from you. He'll go through life branded by the shame of being your son . . ."

Another blow convulsed his head. He shook it and put out his tongue to lick the blood from his lips.

"There are things, Macha, that you'll never be able to understand: defeats that are worth more . . . Sacrifice is, sometimes, more human and more beautiful than triumph."

I was sure: it was him. I recognized his voice. It was the voice of Commander Iñaqui, who had talked to us about the color red: *krasnyi*. Everything changed for me in that instant. It was his suggestive voice, intimate and serene. It was his voice that brought me back, the way an aroma can do after years have passed, to my place in that community of dreamers who sang along to a couple of guitars next to a bonfire in the Nahuelbuta Mountains. It seemed as if I could hear the crackling of that red fire: *krasnyi*.

He wanted to add something else, but a vomit of black blood stopped him. His belly was still swelling up like a pregnant woman's.

"Macha!" shouted Great Dane, beside himself . . .

"MIR, the Front, they all have real leaders," Macha was saying to him, calm now and ignoring the shout. "But in Red Ax the leader didn't exist, right, Bone? Commander Joel was you. Right?"

"You win, Macha Carrasco, but without honor. A man like you . . . ," he spit a little more blood. And, facing him: "Take your victory, you fucking murderer, take it back to your putrid den. The glory stays here, with us."

Macha stood there looking at him, unmoved.

"Pretty words, Bone, but . . . only words."

Reflections of the ambulance siren colored the old living room with red beams. Macha gave a signal and Indio Galdámez came up behind him. I saw the medical technicians coming over with a cot and saline bags. They didn't have much time. I saw Great Dane's enormous, denim-sheathed back, dirty and bloodied, covering Macha. Suddenly, Bone's balding head bounced forward violently, emptied over the wall like a smashed cup. I moved away immediately from the railing, hiding my weapon. Although I managed to catch sight of the suctioning black of Macha's eyes. It seemed like he would swallow my eyes up.

"Who fired?" shouted Indio Galdámez. "Who was it?" And the rage suffocated his curses.

SIXTY-FOUR

I escaped through the hole of the broken skylight, and after clambering and slipping over the roofs, I managed to climb down to Calle Maturana. I arrived before dawn at the house of the Swedish cultural attaché, the one who used to invite Clementina and me for lunch. Hours later, in the consul's car, we went into the Swedish embassy. Anita was with me, wearing her school uniform.

And I see myself now in the plane telling her about Sweden, land of the Vikings in search of amber, the "tears of sea-birds," I tell her. I told her it was the only precious stone of organic matter, and it came from the fossilized resin of ancient conifers that existed forty million years ago, and had gone extinct over ten million years ago, when the ocean rose and swallowed those forests up. "There are insects from that time, ones that are extinct now," I tell her, "that were preserved in a piece of amber. They're still there."

"Alive?" she asks me, her eyes very wide.

SIXTY-FIVE

When the situation finally changed, when the damned dictatorship finally came to an end and the country recovered democracy, a couple of lawyers showed up unannounced at my apartment in Stockholm. They were Chilean. I let them in, resigned. Just like that time when a white Mazda pulled up and I recognized Ronco's voice, I sat down with them obedient as a worn-out ox. They knew my story. I was a victim, they insisted, and I needed to give my complete testimony. They convinced me. Roberto—I was still with him then—really encouraged me to do it. He thought it was my duty, he thought it would do me good.

I traveled incognito to Chile, with bodyguards and a new fake identity, and I testified for hours and hours in front of a judge. I testified for several days. I denounced them. I told what I saw, what they did to me, something, the minimum, about what I did myself. They brought me face to face with some of the thugs, the ones related to that particular judge's cases. I gave blow-by-blow accounts in those trials. I omitted what they didn't ask about, I omitted everything related to other crimes, I omitted my own participation in those events. When they brought in a tall man, very bald, with the little hair he had completely white over his ears and the nape of his neck, thin but with a paunch by now, deep wrinkles on his face, and I recognized Flaco Artaza's smile, I felt pity. He entered in handcuffs. Only then did I find out his real name.

He had spent a long time as a defendant and a prisoner. He greeted me with dignity and a trace of affection. He was upright. He was quiet while I answered the judge's questions. He shrank into himself little by little. But he never lost his calm. He bore it all nobly. "I never thought you would want to destroy my life," he told me on his way out. He wasn't angry but rather sad and disappointed, it seemed to me. "Why me? Why like this?" he said. When he was about to disappear, surrounded by guards, he turned his head and threw me one last, solitary look.

I wavered: Shouldn't I tell them everything and turn myself over to Justice once and for all? There were other cases in which they could be looking for me, though they may not know it exactly, or in which I could provide information. Wasn't it only fair that I should also pay in jail for what I did, though it would mean being away from Anita, away from the Baltic Sea, from my freedom?

At that moment, someone spoke to me and I gave a terrified jump. A scrawny old man had sat down next to me, his matted hair somewhere between white and red, long ears. He was wearing a dark brown suit, dandruff on his narrow little shoulders, a yellow shirt, and a tie with a gold sheen.

"I'm Rat," he told me, "Rat Osorio. You remember me?"

And of course I remembered and would always remember.

"I knew you at Central, remember?"

And when he saw my frightened, surprised face:

"I'm Inspector Pedro Ortiz, of Investigative Police."

He slid a card between my fingers. I was overcome with a shame I had never felt before. Shame of having been subjected by this rat, this thug, shame that his insults had been able to wound me. Disgrace. That's what it was. Not shame: disgrace. I barely contained the feeling.

"I was always a detective with Investigations; during that 'black' time I was only at Central in commissioned service. I was assigned there, that's all. Now I'm in charge of several criminal cases in which ex-agents of Central are directly implicated, get it? My duty is for justice to be carried out."

Quick lights flashed across Rat's restless, astute eyes. There was a slight vibration in his nostrils. Was he smelling me? Again on the side of the victors, a snitch just like me, I was thinking: this wretch, my double, my brother, I was thinking.

I wonder why I am there, why I have informed on Flaco and the others I used to know. Am I hoping for forgiveness? And who could forgive me? He goes on watching me, waiting, he wants to decipher any sign I give. I lower my gaze.

And I'm telling myself again that there's no justification for what I did. Can one ask forgiveness, then, for the unjustifiable? And if so, on what grounds? It would be asking for a gift. Because that's what forgiveness is: a gift. Why should that gift be asked for and not others, which are simply received? And if I did ask for it, what would happen if it wasn't granted?

"Iris, you remember Iris? She killed herself." He put two fingers in his mouth to simulate a gun. "With her own CZ, it was. But they can't fool me that easy, no way . . . I wasn't born yesterday, y'know?" He purses his lips in a disdainful gesture. "If you ask me . . . she got smoked. That chick knew too much, wouldn't you say?"

"And what about Macha, and Gato?" I asked him.

"The Law is looking for Macha and its arm, as they say, is loooong. Big things, ugly ones. Both his alibis fell, you know? Jacinto Hermosilla Ruiz is Macha Carrasco's real name." He tells me this proudly. "As for Lisandro Pérez Olmedo, he's named in old files for thirty-four cases: some nasty things, y'know? For example, the death of a young man who fell, according to Macha's deposition, because he disobeyed the order to stop and he covered the Spartan's flight with an AKM. Macha shot him down—I mean, Lisandro Pérez Olmedo did—from the roof next door, according to his testimony later that night. And they haven't found Macha. He left the country. Illegally, of course. But they'll nab that fucker . . . There are three men, I'm telling you, three experienced agents who used to be in Central and who are looking for him now. We don't know their real identities. We don't know if they answer to disconnected groups of ex-agents trying to protect themselves from the law or if Military Intelligence sent them and is secretly giving them help. It's possible. They deny it, of course. But Military Intelligence must be trying to get rid of evidence and witnesses of what they did at Central. To save the ones at the top, you get me? Those three ex-agents managed to cross the border in spite of the precautions we took, and they left with the order: shoot Macha's mug full of holes before Investigations gets their hands on him, before we haul him in here in cuffs and get him singing, shit. Macha's fucked: by next spring he's either pushing up daisies or behind bars . . ."

"And Gato?"

A shine in his small eyes.

"No one talks about him. He turned, was what I heard." And now in a whisper and looking at me with narrowed eyes, he makes a gesture indicating money: "He's protected. He's collaborating. He'd been doing it for a long time, selling information. He talked about you and gave them your information."

On that trip I saw my parents for the last time, in their separate places, both of them sick. My mother received me very calmly, with a new calm that was perhaps the product of her medicines. She was on saline. She asked about Anita, whom she saw rarely, if ever. About me, almost nothing. She didn't shed a tear when I said goodbye, but she squeezed me tightly. My father, on the other hand, wept from the moment he saw me set foot in his room. The chemotherapy had taken all his hair and his skin was a greenish white. In his arms, the jelly of his old tennis player's muscles. I wanted to go to El Quisco. He wanted us to go together. His little summerhouse was still there, waiting for me. So was the sea. He repeated that several times. In the end I didn't go.

You need to go to the bathroom? Of course! Look, it's easy: end of the hall to the left. You can't miss it. Why are you looking at your notebook? You don't trust me? Take it with you then; here, take it with you if you want. No?

SIXTY-SIX

Did you find the bathroom? See? You can't miss it . . . and your notebook is still there, see?

And Anita? She's good, she has a boyfriend, a Danish guy she met in Chile when she was backpacking in Torres del Paine. For a while they lived in San Francisco, and then they went to Santiago. He works at Santander Bank and she works at EuroAmerica Insurance . . . They seem happy. They work a lot, too much if you ask me. To Anita it's only natural that I'm dying; I'm old, and old people die. But it's me who is dying, fucking shit. That's what changes everything for me. To me, my death is not natural.

And now you've come all the way from Chile to open and shut me, right, *mon chéri?* A crab has taken over my stomach. It's growing like a fetus. Now nothing works right in my organism. I'll give birth to my own death. I was never a crier. Since I was a little girl I hated that old idea that "real men don't cry," which means: women do. Well, not me. But I do now. The memories return: Anita has come back from Chile and my hand caresses the closed door of her room while she sleeps. Did I tell you how after the equinox Roberto and I would start going to the ocean? We'd lay back naked on those rocks that had been polished to perfection by primeval ice and that hold the warmth of the sun. We jumped into the water, and no one existed besides us.

The Baltic sunsets through my window are very long, very gradual. As if the light wanted to hold on just a little longer. For some time now, my eyes will tear up on occasion, and a single tear falls. I brush it away so it doesn't run down my face. I take the little polished silver mirror that my grandmother left me out of my purse and I use a tissue to dry my face. I put on a little eye shadow, go over my eyelashes with mascara. I look out at the Baltic, some ship is coming in or going out, and that's it. It's just a moment. I wouldn't want the other women in the home to notice. Though I'll tell you, I've see a lot of them quietly crying, who knows why.

What? Yes; I laugh with the nurses, I talk with these shriveled-up old ladies, I do a few little translation jobs they still give me, and I talk on the phone with my daughter, so far away. I think about her a lot. I imagine what she's doing: for example, at this hour she must be having breakfast, her muesli with cold milk and honey . . . Or has she changed what she has for breakfast? You know, it never occurred to me to ask her. She is always the one to call me, from Santiago. She prefers it that way. Sometimes I think about Roberto and I want to call him on the phone. The other day, I did. A machine answered. I hung up. Talking to you, I don't know, I feel like I might call again. I'm sure he would want to see me . . . I wonder if we'll have snow this year before Christmas. The snow brings light.

And? Have I earned my money yet? I'll tell you a secret: With what you're giving me for my story today, I'll have thirty thousand dollars. An inheritance for Anita. Not a bad amount, don't you think? Well, it's no great thing, but for me . . . She'll appreciate that I've saved money so I can leave it to her. So here I am, telling you my damned story. Sometimes, like I've said, a stranger is the best confidant. But it's better if you don't write it. Change it, make up something else, find a metaphor. No one will understand. Not here and not back in Chile, either. Not even my daughter, if she ever found out. She knows very little about all this. I never wanted to tell her the story the way it really happened. Too crude for her. I thought: I don't want to make her suffer. Also: Someday she should know the truth, I'm her mother. Someday. That moment never came. Not until now.

You know? My voice caught there for a second, you noticed, right? It was laughter, it welled up inside me and stopped, it wouldn't come out. What blocked it? What would that aborted peal of laughter have been like? Happy people do not speak for me. I speak with the mouth of sacred hate. For me, only someone pursued like a shadow by shame and resentment can speak. Although neither death nor oblivion will be able to erase the fact that I lived and this was my insignificant and shitty life. No one lived it for me. No one will. I'm unrepeatable. I existed. You only live once. And in your own way. Forever. I never became the combatant I promised myself I would be. "Everything for the cause, Irene, everything." I wasn't capable of living up to that credo. You know that by now. I tried and I couldn't. And then I did what I did to my brothers and sisters. But I was the one, I alone though no one knows it, who kept them from putting Bone into Gato's hands. I knew what that was. And I saved my daughter from his jaws. I was forced to choose: combatant or mother. I feel as if only now, finally, am I ready to start living. I was what I was in the only chance I got to be alive. It's taken me an entire life to learn how to live. Maybe.

You're leaving with your notebook nice and full . . . For my quotations? Ha, ha! My being is a pit filled only with quotations . . . Ha ha! What I'm telling you, I repeat, is no good to you. For your novel, I mean. Forget this Lorena. A good novel leaves the door half-open for hope. Not me. You know who the woman talking to you is? I'm a question for you. I'm your Lorena, nothing more.

What time is it? Good grief! The five hours we agreed on are long over. Give me my money and get out of here. Better count it, hadn't we? Only hundred-dollar bills, right? OK . . . They're about to bring me my *merienda*; that's what the Spanish priest calls my dinner: They're bringing your *merienda*, child. That's three thousand . . . My nose is itching. I don't know why I have that itch now on my nose, so I wrinkle it like that, see? And then I scratch it and it's gone. OK. It's all there. Yes, here, leave it here below, please. Thanks.

As for you, go back to Santiago and do what you will with those notes you've been taking. But don't even think of coming near me again, is that clear? I don't want your condescension, not yours or anyone else's. I won't answer your calls. I don't want to see you ever again. I won't even read what you write, if you end up writing anything. That's how I want it. Leave me alone. Go on, get out of here. Now you know: Truth is impossible, *the truth was invented not to be told.*

Look, see how there's light even now over the Baltic?

SOURCES

Although the people and events in this novel are fictional, the author used actual events and true stories as a point of departure. In addition to interviews with various protagonists and witnesses from the period, he made use of the following documentary bibliography: Eduardo Anguita and Martín Caparrós, *La voluntad* (Buenos Aires: Norma, 1998); Luz Arce, *El infierno* (Santiago: Planeta, 1993; translated into English by Stacy Alba Skar as *The Inferno: A Story of Terror and Survival in Chile* [Madison: University of Wisconsin Press, 2004]); Miguel Bonasso, Roberto Bardini, and Laura Restrepo, *Operación príncipe* (Mexico City: Planeta, 1988); Carmen Castillo, *Un día de octubre en Santiago*, trans. Felipe Sarabia (Santiago: LOM Ediciones, 1982; original title: *Un Jour d'octobre à Santiago* [Paris: Éditions Stock, 1980]); *La Flaca Alejandra* (documentary film, 1993) and *Calle Santa Fe* (documentary film, 2007); Ascanio Cavallo, Manuel Salazar, and Óscar Sepúlveda, *La historia oculta del régimen militar* (Santiago: Editorial Sudamericana, 1998); Comité Memoria Neltume, *Guerrilla en Neltume* (Santiago: LOM Ediciones, 2003); Daniel de Santis, *A vencer o morir* (Buenos Aires: Editorial Nuestra América, 2004); Régis Debray, *Alabados sean nuestros señores* (Buenos Aires: Editorial Sudamericana, 1999; original title: *Loués soient nos seigneurs* [Paris: Gallimard, 1996]); John Dinges, *Operación Condor* (Santiago: Ediciones B, 2004; original title: *The Condor Years: How Pinochet and His Allies Brought Terror to Three Continents* [New York: New Press, 2004]); Diamela Eltit, "Perder el sentido," *La Época* (Santiago), July 30, 1995; Eltit, "Vivir ¿dónde?" *Revista de Crítica Cultural* (Santiago) 11 (1995); and Eltit, "Cuerpos nómadas," *Debate Feminista* (Mexico City) 14 (1996), all essays reproduced in *Emergencias* (Santiago: Planeta/Ariel, 2000); Nancy Guzmán, *Romo* (Santiago: Planeta, 2000); Max Marambio, *Las armas de ayer* (Santiago: La Tercera Debate, 2007); Marcia Alejandra Merino, *Mi ver-*

dad (Santiago: A.T.G. S.A., 1993); Pedro Naranjo, Mauricio Ahumada, Mario Garcés, and Julio Pinto, *Miguel Enríquez y el proyecto revolucionario en Chile: Discursos y documentos del Movimiento de izquierda revolucionaria, MIR* (Santiago: LOM Ediciones, 2004); Ricardo Palma Salamanca, *El gran rescate* (Santiago: LOM Ediciones, 1997), and *Una larga cola de acero (Historia del FPMR, 1984–1988)* (Santiago: LOM Ediciones, 2001); Cristóbal Peña, *Los fusileros* (Santiago: Debate, 2007); Roberto Perdía, *La otra historia: Testimonio de un jefe Montonero* (Buenos Aires: Editorial Grupo Ágora, 1997); Cristián Pérez, "Salvador Allende, apuntes sobre su dispositivo de seguridad: El Grupo de Amigos Personales (GAP)," *Estudios Públicos* (Santiago) 79 (2000); "El Ejército del Che y los chilenos que continuaron su lucha," *Estudio Públicos* (Santiago) 89 (2003); "Historia del MIR: Si quieren Guerra, Guerra tendrán . . . ," *Estudios Públicos* (Santiago) 91 (2003); Patricio Rivas, *Chile, un largo septiembre* (Santiago: LOM Ediciones, 2007); Ricardo Uceda, *Muerte en el Pentagonito* (Lima: Planeta, 2004); Hernán Valdés, *Tejas verdes* (Santiago: LOM Ediciones, 1996); Hernán Vidal, *Chile: Poética de la tortura política* (Santiago: Mosquito Editores, 2000), and *Frente Patriótico Manuel Rodríguez* (Santiago: Mosquito Editores, 1995); and Patricio Verdugo and Carmen Hertz, *Operación Siglo XX* (Santiago: Las Ediciones del Ornitorrinco, 1990).

ARTURO FONTAINE was born in Santiago and is professor of philosophy at the Universidad de Chile. He is the author of four volumes of poetry and three novels, and he regularly publishes essays on political and cultural topics. He is on the board of Chile's Museum of Memory and Human Rights. He lives in Santiago, Chile.

MEGAN MCDOWELL is a translator specializing in Chilean and other Latin American literature. She lives in Zurich, Switzerland.